Praise for *A Change of Location*

"Porter has perfectly captured the romance trope of finding unexpected love while traveling to new places. The author also deftly portrays the machinations of a twentysomething career woman who's somewhat closed off to romantic intrigue. Porter skillfully immerses readers in the fictional Milver Vale and vividly evokes British village life, from pubs to fun characters to countryside exploits . . . A charming sojourn to the English countryside for readers who enjoy smart love stories."

—*Kirkus Reviews*

"Hannah's ability to navigate and analyze unfamiliar surroundings and people becomes a driving force in a novel that explores her international sojourns, matters of the heart, and the people and places that motivate her to step away from her former successful patterns and into different relationships and milieus . . . A revealing novel of new possibilities and life that covers unemployment, romance, heartbreak, other cultures, and new lives . . . The perfect ticket for a warm account of movie-making and personal magic."

—*Midwest Book Review*

"A triumph! A Change of Location hits its marks perfectly on both sides of the pond. I had so much fun with Porter's quirky, thoroughly lovable characters that I couldn't put the novel down."

—*Leslie Caroll, author of Royal Affairs.*

"Perfect for romantics who adore stately homes, all things England . . . and delicious budding romance . . . Highly recommended!"

—*The Literary Redhead*

Also by Margaret Porter:

The Myrtle Wand

The Limits of Limelight

Beautiful Invention: A Novel of Hedy Lamarr

A Pledge of Better Times

A Change of Location

The Library of Congress Cataloging-in-Publication Data is available.

ISBN 979-8-9856734-5-6

ISBN 979-8-9856734-5-6 (pbk)

ISBN 979-8-9856734-3-2 (ebook)

A Change of Location

A Novel

MARGARET PORTER

GALLICA PRESS

For my treasured companion in most of my London adventures and so many Somerset escapades.

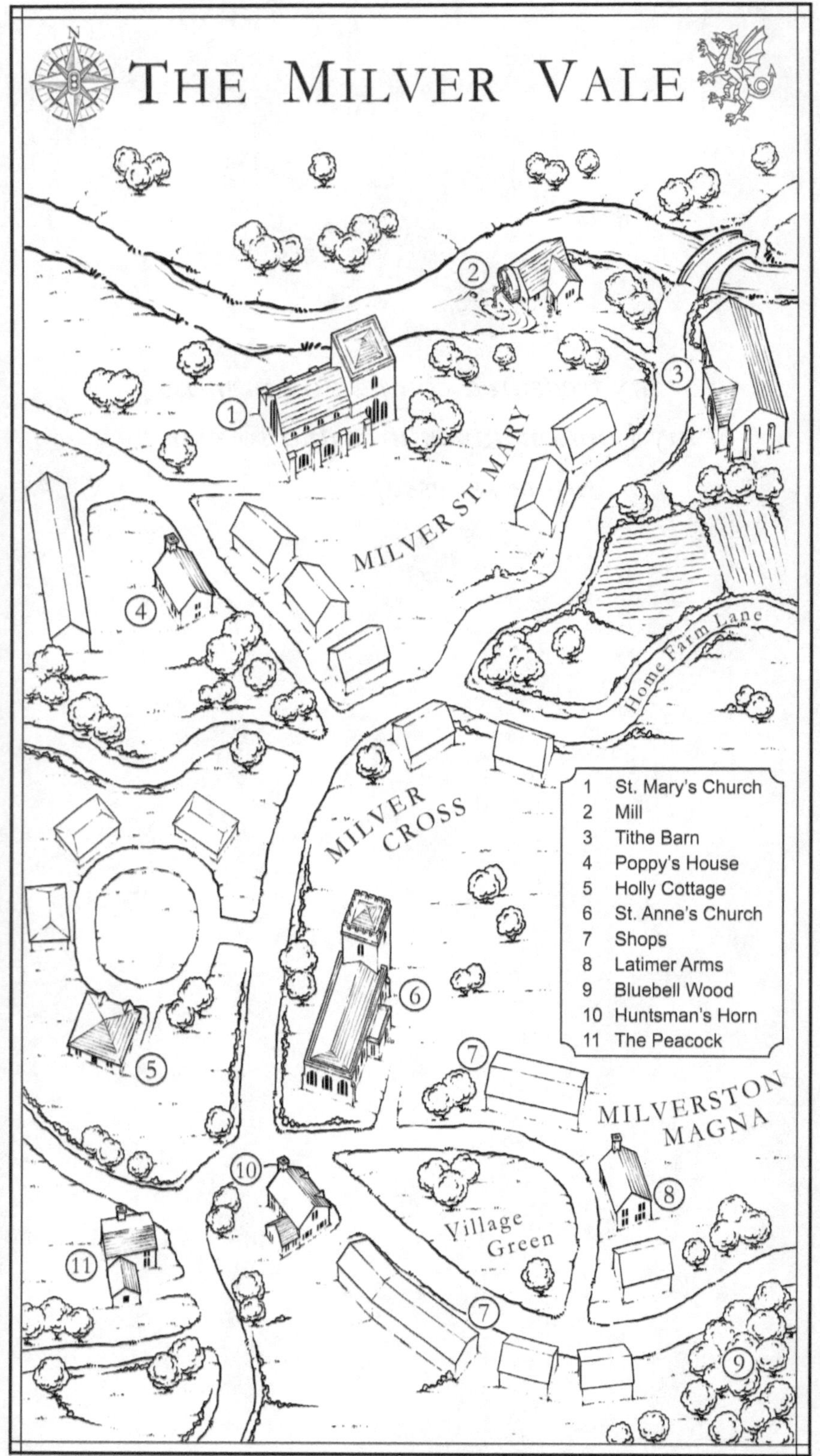

N
THE MILVER VALE
MILVER ST. MARY
Home Farm Lane
MILVER CROSS
MILVERSTON MAGNA
Village Green
1   St. Mary's Church
2   Mill
3   Tithe Barn
4   Poppy's House
5   Holly Cottage
6   St. Anne's Church
7   Shops
8   Latimer Arms
9   Bluebell Wood
10 Huntsman's Horn
11 The Peacock

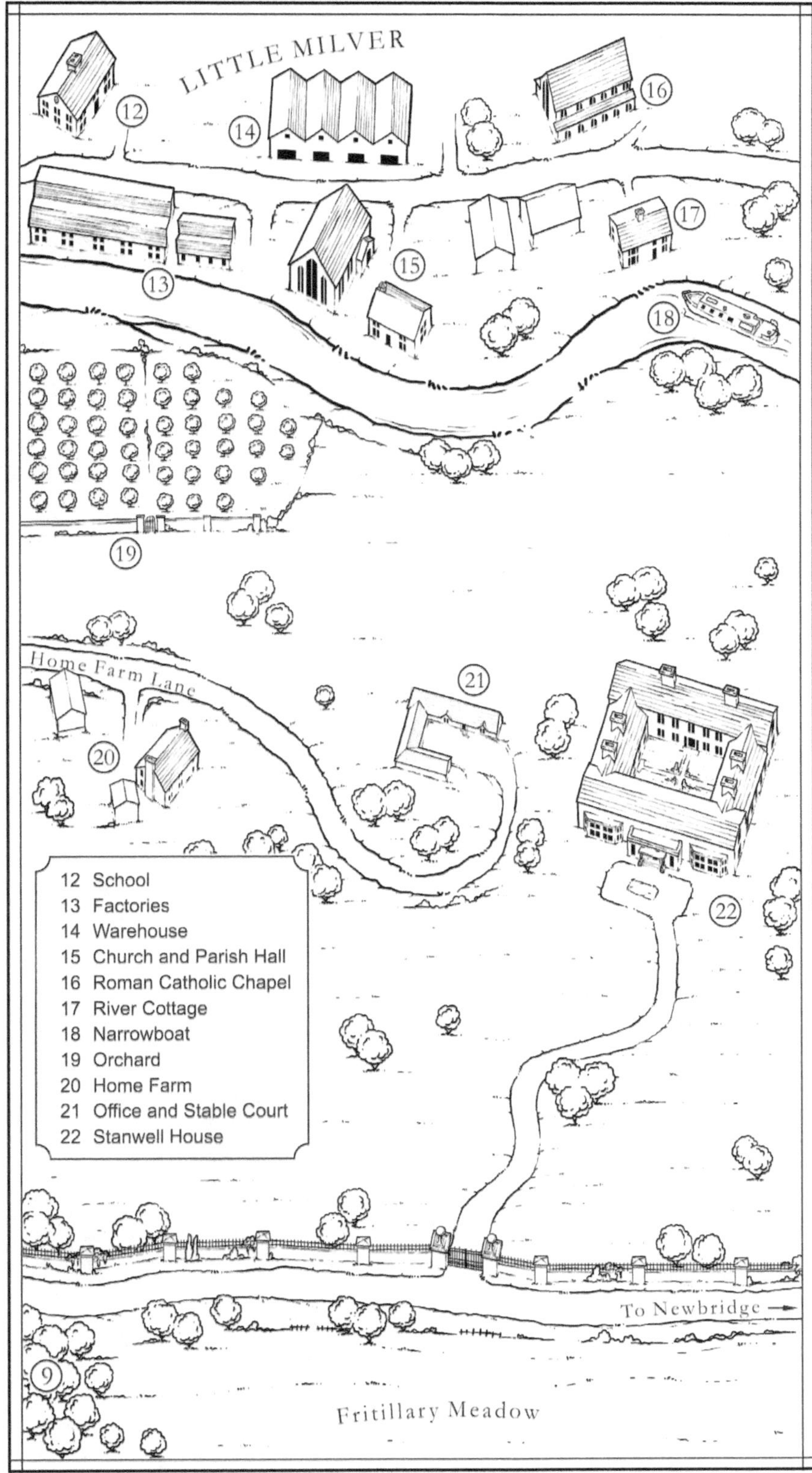

LITTLE MILVER
12
14
16
15
13
17
18
19
21
20
22
Home Farm Lane
To Newbridge
9
Fritillary Meadow
12 School
13 Factories
14 Warehouse
15 Church and Parish Hall
16 Roman Catholic Chapel
17 River Cottage
18 Narrowboat
19 Orchard
20 Home Farm
21 Office and Stable Court
22 Stanwell House

Part 1

*Choosing location is integral to the film:
in essence, another character.*

—Ridley Scott

Chapter 1

Tourists, thrilled to discover quaint and quintessential Englishness, pointed their phone cameras at the brick shop façades lining Latimer Row. Other pedestrians lingered just long enough for a quick selfie before stepping inside one of the establishments, if they bothered to enter at all. The black taxicabs passing along the street couldn't detract from the historic ambiance. However it was briefly marred by the death-defying motorcycle courier perilously—and noisily— weaving through the traffic.

Pausing at the window of Wincott & Sons, Hannah Ballard examined the artful display of cheese wheels, blocks, and wedges. Catching sight of her reflection in the dimpled antique pane, she adjusted the tortoiseshell clips in her unruly hair. When she pushed open the gleaming black door, she was startled by the ding of a brass bell—and the intimidating and confusing array of dairy products.

"Good afternoon, Madam. Are your requirements specific, or general?"

Madam, already in over her head, contemplated a speedy flight to the supermarket several streets away. Helplessly she faced the one employee who didn't wear a striped apron and straw boater. His shaggy brown hair, not as dark as hers, contrasted with the classic gray suit and paisley silk tie. The sign hanging outside boasted that the firm had been *EST. 1753*, so he definitely wasn't Wincott, or even one of the Sons. A great-great-great-great grandson?

"I'm shopping for a party."

"Drinks party?" At least six feet tall, he towered over her—a pet peeve, but he was so easy on the eyes that she wouldn't hold it against him.

She nodded. "I need wine as well as cheese. And fresh fruit. For a business thing. Tomorrow. And I know it's very short notice, which is why my hotel can't provide catering services. The concierge suggested I come here."

"For how many guests?"

"About eight, if they all show up." They wouldn't.

Hannah surveyed the neat rows of unidentifiable wedges in the refrigerated display. She felt unworthy to gaze upon his fine cheeses, or carry any of them away.

"The venue?" he prompted.

"My suite."

The party wasn't her idea. From the other side of the Atlantic Ocean her executive producer had insisted on it, as a gesture of goodwill and to promote their nascent film project and partner studio. Why hadn't she reminded Liz that organizing a social event—in London, of all places— was not part of her otherwise expansive skill set? Craft services was just about the only department that remained a mystery to her. Emailing and texting invitations to her contacts at the location search company was simple enough. If, as she expected, senior staff were too busy to attend, they would probably send their assistants.

"Fine British cheeses are our speciality. We also source products from France, Italy, Spain, and Holland."

She followed the manager as he pointed out shelf after shelf, making suggestions, nodding enthusiastically whenever she recognized a name. Cheddar, Stilton, Brie, Camembert—he had them all. And then some.

"We take particular pride in this one."

When she leaned down to examine the label, a perverse curl slipped from its clasp and fell onto her cheek. Impatiently sweeping it behind her ear, she read, "Milverston Maid. Pretty name."

"From Milver Vale Dairy. Would Madam care for a sample?" Not waiting for her answer, he seized an implement and expertly extracted a pale plug of cheese. His busy fingers were long and nicely shaped. He wore a large gold signet ring, its oval center imprinted with a winged creature standing upright on a single hind leg. Not the same dragon with raised claw that she knew from the Welsh flag, though it had an identical curling tail.

She always noticed hands. Dad's were clean and capable, befitting a veterinarian who treated and operated on animals large and small. Because Mum habitually forgot to wear her gardening gloves, hers were scored and scratched by rose thorns. Decades of boating and lobstering had tanned and roughened and bruised and scarred Grampa's. But whenever she envisioned her uncle's hands, she always remembered that one of them had driven a knife into another man's body. His desperate and impulsive act ruined his life and altered hers.

She accepted the morsel presented to her on a tiny napkin imprinted with the shop's name. The giver's intense scrutiny while she consumed it increased her self-consciousness. "Delicious." Excruciatingly expensive, too.

"I assure you they're the happiest and healthiest of cows. I've met them."

Lifelong familiarity with English accents informed her that his was unusually posh for a shopkeeper. His salesmanship was rooted in a genuine enthusiasm for the product. He mongered his cheese quite effectively. She let him serve her a piece of Milver Blue and nodded her appreciation. Then she tried Stanwell Splendor, a softer goat's milk cheese. When he asked a series of questions about wine, she answered with colors—red, white—incapable of reciting countries and regions and vineyards and grapes and years. Confronted with a baffling printed list from the neighboring wine merchant, she persuaded Great-Grandson of Wincott to make the appropriate selections.

"Your order will include our finest brand of biscuits," he explained, ushering her towards the counter. "And we're able to supply the fresh fruit you mentioned."

"Wonderful."

Hannah envisioned elderly duchesses and tottering countesses leaving the shop, their carrier bags crammed with cheese, hearts palpitating from exposure to his impish smile and amused gray eyes. An aerobically fit jogger of twenty-seven whose work regularly placed her within the orbit of the sexiest men on the planet, she was aware of his charm. But not overwhelmed.

His fountain pen poised over a printed form, he asked her name, hotel and room and mobile phone number, and the hours of her party.

"I trust you're enjoying your time here," he said. "Your first visit to England?"

"I spent a year at Bristol University. Film and Television Department. But I came here many times before. My mother grew up in Somerset."

His expression altered slightly. "Which part, north or south?"

"North. Portishead."

"Have you family there still?"

She shook her head. "My grandmother moved back to Wales to be close to her relatives. My mother's brother lives in Southfields, near Wimbledon."

"Convenient for the All-England Tennis Championship," he commented. "If you're staying that long. Should we file your order in your own name, or that of your firm?"

She extracted a shiny silver Acorn Films credit card from her wallet and slid it across the counter. She hoped the cheese man was suitably impressed. From the depths of her purse came a series of peals from Big Ben, the ringtone she'd set on arrival in London. She made an apologetic face as she retrieved her phone. "Hannah Ballard."

"Me again," Liz Gregorio drawled across thousands of miles.

Mentally she placed her executive producer in her black leather chair, elbows propped on a black marble desktop. The bulging body would be comfortably and expensively sheathed in a jewel-toned silk tunic and matching drawstring pants.

"Nothing's changed," she said calmly. "As I've already told you, pre-production meetings are on track. Stop pestering me."

"I'm not. The site of your next appointment changed—again. For some reason the email came to us. Get your skinny ass over to the Savoy Hotel in twenty minutes, because Owen Parry waits for no one. Nigel's on his way there now. And please tell me it's do-able."

Hannah's eyes lighted on the giant, old-fashioned clock on the wall, and hoped it kept perfect time. "Not unless I leave now, and I do mean this instant. I'm ordering food for the party."

"I swear this is the last time I do your scheduling from a distant time zone."

"What else is there to keep you occupied, besides knitting baby booties?"

"Very funny. Don't forget to mention your Welsh grandmother. The perfect ice-breaker. I'm so jealous. You'll understand why when *you're* twenty months pregnant and *I'm* sashaying around London with Britain's most famous director. Yikes—studio accountant on my other line. I can manage only one trans-Atlantic call at a time."

"Losing your touch," said Hannah, half a second too late. "My boss," she told the man at the till, a term that in no way indicated their close personal relationship and long history of working together. "Head of the company."

"Early for Los Angeles, isn't it? Or extremely late."

"She's in Boston, five hours behind. Would it be all right if I come back later to finish the paperwork? I'm expected at the Savoy for an appointment with our co-producer and Sir Owen Parry." She was sure he'd recognize that illustrious name.

"I've taken down the essential information," he assured her. "A member of staff will ring you tomorrow to confirm delivery time. Your card, Madam."

Her gaze landed on the carved and gilded warrant holder crests mounted on the wall behind him. She'd be sure to tell Uncle Chase about meeting the Royal Cheesemonger, who had transformed her dreaded chore into a memorable shopping experience.

Exiting Wincott & Sons, Hannah began the tricky business of hailing a taxicab in a posh and picturesque street where traffic consisted primarily of costly German imports, bulky Range Rovers, and the occasional Rolls Royce or Bentley.

"Shall I file that order for you?"

Watching his customer's attempt to secure transportation, Martin was slow to answer. "Not till I've changed it to a Jubilee."

"She wants a Chelsea," the shop assistant corrected him. "Wine, cheese, biscuits, and fruit. The Jubilee includes smoked salmon, lemon wedge, and champagne. And Belgian chocolates."

"I know."

They watched a cab swallow the petite American and carry her away from the Row.

"Wish I had curls like that."

Her wistful non sequitur amused Martin. Beneath the straw boater, the girl's straight blonde hair was pulled back into a blunt stub like a shaving brush. Tugging it playfully, he said, "India, there's nothing wrong here that purple dye couldn't improve."

"You'd know all about that, wouldn't you?" she retorted.

Someone had written *Happy Birthday!* in red marker on a tabloid newspaper clipping and sellotaped it to the staff notice board. Taken years ago, it was an unfortunate relic of his exhibitionist phase. If not for the identifying caption, nobody would recognize him in that wild-eyed, pasty-faced teen with purpled hair and goth garb lurking outside a Soho club.

Typing details into the computer terminal, he said, "She'll need the extra bits."

"But can she afford them? Like Mr. Cole always reminds us, not every American who comes into the shop is rich. That's why so many of them moan about our prices. And the exchange rate." India added, "I could get sacked for letting you muck about with this order. I've got problems enough without that."

The redness around her eyes had faded, but her nose was still rosy. An hour ago he'd found her in the upper room where cheeses matured, weeping her heart out. Boyfriend trouble. He'd had no useful advice to offer but hoped talking things out had helped.

"You won't get the sack," he said firmly. "But if you ever do, I'll have a word with our near neighbor the wine merchant. Better yet, the haberdasher. You could give up that apron and boater. Imagine the thrill of measuring gents' inseams all day!"

India's pink nose pinched in disdain. "Wrinkly old toffs."

"You might not enjoy it, but they would. Not all their customers are ancient. Where d'you think I bought my suit?"

"I'm happy where I am, thanks all the same."

"If you let me deal with this order in my own way, I'll tell Old King Cole you deserve a rise in salary."

"That's blackmail," she accused him. "Paying higher wages would mean the bosses couldn't afford their ground rent. Your loss."

"Hadn't thought of that."

"Fine businessman you are."

"Don't fret, I won't charge Ms. Ballard for the Jubilee. Acorn Films will get billed for the Chelsea she requested. I'll make up the difference myself. And you'd best keep schtum about it." He scrunched his face into a frown and intoned threateningly, "Or you might regret it."

She laughed and cheekily mimed a curtsy. "Milord need not concern himself. These lips are locked."

After emerging from the Savoy's oppressively refined premises, Hannah crossed the Strand to a sushi shop for a quick bite before she descended to the depths of the underground. Changing at Piccadilly station, she navigated the crowded maze of tunnels to the platform she wanted, arriving in time to hear engines roar and feel the blast of air as the westbound train pulled up. Rush hour hadn't started and seats were available in the carriage, but there was no point sitting with Green Park just one stop away.

She retraced her earlier path to Latimer Row. As though decreed by a lighting designer, late afternoon sun streamed artistically across the distinctive Dickensian shop fronts.

At Wincott & Sons, an older gentleman presided at the counter. Alerted to her arrival by the shop bell, he nodded in acknowledgment before placing a customer's purchases in a jute carrier bag printed with the shop logo. After the transaction was completed, he asked Hannah how he might assist her.

"When I was here earlier today, a man helped with my catering order. For Acorn Films. The manager, maybe?"

"His lordship left a short while ago."

She assumed he was giving the staff's nickname for their colleague, doubtless due to the posh accent.

A young blonde stepped forward. "Are you here to make a change?"

She nodded. "My numbers increased. I hope that's okay."

"Absolutely. Lord Milverston's not a member of staff. But he pops in from time to time."

"The Row is owned and managed by Latimer London Estates, Limited," her colleague told Hannah, with obvious pride. "The Marquess of Milverston, head of the Latimer family, is our landlord. He takes a very personal interest in each of the businesses."

Milverston, like the cheese. Latimer, like the Row.

She was aware that a few fortunate aristocrats still owned chunks of Mayfair, plus she had a passing familiarity with English eccentrics. Lord Milverston was apparently the sum of those types. She doubted an Acorn Films credit card and name-dropping Sir Owen Parry had impressed a man with a title whose ancestors must've arrived with William the Conqueror. So had one of hers, but the Norman invader at the root of her own family tree hadn't amounted to much. Nobody except his direct descendants had ever heard of him. As for her nameless and undocumented Welsh forbears, they had inhabited their native Montgomeryshire hills since the beginning of time, and for generations had battled their English enemies.

"My guest list expanded to twelve," she announced.

The girl scribbled a note on her pad. "Very good. We'll make sure you receive the correct amount of food and beverages for that number."

Next door, at the florist's, Hannah could converse more confidently with the proprietor than she had when purchasing cheese and wine. She admired fresh-cut parrot tulips and inspected the potted flowers—cheerful yellow primroses and fragrant pastel hyacinths.

The display of gardening books, all available in the adjacent shop—according to a hand-lettered card—featured Wendy Edney's popular horticulture titles. Each of them, Hannah was aware, had been lovingly dedicated to her daughter and husband.

Rewarding herself for the satisfactory completion of her daily assignments, she purchased a handful of overpriced Tête à Tête jonquils.

"He must like you a lot," commented the rumpled, red-faced American man who followed her into the hotel lift.

It was an opportunity to prove her feminist cred and explain that she'd bought them for herself. But conversations between hotel floors were brief at best and awkward at worst, so she smiled and shrugged and lifted the golden flower heads to her nose. She inhaled their distinctive fragrance, and was instantly transported to a springtime garden near the coast of Maine.

Chapter 2

Entering her dim and silent suite, she tossed her bag onto the sofa. She parted the heavy curtains at each window, blinking at the sudden blaze of light. After zipping from Mayfair to Soho to Latimer Row to the Savoy, then again to the Row, and from there to here, she wanted to sit down, put her feet up, and chill. Later she'd deal with unanswered texts and unread messages and a cascade of emails she hadn't had time to review. Using the landline, she pressed the room service button and requested a bucket of ice and a bottle of Sancerre. Her order was fulfilled with the promptness to which she'd grown accustomed.

She had a sitting room that extended into a small dining room, and a large bedroom, all decorated in a restrained Art Deco style. The marble-tiled bathroom contained a large shower enclosure and an enormous tub. Her opulent surroundings were a delightful but jarring contrast with last week's cramped budget motel, with its clattering air conditioning unit and thin towels. Traversing London by taxicab and tube couldn't obliterate fresh memories of steering a rented SUV along a rain-soaked dirt road. Instead of today's business casual outfit and heels, she'd worn faded jeans and a loose Mexican cotton shirt.

In Texas the pace of her days had been far less hectic. The gregarious folks she met there had been talkative, yes, but endlessly, eagerly hospitable throughout her location scouting assignment. Despite the grim plot and somber tone of the television movie, the locals were endearingly thrilled by the prospect of someday seeing their tiny crossroads town on the small screen. Her guide had practically adopted her, inviting her to a church potluck where she enjoyed the finest meal of her trip, and every day since their parting had sent a chatty email. Embedded in the latest was her photo of Hannah sporting a ten-gallon hat while straddling a split-rail fence, with grazing longhorn cattle in the background.

Chase will get a kick out of that one, she thought. I should send it to him now.

With a couple of clicks, her brief message and the attachment were on their way.

Before her departure from the Dallas-Fort Worth airport, she'd emailed his workplace, attaching her picture of an armadillo—for a Mainer, nearly as exotic as the alligator she'd photographed a few months ago near Savannah. She wasn't likely to come across such bizarre subjects during her many months here in England.

Over the past ten years, her uncle had been recipient of any and all details of her life and work that she thought might amuse or interest him. During his incarceration, she'd regularly sent written letters and printed photos. As a college student and during her yearlong study in Bristol, she'd reported on her theatre productions and student films. Since graduation, she'd kept him informed about the film locations she scouted and movie and television stars who unintentionally strayed into her path. She regularly updated him on significant events in her personal life, such as her dramatic New Year's Eve breakup with the man she'd dated longer than she should have.

Four months without kisses, she thought bleakly, stepping out of her high heels. And everything else decent kissing led to.

Rising from the sofa, she shed her long-waisted black jacket and removed the little black dress and wrapped herself in the oversized complimentary bathrobe.

Anticipating a lengthy and soothing soak, she turned on the taps and made her way to the sitting room for her cell phone. She ought to provide Liz with a brief update.

Returning to the bathroom to check the water level, she blurted, "This tub is filling fast. It has jets! And I'm drinking wine."

"I hate you," Liz retorted. "Talk to you tomorrow."

Before she placed her phone on the vanity, she felt its vibration against her palm as Big Ben clanged. She didn't recognize the number on the display. "Hannah Ballard," she answered. Cautiously she dipped her toes in to test the temperature before easing the rest of her body into liquid warmth.

"Martin Latimer, of Wincott & Sons," said an English-accented male voice. "You visited the shop this afternoon. Twice."

She inserted one leg into the water, then the other, trying not to splash. Before the rising steam choked her, she managed to say, "Lord of the Cheese?"

After a quiet moment he said, "In a manner of speaking. Did India tell you?"

"Yes, if she's a blonde kid in apron and straw hat. I assumed you were Great-Grandson of Wincott." Her low laugh sounded excessively and unintentionally seductive. She blamed the Sancerre.

"Dead for centuries. No relation. I was born a Latimer."

"Lord of Latimer Row." Aware that she was naked as well as almost tipsy, she switched to an assertive, business-like tone. "I hope there's no problem with my order."

"Consider this confirmation of your delivery tomorrow. Very likely by your humble servant."

"Oh. In that case, I wonder whether you could—" Did she dare?

"If you're adding more guests, I need to find something to write with."

With alcohol speeding through her bloodstream and hot water melting her inhibitions, she dared. "Are you able to attend the party? Not just for the delivery, but as my guest. I've put out a distress call to every male I know in London. Neither of them responded. When I think of all those women showing up in my suite . . ."

He laughed, loudly and long. "Delighted to assist, Madam. My only plan for tomorrow afternoon was checking the ripeness of all the cheese stored in the Wincott vault."

Recalling his fondness for it, Hannah was flattered.

With an apology to his dinner companion, Martin tucked his mobile back into his jacket pocket. "An early night for me. Party tomorrow. Must conserve my strength."

"That's unexpected," retorted Daniel Wheeler. "Your infinite nights—and mornings—in the discos are the stuff of legend."

"Clubs," Martin corrected before sipping his single malt, aged to perfection in an obscure but renowned Highland distillery. "That's the preferred term these days."

Over a superb dinner they had covered the serious topics—investments, property valuations, taxes. Even with capable, calculating Dan advising him, he often had to deal with essential matters that had pushed his father into an early grave.

"Whose party? Anyone I know?"

"American bird. With Acorn Films."

"You're trying to pull an actress? Good luck to you."

"If I shagged one of Cole's lady customers, he'd banish me, along with all the Milver Vale cheese. For my dairymen's sakes, I dare not exercise my lordly rights up and down the Row. I can't risk the sort of lurid headlines that would result from a charge of sexual harassment. 'The Sex Mad Marquess of Mayfair.' Or 'Lusty Latimer on the Prowl.'"

"Thirty is a milestone birthday," Dan reminded him. "Best get busy."

"Skirt chasing?"

"Making little Latimers. At your advanced age, you need to settle down with a well-connected, parentally approved, countryside-loving lass."

"The lasses with whom I'm presently acquainted are social media influencers who trade on their titles to accrue followers. They look like anorexics. As far as I can tell, they're only interested in posting selfies. Partying. Clubbing. Not my scene."

"It was. Before you broke up with Natalie."

"She got cross if I wouldn't go out with her and her cadre of friends. Dull as ditchwater, all of them, and just as shallow. I had heaps more fun during my misspent youth. When the music was better. And if you heard I was responsible for ending our relationship, you were misinformed. She met an Italian duke during her Alpine skiing holiday at Christmastime. On Valentine's Day she married him."

His dismay at being discarded by the *duchessa* subsided weeks before her lavish wedding, which he and several of her former romantic partners had attended. He'd been sorely tempted to offer condolences to her bridegroom in place of congratulations. In his less-than-objective opinion, Natalie's character flaws included a lack of consideration for people's feelings and a misplaced sense of her own fabulousness. Her newlywed status might satisfy her craving for attention to some extent, and it ensured a desired prominence in the social columns. But he questioned the durability of her hasty marriage.

"How long do you remain in town?" Dan asked.

"No more than a few days. I was urged to attend my board of directors meeting in person rather than via video call. I'll be dashing back to Somerset as soon as I can get away—lots to do there. The proposal for the Little Milver factory renewal is nearly finished, soon to be shared with the larger planning committee. Mother's coming over from France to assist with the Milver Vale Flower Fete. And I need to prepare my presentation on the eco-tourism venture for the Milverston parish council."

"All work, no play," the solicitor warned, reaching for his whisky and soda.

"I could level that criticism at you." Martin shrugged. "Me, I'm making up for lost time. I messed about with odd jobs and travel as long as I could. I didn't fancy ending up like Rufus, one of the truly idle aristocrats. His greatest achievement was his longevity."

Said Dan, in a voice of supreme satisfaction, "By living seven years after he deeded the entire Somerset estate and the Cumbrian castle to you, and putting the London properties into a trust, he saved you a fortune in inheritance tax."

Martin raised his glass. "To the late Marquess. Every year at my birthday Rufus purchased a case of champagne from the Latimer Row vintner, who sent it to Stanwell. He always arranged for me to receive one bottle from the batch. Even when I was a boy."

Martin had been enormously fond of his uncle, who was also his godfather, and he'd enjoyed his rare and brief childhood visits to the ancestral country house. Infrequent interactions hadn't bridged the extreme gap in their ages, upbringing, and interests, although Rufus had been dutifully avuncular. He was present for entrance day at Eton and turned up for a tennis match the following spring. During the next term Martin's father died—prematurely and unexpectedly. Rufus assumed various paternal roles, attending parents' dinners, and offering advice on which Oxford college might best suit the heir apparent of a titled bachelor who possessed multiple properties. Whenever family members accused the future marquess of being wild and odd and unreliable, Rufus had responded with a strong defense, earning Martin's everlasting gratitude. In return, he'd steadfastly guarded Lord Milverston's privacy and dignity, before his demise, and ever since. He'd never confirmed the faint but persistent rumors about his uncle's sexual preference.

He must've been damned lonely, Martin reflected during his solitary walk past packed restaurants and dark shopfronts. Wish I'd realized it much sooner.

Like the majority of Mayfair's aristocratic mansions, the original Latimer House had been demolished. Its replacement, erected in the 1920s, was an imposing mixed-use structure with ground floor offices and luxury apartments above.

"Evening, sir," the night porter greeted him.

"Any winners today?" Martin inquired.

"Not a one." Lorcan, who frequented the betting shop, aspired to buy shares in a racing syndicate. His fiancée had other plans for their savings.

"Better luck tomorrow."

Although Martin's *pied-à-terre* was a luxury, not a necessity, he wouldn't relinquish it. Almost weekly, Dan forwarded lavish purchase offers from upper crust estate agents with covetous clients, or developers with grandiose and destructive plans, but he declined them all. Someday his mother might return to England, and though she tolerated rather than relished London, changes to her health might make living here expedient. Besides, he felt responsible for maintaining the centuries-long Latimer link to the building.

At the onset of World War II, after the government had

requisitioned both country houses, his intrepid great-grand-mother remained at Latimer House, ever attentive to the news bulletins on the wireless, alert to possible clues about her husband's location at the front. Whenever German bombs rained upon the city, she and her servants took up their gas masks and descended to the subterranean boiler room. When the war was over, she made her way to the train station to welcome her returning hero, whose uniform was adorned with multiple medals for meritorious service.

In due course, their son inherited the place, discarding all traces of his flighty marchioness after she deserted him for a not-so-secret lover. Although his near neighbors decamped to modest digs, he stayed on, tended by his equally aged servants, attending the House of Lords and dining at one of several prestigious clubs to which he belonged.

Martin's mobile, silent since the brief dialogue with Hannah Ballard, buzzed with an incoming voicemail. After two listens, it persisted in confounding him.

"Mart—Jess. Dreadful news. A hack from *Posh* has been hounding me incessantly for juicy quotes about you. Unbelievably pushy. *And* she wants photos. I refuse her every request. You know how persistent those gossip trollops can be! Consider this a warning to lie low. Or are you already hiding out at Stanwell?"

He and Jessica had paired up in a casual way before he became seriously involved with Natalie, and they maintained a fond and easy friendship. Her concern about an interview request from a glossy fashion and society magazine struck him as excessive. Precisely how this related to him, or her, or them, he couldn't comprehend.

Chapter 3

Lord Milverston had stood her up. The rat!

Wincott & Sons was represented by Karl, a blond Nordic god with a sexy Scandinavian accent. He'd supplied Hannah with ample food and wine, as well as bottles of champagne she didn't recall ordering. His equally presentable uniformed colleague arranged trays with cheese and biscuits and fruit, replenishing them as needed. At the moment, the pair were circulating with trays of pink salmon slivers on little pieces of crustless bread. She hadn't requested the fish, either.

Concerns about low attendance had been unnecessary. In response to her urgent pleas, her cousin Will had arrived with an entourage. They had signaled news of abundant alcohol and available women to their acquaintances. She saw manicured thumbs tapping mobiles and fluting voices alerting office mates about the presence of male guests. Her modest gathering had morphed into something noisier—and more potent—than she'd intended.

While tilting her phone to frame an artsy shot of a floral arrangement, she was distracted by a plummy British voice saying, "I'm here to register a complaint." She spun around.

"About what?"

The marquess grinned. "Depictions of English twenty- and thirty-something in films. Grossly misleading. All so gorgeous, witty, well-dressed, and matey as hell. They hold no jobs yet reside in up-market neighborhoods like Snogging Hill and Westbourne. They bang on about their love lives at dinner parties. And though they seem to be utterly devoid of family ties, they're forever turning up at weddings. Or funerals."

"Because that's what American audiences expect you to do," Hannah replied, retrieving her glass. "Go ahead, tell me all about your reality. How do upper-class Brits pass their time?"

"Abusing alcohol and less lawful substances. Smashing up expensive motorcars. Submitting to detox regimes. Nattering to therapists. Maxing out credit cards. Faffing about with cryptocurrency. Not me, personally," he was quick to add.

"People in overseas territories get a skewed representation of Americans. We aren't *all* action heroes or soldiers or addicts or sexpots." Conscious of a waspish edge to her voice, she said, "Sorry if I sound defensive. I'm suffering from a case of social anxiety."

"Perhaps you should drink something stronger than sparkling water, to buck you up."

"I did. Karl looked so devastated when I declined to sample his wine that I had a couple of sips. I couldn't refuse a man who looks like that."

He surveyed the humming throng. "You lured me here under false pretenses. The place is heaving with blokes."

"I panicked and called in reinforcements. My violinist cousin—chatting up the redhead—brought along a few of his colleagues from the symphony. You might say fostering relationships is an essential aspect of my job."

"You're a matchmaker?"

She laughed. "Yes, but not that kind. I'm a location finder—a scout, as we say in the States. Recently promoted to location manager." She still got a charge of pleasure from announcing her title. "For the film currently in pre-production, I'm heading our Locations Department."

"Impressive."

"Not to people in the industry, although it's a crucial function. Massive responsibility." She'd discover how much more at the end of the summer. Her present tasks were routine and familiar, easily transferable to a different country. "My name will appear in the closing credits. Somewhere in the middle, after Postproduction Accountant and before Extras Casting. My guests are personnel from the film location company making recommendations of suitable sites. Tomorrow I start touring the ones that match my chief criteria: picturesque, photogenic, and period correct. With ideal logistics."

"What sort of movie?"

"Historical epic, eighteenth century. My mission is identifying the perfect house to shoot in and around."

"Looking for a stately home, are you?"

Hannah nodded. "Preferably with a scenic village close by. And a great deal more. Not that I expect to find everything we need all in one place. Typically, we shoot in multiple locations and the footage gets seamlessly mushed together in the editing process. After I've assessed recommended sites, I select the ones that suit the project and present them to the producer, the director, and department heads."

"Who's starring?"

"Casting announcements will be strategically timed for maximum impact." Smiling, she added, "If you stop asking questions I'm not allowed to answer, I'll put you on the ticket list for our London premiere."

Will, separating himself from the redhead, came to her rescue.

"Awesome party," he told her. "Lots better than my

mates and I expected." He bobbed his head at Lord Milverston. "William Edney."

"Martin Latimer."

"I say, Hannah, might Davey and Jos and I steal Bridget and a couple of her friends? There's just enough time to grab a bite before we're due in the orchestra pit."

"Fine with me." She handed over her phone. "After you take a photo I can send my boss, proof of how well I'm doing my job."

"Shall I step aside?" the marquess murmured.

"No way! You're my one celebrity. I'm exploiting you." She edged closer to him.

Will obediently positioned her phone. "Say 'Cheese!'"

Hannah and her lordly guest exchanged smiles.

"Look over here." Will completed his assignment and returned her device. While she scrolled through the images, he said, "When you're in touch with Aunt Gwen and Uncle Neil, give them my regards. And do ring my parents before you leave town. She and Dad hope to see you before you get any busier. Gran, too, if you can manage it."

"I will. I'm definitely planning to make a plan to see Mum's family while I'm here."

Her cup of satisfaction was brimming, just like the champagne flute the marquess had plucked from Karl's tray.

He held it towards her. "Drink. If only to salve your disappointment about my lack of celebrity status. Despite the title, I'm a complete nonentity. Which is why I can loiter in Wincott & Sons and force Milver Vale products onto anyone who wanders in."

"Blessed are the cheesemakers," she said merrily, touching the rim of her glass against his.

"I sincerely hope so."

"Marquesses aren't very high profile," she commented. "Not like dukes and earls."

"In the eighteenth century most marquessates got

upgraded to dukedoms. For reasons beyond my knowledge, ours wasn't. In France, I'd be a marquis, not such a rarity." He sipped his champagne before saying, "I daresay you interact with hordes of truly famous people in Hollywood."

"I only travel to the West Coast under duress and stay not a moment longer than absolutely necessary."

"Why is that?"

"A Yankee thing, I guess. Half-Yankee," she corrected herself. "My dad, despite being a descendant of colonists who fled this land centuries ago and revolutionaries who battled your side, married a Briton. My mother is Wendy Edney. The garden writer and television personality."

"Poppy will have heard of her. She's a keen gardener."

Of course there was a wife—a marchioness. He was an attractive aristocrat with a chin, a sense of humor, and a bad boy grin. And atmospheric gray eyes staring down at her.

Seconds dragged by before he said, "That explains how you managed to recreate the Chelsea Flower Show here. Primroses, daffodils, tulips, springing up on every table."

"A trick of Mum's," she confessed. "Pile the mossy stuff high, stick the pots and vases down deep and cover them. Cheap and easy. Excuse me, I need to mingle."

Unlike your lordship, she added silently, I've got a real job.

Martin sizzled with hopeful speculation when watching Hannah Ballard, a bright note of shimmery coral in an ever-shifting sea of charcoal and black. Her short, sleeveless silk dress exposed toned arms and slender legs. She ran her fingers through her manic dark curls, her expression inscrutable as a weedy wanker with a prominent nose and big ears cornered her. She was an alien from a strange and distant world populated by creative geniuses and moguls with limitless power and money.

Wouldn't it be brilliant, he told himself, if she sprinkled some of her stardust over me?

He understood what she needed far better than she did. And he had precise needs of his own.

Feigning interest in the tray of smoked salmon, he considered possible methods of persuasion. Applying liberal amounts of alcohol in hopes of winning her over would be ungentlemanly, and she wasn't much of a drinker. It might be better to take the most direct approach, and boldly state his proposition.

As the crowd thinned Hannah handed out flowerpots to departing women. She offered the remains of the cheese and fish and biscuits to the people clustered around the serving table.

"Take fruit, too," she urged. "I can't eat all these leftovers. I'm leaving early tomorrow."

Marching forward, he seized a tray of Belgian chocolates. "Don't give these away."

"I'm not *that* generous," she admitted.

"Might it be possible to speak with you privately?"

"Sure," she said airily. "Wait down the hall, I'll be there in a sec."

Martin conferred with Karl about storage of the unopened wine bottles prior to their being returned to the vintner. After a brief stop in the palatial lavatory, he made his way along the corridor. In the bedroom, he found club chairs and a sofa arranged around a reproduction butler's table, and a king-sized bed with a nubby satin counterpane. An alcove was arranged as a work space—it contained a small glass-topped desk and black chair. Through a half-open window he could hear the drone of traffic in Piccadilly. A gust fluttered the gauzy curtain, depositing several loose papers onto the floor.

Hannah surged into her inner sanctum. "Karl says you're wholly responsible for the additions to my catering order. In the past twenty-four hours I've become Wincott & Sons' greatest fan."

"Our reputation for quality is over two centuries old," he responded in his smoothest salesman voice.

"I'll quote you when our production accountant squawks at the cost." She collapsed into one of the leather chairs. "Will I get a hard copy of the invoice?"

"Not from me, I don't have anything to do with paperwork. Karl will leave an envelope in a conspicuous place. The chocolates you kept won't sustain you for very long. Fortunately, I know a superior French bistro in Shepherd Market."

"Thanks for the suggestion, but it's the room service menu for me." Her tone was polite but implacable.

"Drinks instead? I'm familiar with several pleasant pubs, steps away."

"I wish I could join you, but I've got calls to make. Clothes to pack. I'm booked on a morning train to Reading."

"Really?"

"Ree-leee," she mocked him, her accent spot-on.

"I was born there. Stayed till I was five years old."

"I'll be picking up my hire car. Never fear, I pose no danger on your motorways and narrow lanes. I have experience with right-hand drive and manual transmission. Mum gave Dad a clunky vintage Morris Minor for their tenth wedding anniversary."

Her parents sounded like fun, a pity she wasn't more like them. He'd better get to the point before she chucked him out.

"Miss Ballard—"

"Hannah. We moved past a business relationship when you came to my party."

"Your visit to Wincott & Sons yesterday was a stroke of luck. For each of us."

"Do you say that to all your lady customers when you get them alone?"

Martin shook his head emphatically. "The shop's clientele are strictly off limits."

"Even the posh ones, with titles?"

He didn't waste time on an answer. "Hannah, I've got something spectacular I want to show you."

Sitting straighter, she eyed him suspiciously. "What is it?"

"My most significant possession. I'm very attached to it. And it's attached to me."

She leaned forward, eyebrows arched. "Big?"

"Enormous," he boasted.

"Size isn't everything."

"Your opinion about that will change when you've seen it."

Leaving her chair, she grabbed a notepad and pen from the desk. "Directions, please."

"I can keep it up a lot longer."

She groaned. "No more double entendres. Tell me where I can find your enormous prized possession?"

"Somerset." He extended his right hand to show his signet ring. "The county emblem. Dragon rampant."

Her eyebrows shifted upwards before she echoed his question from yesterday. "North or south?"

"South. Milver Vale."

"Where the cheese is made."

He nodded. "Stanwell House is close to Yeovil and not far from the Dorset border. I'm confident it meets your every requirement. Picturesque and photogenic, with gobs of period appeal. Royal associations, too. King Alfred traipsed across the property. Henry the Eighth used it for a hunting lodge before selling it to Sir Rufus Latimer. Edward the

Seventh popped in once—there's a menu of the dinner he was served, which must have lasted for hours. I shouldn't wonder if Edward the Eighth shagged Wallis Simpson in one of the bedrooms when they visited, before his abdication."

"Website?"

"None. It's my private home, in no way connected to the National Trust or English Heritage."

"If it's architecturally interesting, I'll be able to find pictures on the internet."

"Nobody can get near enough to photograph it, and fewer still have been inside. A footpath cutting through the property is a right of way, accessible to walkers and ramblers. At a considerable distance from the house, which isn't visible."

"Freshness and uniqueness are rare and desirable commodities," she acknowledged. "I already rejected one historic house because it's so frequently filmed. Advertisements, magazines, movies. My producer doesn't want the audience noticing our country mansion is the same one from a Jane Austen flick. Or the Bridgerton saga. Or a Charles Dickens series on public television."

"Any existing footage of Stanwell would've been shot decades ago, by guests of the family. It's in dusty attics or cellars, disintegrating."

With an intensity that proved his optimism wasn't misplaced, she asked him to estimate the driving time from Bristol.

"Something just under or over an hour, depending on the time of day and the route. Is that important?"

"Our production is based at Hartcliffe Film Studios in a Bristol suburb. A major facility, with office space, sound stages, wardrobe. The works. We'll construct interiors there as necessary. But if I do my job well, we won't need many." She reached for a sheaf of papers. "The entire story takes place in a rural area. In addition to the big house, I'm looking for a site with farmers' cottages, preferably with thatched roofs. A tavern. A barn with hayloft. Parish church, ideally with tombstones all around. Water—either a pond or stream will do. And some sort of woodland, for the gamekeeper's hut. He's a major character."

"Certain areas within the Milver Vale are forested. Can you use a river? I've got one."

Phone in hand, she pressed the screen with her thumb. "I need to look at a map. Where is your territory?"

He took out his own device. Swiping outward, he enlarged the image so she could read the place names. "Milverston Magna oozes character. It's got a village green surrounded by shops and two very historic pubs. Milver Cross and Milver St. Mary have a few thatched cottages. Near the river there's a working mill and millpond. Our oldest churches are quite pretty. Each village is a separate parish, with a single lady vicar serving all. And there's an ancient tithe barn."

"What about a courtroom? A jail?"

"Newbridge has a well-preserved eighteenth-century assembly room. And a market hall, originally built for selling sheep fleeces and produce. Plus several historically listed buildings. Brick, stone, even some half-timbered ones."

"I've included two open days in my itinerary, in case an appointment is postponed or I get a hot tip from my primary contact at the location company. I can tack your Stanwell and Milver Vale onto the end of my tour."

"Trust me, you're saving the best for last."

Lifting her head, she said, "The places on my longlist were selected by expert location finders."

He leaned over the desk and used the hotel pen to scribble the estate office phone number on the pad. "If you've got questions, ring Poppy Deane. She'll get you sorted. I can book a superior room at the Latimer Arms in Milverston

Magna. Nothing like as grand as this place, but very highly rated. Bed and breakfast?"

"Bed only. I'm no tourist, stuffing myself with the full English. All I require is a pot of yogurt from the village shop. My tastes are simple, and I'm easy to please. Except," she concluded in a tone of warning, "when it comes to choosing locations for the most important film of my career."

Chapter 4

After a surprisingly sunny, trouble-free tour of hamlets and houses, the weather—and Hannah's outlook—abruptly changed. Not only because of gray skies and intermittent rainfall. This was the tenth anniversary of Chase's sentencing.

Today her mind frequently darted back in time to that chilly April afternoon when she'd helped her grandfather stack his lobster traps. Without her uncle's stream of jokes, the job had taken longer than usual. She remembered how the breeze rippled the water beyond the dock and the shimmer of sunshine on the surface. The screeching gulls drowned the droning voice coming from the portable radio—until Grampa turned up the volume. A decade on, she could still hear the words with perfect, piercing clarity: *Chase Ballard, convicted of manslaughter . . . a ten-year sentence . . . transferred from Cumberland County Jail in Portland to the Maine State Prison in Warren . . ."*

He'd taken her fishing in his motorboat and helped her haul in her catch. Shown her the best places on the river to spot eagles and ospreys and herons. Supervised her 4-H projects when her parents didn't have time. An only child, she'd felt so lucky to have big brother and uncle rolled into one. Someone to have fun with. Whose shoulder she could cry on—not that she often did.

She twisted the car radio's volume button. As the final notes of an upbeat song faded, a pair of presenters began rehashing the latest developments in the widely publicized Sterling Scandal. Several days ago, darting into a bookshop in the Reading railway station, she'd noticed large boldface headlines on the tabloid newspapers and garish color photos of a member of Parliament and his glamorous lover, whose connection to an infamous crime family had recently been uncovered. Hannah hadn't imagined that her opinion of the British press and its characteristic obsession with the private lives of public figures could sink any lower. Current events proved otherwise.

Her expectations for Stanwell House weren't high, a judgment based on a few low-res images produced by her internet search, and doubts nagged her as she approached the final stop on her tour. Shooting interiors and exteriors at a private residence would be a hell of a lot trickier than at any of the sites recommended by the location agency.

During a phone conversation with her location finder—without naming Lord Milverston or his house—she puzzled over his motive for readily opening his property for inspection.

"Flat broke," the woman declared. "Desperate to replace the lead roof, or get rid of the dry rot. I reckon his bank overdraft is giving him and his accountant seizures. Those huge places cost several fortunes to maintain. That's why we've got such a large list on our books, and you're so spoilt for choice."

Hannah disliked being the beneficiary of someone else's misery, although she was aware that an infusion of money from the film production would benefit the property owner.

"If he hasn't opened his precious house to the public,"

her contact went on, "he doesn't want the common folk traipsing over his hallowed acres and marching into his great hall to mock or criticize the portraits of his noble and not very woke ancestors. You're the lesser of several evils."

"His estate's proximity to Hartcliffe Studios is a significant plus."

"The only one, is my guess. Internet access in the countryside can be unreliable. It's impossible to manage a production without a strong signal, for all the reasons you know well enough. The house will contain all kinds of valuable objects to be guarded. Also, if its overall condition has deteriorated, there could be hazards. Outdated wiring. Flaking plaster. Creaking floorboards."

Hannah considered these nightmarish warnings as the scudding clouds congealed into a dense darkness. Raindrops crashed onto her windshield, blotting out the landscape. She could just make out a single-track road, miraculously signed for Milverston Magna.

"England in springtime," she sighed, rolling through the sodden green landscape.

Parallel hedgerows lined the narrow, twisting lane. It brought her to a paved road, at which point the satnav instructed her to make a right turn. She glanced at a Roman Catholic chapel and beyond it an Anglican church, both Victorian and neither old enough for her purposes. She passed a cluster of semi-detached houses, a school, and dilapidated factory buildings. This village was a dud.

Crossing the narrow bridge over the broad River Milver, she spied a lofty watermill and arching willow trees. Beyond these stood the enormous building that matched Martin Latimer's description of the tithe barn, she arrived at a place where several roads converged. Keeping to the same one, she hoped for the best.

Despite being partly obscured by the torrent, her destination looked promising. The parish church, built of stone, sat near the triangular grassy common, bordered by shops on two sides. The Latimer Arms stood at the short end.

Her relief and sense of achievement were short-lived. On reaching the car park she checked the dashboard clock. "Damn," she muttered. Fifteen minutes late for her appointment. No time to check in, or to stretch her legs, or do anything else. Frantically she searched her phone for the directions to Stanwell House.

She backtracked until she found a muddy single-track road, aware that pheasants and rabbits lurked in the fields on the other side of the hedges and could dart out at any moment. A house and farm buildings lay tucked into a fold between low, sheep-dotted hills.

Her next landmark appeared soon after, two stone pillars marking a paved drive that eventually brought her to a sizable stable yard. The surrounding outbuildings were in excellent repair, the gray-green paint on the wooden doors and the window trim looked fresh. Solar panels topped the longest rooftop, and she noted an electric vehicle charging station.

From her brief telephone contact with the estate manager, Hannah had envisioned a more mature Poppy Deane. The young woman braving the drizzle to greet her was as tall and slender as a fashion model, if not as ethereal.

"The way the rain was sheeting down earlier, I suspected you'd be delayed. I've got the kettle on already. You'll be wanting tea."

Hannah followed Poppy into a cream-painted office with attractive pine furniture and state-of-the-art computer and screen. Colorful Berber rugs brightened the sanded wooden floors. In a corner sat an empty dog basket and water dish. "Nice work space," she commented when the estate manager returned from a back room carrying two mugs.

"Shared. Dennis, our numbers-cruncher, comes in three days a week. A local girl performs general office duties as needed." Poppy's brown ponytail brushed her shoulders as she turned to the large, framed map on the wall. Her forefinger slid across the glass. "Home Farm Lane brought you here. If you'd followed this bigger road bordering the green in Milverston, you'd have noticed the front gate and the fencing. It's the main route to Newbridge."

"What's there?" She couldn't recall what the marquess had said about it.

Poppy smiled. "An extremely *old* bridge, and a weir. The historic Market Hall and the Assembly Rooms, mixed in with some fairly unobtrusive modern construction. The railway station sits at the farthest end of the High Street. Which also has shops and offices, an Italian restaurant, a curry house, café, pubs, and a wine bar. A few years ago, Newbridge won a Tidy Town award. There's also a busy roundabout on the outskirts with petrol stations, megastores, and a chain hotel."

"I'll be checking it out."

Leading Hannah to the empty desk, she said, "You can use Dennis's computer to look over Dad's masterwork." She pointed at a flash drive. "Our Milverston Estate archive, hundreds of photos and descriptive documents. All the dodgy pictures are mine. Feel free to trawl to your heart's content. Take your time."

Hannah scrolled through countless images of old-fashioned cottages and stone houses and farm buildings, each captioned with its date of construction, map reference, and current tenant. A lengthy document contained a property inventory with historical notes.

"This is fantastic," she said, when she'd acquainted herself with the types of structures that could prove most useful.

"My father, the estate manager before me, was mad for record-keeping. There seems to be some sort of cataloguing infection round here. The late marquess had it, too. When

Mart began turning out his uncle's desk, every drawer had a printed list of its contents. An affront to his adventurous soul."

Her fond and familiar reference to his lordship did not escape Hannah's notice. Was this attractive and trusted employee also his girlfriend?

The ringing telephone demanded Poppy's attention. "Milverston Estate office, Poppy Deane speaking." She tapped her fingers firmly against the desktop, listening, then said, "Well, I do appreciate your informing us, but Lord Milverston isn't available for an interview." After a brief silence, she said calmly, "No, I've nothing to share. Sorry." With an intimidating frown, she stated, "That isn't a subject about which I care to speculate. No, I'm *not* his lordship's public relations person. He's got no PR. I'm afraid I really must ring off now. You've caught me during an important meeting."

After the call ended, Hannah told her, "I'm flattered."

"I always say that when badgered by the press, even if I'm sitting here alone. More polite than 'bugger off.'"

"How's the reception on mobile networks around here? Is there consistent internet service?"

"Exceptional. Superfast connectivity via standard broadband and fiber. We're located in a small-scale commuter belt between densely populated towns, and within an hour's drive of Bristol."

After another half-hour Hannah stepped out of the office. She had accepted Poppy's invitation to a tour so she could take her own photos.

She paused in the stable yard, so absorbed by her surroundings that she easily erased the persistent rainfall and the anachronistic elements in the scene—her red rental car and the gray Volvo, the charging station and electrical wiring. Faint neighs from the horse barn carried her backwards through time. Here, as elsewhere in her travels, scenes from the film script took shape in her mind. She could imagine the characters coming to life in this place.

I haven't seen enough, not yet, she cautioned herself.

She needed to explore Stanwell House, looming so tantalizingly close. Even from this vantage it looked promising, but until she saw the rooms she couldn't tell whether it would suit the production team principals. She didn't want to begin her challenging new role in defensive mode.

Returning to the Latimer Arms she inspected the hotel bar—beamed ceilings, fireplace, row of taps—and peered into the restaurant—snowy tablecloths, brass candlesticks, busy floral wallpaper. The menu offered such temptations as spring lamb and river trout. She was hungry enough to order both.

Her room, abundantly furnished with oak and chintz, suited her. She was about to unzip and open her roller bag when her phone rang.

In his hearty voice, the Marquess of Milverston hoped that her accommodations were satisfactory.

"Very. No complaints whatsoever."

"You got the flowers?"

"Um—" She spotted a vase containing branches of apple blossom. "Thanks."

"You'll see the whole blooming orchard tomorrow. And lots more."

She was struggling to come up with a response when he invited her to dinner.

"Aren't you in London?"

"At the house, barely a mile away as the magpie flies. Don't turn me down this time."

"This time? When did I—oh." His post-party offer to feed her, which she'd declined. Then, as now, his energy and enthusiasm had been incompatible with her weariness.

But when she recalled his engaging grin, his smoky gray eyes—and that title—she couldn't refuse. How often did she get a chance to dine with a genuine aristocrat? Never. What's more, it was his job to impress her instead of the other way round. Perhaps he'd already killed a fatted calf or sheep. Or trout.

"When should I come round to collect you?" he asked.

"That depends on whether you'll take me as I am. I haven't even unpacked."

"Be there in ten minutes."

Desperate to erase visible effects of her day in the damp, Hannah made a valiant effort to tame her rain-frizzed hair. She refreshed her make-up and checked her jacket and slacks for creases. From the depths of her precisely packed bag, she extracted heeled shoes—unworn since London—sacrificing comfort for an increase of inches and exposure of her latest pedicure. Familiar with the pervasive chill of big English houses, she grabbed her wine-colored pashmina before hurrying down to the lobby.

A disappointingly ordinary black car idled near the door. Neither a Jaguar nor a Rover, it was manufactured domestically by Vauxhall and confirmed her suspicions about Lord Milverston's precarious finances. A familiar scent indicated that one of his regular passengers was canine.

Cheerily he inquired, "What's your impression of the Milver region?"

"Terrible place to shoot a film. Too much rain."

He laughed. "Not always. Tomorrow will be bright and dry."

"It certainly couldn't get wetter."

"Indeed, it could. And assuredly will. You're experiencing what we call a mild spring shower." The heavy drops battering his windshield contradicted him. "Did driver training in your parents' Morris Minor stand you in good stead?"

"So far, so good. I stay off your terrifying motorways as much as I can. Despite the fact I often drive in Boston, which has the craziest drivers in the entire United States."

"I can easily believe that. Quite shocking."

"You've been there?"

"Ten years ago, very nearly. Reckless motorists and deep potholes and towering buildings. That sums up my experience."

"No cruise on a Swan Boat in the Public Garden?"

He shook his head. "Never saw one."

"You must've been there during the off season. They stop running in September."

"Late autumn, which to us felt like winter. I hadn't any time for sightseeing. I definitely wasn't in the mood. In retrospect, worst year of my life."

"Mine too," she confessed.

The aftermath of Chase's trial and sentencing. The unraveling of family relationships.

She tugged her thoughts from the past and tried to discern the landscape between swipes of the wipers as her lordly driver sped along.

He halted at the metal gate set between a pair of tall stone pillars. "Visiting dignitaries arrive at the main entrance." Picking up a remote-control device from the center console, he pressed the number pad and the iron bars parted. When he'd passed through the opening, he tapped the pad again to close the gate.

The distinctive façade, recognizable from the photos Hannah had studied earlier, loomed ahead. A coat of arms was carved in stone above the archway. "Enormous indeed. As described."

"Compared to Castle Latimer, practically a hovel."

"You have a castle, too?"

"Had. I sold it."

Like his modest automobile, this revelation confirmed his insolvency. "That's too bad."

"No loss. A mid-Victorian monstrosity inconveniently located in the remotest reaches of Cumbria. A popular shooting estate, from Edwardian times up to the First World War, when people traveled in their private rail cars and had armies of servants to make them comfortable. The luxury hotel company who owns it now did it up beautifully. With an exclusive world-class golf course. And a spa." His palm struck the steering wheel. "Damn—forgot an umbrella. Not the best way to make a favorable impression."

She pulled her pashmina over her head, and together they hurried through the rain. He poked at another security keypad and ushered her through the tall oak door.

Drawing back her shawl, Hannah gazed upon the mellow splendor of a Great Hall dating from Tudor times. A minstrels' gallery enclosed with a railing stretched across the room, directly opposite a tall oriel window, rows of clear panes and above them a line of heraldic shields in colored glass. Straight-backed Jacobean chairs with carved arms and legs stood against the wood-paneled wall, and leather armchairs flanked the massive fireplace. Paintings of soldiers on horseback lined the walls, and weaponry arranged in complex patterns decorated the area above them.

"You're well prepared for any trouble that comes along," she observed, slashing the air with her arm.

"It's here now—trouble on four legs." A gangly, furry creature plummeted down the carved staircase and raced across the stone-paved floor. "Meet Ariel."

Hannah stood her ground. Greeting the caramel-colored dog by name, she extended a friendly hand. After some curious snuffling, Ariel waved her tail, an invitation to pet her elongated head. "What breed is she?"

"Numerous. A complete and utter mongrel. Which is to say, a lurcher. Yes, yes, I'm home again. We were apart for all of twenty minutes—however did you survive, my darling?" He knelt so the dog could lick his chin.

If he talks like that to his girlfriend, and caresses her as gently, Hannah mused, she must be in a constant state of bliss.

Rising, he said, "Ron laid a fire in the drawing room so I can show it off. I don't often use it, with just the two of us living here."

Ron? Hannah's speculations about his significant other abruptly shifted from girlfriend to boyfriend. Or male partner. Or husband.

Leading her through a dining room of daunting grandeur, he continued, "Our main security chap is on hols, but his substitute must be somewhere about the place."

"You have a bodyguard?"

"Oh, no, not me. My value is negligible. It's the contents he protects—Old Master paintings, antique furniture and silver, French porcelains. Portraits and miniatures in jeweled frames. Not that we've had any serious issues at Stanwell. But rural crime is endemic, unfortunately." He indicated the array of bottles lined up on a mahogany cabinet. "Gin, whisky, sherry, wine?"

"Wine, please." A risky request, her stomach was hollowed out by hunger. She perched on a Chippendale style sofa—certainly genuine—and examined her surroundings. A crystal chandelier dangled from the ceiling, and her feet rested on a carpet woven with swags and garlands reflecting the plasterwork motif overhead. Stroking Ariel's fluffy neck, she said, "I need to look at your rooms in the daytime, to make a thorough assessment."

"You will, in the morning," he assured her, busy with tongs and ice. "Afterwards, Poppy's going to tour you though the villages and show you some highly presentable farmhouses. Later in the day, when I get back from Newbridge, we'll take you to one of the pubs. No better place to sample our local culture. And color."

When he presented her wineglass on a round silver tray, she said, "What a letdown, not being served by a Carson. Or Jeeves."

"My man is either faffing about in the kitchen, or he already retreated to his private quarters. I'm cooking, by the way. The dough is already prepared and waiting. You don't mind pizza?"

"Love it." She hoped she wouldn't keel over in the time required to make and bake one.

"Ron's official title is house manager," he explained. "The rest of Stanwell's staff is decidedly international. Nico, his assistant, is Greek. Freya, the housekeeper, was born in Norway. Gosia, our daily maid, came from Poland. Kateryna, a Ukrainian refugee, helps with whatever needs doing after classes—her college in Kyiv provides remote learning. Shona, in charge of our horses, is Scots and deeply proud of it. The cook, head gardener, and two under gardeners are English."

"How many horses?"

"Mine, Poppy's, and two lodgers. We'd take in more, but most people here have their own stabling. Do you ride?"

"When I'm at home." Which she rarely was, by intent. "Years ago, I had my own pony. Now there's only Rascal, Mum's gelding."

"Ours need regular exercise. If you're so minded."

She shook her head. "No gear."

"Borrow Poppy's. She's got loads. Her one extravagance."

Hannah laughed. "If you think I'd fit into her clothes or her boots, you're awfully unobservant."

"My faith in female ingenuity is massive." Seating himself, he crossed long, corduroy-clad legs. "Did you locate any hot location prospects during your travels?"

"I'm still evaluating," she answered carefully.

With phone and digital camera, she'd taken as many as a thousand photos and had recorded video of exteriors, interiors, and landscapes. She had filled her notepad with information gleaned from her agency liaison and managers of historic properties. Specific spaces lingered in her mind—a ballroom here, a kitchen there. One particularly attractive Cotswold village frustrated her by being too popular and crowded in the summer, probably unwilling to close off its famous street to traffic. The remote northernmost regions posed insurmountable difficulties—transit time and dubious weather.

"I suppose you carry a copy of the script."

She nodded. "The current draft. Mostly I rely on a breakdown of scenes, annotated with my notes taken from the novel's narrative descriptions of places."

"I'm reading it," he announced. "The day after your party I headed to the bookshop in the Row and interrogated its manager till we worked out the title. *Forsaken Fortune.* Who'll play Rosalind?"

"I'm not supposed to say. But just between us, when I met with the casting people in their Soho office, they were very excited."

"You should use that bosomy Australian bird who took her kit off in a movie I saw on Channel Five." He named a blockbuster from four summers ago, targeted to fourteen-year-old boys.

Hannah required no further proof of heterosexuality. "I never saw it. Our British director—"

"Sir Owen Parry."

She nodded. "According to him, Hollywood A-listers will object to the nude scenes and the sex. They tend to be protective of their bodily assets. Except when dressing for awards shows."

"When you make your movie here at Stanwell, I'm keen

to watch them shoot the hayloft scene. Steamiest pages in the book. So far."

"No onlookers. Just the director, camera and sound, and the intimacy coordinator."

He left his chair to tend the simmering fire. "*I* don't object to spectators when I'm performing. Come and be a witness while I prepare your dinner."

Chapter 5

The bright and spacious kitchen impressed Hannah with its contemporary wooden cabinetry and state-of-the-art appliances. Beneath well-positioned light fixtures, the milky marble worktops gleamed.

"I wouldn't call this Jacobean."

"Elizabethan." He grinned. "Elizabeth the Second. This used to be the servants' dining room, formerly connected to the old kitchen and its adjacent components. My late uncle had walls bashed down to create this space for cooking, eating, and entertaining. I upgraded the equipment, changed the cupboards, and called in the painters. You'll be relieved to know that the original and quite historic areas are basically intact. Stillroom, buttery, pantry, and so on."

Ariel stretched out on one of the floor mats, inserted her muzzle between her paws, and watched her master. He opened drawers and removed the necessary utensils with a confidence surprising in a man who employed servants.

When Hannah asked how often he cooked for himself, he replied, "In the evening, when it's usually just Ron and me, we take turns. Jan comes early enough to do our breakfast, then lunches for me and the staff, and tea before she goes home. She does the shopping and keeps me amply stocked with the choice items I request, though not without grumbling. She's a proponent of plain cookery. Yet she was busy all afternoon with a chocolate thingummy meant to astonish you. Not only did she lecture me on properly turning it out of the pudding basin, she left written instructions for heating the sauce."

Hannah liked that he referred to his employees as though they were family members. "How can I help?"

He looked up from his blob of dough. "You could pour the wine into that jug and place it on the table."

She filled the colorful ceramic pitcher as instructed and carried it to the dining area, her heels clicking against the stone floor. An enormous trestle table, a modern reproduction of the antique version, surrounded by ten chairs, was set with two square plates, cutlery, and stemware.

"There's a wine cellar," she guessed.

"A subterranean vault, my uncle's pride and joy. Ron deals with the brokers and makes recommended additions. Me, I nip into the wine shop in Milverston—mainly for *prosecco,* in memory of my time in Venice. For about a year I worked in a restaurant on the Grande Canale, where I committed various brutalities against seafood. Already dead, of course."

Hannah could easily picture him in a white apron, cleaving off fish heads like a manic food channel chef.

"In Naples I studied the art of pizza-making." With experienced hands he flattened out a thin crust. Painting it with a light coating of what appeared to be puree of fresh tomatoes, he displayed all the joy and artistry she'd lacked during her stint in a busy college town pizza parlor.

"Oven door, please."

She confronted the bewildering selection. "Which one?"

"Second one down, on your right. Then you can get my mozzarella. There's prosciutto, too, if you like it."

The stainless-steel fridge was stocked with British staples and an array of interesting foreign foodstuffs. She located the lump of pale cheese and thinly sliced ham wrapped in greaseproof wrapping.

He studied the salad greens spread across the counter. "Rocket and chicory. Well done, Jan."

"Let me prep your 'shrooms." She cleaned and sliced them, tossing neat slivers into the salad bowl with the halved cherry tomatoes. "My restaurant job wasn't as exotic as yours."

"That makes us even. I once did a job on a film. If you count lugging camera equipment through jungle thickets."

"Really? Where?"

"Thailand. I joined a documentary crew for a fortnight. Interesting blokes, ever so glad of an extra pair of hands and a strong back."

"Venice *and* Thailand? That was some gap year. Your—" she hesitated, uncertain about the correct terminology. "Poppy said you were adventurous."

"My vagabond days came after university, from which I made a premature departure. Two years at an Oxford college persuaded me to pursue life studies instead of my degree."

"Your parents let you drop out?"

"My father died while I was at Eton and thus was spared the humiliation. After my mother fell sick—she's all right now, thank God—I couldn't concentrate on my reading or my lectures. My tutor must've been relieved when I packed it in."

"It's not as though you needed a diploma. You were destined to inherit this place. And that street in London. Latimer Row."

"Exactly what Uncle Rufus said."

Leaving her to toss the salad, he removed the partially baked pizza from the oven. Hannah watched him lay on slices of mozzarella, prosciutto, fresh basil and oregano, her hunger pangs intensifying.

"A few minutes under the broiler," he said, returning his creation to the oven.

She voiced the question that had been on her mind since the day they'd met. "What's it really like for you, holding an aristocratic title in the twenty-first century?"

The skin around his eyes crinkled as he considered the matter. "I'm still learning. Certain inherited responsibilities require me to go to London at intervals, but I prefer my work here in the Milver Vale. And a good thing, because Ariel suffers terribly from separation anxiety." He directed a fond glance at the dog, whose floppy ears lifted when she heard her name.

Hannah judged the meal perfect in every detail. It satisfied her raging appetite and her demanding palate. He'd crisped the dimpled crust beautifully, in the true Italian style. The vinaigrette complemented the fresh and tangy salad greens.

Intrigued by her earlier fleeting glimpse of his serious side, she tried drawing him out about his local interests.

"I'm involved in property development ventures. In no way as exciting as movie-making."

His comment didn't ring true to Hannah. This was their third encounter, but already she could tell he wouldn't commit himself to anything he wasn't passionate about. At Wincott & Sons, he introduced people to cheese with infectious enthusiasm. During her party, he'd dialed up his charm so high that she'd decided to look at his house. Here, in his kitchen, he'd energetically displayed his wizardry with food.

Their backgrounds and lifestyles couldn't be more different, but intense dedication was one thing they shared. An attractive quality—especially when combined with a wicked smile and uninhibited laugh.

Deftly shifting the subject away from himself, he asked, "What made you choose a career in film?"

"It chose me. A long time ago. I was just a scrawny Maine kid when a public television crew from Boston came to our farm to film my mother's gardening program." She told him how she'd advised the director, telling him precisely when sunlight hit the delphiniums.

"Life-altering," he commented.

"As it turned out. Liz Gregorio was a junior producer, and nice enough to mentor a nosy brat with a mouthful of braces. Most kids I knew spent that summer at camp or on the beach or roaming Disney World. By staying home, I got my start in showbiz."

After her mother published two popular tie-in books, a cable network offered a bigger budget and a wider audience. The re-imagined series featured visits to gardens and greenhouses, and in-depth interviews with landscape designers and university horticulturalists.

"I mimicked a grown-up voice and took care of phoning and scheduling. Mum and I drove all around the Northeast, following up leads and scouting for the most photogenic gardens to shoot. The production company paid me a per diem and put my name on the credits."

"Sounds like you earned it."

At this point, she resolved to be extremely cautious about what she revealed. Mum's career and their closeness had been casualties of the events she had no intention of disclosing. In the aftermath of Chase's sentencing and incarceration, she'd fled Bear Knoll, fueled by fury and burdened by guilt.

Breaking the silence, she went on, "I attended a college renowned for its classical and extremely picturesque architecture. A film production unit spent over a week there shooting exteriors and crowd scenes, and my drama department friends skipped classes to be extras. Because of my credentials, I scored the job of gofer for the location manager. I spent my junior year over here, at Bristol University."

"Studying television and film."

"That's where I first met Sir Owen Parry. He spoke at a directing symposium I attended and served on the judging panel for end-of-term student films. Mine was a finalist. The summer after graduation I had internships on two movies—one in Maine, the other in Nova Scotia. After that, a Portland production company hired me to scout for advertising shoots. Sometimes I did copywriting and video editing. I transferred to Boston to take a job at an even bigger shop, for much better money."

Wine turned her into a chatterbox. Her host seemed not to notice—or mind—that their conversation had turned into a monologue. She let him re-fill her glass.

"Liz kept in touch with me after she left for L.A. She hired me as a scout for the New England-based mystery series she produced for a basic cable channel. She moved up the studio system ladder, made solid contacts, and banked her salary. Her dream was to become an independent producer, based in Boston. That's where she established Acorn Films. Her low budget features won prizes at Sundance, and over time she accumulated Independent Spirit Awards and Emmys. Two years ago, her baseball player biopic hauled in a bunch of Oscars."

"Which categories?"

"Cinematography, editing, script adaptation, supporting actor—four statues out of ten nominations. She optioned *Forsaken Fortune,* and a major studio acquired distribution rights for a stupendous amount of money. The industry has high expectations." Chin in hand, she confided, "Hard to believe I'm attached to such a high-profile project. Overseeing the location department is a huge deal. Not that it will change my relationship with Liz. If you saw us together, you'd think we're best friends. Accurate, in a sense, although she's also my employer. The boss."

Helping him carry empty plates, she was thankful he hadn't asked about her long-range goals. Despite her abilities as an organizer and facilitator, her ambitions were modest. Unlike Liz, she'd never aspired to become a producer. For a decade and a half, she'd watched her friend handle pressures large and small, battling the outsized egos, crunching the numbers in ever-expanding budgets. Mindful of the potential dangers of industry prominence, Hannah balanced career progress with her need to avoid the limelight. Attracting too much attention meant risking scrutiny that might extend to Chase, her ex-con uncle, punished for taking another man's life and on the verge of reclaiming aspects of his own. Fortunately for her, location scouts and managers were below-the-line personnel, invisible to the press and the general public.

"What happens after you find the sites you require?"

"It's not entirely my decision. Before I make a presentation, I analyze the terrain and the roads and potential parking areas, electrical and technical facilities. Cast and crew accommodations. I work with the production secretary on costings and budget so I can negotiate fees and contracts and access. I relay all necessary logistical information to the unit manager, and the technicians, and the transportation team, and the caterers. There's a risk management component, too. Safety and security are essential, and we must follow government and union health regulations and guidelines."

"Keeping track of all those details must do your head in."

"I'll delegate. The assistant location manager helps with the people part of the job. I'd like to have a trainee or intern as well, a young and eager someone who can get entry level work experience. We'll confer with everybody whose property we want to use, or whose business would be affected.

We explain the process, the timetable, the anticipated shooting schedule. It's essential to make clear what will happen, when, and for how long. The people whose locales we use hate surprises and misunderstandings as much as we do. Excellent communication up front saves worlds of trouble later."

He nodded. "I'd be grateful for clear communication right now. Should I serve our pudding straightaway, or after I've shown you some of the rooms?"

"After." Moving about might clear her head.

He put all the food away and placed their plates in the dishwasher. "Lurchers are notorious scavengers and food thieves. Turn your back for an instant, and Ariel will snatch whatever's in view. She's greedy. Like her master, Poppy would say."

"You're stark, raving mad!"

"I daresay," Martin responded as he and Poppy squidged through the thick mud created by overnight rainfall.

"You can't have a movie crew invading Stanwell. The lorries and caravans will tear up this Home Park. And the green. Not to mention the unpaved roads connecting the villages. The boom microphone will knock your chandeliers about. They'll roll cameras into your antique furniture. Old Rufus must be gyrating in the family vault."

"Why would he object? You know how much he appreciated artistic types. So do I."

"Isn't this all about shagging that movie woman?"

"You're the second person to charge me with an ulterior motive."

"Who else?"

"Dan Wheeler."

"You're not denying it," Poppy pointed out.

He couldn't, not truthfully, because he had thought about it. Frequently. "I swear, I didn't lure Hannah Ballard to Stanwell because I'm sex-starved. She's far too sophisticated to be interested in a simple country lad like me." Ignoring her guffaws, he added, "I lust after her film production."

"To the extent that you'd risk your precious privacy?"

"Temporarily. A short-term inconvenience with long-term benefits."

She halted so abruptly that they nearly collided. "I don't see any, Mart. Not even if they pay you pots of money."

He surveyed the landscape, aware that their companions had deserted them. "Where the hell are those dogs?"

"Ariel must've led Millie into trouble. Too adventurous by half. Just like her master."

Despite Poppy's accusation, he knew he didn't set a bad example for his dog. Quite the contrary, he'd trained her well and taught her proper manners. If they shared some personality traits, it wasn't his fault.

The lurcher bounded ahead of the sleek black Labrador loping towards them in response to Poppy's call. Unlike the panting Millie, Ariel wasn't winded. She pranced about as if eager to race or chase.

As they proceeded along the footpath, Poppy asked when filming would start.

"Late summer. Eight weeks, at a minimum. Followed by editing and scoring and I don't know what else at the studio in Bristol or some other place. Hannah's boss, the executive producer, will screen the movie at the festival in Cannes about a year from now, for international distributors. Followed by a limited release in autumn, to qualify for the Academy Awards. With wide release before Christmas."

"You've picked up a new vocabulary," she commented, at her driest. "Why are you grinning like a demented monkey?"

"I'm thinking about something significant that will occur in this district next year."

"The official opening of the Milver Vale Recreational Area."

"After that."

When she turned, he read the comprehension in her expression. "Right. Autumn Harvest Week. The prince comes for the ribbon-cutting at the Rural Heritage Center."

"Exactly. At about the time of the royal visit, *Forsaken Fortune* will be getting a big promotional push. Our villages could be featured in a major motion picture in cinemas across America and the U.K., in Europe, and far beyond. If the film receives Oscar nominations, there's added publicity—opportunities to promote our ecological tourism ventures throughout winter and spring, when people are planning summer holidays. And it costs nothing."

"Except what's left of your sanity," Poppy muttered. "And your solitude."

Martin kept a watchful eye on Ariel, whose cocked ears and erect tail indicated that she would fly at any unwary rabbit. "This motion picture is destined to have a long life, possibly eternal. Eventually it will be accessible through video streaming on ServeFlix. That's a perpetual advert." He drew an invigorating breath of morning air, and continued, "London day-trippers will come to the museum to see rural life and farming displays and learn about regenerative agriculture. Our experts will demonstrate how to thatch a roof and construct a hurdle and milk a cow. After watching flour being ground at the watermill and cheeses being turned, they'll want to take the products home. Nature lovers will come here for rambles through the woodland and pony-trekking in the Milver Vale and walks along the river."

Her tone reflective, she admitted he could be right.

"Now I've got you thinking I'm clever, not crazy."

"Clever *and* crazy," she said pointedly. "They aren't mutually exclusive."

He was accustomed to her frank criticisms and unbothered by them. Their friendship was at times complicated by the fact of her being his employee, but the rare quarrels and quibbles soon blew over and were just as swiftly forgotten. Three years younger, she was practically as tall as Martin, with long, strong legs. Pretty in a wholesome, healthy way, she had a sprinkling of girlish freckles across her cheekbones and a tiny gold stud in one nostril. As usual, she wore her brown hair tied back in a tail.

Over the past two years she'd proved herself a worthy successor to her father, retired from service and living in sunny Portugal. Her forceful personality and keen intelligence served her well in a traditionally male occupation. Poppy handled her office duties effectively, but every minute at her desk kept her from the task at which she excelled—working with people. In a multitude of ways, she was Martin's ambassador to a scattered community with conflicting needs and expectations.

Each of the four variously sized villages forming the estate had its distinct identity and appeal. Prosperous newcomers, bolstered by their London salaries, had improved the older and more substantial properties scattered along pleasant lanes leading in and out of Milverston Magna. Its vitality was ensured by the shops, grammar school, the Anglican church, a pair of public houses, and the inn with its restaurant. A short distance from there, a crossroads hamlet consisted of several houses and surrounding farms. Milver St. Mary had its historic parish church and watermill, a farm shop, and plenty of modern suburban-style housing. He and his working group envisioned the cavernous tithe barn as the primary rural skills demonstration area.

Little Milver, victim of a failed industrial estate and the demise of textile manufacturing, was the runt of Martin's litter. It was also the current focus of his attention and activity, and crucial to his larger ambitions. Believing its spacious, salvageable buildings might be attractive to artisans, he'd begun renovating a vast mill building into studios for painters and potters and craftspeople with gallery and shop space included. The de-consecrated church and unused parish hall would become the heritage center. Planning permission had been obtained for a sensitively designed and attractively priced housing estate.

The moment the petite, curly-headed American had mentioned her film, he'd recognized the potential of placing his section of Somerset before an increasingly heritage-mad and recreation-focused public.

"I'm not seeking your approval, Popster. But I want you to understand what this means to me. To us."

"I'm beginning to. How does Dan Wheeler feel about your scheme?"

"I haven't told him anything. And won't, until we get onto Hannah Ballard's short list. It's early days yet, and nothing's certain."

As they approached grassy land dotted with grazing sheep and their lambs, they called back the dogs and put each one on a lead. The woolly, bleating beasts bored Ariel, but she was a sight hound and if she sighted something interesting, she'd hound it. And in the process, upset the animals and enrage Martin's tenant.

Poppy bent to adjust Millie's collar. "If this movie has gruesome murders and torrid sex scenes, your precious publicity might do us more harm than good."

"I've been reading *Forsaken Fortune*. Classic stuff. Page after page of love and lechery, birth, betrayal, and death. I've made it through the murder trial, and I predict a public hanging will soon follow. There's a mysterious chap who lurks and limps about, looking and listening. The village idiot."

"The perfect role for you," she teased.

"Just what I was thinking," he said, affecting a hobble. "As lord of the manor, I deserve a walk-on."

"At the very least," Poppy agreed.

Chapter 6

Lord Milverston ushered Hannah up and down his carved staircases, in and out of rooms designed for receiving illustrious visitors, elaborate dining, formal dancing, sleeping, and praying. For a historic house still in private ownership, its state of preservation was remarkable. She had no concerns about camera dollies crashing through rotted floorboards.

The man and his dog watched her measure the length and breadth of the rooms. She took digital photos and recorded video. She jotted notes and questions. In rapid succession she saw the Tapestry Hall, the Duke's Chamber, and the King's Room.

"Stanwell is a corruption of St. Anne's Well," said her host, ushering her into the Long Gallery. "The surrounding lands belonged to an ancient abbey dedicated to her. After Henry the Eighth dissolved the religious houses, the monastic buildings were dismantled or demolished. Except for the great tithe barn near the bridge crossing the River Milver."

She didn't refute his erroneous assumption that her colleagues cared about his ancestor Sir Rufus Latimer, who purchased the vast property from the murderous monarch and built his magnificent house from honey colored hamstone, locally quarried. Or the son who added a long wood-paneled gallery for entertaining King James the First in regal style. What mattered to the lighting technician was its size and the number of mullioned windows, and the quality of the light. The set decorator would ask her whether these antique chairs and chests and paintings could be filmed. The sound technicians, she suspected, would be pleased by the mellow acoustics.

While examining the diamond-shaped glass panes, she saw someone on a four-wheeler, zipping through tall grass. In an instant she was tugged back to the twenty-first century.

They went downstairs so she could look at what her guide referred to as the old kitchen. It retained an enormous fireplace and baking ovens. Connected to it was a series of smaller rooms fitted with wooden cupboards.

"Here, in the scullery, Charles the Second dined on fricassee of duck. After his defeat at the Battle of Worcester, he was in danger of being captured and executed like his dad. He disguised himself as a manservant and traipsed through the west of England, seeking shelter from Royalist supporters. He spent the night not very many miles from here."

"Is there a ghost?" she wondered.

"None that I've ever heard about. They're only necessary if you want to attract the paying public."

"You must've had fun here as a little boy. All the nooks and crannies and hiding places."

"I lived in Reading, then London, and visited twice a year at most. For complicated—and quite boring—reasons, the estate was legally transferred to me before I was out of my teens. But I didn't take up residence here until Uncle Rufus died." He opened a heavy wooden door, holding back until Hannah and Ariel had passed through. "Your images of all my worldly possessions won't fall into the wrong hands, I trust."

"Never." She checked to see if he required further assurances—apparently not.

They cut across an inner courtyard to reach the opposite wing. Stone-paved paths bisected the green grass, and statuary adorned each neat rectangle of lawn.

"So peaceful and quiet here. What a perfect place to spend lockdown."

"You'd think so, but in fact I worked as hard as I've ever done. Actually, much harder. So many online meetings filling my diary. Doing the costings for various projects in this area. Watching the price of everything going up and up, and then recalculating. Filling out applications for grant money. Not that I've any right to complain. It was harder on Londoners. Half of Latimer Row was shuttered, or as good as. The firms that didn't trade in necessities or consumables got round to renovating their premises—when they could get laborers and source the materials. What about your job? You must've had plenty of pandemic downtime."

"Liz kept me at Acorn Films, in a different capacity," she said, following him into another section of the house. "Marketing assistant. Among other tasks, I scheduled press interviews with talent whenever our movies or tv shows were made available for home viewing. I produced a few of them myself. Like you, we went into planning mode, biding our time. We shut down the limited series for ServeFlix, and nearly a year passed before our productions could start again." After looking at several unused rooms, where dust cloths protected the furnishings, she asked, "Where's a good spot to photograph the exterior? I'd like to get a panoramic shot of the entire house."

"You'll have the best vantage from the drive, halfway to the entrance gate. I'll take you after you've seen the gardens and grounds."

They exited onto a broad, stone-paved terrace furnished with tables and chairs and benches. At each corner stood an urn of parrot tulips in bloom. A wisteria vine with a broad, twisted trunk hugged almost the entire exterior wall. Numerous pale panicles on its lateral branches promised an abundant display of flowers.

"You won't mind if I share garden photos with my mother?"

"It would be an honor."

Long borders of spring bulbs and perennials and roses lined a grass walk leading to the Georgian-era orangery, flanked by large and amply-budded lilacs. There was a dovecot and a water garden and a tennis court. Shrubbery at one end of a flat stretch of ground screened the swimming pool.

"This was once the bowling green. Later, it was used for archery, judging from old photos of Victorian ladies posing here with their bows and arrows. In the 1920s, poolside parties became popular. Not a problem from your perspective, I hope."

"It's well hidden."

"We concealed the solar array that powers the house just as carefully. If I weren't pressed for time, I'd challenge you to find it."

"I've seen the rooftop panels."

"Those are only for the stable and a staff flat and offices. And vehicle charging."

Making their way to what he referred to as the South Front, they met the house manager, a cheery chap in his late fifties, who described himself as Ariel's nanny.

"And mine, on occasion," his employer declared. "As you see, Ron, our visitor survived my cookery."

"One of the best pizzas I've ever had," Hannah volunteered. "And the chocolate sponge with fudge sauce was divine."

"Jan prides herself on her puddings," the older man responded.

"Tell Hannah how you've put on half a stone since coming here, all because of her cookery. I'm leaving Ariel with you. Sorry, my precious, but you're not welcome at the Home Farm."

"Why not?" asked Hannah.

"Harold, the present occupant, loathes lurchers. To him, they're poachers' dogs, four-legged gypsies who get up to mischief in the daytime *and* after dark. When I brought her to live here, I was afraid he'd give notice to quit." Turning to Ron, he said, "While I'm at my lunch meeting in Newbridge, Poppy will drive Hannah to the other villages and some of the farms and barns. Tonight we're taking her to a pub. I'm bound to come home rat-arsed."

"I appreciate the warning, m'lord." Ron spoiled this Jeeves-like response by grinning at Hannah.

"You can open the front gate for us. I'll be sure to close it with my remote as I drive past on my way to town."

She had to walk at a brisk pace to keep up with the long-legged marquess. Craving a jog, she cast envious eyes across his private parkland and pathways.

"We won't mow until later in the year," he told her. "Maintenance has given way to a more environmentally sensitive form of land stewardship. Abandoning pesticides and fertilizers, so the grasses can grow and reseed. Planting native trees. Encouraging the spread of wildflowers. This area has become a haven for pollinators."

"I can see that." She trained her camera lens on a blue butterfly with white-edged wings, flitting over a clover patch.

When she had all the shots she wanted, she posed her host with his house as a backdrop. He amused her by making silly faces.

"Consider it my audition for the village idiot."

"I'm not responsible for casting. But it would definitely impress our audiences if we're able to include 'Marquess of Milverston' on the credits."

"In that case, never mind. Martin Latimer is the name I answer to. Don't forget."

"Okay." His instruction reminded her of the way her mother, famed garden guru Wendy Edney, preferred the anonymity of being Gwen Ballard.

"Let me see." When she passed her phone to him, he groaned. "I look like one of those chaps cluttering the pages of *Country Life* magazine. Might I persuade you to delete that?"

"Not a chance," she said breezily.

She intended to email it to the Palindrome Posse, the supportive sisterhood she'd belonged to during her college years. Eve, a divorced teacher, and Mim, a single lawyer, were her confidantes and cheerleaders. Because Hannah was a constant traveler, the Posse maintained contact by group text and video chat. Whenever they could arrange a gathering, her friends expressed envy of her unpredictable and seemingly glamorous job. Photos of the marquess and his mansion was proof that sometimes it could be both.

"You'd never guess nowadays, but I was quite the spectacle during my misspent youth," he was saying. "Long black coat, eyeliner, magenta hair. Extremely goth."

He took her across the road to a field carpeted with jagged bell-shaped flowers. Most were a mottled maroon color, but the occasional white blossom provided a contrast.

"The fritillary meadow. It's a variety of native wildflower, commonly called snake's head lily."

"Mum grows it, but nothing like this many. Who planted them?"

"The Almighty, I suppose. They've been here forever. Picking is discouraged, unless for decorating the church altar on Sundays. I'll grant special dispensation if you'd like to gather a handful."

"Photos last longer." She knelt for close-ups and macro shots, focusing on the patterned petals and the undersides.

He asked to see the images. "You're quite good."

"Plenty of practice. As a kid, I entered my prints in exhibition at the local fair and won batches of ribbons. I joined my college's Shutterbug Club and provided pictures for our class newsletters and the yearbook."

"What are your favorite subjects?"

"Anything in range of my lens. Critters, birds, boats, people. Flowers."

"My pastime isn't as creative, or portable. Coin collecting." He shrugged dismissively.

"It's educational."

"Not in my case. I'm thick as the proverbial plank. Ideal for your village idiot."

Reclaiming her phone and the digital camera, she said, "You don't give up easily, do you?"

Hannah Ballard had turned out to be far more than the sum of her parts—and Martin was constantly aware of those. Strange, that such a rational, down-to-earth, pragmatic woman toiled for the make-believe merchants. Tramping through the Home Park, he regretted the necessity of handing her off to Poppy, whose reluctance to see his domain transformed into a film set hadn't fully subsided. He trusted her to take Hannah to all the points of interest but worried she might unintentionally sabotage Stanwell's chances with a lack of enthusiasm.

Wearing an intent expression, the location scout prowled through the Home Farm's agricultural buildings. Oblivious to his inspection of her clinging shirt and bum-hugging khaki trousers, she climbed the ladder to the storage loft. Determined to capture her all-important images, she crouched, knelt, and otherwise contorted herself in alluring ways.

Single-mindedness, a quality he also possessed, looked especially attractive on Hannah Ballard.

Plans, proposals, and presentations had overtaken and consumed him. He hadn't socialized much since his ill-fated romance with Natalie—he didn't count pub nights with Popster or London dinners with Dan. This intriguing American had breezed into Wincott & Sons, providing him with a project well worth pursuing. Potentially more than one.

"At Wincott & Sons, you mentioned herds of happy dairy cows, the source of all that Milver Vale cheese. Where are they?"

"Ask Poppy to introduce you."

He didn't realize she'd halted until he heard her say, from behind, "That's a dog."

"Where?" He tried to follow the direction of her stare.

"Over there. Lying in the grass." She jogged away from him. He followed.

Approaching the inanimate black mound, he realized with dismay that it was Poppy's Millie. He placed a hand on her side, seeking life in a horrifyingly still body.

With sudden force, Hannah knocked his arm away. *"Don't touch!"* In a calmer voice, she added, "Sorry, I didn't mean to hurt you. An animal suffering from shock is unpredictable, and you could be severely bitten. My dad's a vet."

"I have to do something," he retorted.

"Wrap your jacket around her head—loose over her eyes, against the muzzle. But not so tight she can't breathe." After he obeyed, her delicate hands explored the inert body. "I didn't notice blood in her mouth or ears, though that doesn't rule out internal injuries. Strong heartbeat. Lungs are working." Gently she tugged a back leg, and Millie uttered a low warning growl. "Broken, I think, or dislocated."

He yanked out his mobile and auto-dialed the estate

office. "Millie's hurt. Drive down to the Home Farm straight-away. We need transport."

"Oh, God," Poppy wailed. "I've been looking for her everywhere. What happened?"

"Struck by a car, I suppose. She must've dragged herself from the lane to the Home Farm pasture. One leg appears to be damaged."

"I'm on my way."

When she rang off, he murmured to the dog, "Hang on, old thing. Popster can't manage without you." If Ariel were lamed and lying helpless in the grass like this, he'd be insane. "Who the *hell* does a hit-and-run so close to private property? In broad daylight."

With irritating calm, Hannah replied, "Mean people suck."

"Sorry?"

"Bumper sticker on my housemate's car."

Poppy's mud-spattered Volvo zoomed down the lane. She leaped out and raced over, her face a mask of anguish.

"Why's her head covered? Don't tell me she's dead!"

Hannah explained, "To keep her from snapping at us."

"Millie's not a biter."

"Physical pain can cause abnormal behavior."

Poppy flung herself on the grass. "I'm here, sweet girl." The dog's tail thumped the ground weakly. "You've been knocked about, that's all. Be brave, and Dr. Allason will patch you up."

Martin placed a hand on her shoulder. "Hold her head while I lift her up, and don't remove my coat. She won't like being carried."

The dog's breath came in gasps as he carried her to Poppy's car. Struggling in his arms, she pawed at the material obstructing her vision.

"If she tries to get up or move about," Hannah said

when Poppy and Millie were settled on the back seat, "don't let her. Keep talking to her."

Exceeding the speed limit, Martin made good time until blocked by a slow lorry on a busy stretch of road. Glancing to his left, he saw Hannah's fingers frantically tapping at her phone. Behind him, Poppy alternately soothed her pet and cursed whoever had callously run her down.

Hannah swiveled around, saying, "If Millie had a morning meal, your Dr. Allason won't be able to knock her out for a while. Regurgitation under anesthesia is a greater danger than a fracture."

To stop Poppy from exploding again, Martin said, "Hannah's dad is a vet."

"I'm texting him now, but he's not responding. At this hour he must be milking the goats."

"You keep dairy goats?" he asked, in an effort to distract the frantic Poppy.

"Susie, mature and sweet. Marilyn, young and movie-star beautiful, and like her namesake has perfect—teats."

Luckily there were no other emergencies at Beechwood Veterinary Clinic. After Poppy and Millie were admitted to a consulting room, Martin and Hannah sat down to wait.

Across the room, an elderly man's white head was bent over a newspaper. Splashed across the front page was the latest Sterling Scandal headline:

MP'S MISTRESS: HOW THE MOB MAIDEN GOT HER MONEY.

A lady with a cat carrier exhibited a morbid interest in the details of the Labrador's injury. Martin reluctantly entered a dialogue, underscored by creepy yowling from her Siamese.

Hannah fared better with a young mother and her toddler, accompanied by a hedgehog in a shoebox.

The woman told her, "I found out on the website that Dr. Allason treats indigenous wildlife without charging a fee."

Hannah ran her finger across the creature's spines. "We don't have these scurrying around where I come from," she said. "Old Mainers call our porcupines hedgehogs. They're lots bigger, and not as cute. Covered with long, sharp quills."

"You're an American? Lily, this lady lives across the ocean. She can tell you all about Disney World."

"I'm afraid I can't," Hannah said apologetically. "I've never been there."

Excusing himself from the nosy cat woman, Martin went into the corridor to cancel his lunch appointment.

"Sorry to say I won't make the meeting, Thomas. Poppy Deane's dog was struck by a car or lorry, and I've got to fill in for her this afternoon. I'd be most grateful if you'd contact the building society chaps to extend my apologies. Find out how soon we can re-schedule."

Creating a finance package for his new housing estate's future residents was a priority. But poor Poppy had to stay here. Hannah hadn't seen the significant local landmarks, and it was imperative to land that film production. He phoned Ron at the house to report the accident and his change of plans and went back to the admitting room.

Poppy, at the reception desk, whirled around to say in relief, "She'll be okay—eventually. Dr. Allason looked her over himself. She's in the imaging theatre being checked for hip damage. Later she'll have an operation to secure the broken bone with pins, or a metal plate."

"How are you holding up?"

"Awfully rocky. Thankful she'll be all right, in time. I'll stay to hear the results of her scan, but you needn't. You've got your lunch in Newbridge."

"I called it off." When she opened her mouth to object, he assured her, "Postponed, not canceled. Ron's on his way to fetch Hannah and me. After Jan feeds us a midday meal I'll continue the tour guiding."

Shaking her curly head, Hannah said, "You don't have to. I've got my hire car and its satnav. Plus a detailed Ordnance Survey map."

"Even so," Poppy responded, "you'll probably get lost. Mind you, it's just as likely to happen with Mart."

He ignored that comment, untroubled by her habitual put-downs. "Don't concern yourself with us. Stay here, and find us at the pub later. If you feel like it."

She kissed his cheek. "Ta." With a sideways glance at Hannah, she added, "Dr. Allason says you gave excellent advice. Sorry I was such an ungrateful bitch."

"If any of our dogs was hurt like that, I'd be a complete mess."

"What breed?"

"Two shelties and a border collie—a volatile mix. They're living their best lives on my parents' farm. Because of all my travel, I can't have a dog."

"Too bad for you," said Poppy with feeling before she sat down to continue her vigil.

Chapter 7

"Where do the local people work?" Hannah wondered, after a thorough examination of the surrounding countryside and villages. "Not the farmers, or the teachers and shopkeepers, but all the rest."

"It varies. People commute to Newbridge, which is quite close, or to larger towns. Yeovil and Wincanton and Sherborne are less than half an hour's drive. Taunton and Bath are slightly farther away. By car it's just over an hour to the heart of Bristol," Martin said.

"What about a train?"

"About the same, direct service from Castle Cary or Taunton. I have great hopes of building up and sustaining a local workforce. To that end, I collaborate with area employers, in various enterprises. We strive to retain our young people through training programs and apprenticeships."

"You must've had an influx of city people during the pandemic, when so many jobs could be performed remotely."

"Oh, yes. Swarms of Londoners moved to the West Country. Bristolians, too. Our region is a certified area of Historical and Natural Significance," he boasted. "The available stock of high-value, attractive homes was already limited, and prices rose accordingly. But due to a gradual outflow, there's less competition. Countryside living, long-term, doesn't suit everyone. And working from home is no longer the norm."

Residents in Martin Latimer's part of Somerset were recognizably similar to most of Hannah's family and friends and acquaintances in Maine. Here, as there, people either lived in quirky or historic older houses or modern ones. Farmers raised and gathered their crops. Factory employees fretted about job security. Horsey folks rode and showed. Commuters zipped from country to city and back again.

He pointed out a pasture of grazing milk cows and the meadow populated with ewes and their lively spring lambs. He took her to a farmyard and encouraged her to climb onto a stone mounting block. Standing under flowering pear trees, as pale petals floated to the ground, she imagined them laden with fruit in the final weeks of filming. She roamed an ivy-clad burying ground beside an ancient church and marveled at the size and age of the yew trees on either side of the lych-gate. She explored the Georgian rectory's walled garden, which would delight her mother.

The massive tithe barn on the road from Milver Cross to Little Milver was suitable for the harvest supper scene. She'd photographed the stone bridge spanning the River Milver, and on the other side assessed a vacant warehouse, not yet converted to an antiques center, and an abandoned factory. In either, or both, the construction crew could create interior sets. She found sufficient parking for the generators and trailers for the actors, make-up team and wardrobe.

"We have a strong commitment to adaptive re-use," he told her. "The deconsecrated church and disused parish hall received planning permission for alteration. Work on the heritage center is likely to start this summer, but I have the authority to delay it by a few months. If you gave me a good reason."

"You are persistence personified," she commented.

For her benefit, this man in dire financial straits had missed a meeting with bankers. If she hadn't already fallen so hard for Stanwell and the Milver villages, sheer guilt would compel her to put them ahead of all other sites she'd seen.

He brushed off her thanks for the tour of his territory. "My pleasure. I've just thought of something else you might like. Ever seen otters?"

"Lots of times. Not English ones, though."

"We can look for them. If you don't mind mud."

"In Maine, we have an entire season devoted to it, the weeks between snow melt and spring flowers." Her khakis were already speckled with dirt and damp at the hems. Her face felt flushed from all the walking, and she didn't want to think about her hair.

He led her along a riverside footpath. "After years of decline, their numbers are increasing. Playful little buggers. In winter, they slide on their backs in the snow, right along this bank." He pointed to a grassy slope.

"You've seen them doing it?"

"If by 'doing it' you mean snow sliding, I haven't actually caught them in the act, though I've seen evidence when snow lies on the ground. It rarely does, this far south."

At the place where the river broadened, near a clump of willows, stood a small brick dwelling. Nearby, resting in the water, was a red and black vessel. *Emotional Rescue* was painted on its hull in bold, bright lettering.

"My former home."

"The cottage? Or the houseboat?"

"*Em* is a canal narrowboat. I bought her years ago and performed some of the restoration work myself. After Mother moved from London to France, I rented a residential mooring in London's Little Venice."

"I've been around boats all my life. Can we go inside?"

"I haven't got the key with me. Agnes, the River Cottage

tenant, has one. She manages the charity shop in Newbridge, so she's not there now. I come by occasionally to potter about. Polish the brass fittings, freshen the paint. Once in a while I drag Poppy along. But she prefers horses."

Hannah recalled the kiss his estate manager had bestowed back at the vet's office. Proprietary, or a simple expression of gratitude? Their relationship was an unsolved puzzle.

"Cost me a packet to move *Em* from the city. Somerset hasn't many canals, and the nearest ones are derelict, so I placed her here. The water is relatively shallow, except during the occasional spring flood, so she just sits, which is bad for her engine and electrics and stove. She needs to be on the canals again, piloted by somebody as attached to her as I've been. I contacted a broker at a Bristol boatyard to discuss selling her, then got too busy to follow through. But I will."

Around teatime he dropped her off at her hotel, promising to return later. Hannah changed her dirty trousers for comfy flannel loungewear, and stretched out on the bed with phone and laptop to review her photos and videos. In her relaxed and reflective state, she was tempted to withdraw from the promised foray to the local pub. The prospect of several hours in prickly Poppy's company wasn't appealing. But telephoning Martin with a made-up excuse would be futile—his coaxing was too persuasive, and she always gave in to it.

Refreshed by a shower, she dried her hair and considered her dwindling wardrobe options. She managed her mix-and-match outfits on a four-day rotation. Hand-rinsed tops, damply clinging to the radiator, decorated the bathroom, along with most of her underwear collection. From her bag she excavated a lace-edged camisole and combined it with a skirt and a jacket buttoned up to hide the lingerie underneath.

Several minutes before the appointed time she wandered

down to the lobby. Martin was there already, studying a tourist brochure.

"Just me," he declared. "You'll be relieved to hear that Millie came through her surgery with an excellent prognosis. Slight change of plan—I booked a table for two in the dining room here. But I'd like to take you to my favorite pub first. Popster's too knackered, meaning we can go across the green to The Peacock. She always insists on The Huntsman's Horn. It's all right, though too tarted up for my taste. And I prefer real ale."

She approved of his choice the moment she saw the authentic hodgepodge décor of what he described as the oldest public house in the district, which was clearly the warm, noisy heart of this village. A cheery tapster interrupted his conversation with the men assembled at his bar and hailed Martin by name.

Hannah requested a half-pint of cider and let him pay. She intended to treat him to dinner.

"I'll send young Andy over with menus," the barman said, eyeing the level of the amber liquid as he pulled on the tap. "He's in a bad skin tonight, won't say what's wrong."

"We're dining at the Latimer Arms. Hannah can try your cookery another time."

This comment revealed his firm belief that she would be returning.

"Heavenly," she said after a hearty chug. "And there's a dartboard! I haven't played in ages."

Both men stared at her, obviously surprised by her admission.

"My uncle taught me," she explained. "He's a champ, and has trophies to prove it." Now that Chase was out on work release, maybe he could compete again. He hadn't been able to play while incarcerated at Warren, or after his transfer to Machiasport.

"I'll take you on," Martin offered.

Immediately regretting her enthusiasm, she told him frankly, "I'm rusty."

"Let's fling some arrows. No scorekeeping. This time."

Her coordination was disgraceful. Nevertheless, she almost managed a bullseye, a triumph to report in her next email to Chase.

With a nod at the gloomy young waiter loitering between the bar and the kitchen, Martin called out, "Cheers, Andy. Working for Jack, are you? He needs more help round here. Good to know you're able to unglue yourself from the seat of that quad bike."

"You saw me? Today?"

"I won't tell your dad."

"He lets me," Andy said defensively. "Sometimes. But he says if I don't study enough to pass my exams . . ." His voice trailed into awkward silence.

"There's a running bet that you will."

Answering a summons from his boss, the young man shuffled away, shoulders rounded.

"He's the son of my Home Farm tenant. Harold Riddell."

"Who loathes lurchers," Hannah recalled.

On their way out, a fellow at the bar stopped Martin to ask after Millie.

"A clean break and well-mended. She's young and healthy and strong."

"Just like her mistress, eh?" The questioner winked at Martin. "How'd it happen?"

"Hit and run. Poppy's frustrated that she can't blame my Ariel."

After pondering the numerous temptations on the hotel restaurant's menu, Hannah ordered pan-seared trout. She let Martin choose the wine.

"To Acorn Films." He touched his glass to hers. "And future associations. I know, I know. Not your decision."

Meeting his gaze, Hannah said, "I'm willing to answer

any questions you might have. Except for specific contractual stipulations—the day-rate we'd pay, legal liabilities, security protocols. Those get worked out later."

"I'm less concerned with the fees than with how filming might affect tenants and neighbors. Presumably they can opt in or opt out."

"The locations department will hold public informational gatherings, and meet with individuals as necessary."

"You'll want to keep the local constabulary fully apprised."

"Their cooperation is essential to a smooth shoot. We depend on them to close roads and assist with traffic control."

"Do you suppose your boss, the famous producer, will look favorably on Stanwell?"

"Possibly," Hannah hedged. "We don't often disagree. Although I didn't encourage her to pursue this particular literary property. Liz adores adaptations and the challenges they pose. I prefer original screenplays."

"Why is that?"

"Artistic freedom. No built-in audience expectation, or the inevitable comparisons to the source material. Most people say the book was better, and often they're right. But Liz has great instincts. And she persuaded Owen Parry to direct *Forsaken Fortune.*"

She watched him tip the wine bottle towards her glass. Hadn't he realized that alcohol increased her verbosity?

Throughout their meal he interrogated her about the film process and the shooting schedule. At his insistence, she tried the treacle pudding. As they waited for coffee to arrive, he excused himself. On his way back to their table a couple accosted him. At her London party, he'd denied celebrity status, but on his own turf he obviously possessed it. While he was otherwise occupied, she slipped away to the ladies' room for a brief check in with the Boston office. It wouldn't hurt to mention Stanwell to Liz, in advance of her official report to the team at Hartcliffe Studios.

Cell phone pressed to her ear, she listened to what sounded like an instrumental version of the theme song from one of Liz's movies.

"Who are you holding for?"

"Who's speaking?"

"Pam."

She conjured the image of a lanky twenty-something wearing headset and microphone. "Pam, Hannah Ballard. Can you put me through to Liz? Just for a sec."

"Ms. Gregorio isn't here," the girl answered. "Yesterday she checked into the hospital. For, like, observation."

"Premature labor?"

"Not sure. I could connect you with her assistant?"

"Not now. Have her call me later if there's news about Liz and the baby. Never mind the time difference."

"Sure. You're in L.A.?"

"England. She has my number."

Hannah ended the call. She speed-dialed Liz's cell—no answer. After leaving a brief and excessively cheery message predicting all would be well, she made her way to the table and shoved her phone into her handbag.

"Not good," she muttered, not bothering to conceal her apprehension.

"Something wrong?"

"Hard to tell. I hope not. First Millie, now Liz." Reaching for her wine, she said, "Her baby isn't due for at least a month. But for some reason she's already been admitted to the hospital."

Chapter 8

Hannah shared her miniscule Hartcliffe Studios workspace with the assistant location manager, a Scotsman whose blatant attractiveness in no way compensated for the hassles of their enforced companionship. Alistair McLaren's accent evoked the hills and glens of his native habitat somewhere "nair In-vair-*ness.*"

On a dismally gray afternoon she made her way to their cramped quarters, striving not to spill two paper cups of commissary tea. At the door she halted in silent and suspicious watchfulness. He sat in her chair, elbows leaning on her desk, intently studying her laptop screen.

Unabashed about snooping, and getting caught, he told her, "I'm looking for the updated shed-yule for our Stanwell visit."

She refused to let him off the hook just because he was gorgeous. "You could've asked for it." After replaying his excuse, she asked, "What do you mean, *our* visit?"

"Nigel didn't tell you? Or Owen? I'm included in the search party."

She bit back her frustration at being left out of the communications loop yet again, certain that any complaint would be repeated to her overlords. Avoiding potential land-mines and quicksand was by now instinctive, and though sucking up wasn't technically included in her job description it might as well be.

Eventually, she and the rest of the crew would leave this vast complex of warehouses and soundstages for the film location, where camaraderie would develop. It always did. Conflict, too.

She presented the steaming paper cup to Alistair.

"Ta," he responded.

He hadn't asked her to bring it to him. She'd volunteered, from a determination to maintain friendly relations during her current confinement here at Hartcliffe Studios.

Days were busy and long, crammed with presentations and meetings and conference calls. Whenever she heard a burst of laughter from one of the office suites—often as she passed by—paranoia rose, with an accompanying suspicion that she might be the target. Blaming the pervasive cheerlessness of her surroundings for her mood's downward spiral, she reminded herself that the real fun of filmmaking was yet to come, on location.

At least she'd received positive news from Boston. Liz, discharged from the hospital, rested comfortably—and impatiently—at home. Several times a day she messaged Hannah, and when the time difference allowed, they logged on for a video chat.

Solitary evenings in a budget motel adjacent to a noisy motorway roused nostalgia for the comfort and quiet of the Latimer Arms. She found herself missing Martin's infectious smile and vibrant personality. Poppy, her contact at Stanwell, seemed even brisker and more businesslike on the phone than in person. But when Hannah asked after Millie, the estate manager's coolness thawed.

Alistair transferred his impressive bod and his tea to his workspace behind the partition. She heard his muffled curses as he shuffled papers. "Here it is," he announced, and his dark, close-cropped head bobbed above the partition. "Our shed-yule."

"Fab," she said absently, logging into the Acorn Films email server. Nothing new. Her personal account contained a note from her mother reporting long-awaited signs of spring in Maine. She typed a hasty and marginally coherent reply.

"Our minibus to Stanwell House and the Milver villages leaves at nine in the morning," he called over. "How long a drive?"

"Fifty minutes. An hour at most."

"But according to this, we don't arrive there till half-ten."

"Because there's a brief stop in Newbridge High Street to inspect a room in the Guildhall. If we use it for the magistrate's court, that's one less interior to construct. In the same street there's also a potential jail exterior. I've got pictures."

Alistair emerged from his corner to look at them. Standing behind her, he placed his hands on the back of her chair. "Right," he said when she pulled up her photographs of an imposing stone structure. "You included it in your presentation. Which, I must again tell you, was brilliant."

Hannah wasn't the only one sucking up.

When not contending with a multitude of details, she worried that she might have oversold Stanwell to her production colleagues. She couldn't afford to lose whatever amount of credibility she possessed around here.

Alistair fielded a call on his mobile—from their tech scout, judging from his answers to a string of questions about tomorrow's recce. She waited, expectantly, for him to pass the phone to her. During the protracted conversation, her jaw clenched tighter and tighter.

"Brill," he said, "I'll find out from Hannah. Cheers." He rang off. "He's asking if there's an electrical schematic for Stanwell, showing all the mains."

"Even if one exists, that doesn't mean we'll get our hands on it. The property owner is extremely security conscious. Besides, it's not essential. Our generators will produce the necessary power."

"So you don't actually know the state of the electrical system."

"I've already told Barry," she shot back, annoyance acidifying her tone. "The entire house and the outbuildings were re-wired when the heat pump system and a solar array were installed. The place is practically carbon neutral. In addition to being attractive and historic."

"You're really fixated on that old pile, aren't you?"

She regarded him with hostile eyes, resenting the implication that her wholehearted recommendation might be subjective. "I've scouted locations for well over a decade. I'm no newbie or novice. Of all the places I saw within a reasonable travel distance, Stanwell House and the Milver Vale satisfy our every requirement. They're convenient to this production office and these studio facilities."

"Convenient for you as well," he murmured. "Makes the logistics loads easier."

Her voice tightened even more. "I based the recommendation on serving and supporting Liz Gregorio's vision for this film, and Owen Parry's requirements. Full stop. I know damn well there's no such thing as an 'easy' location. Each one has built-in challenges. Some are obvious at the outset, and the rest will materialize over the course of the shoot. It's my job to minimize them." Pleased with this speech, she defiantly stared him down, daring him to refute anything she'd said.

"No wonder you've got so far, so young, wee lassie," he said, in a patronizing tone that seemed calculated to fan the flame of her anger.

The reason I've got so far, she almost retorted, is because

I'm smart enough to defend my actions as necessary and to ignore deliberate provocation.

Forcing herself to smile serenely, she turned her attention back to her computer screen. Reviewing her checklist, she highlighted items she intended to complete by day's end. She heard him leave the office. He often did, offering little or no explanation of his activities. Too distracted by her own responsibilities to keep track of his, she was glad to be spared inquiries about what she was doing, and why.

Before the van rolled out of Newbridge, Hannah leaned forward to make sure the driver was aware of the preferred route, a lesser road two thirds of the way through the roundabout on the outskirts of the town. It had the advantage of winding through the picturesque terrain between the town and Stanwell House. Her fellow passengers absorbed the surrounding vistas—rounded hills with grazing sheep, a group of cattle standing in the shade cast by a grandfather oak, and the foamy white hawthorn blossom in the hedgerows. Occasionally a bend in the road offered a glimpse of the River Milver.

The security officer met them at Stanwell's front gate, and waved them through.

"Slowly, slowly," Owen Parry said as the van proceeded up the drive. "It's even more palatial than photographs indicated."

His fellow passengers responded with a combined murmur of appreciation.

Hannah held her hand up to the window and waved to the house manager, standing in the shadow of the arched doorway.

Ron stepped forward to offer a general welcome. Singling her out, added, "Delighted to see you again, Miss Ballard."

She performed the essential introductions, and the tour proceeded as planned. Her colleagues trooped from room to room, and her pen flew as she jotted down keywords from the director's comments and questions. These were primarily directed at Alistair, who frequently stepped aside to dictate notes into his phone. The lighting designer took meter readings, the audio tech moved up and down the Long Gallery with his handheld recorder. The art director pointed his mobile at ceiling frescoes and artwork and sculptures and ornate carpets.

Nigel Rossiter, the co-producer, nodded at Hannah and smiled his satisfaction before descending the staircase to the Great Hall.

When the group reassembled near the front door, the set decorator enthused to the art director, "Fantastic furniture. Several centuries mixed together. Exactly that authentic and lived-in look we want."

Ron gave the group time to assess the dining room, then led them down a stone stairway to the original kitchen and buttery and stillroom.

"Marvelous," murmured Owen Parry. "Real possibilities here."

A rare accolade, one that Hannah took to heart.

Their guide led them to the modern kitchen, brightened by the natural light pouring in through its tall windows, where a smartly-dressed Poppy Deane waited, with a meal laid out buffet style across a marble countertop. They lunched on prawn and artichoke salad, salmon paste spread on toast points, raspberry tarts, and a selection of pale, light wines. Martin, contradicting his claims of idiocy, had correctly guessed that alcohol would enhance the visitors' favorable impressions of his property.

Where was he?

She'd counted on him to make an appearance, decked out in his corduroy trousers, exerting his charm and awing her crew with sprinklings of *noblesse oblige*. Although her companions seemed to be sufficiently enraptured by Stanwell without it.

After she'd declined Ron's offer of wine, he said, "You might like our elderflower cordial, with sparkling water. Quite refreshing. And locally produced."

Sipping the faintly sweet, floral-flavored beverage, she repressed the urge to smooth her hair. She'd passed countless antique mirrors this morning and knew the assortment of pins and combs holding up her curls were letting her down. She needed a trim, and soon. A shorter, undemanding style was more suitable for the weeks and work ahead. Because as soon as they locked down the necessary sites, her workload would increase and personal time would evaporate. Filming on location was a singular combination of summer camp and siege—laborious, uncomfortable, exhilarating, exhausting.

Poppy, cornered by Alistair, was responding to a stream of queries.

Hannah approach them and asked, "How's Millie?"

"Hobbling about, but her gait improves every day. Her shaved fur's growing back. You should pop into the office to check her progress."

Martin was the one she most wanted to see, but hope of doing so diminished with each passing minute. Neither Poppy nor Ron had introduced his name into the conversation.

He must have gone to London to escape the intruders, she concluded.

When her well-fed group stepped into the stable yard, the presence of his car indicated he could be somewhere on the premises. What activity of his took precedence over this all-important visit from the decision-makers? And where was Ariel?

"Easy, my darling." Martin gripped the restive dog's collar as she moaned her desire to drag him onto the balcony. She pressed her damp nose to the glass pane. Like him, she was spying on the scrum of people gathered in the drive.

He focused on Hannah's small but commanding figure, chivvying all the chaps into the minibus. Her wild curly hair was the one unrestrained aspect of her appearance—she wore severely professional garb today, the austere charcoal gray trouser suit.

In his own way and for different reasons, he was as curious as Ariel. What did her film company's brain trust think of Stanwell? He'd battled his urge to intrude upon their tour, or join in the meal he'd organized so carefully. Plenty of modern Britons clung to the idealized concept of a classless society, and he wouldn't spoil Stanwell's chances by inadvertently rousing prejudice against aristocrats. Or making an ass of himself.

Ron brought his lunch tray moments after the team boarded the minibus and set off for the Home Farm.

"What's the verdict?" Martin inquired, with false nonchalance.

"Our guests complimented the food. You don't care to come downstairs for yours?"

"I'm not depriving you of this rare opportunity to buttle for me."

Ron unceremoniously handed over the cutlery. "Film people are chatty and their conversations are transparent and revealing. By now Poppy will have resigned herself to what appears to be a certain outcome."

"I won't send for my legal adviser until there's substantive proof of intent." As Ron moved to the door, he asked, "Could you tell if they're visiting other properties?"

"Sir Owen Parry compared us to a house called Westerleigh. I deduce that he prefers Stanwell."

"That's something." As soon as he finished his prawn mayonnaise sandwich, he'd investigate the chief competition on the internet.

Ariel took up a position beside his knee, watching for any stray crumb that might fall her way.

"Patience," he murmured. "If this turns out well for us, by summer's end you can scavenge food from catering vans."

During the tour of Milver Vale villages and potential interior and exterior locations and scenic vistas, Hannah asked Poppy to introduce the group to local residents who might be receptive to having their properties appear on film. Several were eager, others indifferent. The ones familiar with tabloid papers and entertainment websites were aware that the director was married to an equally renowned actress.

An apple grower asked eagerly, "And will your missus be starring?"

This wasn't the only time Owen Parry had heard the question—probably the fourth. "She not available, I'm afraid. She'll be working in Tuscany."

His mobile chirped, an incongruous sound in so pastoral a setting, and he retreated deeper into the orchard for privacy.

Hannah checked her own phone, which had silently registered an earlier text from Liz: *In labor. Ouch! Back 2 hosp. More l8r.*

A full week from her due date. It was pointless to obsess about her friend's ordeal or speculate about its duration and intensity. Taking into account the time difference, the producer and her professor husband might already be cuddling their bundle of joy.

While the technicians inspected a vacant industrial building, Alistair cornered her.

"We'll be here for a while. Best warn the driver."

Her gofer days were far behind her. "Take care of it for me. Please," she added, as pleasantly as she could.

"I'm shadowing Nigel. His request."

Although the tone was apologetic, not triumphant, she seethed.

How can I work comfortably with him, she wondered on her way to their minibus to report the delay.

Poppy, leaning against the vehicle, smoked a cigarette she'd bummed from the driver.

"I gave these up ages ago. On rare occasions the craving returns, and I succumb. Do you smoke?"

"Just once." Her words sparked a memory. Chase seated on their favorite rock, shielding his lighter from the winds whipping across Casco Bay. He'd offered his pack. As she tentatively drew out a cigarette, he warned her she wouldn't like it. He was right.

Poppy muttered, "When I stopped, the person I did it for never even noticed." Grinding the butt against the bottom of her shoe, she added, "Smoking is strictly forbidden at Stanwell. Make that clear to your crew."

Owen Parry, Nigel Rossiter, and Alistair exited the factory. The Scotsman loomed over them, exuding the self-confidence that inevitably eroded Hannah's.

Poppy, watching her closely, asked, "Is Sex-on-Stilts your boyfriend?"

"We've hardly known each other a fortnight." Time enough to decide she disliked him. "He's my subordinate. And way too tall."

"No such thing, from my perspective. I suppose you've got someone special waiting for you to return to the States."

"I'm always on the road. In the air. Moving around the country."

"Right. No dog, either. Men require more attention and training than the average animal, don't they? So why are women considered high-maintenance?" Poppy grinned. "We're so practical and adaptable."

Hannah suspected Martin Latimer could be a closet chauvinist. An archaic title and aristocratic lifestyle were no excuse for an outdated view of womanhood. But that was Poppy's problem, not hers.

Chapter 9

Dan Wheeler's silver Jaguar slid into the stable yard at the same time Martin returned with Poppy from a lengthy ride on their favorite bridle path. On receiving the good news he been hoping for, he'd fired off an urgent summons to his legal advisor.

Martin dismounted, saying, "You didn't waste any time getting here. Please accept apologies for summoning you at fish spawning season, when freshwater angling is prohibited."

"I never mind coming to Stanwell." Dan held a leather briefcase over his crotch to guard against Airel's probing muzzle.

As soon as Poppy's boots hit the ground, she said, "I'm ever so glad you're here, Dan Wheeler-Dealer. I rely on you to pound sense into this dense skull." She pointed her riding crop at Martin's head, still encased in his protective riding hat.

Dan laughed. "That's your job. I lack qualifications." Turning to Martin, he asked, "How did this film company discover the Milver Vale? Your message contained very few details."

When he'd unfastened the girth, he gave Étoile's side and

barrel a gentle rub. "It started about several weeks ago. On my birthday, I told you about the American who popped into Wincott & Sons to place a catering order. She's the location manager, and mentioned the sort of property she required. I invited her to Stanwell to look over the house and the villages. She liked what she saw. So did the army of production people that she brought here later. They're ready to commit."

Shona the groom stepped out of the barn to take charge of the horses. Nico, the assistant house manager, removed Dan's travel bag from the car boot so it could be taken upstairs to the bedroom he always occupied when visiting.

"Let's go to Poppy's office," Martin said, "and I'll explain exactly where the filming is likely to take place."

Millie limped over from her basket to offer the visitor a less invasive welcome than Ariel's. Standing at the large estate map that extended across one wall, Martin pointed out the village properties and farm buildings already identified as potential locations, and areas designated for cars and vans and lorries.

"I contacted the Historic Properties Association," Dan told him, "and requested their guidelines about day rates and insurance for damages, and so on. They forwarded the pertinent pages." He tapped his briefcase. "We want to negotiate with Hartcliffe Studios and Acorn Films from a strong and fully informed position."

"Of course. But I won't put obstacles in the way unless there's reasonable cause. *Forsaken Fortune* will put Stanwell and Milver region on the tourism map and anchor them in the public consciousness." He took a cooling swig from his water bottle and set it down. The top of Poppy's desk was irritatingly free of the cluttered papers, writing utensils, mechanical devices, and detritus that covered every workspace he used.

She crossed one long leg over the other, both encased in

tight-fitting jodhpurs. "His heart's set on this. No argument of mine will deter him."

"I'm not getting involved in your disputes," Dan stated. "I can only make sure he doesn't later regret turning this region into a movie set. I'll insert a stringent and ironclad security clause into the contract. All production personnel must be fully vetted. We'll stipulate that guards will be posted on these premises at all times, inside the house and on the grounds. Remember what happened at Longleat? During a location shoot there, a rare drawing vanished from the house, never to be seen again."

"Every day, all over Britain and Ireland, movies are being produced at historically significant properties with collections of far greater value than mine. Most paintings and *objets d'art* are family relics, not national treasures. Those are shut away in a protected storage facility—as you well know—until such time as they are lent to museums. Or sold."

Dan pressed his lips together, as always happened when Martin referred to disposing of the rapidly appreciating assets he'd tucked away.

Poppy excused herself and drove off in her gray Volvo to soothe a fractious tenant. Martin took Dan to the house, where he exchanged the usual pleasantries with staff, eager to ensure his comfort during his stay.

Martin cleaned up and changed into smarter attire than he normally wore in the country. Dan was a private club man, not really a public house man. Like proper gents, they consumed pre-dinner libations in the library.

In the morning, after breakfast, he dialed Hannah Ballard's mobile number.

"Hello," she said, apparently quite startled. "How are you?"

"Dead chuffed. This time yesterday, a Scotsman rang Poppy, saying Stanwell and environs are selected as the primary shooting location."

"*Alistair* contacted you? Already?" After a prolonged silence she said, "I'm glad. For both of us."

"We haven't agreed upon a price. Whatever your lot propose, my solicitor will insist on more. I gather you'll be based here for—well, I've forgotten how long. No matter. You know all about it."

He detected an edge in her voice when she replied, "You'd be surprised what they don't bother telling me. Pre-production is well underway. In just over three months, our trucks and trailers will appear."

"Some of my tenants are reporting their offers to Poppy. One holdout so far. He refuses to take down his satellite dish."

"That's not uncommon."

"All well with you?"

"Liz, our executive producer, had her baby this week. Alexandra Elizabeth. They call her Lexi."

"I'd say a joint celebration is in order. A festive night out in London." He paused for effect, then said, "With a prince."

"You're not serious."

"I have in my possession an invitation for Lord Milverston and one guest to the Countryside Development Coalition's annual awards dinner later this week. His Royal Highness will be present, long enough to make a few remarks."

"Shouldn't Poppy be your plus-one?"

"I couldn't persuade her—unless my life depended on it—and probably not even then. She loathes this sort of affair."

"It does sound exciting. Unfortunately, my travel wardrobe doesn't include a ball gown and tiara."

"Surplus to requirements." He studied the curving black script engraved on stiff cream card stock. "A black-tie event, one step down from white. If you don't mind leaving in the morning, we can travel together. I'll book first-class train tickets from Bristol Temple Meads and meet you there. I need to get to town in time for a lunch meeting with the Specialist Cheese Producers. Our evening festivities begin at eight and might not finish until after the last westbound train." Carefully avoiding any suggestive overtones, he added, "You're welcome to spend the night at my flat. Five bedrooms."

"Oh." The monosyllable hung in the void. "Let me check my schedule. I'll get back to you."

"I couldn't think of any other way to thank you for choosing my territory as the *Forsaken Fortune* location."

"You've got it backwards," she told him. "When you said our meeting at the cheese shop was lucky for me, you were so right. Stanwell and the surrounding area are perfect, and I got credit for discovering it."

A long wait, thought Martin, until caravans and cameras and crew members and actors arrive. Bringing Hannah Ballard with them.

"Enough of a change?" the scissors wizard asked, his mirrored face looming over Hannah's shorn head.

"Perfect," she said fervently, eyes glued to her freshly chopped curls, framing her face in an interesting way. The transformation enthralled her.

"We'll want you back in about three weeks, to properly maintain the cut." He beckoned to an underling and moved on to his waiting client.

"Book ahead next time," advised the assistant, whose

bone structure she envied. "Antoine rarely has a cancellation."

No wonder, thought Hannah.

Time spent in South Kensington had been productive. At Harrods she'd found a baby gift for newborn Alexandra. In an upscale charity shop offering gently worn couture, she scored a jade silk sheath that was offensively—rather than criminally—expensive.

In the High Street she found a pair of gold satin shoes with extraordinarily high heels. Liz, a magnet for exclusive invitations, enjoyed evenings out, and Hannah could justify her costly acquisitions in the expectation of future dressy occasions. At a day spa she splurged on top-to-toe treatment—facial, massage, manicure, pedicure—emerging with glowing skin and soothed limbs.

And now I've got fabulous hair, she exulted, gathering up the assortment of shopping bags.

Her re-conditioned feet carried her from Beauchamp Place to busy Brompton Road. Attracted by the colorful window display of a shop featuring goods imported from India, she chose a silk wrap—jade green striped with gold— to complement her new dress.

Unable to carry anything more, she hailed a taxi. "Latimer House, near St. James's," she told the driver, depositing her bounty on the floor.

He sped through the traffic, squeezing between red buses and navigating clogged lanes with admirable efficiency. "On holiday?" he asked.

"Working," she replied. "My company is making a movie over here."

"So, who's in it, then?"

"Caroline Bryden and Lucas Daltrey."

Dream casting, as Liz frequently declared. Caroline, a porcelain-skinned redhead directly descended from a Victorian aristocrat, possessed two BAFTA awards, a Best Supporting Actress Oscar nomination, and appeared on every producer's short list. Lucas, a popular West End thespian with dramatic and comedic chops, hadn't collected any statues—yet—despite receiving critical acclaim for every stage performance and several screen appearances. *Forsaken Fortune* provided him with his breakout role.

"I've been in movies, with my cab," her driver volunteered. "On telly, too." He pulled aside the glass partition and passed his card through the narrow gap. "I'm reliable."

"Thanks. Ours is a period film," she said apologetically. "Horses and carriages and wagons."

"I've heard it said London traffic is slower nowadays than it was in olden times, when there was hansoms and carts and mounted policemen filling these streets."

Buckingham Palace's iconic façade filled the window. A swarm of tourists gathered at the gate, waiting for the changing of the Guard. Hannah was suddenly conscious of her distance from the farmhouse on Bear Knoll.

She imagined her mother weeding in the rose beds and her father shoveling aged animal manure onto the vegetable patch, both of them making the most of the time before the dreaded black flies launched their annual onslaught. At this hour Grampa would be at Ballard's Landing, puttering on *Jenny's Dream*. As for Chase, she had no idea what he'd be doing. His laconic responses to her recent texts and emails offered no details whatsoever.

The Latimer House porter opened the glass-paneled door. The lift swept her up to Martin's floor, and she let herself into his flat with the extra key he'd given her. After arriving at Paddington Station, they'd come straight here in a taxi, depositing their overnight bags before going their separate ways. Now she had the opportunity and the privacy to explore.

In the drawing room she found English classicism, elegant but not oppressively so. Pale blue damask upholstery complemented swagged gold-fringed curtains. Landscape paintings adorned each wall. Her association with Liz, a true-born Brahmin and prominent film industry fixture, had exposed her to luxurious surroundings, but nothing like this. She was drawn to the mantel by a row of photos in antique silver frames. An Edwardian beauty in a bridal gown, her lace wedding veil anchored to her head by a diamond tiara. A lad in long-tailed coat, posed in front of a brick build-ing that might be at Eton, possibly Martin's grandfather. The portly gentleman seated on the Stanwell House terrace, holding a cocktail shaker, must be the late marquess. A boy with a familiar grin stood in a punt, grasping a long pole, as an attractive young couple looked on—Martin with his parents.

She identified his personal lair by its lived-in atmosphere and its contents—desktop computer, state-of-the-art wide-screen television, audio equipment and compact speakers that surely produced the purest sound. Large-format pho-tographs of exotic places shared the wall space with framed concert posters. A cursory examination of her host's book-shelves told her that his reading preferences were travel and music.

The extensive and disorganized collection of compact discs was similarly revealing. In this era of music streaming, he retained a full catalogue of sensitive, angst-ridden British singer-songwriters—she spied Joe Jackson, Mark Knopfler, and Peter Gabriel in the mix, members of the same gener-ation of rock musicians her father favored. The New Wave and Goth traditions were amply represented by The Cure and New Order, Elvis Costello and The Psychedelic Furs.

She suspected Martin had chosen the sleek, ultra-modern kitchen appliances. Her gaze landed on two candid photos attached to the fridge door. In one he wore chef's garb, pre-sumably taken during his stint in Italy, in the other he and Poppy were mounted on horses.

The largest of the five bedrooms appeared to be his. She moved on to the next, decorated in a more feminine style. The neglected atmosphere of the two smallest indicated that they had been allotted to children or a servant. Hannah's contained a charming Biedermeier-style suite of matching furniture: sleigh bed, dressing table, and tall chest of drawers. She tossed her shopping bags onto the striped coverlet and eased her feet out of her jogging shoes. Time to check out the shower room—and the water pressure.

Thoroughly refreshed, she wrapped herself in a voluminous towel and tried to replicate Antoine's styling. He'd used product and she hadn't brought any. Martin didn't seem the type to keep it, judging by the shagginess of his hair.

Doesn't matter, she told herself, finger-fluffing her damp curls. Nobody at the dinner will know who I am, or remember I was there. And it's not a date.

When a telephone rang, she decided not to answer it. If Martin wanted to contact her, he'd call on her cell. After the fourth chime, the answering machine clicked on. She stepped into the hall to listen.

"Martin—Jess. You're never where you're *supposed* to be. And why is your mobile always switched off? Poppy swore you were in town today. I can confirm that *Posh* is definitely running a photo feature on Natalie's wedding, in the same edition as that article I told you about. The writer contacted me, asking for pictures. Of you. Or you and her. Consider yourself warned. Let's meet up soon, haven't seen you in the longest. Smooches."

As far as Hannah could tell, Martin's circle of friends was exclusively female. Poppy, Jess, Natalie. Was he currently sleeping with any or all of them?

Hearing the door of the flat open and close, then a series of footsteps, she tucked her towel more securely and returned to her room.

"Hannah?" Martin called out.

"Don't come in!"

"Is something wrong?" His voice too close for comfort.

"No."

"I popped in to find out if you're managing all right."

"Definitely, thanks."

"Help yourself to anything you like. I'll be back—I'm off to Wincott & Sons. Won't stay too long."

After she heard him retreat, she could breathe naturally. In retrospect, she recognized her error in prowling half-naked around his flat. If he'd seen her, he would have assumed it was a come-on.

Chapter 10

Even though he'd been perfectly satisfied with the customary version of Hannah Ballard, he was even more appreciative of the one he found when he returned to the flat. The sight of her sparked contradictory reactions—eagerness to show her off, the desire to keep her all to himself.

"You're entirely too exquisite to take to a pub." She smelled so marvelous that he couldn't bear to march her through the thick and noxious fug of cigarette and cigar smoke polluting the pavement in front of the Red Lion.

"I didn't know that was the plan."

"We'll be dining at the Ritz, so we might as well start with drinks in the Rivoli Bar. Can you walk in those heels?"

She looked down, saying ruefully, "Hope so."

Seated in an alcove of the Art Deco bar, sipping the peatiest of single malts, he could forget his mighty struggle with shirt studs and bow tie and cummerbund. He asked Hannah how she'd spent the afternoon.

She ducked her head self-consciously. "I splashed money around like I was Liz Gregorio. She can afford it. But I can't."

"I thought movie people were loaded."

"Not the location scouts. Or the location managers. My

parents wonder how I manage to pay for rent and food. Boston living doesn't come cheap."

"I imagine they're proud of your accomplishments."

"I'm not so sure. On the rare occasions when we're together, I avoid the controversial topics. My chosen career used to be one of them. Perhaps it still is."

"I had the impression American families are close-knit and huggy. The opposite of stifled, repressed Brits."

"No nationality has a monopoly on dysfunction. There's a reason I left home at seventeen, dropping out of high school to go to college."

"At least you weren't sent away before you were able to count your years in double digits. Like I was." Martin jiggled the amber liquid in his glass. He wouldn't admit the intense loneliness of his Eton years. Changing the subject he asked, "Am I allowed to tell people about the filming at Stanwell?"

"If you want to. Cast and crew accommodations are already reserved in Newbridge. The stars and production principals will have rooms in the fancy manor house hotel on the edge of town. Everyone else stays in the other one."

"What about you?"

"The other one. By the motorway."

They joined the queue forming outside the reception room, and had their names checked against the guest list. Martin emptied his pockets, and Hannah opened her tiny handbag for inspection. A security man discreetly wanded them before letting them enter. Hannah's silk gown shimmered in the light of the giant chandeliers, and Martin noted the flash of sparkling threads woven through her gauzy shawl.

"Wow," she said under her breath. "The jewelry!" She fingered a gold earring. "I'm under-adorned."

Spotting a particular glittering female, he muttered, "Hell and damn."

"What's the matter?"

"It's my grandmother." He seized her hand and pulled her aside, closer to the dining room. "I hope she didn't notice us."

Hannah looked up at him through narrowed eyes. "You don't want to be seen with me?"

He shook his head. "You've got the wrong end of the stick, my girl. It's not you, it's *her*. If I'd guessed she'd be here, I'd have warned you in advance." That sounded terrible. "I mean, prepared you. For the experience." He waylaid a passing waiter and removed two glasses of wine from the tray. "Let's fortify ourselves."

"Why do we need to?"

Before he could explain, he was approached by an acquaintance, who offered an effusive greeting.

"Martin, so very pleased to see you! How're you managing at Stanwell?"

"Perfectly well." His grandmother could've cleared up his confusion about whether he should present a commoner to an earl, or vice versa. Not that it mattered. Reg was usually too inebriated to care about protocol, and no Yank—even a half-British one—would detect a breach of etiquette. "This is Hannah Ballard, from Boston. The one in America. Hannah, Lord Redruth."

"What brings you to Blighty, Hannah?"

"Moviemaking," she replied.

Intrigued, Reg asked, "Have I heard of you?"

"Unlikely," she said with a dazzling smile. "I'm responsible for location shoots, working behind the scenes."

"Right. Well, you're certainly lovely enough to be an actress. Eh, Martin?"

He bobbed his head. "Stanwell will be a setting for her company's next film."

"Well done," Reg responded, impressed. "I say, Hannah, my property in Cornwall has been in our family for centuries. We've turned most of the house into an exclusive hotel, catering to the high-end trade. Do stop by—as our special guest—and have a look. I'll wager you'll want to use Morthana House for a location."

Politely noncommittal, she replied, "I'll keep it in mind."

Reg's hazy eyes fell on Martin. "I hear you're doing up one of your properties as a sort of museum."

"Developing a local history center."

"Will it pay, after the capital expenditure?"

"We aren't expecting to turn a profit, not in the short term. It's a much-needed source of employment and will energize the local economy."

To his relief, Reg shuffled off to greet somebody else.

Hannah asked, "Is Lord Redface a close friend?"

"Redruth. We barely know each other. When drinking, he tends to forget that."

"Is there a Lady Redface?"

"At least two. His most recent wife refused to overlook his call-girl habit. There's an opening for a third, if you're interested. An earldom. With a hotel attached. How can you resist?"

"Cornwall has call-girls?"

Martin laughed loud enough to draw stares. "If it did, Reg would spend more time there."

She sampled a shaving of smoked salmon wrapped around a celeriac wedge before asking him the purpose of the Countryside Development Association. "It seems like a misnomer. Country folk in Maine don't look anything like these people."

"Membership is hereditary. My grandfather was a founder. My uncle was actively involved. I'm representative of a subset of younger, forward-thinking property owners. Our committees do massive amounts of work, and we let the codgers enjoy the visibility. And take much of the credit. A senior member of the Royal Family is always our patron. It used to be the Queen Mother, who was awfully fond of my late uncle when he was a young man about town. Most of her favorites were gay men. Or gin drinkers. Preferably both. Rufus was ideally qualified." Lest she suspect him of speaking too disrespectfully, he added, "Not a secret to those who knew him well and loved him. But he never publicly outed himself."

"Did he have a partner?"

"Not during his last years. If Alicia makes derogatory remarks about 'my son, the pooftah,' you'll know who she means."

"Alicia?"

"My grandmother. The Dowager Duchess of Wellford. Through her marriages, she worked her way down the peerage ladder and back up again. Just now she perches at the very top of the social pinnacle. Three husbands to date. Number of lovers—unknown. Possibly incalculable. Even by her."

Her eyes opened wide. "I never heard anybody talk about their grandmother that way."

"Nobody's got one like Alicia. Her affairs, before and after my grandfather divorced her, were legendary. By the time I was incarcerated at Eton, she was gone. Though she's never terribly far off. Whenever she needs attention, or suffers from extreme boredom, she turns up at a christening or a wedding or funeral, current husband or paramour in tow. We remember those events by what she wore, who she brought, and whose composure was most shattered by something she said or did. You claim to have issues with your family. How do you rate mine for dysfunction?"

"You win, hands down," she said airily.

His silver-haired grandparent floated over like a geriatric fairy, in layers of silk chiffon. A large ruby pendant dangled from her diamond necklace, and the bracelets circling her thin wrists were laden with matching gemstones.

"Darling, *splendid* to see you. And I must say, you look awfully distinguished, which is a nice change. Who have we here?"

"We have here Hannah Ballard. All the way from America."

"Dear me. Isobel has kept quiet about this one. So *like* her."

"Mother hasn't yet had the pleasure." He explained about the impending film production.

"How thrilling. Movie people are *fascinating*. I had a—an admirer in Portofino, a director. Or was he a producer? Italian, devastating charm." The memory brought a sparkle to Alicia's dark and piercing eyes, which had lanced Hannah. "You must find England quite baffling. So different to where you live."

"Not much," Hannah responded. "That's why the colonists called it *New* England."

"Her mother hails from Somerset," Martin volunteered. "You'll have heard of Wendy Edney, I'm sure."

"Dear me, yes. That lovely little garden girl on the television. And she's over there now? Extraordinary. Whatever does she do?"

Hannah smiled. "Everything she did when living here. She designs gardens and presents television programs. She writes articles and books, and she goes on lecture tours."

Martin relished Hannah's deft handling of his grandmother. With an unfaltering smile and calm voice, she resisted the older woman's attempt to patronize her. The busybodies observing them so closely would be amazed to know Alicia was being challenged by this tiny American. Hannah could certainly hold her own if he succeeded in introducing her to the prince.

Alicia's escort was the only stepson with whom she remained on speaking terms, a paunchy middle-aged chap burdened with supervision of the family estate. Its lawful owner, the current title holder, had absconded to Italy to lux-uriate in *la dolce vita*. Alicia, no doubt, maintained the rela-tionship out of pure self-interest. If she was stalking a fourth spouse, which wouldn't surprise Martin in the least, she'd want to stage her campaign from an absent earl's majestic house. Was her intended victim among the wrinklies popu-lating the room?

"What do you think of her?" he asked Hannah when the duchess drifted off.

"She could be a character from an Evelyn Waugh novel."

"Close. Straight out of Nancy Mitford. She's a bolter."

"Do all these people have titles?"

"I've no idea. It's not a prerequisite to owning or inher-iting country property. Shall we find our assigned table?"

He refrained from placing his guiding hand on her back. No touching—not with Alicia's beady eyes upon him. He'd cautiously established that their connection was wholly pro-fessional. Peering down the front of Hannah's dress, leaning too close, smiling at her too often—forbidden behavior. Which of course made him want to do all three at once.

Sirs, lords and ladies, dukes and duchesses, and a royal highness. None of Hannah's adventures as Liz's plus-one compared to this once-in-a-lifetime experience. She didn't mind that conversation in her vicinity was mind-numbingly dull. Or that as an American, her nationality wasn't exotic enough to rouse interest. Her profession generated a flicker of curiosity in the ancient gent seated on her left, but the attempt to clarify her function failed. At a loss, she dropped her mother's name. This inspired a droning description of a garden with a rockery, in a voice so over-the-top posh that she struggled to maintain a straight face.

During the prince's brief remarks, her thoughts strayed

homeward. The Palindrome Posse would be beyond thrilled to receive her description of the world-class hotel, impressive titles, wines older than she was, and gasp-inducing jewels everywhere she turned. Eve would carp about the patriarchy and hereditary privileges accrued through colonialism. Mim would relish the fashion notes.

Chase couldn't care less about English elites or her temporary proximity to royalty. But she would certainly let him know about this night. She'd email a press photo of the prince, she decided, with the caption *We had dinner together!!!*

She wondered how these society people would react if they discovered she was a killer's niece.

Maybe, Hannah surmised, I'm not the only one with a dark secret. Every kind of scandal could be lurking behind extensive pedigrees and formal manners.

As soon as the meal concluded, the diners left their tables. When one of Martin's contemporaries claimed his attention, Hannah deemed it a prudent time to visit the powder room. It was as gorgeous as she'd expected. Two women of a generation between her mother's and Alicia's briefly acknowledged her presence before resuming their languid dialogue. They were discussing Daphne, who couldn't give up shooting despite being "passionately green and now half-vegetarian."

Closing herself in a stall, Hannah pondered the term's meaning. Did they mean Daphne ate half-portions of meat, half of veg? Meat at every other meal?

At the sink she washed her hands with floral soap and eavesdropped on their gossip.

"She's awfully keen on hunting, too," reported the plump one with the bulging bust.

"I do wonder how those children will turn out. Will they ever feel a connection to their heritage, or any sense of responsibility?"

"I shouldn't think so. Little gypsies, the lot of them. I predict they'll be trekking about in the Himalayas or haring off to ashrams."

"We did it ourselves, Clarissa," pointed out the woman wearing sapphires in her earlobes, on her fingers, and around her neck.

"Marrakesh," her friend said reminiscently. "Not a care in the world. Oh, the heavenly hashish!"

No one would have guessed, thought Hannah, that these upper class, bejeweled females shared a drug-infused hippie past.

She emerged to see that the landowners were departing en masse. She followed Martin to the main entrance where a line of vehicles waited, and the hotel doormen opened and closed the doors of chauffeured cars or taxicabs.

"I'm glad you were with me. Seriously. Otherwise, it would've been the usual nightmare. What did you think of it all?" he asked after they crossed from Arlington Street to St. James's Street. "Be honest."

"I have no point of comparison. It was unprecedented."

The air felt refreshingly cool. Down the street stood the towering brick palace gatehouse. Tudor crenellations at the top reminded her of the rooks in Dad's chess set. The clock face glowed like a full moon.

"Alicia terrifies me. If she's not on the phone to La Rochelle tomorrow morning, I'll be astonished. Mother will learn about your movie from her."

"Tell her about it yourself. Tonight."

"She's an hour ahead of us. It's too late to ring."

"Will she mind about the shoot?"

"Not a bit. She never lived at Stanwell and has no strong attachment to it. Whenever she visits, she frets that I'm excessively burdened by all the responsibility."

"Are you?"

"Not on the good days. We've had lots of those lately."

He pulled open the impressive glass-and-wood front door of Latimer House. "Evening, Lorcan. Any winners today?"

"No, sir. Had a promising tip for tomorrow, though."

In the lift, Martin enlightened her about the night porter's racing fanaticism.

She stifled a yawn.

He noticed.

"Sorry," she sighed. "Time for this Cinderella to turn back into a pumpkin. That's what my dad calls me. Punkin."

At that moment she realized that within seconds they'd be inside his apartment. Alone together. Late at night. With five bedrooms.

This is *not* a date, she reminded herself again. No reason for either of us to feel awkward.

"Another drink?" he asked, switching on the kitchen lights. "If you don't care for more alcohol, I keep powdered cocoa mix in the cupboard—quality stuff. And if you can bear the mess, we can listen to music in my sitting room, or catch the news on the telly."

"Sure. But I need to change into something—"

"Comfortable?"

"Something else," she said, conscious of a sudden burst of nerves. Her excessively high heels carried her unsteadily down the hallway.

Chapter 11

For undisclosed reasons, Sir Owen Parry had made his first appearance at Hartcliffe Studios, taking possession of an office that had been prepared for him in advance. Hannah, summoned to a private meeting, pretended she didn't have a dozen unmarked items, at a minimum, on today's checklist.

The director never failed to dress impeccably, as befitted a man knighted by the late queen for his service to the arts. Today he wore a sweater of quality cashmere, pale blue. She wanted one just like it.

"After consultation with several parties involved in our production, a difficult but necessary decision was made with regards to your role. I'm informing you myself, to prevent any misunderstanding."

Unsure how else to respond, she nodded.

"From tomorrow, Alistair McLaren will take on the position of location manager."

The stark pronouncement refuted the British habit of indirect speech. He wasn't beating around the bush, as Grampa might say. Although her breath had become trapped deep in her chest, at the bottom of her lungs, she managed to blurt a single syllable. "Why?"

"Your lack of experience overseeing an entire department

and a complex shoot, in this country, raised concerns. Not that Liz exaggerated your abilities, which you have proved."

"I'm half-British," she interrupted. "I've been coming to Somerset all my life. Alistair's from Scotland." These justifications were pitifully lame and not at all persuasive, but she didn't care. "I've worked on location since I was thirteen. As a professional."

His cashmere-covered shoulders shrugged. "Not over here, apart from your student projects at Bristol. Alistair has numerous credits in British television and film."

"Never as location manager," she pointed out. "When did you decide to dump me? What did Liz say about it?"

He frowned. "I have complete authority to act on personnel matters while she's taking her maternity leave."

"She doesn't know."

"We expect you to remain with the production. In another capacity."

Who the hell was included in that "we" he kept repeating? She suspected he'd inflated the number of decision-makers.

"After reviewing the options," he continued, "we've settled on one that best matches your abilities and prior role."

"Alistair's assistant? No thanks."

"If you're concerned about salary—"

She stalled him by standing up. "As far as I'm concerned, I've been made redundant. Tomorrow I'll check out of my hotel. And return the hire car."

"Is that what you want to do?" He seemed genuinely surprised. His voice took on a paternal tone when he added, "Take time to consider what you're giving up."

"No need," she said firmly. Her list of priorities had suddenly shrunk to one—getting off the premises as swiftly and unobtrusively as possible, with her dignity intact. "When you came to the directing symposium at Bristol University, and gave such a glowing evaluation of my short film, it was my dream to work with you. At least I can say I had the privilege. For three weeks."

She turned and hurried out of the room.

Retreating to her workspace, she was relieved to find it empty. Otherwise, she'd be tempted to strangle the perfidious Alistair with one of the long cables littering the room. She suspected he'd intended to push her aside from the moment she arrived at Hartcliffe Studios.

Despite the powerful urge to contact Liz, she wouldn't.

Owen can tell her what he's done, she thought vengefully. Or make Nigel Rossiter do it. And they'll have to listen to her vent all the outrage that I had to hold back.

Far more worrisome, her immigration status had instantly become problematic. Her visa permitted her to work in Britain temporarily, as a creative sponsored by a sanctioned entity—Hartcliffe Film Studios. Her six-month stay was contingent on employment, and she was clueless about altering her status. Money wasn't an immediate concern. The payroll department had recently deposited two weeks' salary to her online bank account. Acorn Films would absorb credit card charges for her car and hotel, tonight's dinner and breakfast tomorrow.

Grabbing her satchel, she shoved her laptop inside and pocketed her cell phone, desperate to get away before Alistair returned. He required no briefing before she made her escape. He was the beneficiary of her diligent planning and preparation. She'd shared all her files and notes. They were stored on his laptop and his phone and his tablet.

Liz will make it up to me, she consoled herself. This isn't the end of my—oh, hell, I've been bumped from the picture of a lifetime. It's destined to rake in millions of dollars and scoop up every award going. And my sole contribution—securing the perfect location—will be forgotten.

Gran's cheeriness was a temporary antidote to despair, and her delight at Hannah's visit provided some solace. A fast-forward version of Mum, she possessed an identical smile and boundless energy undiminished by age. Widowhood had prompted her return to her native Montgomery and this house within strolling distance of her brother and sister-in-law.

"Barbara wants to show me the present bought for George's birthday. Coming with me?"

Hannah shook her head. "I haven't finished these." She jabbed her vegetable peeler at the mound of potatoes on the oak tabletop.

She continued her scraping, half-hearing the radio news bulletin. It concluded with a recap of headlines from around the world and, inevitably, an update on the Sterling Scandal. A Parliamentary inquiry would determine whether the honorable member had funded his re-election with dirty money from his mistress's brother, awaiting trial for the alleged murder of a "business associate."

The afternoon play, much to Hannah's relief, was a comedy. Out of habit, she visualized its setting, placing the characters and the action in West Country locations.

Her phone buzzed—she'd temporarily silenced Big Ben. Confident that this was Liz's long-awaited call, she didn't glance at the number before answering.

"Hey there!"

"Hannah." Martin's disembodied voice filled her ear. "Where are you?"

Startled, she replied, "My grandmother's kitchen. In Wales. You?"

"Stanwell. Yesterday a gigantic Scot turned up to prowl my house and grounds, claiming to be the location manager.

That's odd, thought I. You don't look anything like the diminutive young lady who's been telling me the same thing for the past month. He never mentioned you."

"I'm not surprised. Alistair stole my job. The fix was in from the start."

"Why didn't you let me know? When will you be back in Somerset?"

"Looks like never. I was booted off the film."

After a quiet moment, he said, "Please tell me you're all right."

"Half the time my head feels like it's about to explode with questions like 'What if?' and 'Why me?' and 'How *dare* they?'" She picked up potato peelings and arranged them artistically on the wooden surface. "Sir Owen offered an alternative, but I refused. After being Alistair's superior, no way could I continue as his subordinate."

"I should think not."

"I told Gran I'm having a break from work. True enough."

"I'm really sorry. And very disappointed. I looked forward to watching you manage this location."

He had no idea how those well-meaning words stung. She'd spent several wakeful nights imagining herself embedded in Milver Vale. "If I'd stayed on the film, I would've been busy for up to sixteen hours at a stretch. No time for socializing."

"What are your plans?"

Her laugh emerged as a mirthless huff. "Flying back to Boston. Looking for my next gig. Living down this disaster."

"Here's a better idea. I detect the hint of a Welsh accent, evidence that you need to depart quite soon. You belong in Zummerzet, as our locals say. At Stanwell."

"That's the *last* place I want to be."

"Harsh."

"I can't help feeling bitter. And jealous. I'm no longer connected to *Forsaken Fortune*. You are."

"If not for you, I wouldn't be. I'm still in your debt."

"You gave me a memorable night in London. The Ritz. All those lords and ladies. Even a prince. Your grandmother."

He groaned. "Making amends for that excruciating episode requires a major effort. As you know, this place is a veritable resort. Tennis, swimming pool, horses, dogs. Delicious dinners. Healthful country rambles. Your choice of bedroom. I've got twenty of them."

"Don't you *dare!*"

"I'm not propositioning you. Honestly."

"I wasn't talking to you. Clive, Gram's Burmese cat, is in crouch position, about to leap onto the kitchen table." She eyed the tensed mound of gray fur on the adjacent chair. "It's a lovely offer, Martin, and generous. I'm grateful. But I can't accept."

"What's more, our annual Flower Fete is coming up. You can experience the madness—I mean, the fun of it."

"You might get in trouble for harboring a fugitive. Hartcliffe Studios sponsored my work visa, and I no longer work there. Meaning I'm in breach of Britain's immigration laws."

"No better hideout than the Milver Vale. The authorities will never think to look for you here."

Accustomed to his stubborn persistence, she didn't feel ready to capitulate. She heard the front door open and close, signaling her grandmother's return.

Martin's silence made her wonder if her phone signal had failed, until he prompted, "Well?"

She was heartened by evidence that she wasn't entirely friendless on this side of the Atlantic Ocean. "I'll think it over and let you know in a day or so."

"Even better, text your train details as soon as you work them out. I'll collect you from Newbridge railway station. See you soon."

Gran stepped into the kitchen and saw her put down the phone. "Are they calling you back to work?" She tied on her pinny, printed all over with calico cats.

"A friend invited me to stay." Hannah picked up a spud and the peeler. "I haven't decided whether I'll go."

"It's been a treat, having you here, but I've got plenty to keep me busy."

"Oh, I know. Book group leader. Secretary of the Outing Club. RSPCA volunteer. My presence is surely cramping your style."

One dry, cool hand reached down to cup her cheek. "Don't be daft. Spending time with my clever and successful grandchildren is a rare treat. Our Will is an accomplished orchestra musician, making a name for himself in London. You're rising high in the movie business. No granny could be prouder."

Hannah's conscience chewed at her. Informing Gran about her jobless status ensured it would be communicated to her parents. A few days ago, she'd phoned to tell them her whereabouts but felt too emotionally raw to stir up a family drama.

After scheduling her flight to Boston, she'd let them know she was no longer working on *Forsaken Fortune*. She didn't have to explain why.

Gran's house felt more like home than Bear Knoll. Since her toddler years she'd been crossing the ocean. While Mum toured Britain to promote her books and design client gardens, Hannah had stayed in Portishead with her grandparents, accompanying them to Montgomery to visit her great-grandparents and Great-uncle George and Great-aunt Barbara. She'd spent a memorable childhood Christmas in Wales, staging a legendary meltdown when refused a glass of port like the adults drank while viewing the Queen's Speech on television.

The predictability of her days with Gran was a pleasant change from constant travel and regular confrontation with the unexpected. After breakfast—whatever the weather—they strolled to the shops clustered around the Georgian town square and visited the library. In the afternoon, Hannah jogged up to the castle ruin and back, or to the vineyard. Sometimes she trudged across a section of the Offa's Dyke trail. At night she sat on the sofa, stroking Clive the cat as long as he wanted her to. Gran, an avid crime series viewer, sat a cushion away with her knitting.

Gran filled a basin with water, and they both sliced the peeled potatoes, placing each wedge into the bath.

"How is your uncle managing, now that he's out of prison?"

Hannah reached for a naked spud. "At Christmas he got a part-time job in Old Town, at the canoe factory. And he's doing community service on the Indian Island Reservation."

"I remember him during your parents' wedding week, quite the liveliest and most popular person at every party and gathering. So different to Neil. Given the age difference, they scarcely seem like brothers."

"He's a firecracker, for sure. Or was." Hannah pushed back her hair with damp and starchy fingers. "Grampa needs more help with the boat. Not enough younger people take up lobstering or scalloping, and the ones he hires don't stick around long. Dad used to go out with him on Sunday, when the vet practice is closed. But after he injured his hand, Grampa wouldn't take him on board."

"I didn't know about that."

"Nothing too bad. A bruised wrist and a shallow cut that didn't even need stitches. We're hoping Chase will move back to Falmouth, but nobody's going to pressure him."

"How would the community react, do you think?"

"Everybody knows he didn't kill with intent. He was charged with manslaughter, not murder. He participated in the University of Maine's Prison Education Partnership, taking business courses. When he goes home, he'll be just fine."

She hoped her prediction wasn't overly optimistic.

Martin, standing in the Newbridge railway station car park, watched Hannah efficiently steer her wheeled case around the rain puddles on the platform. During her prior visit to Stanwell, he'd become acquainted with a diligent, work-obsessed location manager. He didn't doubt that he'd enjoy the company of this different model, unemployed and stranded, just as much.

"Any trouble on the railways?" He stowed her single piece of luggage in the boot of his car.

"My connection at Birmingham was so tight I almost missed my train to Bristol. Temple Meads was madness."

"Did you get lunch?"

"Gran sent me off with egg and cress sandwiches and homemade flapjack," she answered. "I could do with a coffee, though. I didn't finish the swill I got from the refreshments trolley."

"There's a café down the street. The Dancing Dragon."

"A civilized stroll sounds wonderful. When not sitting in a cramped seat, I was racing from platform to platform."

He pocketed his key fob and wandered towards the pay-and-display kiosk.

Pointing at the sign hanging above the pavement, Hannah said, "Somerset's symbolic creature. The one engraved on your ring. A Latimer heirloom?"

"Sort of." He fingered the gold band. "Though not an antique. A couple of decades ago, the tenants and estate workers took up a collection and commissioned it as a Christmas gift for Uncle Rufus. I decided to wear it as a tribute to him. And the people of this district."

Lunchtime diners had deserted the coffee shop, and the teatime rush hadn't begun.

Turning her face to the window, Hannah said, "Now that I'm a charity case myself, I should visit the shop across the street."

Misfortune had dimmed her spark. "Agnes, my tenant at River Cottage, runs the place. Looking for anything in particular?"

"Whatever is cheap enough and not too casual. I'm sick of the work outfits I've been dragging around everywhere I go. But as your lordship's guest, I need something more respectable than jogging clothes."

"You're a runner?"

"No time to be, until I went to Wales."

"The Pub Dashers will be out in a fortnight, training for our monthly point-to-point. Which for us is a pub-to-pub. You should join us."

She leaned against the chair. "I won't be here that long. I came for the Flower Fete. When is it?"

"At the weekend. But you're staying on afterwards."

She sipped her coffee before replying. "I've got to face up to reality. When I was with Gran, I could pretend nothing's wrong. This morning, the moment I sat down on the first train of the day, all the heavy facts of my situation came bearing down on me. I need to get back to Boston. Soon."

Jaz, the server, came by to refill their mugs. "Fresh brewed."

Hannah shook her head.

"No more for me," he said.

"We don't see you often enough," she complained. Her spiky platinum hair and kohl-daubed eyes contrasted with her genteel, lace-curtained establishment. "Tell Ron I bought the espresso maker I mentioned to him. My old one, the Brasilia Pronto, is his to borrow if he still wants it."

"I can't think why he would," said Martin, puzzled. "The one at Stanwell is in fair working order, far as I know."

"Flower Fete," Jaz told him. "He means to offer espresso in the same marquee where the teas and coffees are served."

"A break with tradition? Good luck to him, getting past those tea ladies—they're a fierce lot. Why'd you replace your machine?"

"The new one does over three hundred cups per day, twice the number as the Pronto. After Ron uses it, if he does, it goes to a re-seller."

"I'll let him know it's available." He handed over a ten-pound note. "This covers everything. Add whatever's left-over to your Pet Rescue support collection." He murmured to Hannah, "Ariel would insist."

The clouds that had delivered morning showers were parting, but damp lingered in the air. He accompanied Hannah to the charity shop and studied a shelf of second-hand books while she browsed. When she withdrew to the changing cubicle, he had no difficulty culling gossip from Agnes.

"How'd you like to adopt a flock of peafowl?" She inquired.

"I can't think of anything I'd like less."

She cocked a grin. "Lady come in yesterday, carload of city clothes. As I was helping 'er heft them out, she asked did you have peacocks at Stanwell and wondered if you needed zum."

"Nobody needs them. Or their obnoxious screeching."

"Too right, and she learnt it t'hard way. 'Er husband and 'er bought that parsonage up to Blampfyde. Before the removers arrived with all their goods, she'd taken in a peacock and peahens to decorate her gear-den. Ready to wring their necks and serve them birds roasted on a platter, she is, but can't do it without upsetting the kiddies."

Hannah emerged from behind the loose curtain, a printed

cotton shift, a denim mini-skirt, and a selection of colorful tops hanging over her arm.

"Look at all them curdles on 'er," Agnes said in an admiring tone.

On their way to the car park, Hannah asked him, "What are curdles?"

"Curls. She speaks the broadest Somerset dialect of anybody I know. The BBC or a linguistics professor should record her for posterity."

While driving to Stanwell, Martin gave an account of his grandmother's social maneuvers. Alicia was badgering her famously reclusive stepson to host a large party on the eve of the Henley Regatta. And to persuade his elder brother, the earl, to pop over from Italy and make an appearance. "She's got no chance of getting her way with either one."

"I wouldn't be so sure," Hannah reflected. "At the Ritz I watched her prod that poor man in the prince's direction. That reminds me, the dress and heels I wore that night are still at your flat."

"You'll get them back. Hardly a fortnight passes without me being called to London."

"Is your fete like a wedding? Will I need a fancy hat with a big brim and silk flowers, or a dainty fascinator trimmed with arrow feathers?"

"Not unless you want to be conspicuously overdressed. If it's anything like past years, we'll be dodging raindrops for part of the weekend. Or all of it."

Chapter 12

Hannah placed her left foot in the stirrup and climbed onto the Welsh cob, relishing the familiar creak of saddle leather. Although the groom's side-zip short boots fit her, the cuffs of a long-sleeved striped tunic nearly reached her knuckles, and the loose jodhpurs didn't hug her legs. She ran a finger under her helmet's elastic chin strap, checking the tension.

"Take these." Shona reached up to hand her a pair of gloves. "Grip-Fast, a smaller size than Poppy's."

"Thanks."

Meg—her mount—boarded in the Stanwell stables while her young owner was confined to a girls' boarding school. Martin was riding his own horse, a glossy black called Étoile because of the pure white star between her ears. He'd surprised Hannah by turning up in old-school riding attire: polo shirt, olive riding breeches, boots with brown tops. His headwear had a classic peak front, shading his eyes and nose. When he caught her looking, she pretended she wasn't.

"Ready?"

"Lead on, my lord."

"Not if you keep using that term," he retorted.

In Maine, where riding was almost exclusively a female

activity, she rarely saw a man on a horse. Husbands and fathers paid for stabling and shoeing and lessons and the fees to compete in shows. And they moaned about the escalating costs. Although Hannah's dad, who doctored animals large and small, handled equines with calm competence and cared for Mum's Rascal, Ballard men were genetically aligned with boats and the ocean fishery.

When they reached a lane wide enough for riding side by side, Hannah admitted, "I'm nervous about meeting your mother."

"I have great faith in your fortitude. You stood up to Alicia, something I find difficult. You were bold enough to discard a boyfriend on New Year's Eve."

Forcing a smile, she stared at the gap between Meg's pointed ears.

Under the influence of the champagne and wine consumed at the Ritz, followed by a nightcap of raspberry liqueur at his flat, she'd unwisely mentioned the episode. She hadn't explained that Joel's attitude towards Chase caused the breakup. She wouldn't do so now. Or ever.

"At least your chap had a date, even if it ended badly. I spent that night all alone."

She wasn't going to ask him why, reluctant to express interest in his personal life. Perhaps Poppy had traveled to Portugal to spend the holidays with her father.

Tents and booths and tables had been set up around the perimeter of the village green. On the flat grassland behind The Huntsman's Horn, a party of men pounded a set of stakes spaced far apart.

Martin's arm shot up, and they waved back. "Jack Elliston from The Peacock is helping. Not that the pubs are overtly competitive. It's a friendly rivalry."

Other volunteers arranged tables and chairs, and an uninflated bouncy castle sat in the meadow. Delivery vans circled the green and wedged themselves between the newly erected stalls. Men and women bustled about, and a trio of mums with toddlers in prams chatted outside a shop.

Martin guided Étoile away from the activity and onto a narrow bridle path edging the field. Hannah prodded Meg lightly with her heels and followed. The path gradually ascended to a forest of tall trees with straight trunks and gray bark. Their branches filtered the morning sunshine, and blue flowers on slender spikes carpeted the ground beneath them.

"Bluebells!" After a moment of silent admiration, she asked if this was conservation land.

"The beech wood lies outside the development zone. I'm investigating how to place it in a protective trust."

Back at the stable yard they removed the horses' tack and rubbed them down before turning them out into the fenced paddock behind the barn.

On the way to the house, Martin told her, "I was meaning to ask if you'd do something for me, but you might need convincing. There's no time for that now. I've got to clean up before leaving for the airport."

"I'll try and bear the suspense."

Before long, she reminded herself, I'll be the one heading to Heathrow.

Because she seized any chance to be helpful, she volunteered to muck out a pony's stall that Shona hadn't yet done. On finishing, she studied the rows of colored ribbons, faded and fresh, won by either Poppy or Martin.

When she saw him next, he was ambling towards his car, dressed in fresh shirt and trousers.

"Care to come along?" he asked.

"Not like this." She indicated her sagging jodhpurs, streaked with a brown substance that might or might not be mud.

Going into the house, she passed a large mirror that highlighted the incongruity of her riding attire and her luxuriant surroundings. She climbed the staircase, noting the ache in her thighs after a morning in the saddle.

On leaving Stanwell she would miss her bedroom. Light flowed in from the tall, chintz-curtained windows. She slept in a period-correct four-poster fitted with a comfortable modern mattress. By opening the casement, she could look down on the giant wisteria trained to climb up and across the outer wall. When she discovered the topmost branch was within reach, she'd plucked a few of the lightly-scented flowers and put them in the porcelain vase on the fireplace mantel.

A quick shower washed away sweat and grime and the scent of horse. Bodily if not mentally refreshed, she selected one of her secondhand tops from Newbridge and paired it with the denim miniskirt. Powering up her laptop, she carried it to the window seat. A quick scan of online communities where location scouts gathered for networking—and complaining—yielded no useful or actionable information. One more unnecessary reminder that hers was an uncertain vocation.

Hearing voices and laughter from below, she gazed down at the three gardeners removing spent blossoms and staking the tallest plants in preparation for Sunday's big event. The grounds of Stanwell House, off-limits to the public, would be included in this year's Open Gardens Tour.

A ping alerted her to an incoming message. She reached for her phone.

Staring at the image of an infant with enormous eyes of indeterminate color and tufts of dark hair, she breathed, "Hello, Alexandra Elizabeth." Then she typed, "Need to talk."

Instantly, Big Ben sounded.

"She's gorgeous!" Hannah said. "How do you feel?"

"Like shit. And somebody else's shit."

"You can't use that kind of language around your adorable baby."

"By now she's used to it." After a pause, Liz said grimly, "But I'm not accustomed to this postpartum malaise."

"Because of hormones shifting? That can't last forever."

"For some women, it goes on for months. Even up to a year."

"You better not be self-diagnosing on the internet."

"That made me feel worse, so I stopped. Now that our locations are locked, what've you been doing?"

"Absolutely nothing." Here was the moment she'd dreaded. "I'm off the production. Owen fired me. In person."

"You're fucking kidding me."

Hannah gave a brief synopsis of her final meeting with the director.

Liz groaned, then growled, "Why didn't you let me know about this right away?"

"You're on maternity leave."

"I'm postpartum. Not terminal."

"Frankly, I wanted to punish Owen by making him—or Nigel—break the news to you. Guess they didn't have the balls."

"Who in hell is our location manager now?"

"Alistair McLaren. My *assistant*. Owen wanted him all along. It was just a matter of time till I got shoved aside."

"Hannah, I had no idea what you were dealing with. This sucks. Massively."

She drew a shaky breath. "Tell me about it." She wasn't about to burden Liz with the complications of her immigration status, or her dwindling funds. "But I did have a nice visit with my grandmother in Wales before Martin Latimer invited me to Stanwell House for the annual spring festival. After that, I'll be back in Boston to meet your little Lexi. And find a job."

"Don't rush," Liz advised. "Wait till the dust settles at Hartcliffe Studios. Because I'm going to stir up lots of it."

"You can't risk losing your producing partners' goodwill. If you get all defensive about me, that's what will happen. It does neither of us any good." Shifting the subject, she asked, "Are you getting enough sleep? How's Tom coping?"

She listened politely to a fulsome and illuminating description of life with a newborn.

The call ended, and all the difficulties awaiting Hannah across the Atlantic came rolling at her with the force of a spring tide.

Liz, recovering from childbirth, had to cope with unfamiliar responsibilities as a first-time parent, and her unpredictable emotions.

If and when Chase returned to Falmouth and tried to resume his former existence, he'd face a multitude of challenges.

And unless Hannah secured a scouting job, she'd have nowhere else to go except Bear Knoll, the parental home she'd fled a decade ago, to which she returned only when absolutely necessary.

Responding to Martin's texted invitation to afternoon tea, she found him in the kitchen, bracketed by Ariel and Millie, covetously eyeing a plate of scones and the wedge of cheese on his cutting board. Seated across from Poppy at the long table was an older version of the young mother Hannah had spotted in a family photograph at Latimer House. Slender, with regular but unremarkable features in a sun-burnished face, she styled her graying brown hair in a no-fuss bob.

"Hannah, meet my mother. Lady Richard Latimer, according to Debrett's etiquette guide. And *Posh* magazine. She answers to Isobel."

"How do you do, Hannah?"

"Very well, thanks."

"I was more than a little alarmed when I heard Wendy Edney's daughter is helping me judge the floral arrangements."

"Is she? I mean, am I?"

"That's the question I was going to ask you." Martin set down a wooden plank of cheese and biscuits.

"I've never done it before."

"No matter," Isobel assured her. "We have scoring sheets. Entries are identified by numbers, not names, to prevent favoritism. The former vicar's wife and I used to do it together. The current incumbent isn't keen, and I doubt her husband will be." Turning her attention to Poppy, she said, "At Easter I visited friends in Portugal. How does your father like his ex-pat life?"

"Couldn't be happier. Was it a nice holiday?"

"Very. Bridge playing and brass band concerts—a change from *boules* and La Rochelle's baroque music society. I painted watercolor landscapes, which I never manage to fit in between commissions."

Martin explained, "Mother makes portraits. Of children."

Poppy lifted the lid from the teapot to check the brew before filling the cups Martin had placed in front of her.

"Hannah's joining us on the Dashers' trial pub-to-pub run," he announced, presenting her teacup.

"Oh." Poppy's tone was noncommittal.

Hannah divided a scone and applied clotted cream to each half. She accepted the jam pot from Martin, who smiled as she dipped her spoon in.

"Same as us," he commented, "and the fine folk of Devon. Cream before jam."

"Mum's preference. She says it's prettier with the red on top."

"I'm not fussed about it either way," Poppy contributed.

After they polished off Jan's delectably flaky scones and nibbled the other items, Martin wrapped up his precious Milver Vale cheese and returned it to the refrigerator.

Isobel said to Poppy, "I'm eager to see the new kitchen garden Martin told me about."

"Conveniently located a few steps away."

They both stood up. Smiling down at Hannah, Martin's mother asked, "Won't you come with us?"

"I'm doing the washing up."

"Oh no, you aren't," Martin contradicted.

"Drying, then." She opened the cupboard where cloths were stored and removed the top one from the pile.

"Hannah has no capacity for idleness," he told the others.

"That's rich," his mother commented, "coming from you."

Poppy laughed sharply.

Hannah couldn't help glancing towards the broad window while she wiped moisture from each plate and cup. Deep in conversation, the two women inspected the herb and vegetable beds. As they made their way across the lawn to a clump of irises, she thought she detected a prospective mother- and daughter-in-law vibe. If Martin stopped his womanizing and settled down with his estate manager, unpretentious Isobel would doubtless rejoice. Poppy, a countrywoman to her core, spent her working days in close proximity to him. Not only at the estate office, but just as frequently at mealtimes in this kitchen. Although she hadn't stayed overnight since Hannah's arrival, she guessed that Poppy and Martin were essentially co-habiting.

Why did that sting?

Occasionally he veered into flirtatiousness with her, apparently from habit and without any ulterior meaning or motive. Grateful for his hospitality, she depended on his efforts to jolly her out of bleak moods. Which is why she often wished she could stuff him into her luggage and take him back to Boston.

Chapter 13

An overcast sky marked the early hours of the Flower Fete. Hannah joined Martin and Poppy on a pre-breakfast run, but their phones rang so incessantly she wondered why they had attempted it. Poppy received a call that made her mutter ominously about parking arrangements for horse boxes. She peeled off and jogged away towards Milverston Magna.

Flicking brown strands from his damp forehead, Martin said, "I should go, too. There's usually some kind of trouble with the sound system. Better work out any issues well before starting time."

"Definitely, in my professional opinion."

He loped off, leaving her to follow the dirt track, marked with indentations from their horses' iron shoes. The steady pounding of her soles against the earth had a hypnotic effect, and the breeze that ruffled the leaves overhead soothed her. Without her earbuds, she could hear every chirp emanating from the hedgerows, and bleating sheep in the meadow. The sun, gradually emerging from behind the clouds, cast faint light onto the bluebells in the beech forest. Farther on, she inhaled the distinctive fragrance of yellow rapeseed flowers filling a vast field that extended all the way to a distant hill.

After a hasty semblance of breakfast, she returned to the festival ground in time to observe Martin's ascent to the bunting-draped platform. The microphone and speakers were in sync when he declared the fete officially open and offered a brief welcome address that drew enthusiastic applause.

Hannah told Poppy, "I wasn't expecting a crowd this large."

"People come from Newbridge and Yeovil and Frome and Taunton. Down from Bristol, or up from Sherborne." The estate manager was no longer so harried, having solved her horse van crisis. "Did you bring your timetable?"

Hannah reached into the pocket of her charity shop floral shift. "Right here. I'm supposed to meet Isobel at the baking tent in—yikes, five minutes."

Poppy grinned. "You'll need more than a three-mile run to get rid of all the calories you're about to consume."

Reporting for duty, she confronted an array of beautifully-presented cakes and tarts laid out on long tables. Her fellow judge handed over a scoring sheet and offered a brief tutorial.

"Although appearance and taste are the most important criteria, we can give extra marks for creative presentation."

They moved past the row of beaming, hopeful bakers—men and women—to make their initial visual assessment of the items on display. Everything looked delicious. Hannah tasted and scored morsels of fruitcake, custard tart, Battenburg cake, Bath buns, jam tart, iced sponge, Eccles cakes, scones, Bakewell tart, profiterole, Victoria sandwich, fruitcake, and more.

"The Battenburg cake is beautiful," she enthused as soon as she and Isobel stepped out of the marquee to confer.

"Not as light in texture as it might have been. I ranked it fourth. The Victoria sponge was perfection."

"I gave it top marks."

"A pity about the sunken pavlova. What's second on your list?"

"Fig pie. That crust dissolved in my mouth. And the pastry fig leaves were a nice touch."

"We concur." Isobel pointed to her scores. "And we're unanimous about the winner."

Choosing third place and Honorable Mention proved more difficult. Although Hannah had been taught by a baker of British origin, she deferred to Isobel's judgment in particulars. After they handed out the awards, contestants carried their entries to the tea tent to be sliced and sold. Ron, operating his borrowed espresso maker, was mobbed.

Hannah contemplated a visit to the secondhand clothing booth squeezed in between the face-painting stand and the Women's Institute book stall. Shrieks and laughter drew her attention to a long line of children and adults standing near a wooden board painted with a clown figure. Martin's face filled the circle cutout.

"Step up, step up," cried the barker, a dripping sponge in each hand. "Aggrieved about a delay in rubbish collection? Outraged over his lordship's speedy driving? Did that hellhound of his worry your livestock? Have at 'im!"

Martin bared his teeth. "Be warned! I'll impose a higher rent on any tenant who hits me. As for you farmers—if your sponge makes contact, I'll let Ariel loose in your sheep-fold to do her worst. Mark my words, vengeance will be—*crikey!*"

A yellow sponge struck his nose and dropped into the full barrel.

The barker pulled it from the water. Without squeezing, he handed it to the next person in line, a boy in a scouting uniform.

"Trying for a sponge-tossing badge, are you, young Tom?" Martin mock-sneered, drawing laughter.

If it existed, the kid would've earned one. His sponge hit the nobleman's brow with a moist slapping noise.

An elderly lady standing beside her chuckled. "Martin will raise a packet. If we'd got him to do this five years ago, we could've paid for that church roof in half the time."

The sheer efficiency of the proceedings proved this community's ability to cope with the hassles and mayhem that would arrive when filming began. And yet, despite a few common elements, an annual disruption wasn't comparable to a multi-week location shoot.

Hannah checked her cell phone. Within the hour she had to join Isobel for the flower judging. According to her schedule, the gymkhana had begun, so she made her way to the riding ring, past the bric-a-brac tables and craft booths staffed by local charity members and shopkeepers. The stall featuring products from Milver Vale Dairy was a reminder of her introduction to Wincott & Sons and its friendly blue-blooded cheesemonger.

She spied him sauntering along the midway-like alley formed by parallel rows of booths, toweling face and neck. Occasionally he addressed the scowling middle-aged man at his side, who vigorously shook his head at every remark.

"You'll regret creating housing stock for a lower socio-economic population," she heard the stranger say to him. "Introducing an incompatible group to this region is certain to reduce property values overall. And increase the crime rate."

Martin halted. "An opinion I've heard before," he replied placidly. "Discussion forums and survey results from the joint village councils' task force indicate that yours is a minority view. Our housing initiative can alleviate rising prices and enable lower-wage workers to purchase or rent quality homes. Beneficiaries include teachers and public service employees and young couples striving to hop onto the property ladder. That's not to say we're opposed to migration from elsewhere, which fosters community vibrancy."

"The right sort of migrants. Right?"

Hannah and Martin exchanged glances.

Irritation was evident when he replied, "I encourage you, as a newcomer, to stop at the Youth Club booth for raffle tickets. The group's membership is broadly representative of the community. If your children aren't involved, they're missing out on something wonderful."

"My boys attend Cranborough. As boarders. Don't dash off —I've another concern. The fellow whose farmland abuts my back garden doesn't maintain his fields properly. Whatever crop he planted is messy and shaggy and doesn't grow in straight lines like it should. And he lets his livestock roam there."

"Phillip is committed to regenerative farming, dependent on mixed vegetation and plant rotation for biodiversity. Animal manure increases soil fertility. He doesn't use herbicides and pesticides, which leach into the water table or run off into the streams and the river. Caitlyn," Martin called out to a female steward.

A toy duckling perched on top of her bright floppy hat and her basket was half-filled with them. "You've already bought more'n your share of duckies," she told him.

"This gentleman hasn't got one yet. And he'd like to hear about your daughter's experience in the Youth Club. Enjoy the festival, sir." Grasping Hannah by the elbow, he led her away.

"You handled him well."

"Pompous git. I should've told him Cranborough's for boys who couldn't get listed for Eton or Harrow or Winchester."

"Now who's the snob?"

"At least he didn't utter the words 'undesirable element.' Otherwise, I'd have said something rude."

"Isn't rudeness one of the aristocratic privileges?"

"Not nowadays. Do you suppose my short sermon on regenerative agriculture was effective? I could've gone on much longer."

"I know." She grinned up at him. "I'm familiar with your verbal dissertations on that subject."

"How was your cake competition?"

Her arm swept outward in an all-inclusive gesture. "These Milver Vale ladies and gentlemen can *bake!* I won't need another meal for days. Where are we going?"

"To the enclosure at the edge of the field. I'm judging the fancy-dress dog parade."

"Will it be as entertaining as the sponge toss?"

"More so."

"I entered the river race." She held up her duck.

"I filled a bag with them but somehow mislaid it in the tea tent. If my birds are found and re-sold, it'll be extra dosh for the club. What else did you splurge on?"

"Cropped trousers, at Agnes's secondhand clothing stall. Your mother says you're competing this afternoon. Egg-and-spoon?"

"Just the three-legged race. Poppy and I have high hopes."

"I'll cheer you on," she promised.

"We've never won, though we had our best finish last year. Came in third."

The canine costume parade lived up to advance billing. Martin's idiosyncratic method of judging ensured a prize for every entrant—if not a ribbon, a dog biscuit for an improvised category achievement: Floppiest Ears on a Mixed Breed Wearing a Jacket, Best Kilt (one, worn by a Highland Terrier), the Youngest Dog in Pink, and so on.

The majority of Rubber Duck Race participants were children, accompanied by supportive parents and grandparents. They gathered on the arched bridge over the river and waited for the starting signal. After the air gun exploded, Martin emptied his bag of ducklings, causing a mini-riot and good-natured protests. After reviewing the rules, the Youth Club president declared no limit on the number of entries by a single person. His lordship could not, therefore, be disqualified.

Competitors raced along the riverbank path to the finish line, a length of twine stretched over the water. The first duck to float beneath it belonged to a five-year-old girl. Martin awarded her prize, a free family pass to a year's worth of films, donated by the cinema in Newbridge.

"He's never outgrown his ability to make a spectacle of himself," Isobel commented as she and Hannah made their way to the parish church, where the flower arrangements awaited their ratings. "I suppose when he does it round here, it's relationship-building."

"I wouldn't call him an attention-seeker," Hannah replied. "I've met plenty of those in the film industry."

"Several villagers complained to me about your movie. As though I could do something to stop it."

"The prospect of having their satellite dishes and co-ax cables removed tends to make people antagonistic."

"That was mentioned."

"When shooting starts, the objections usually fade. And afterwards, everything gets put back just as it was."

Not once had Martin referred to *Forsaken Fortune,* and she was grateful for his consideration for her feelings. He'd become a true friend, generous and thoughtful, and apparently didn't mind that her presence at Stanwell probably prevented him for carrying out responsibilities as landlord and entrepreneur.

Though lacking her mother's expertise in floriculture, Hannah felt comfortable expressing her opinion of each specimen and arrangement displayed in the church sanctuary.

Isobel stopped in front of a peculiar collection of beer bottles filled with tall leafy spikes. "Oh, he *didn't*," she moaned.

"Those look like stinging nettles."

"My son's handiwork. Should we expose his naughtiness by giving a prize to this aberration?" She removed a pink rosette from her carrier bag. With a wicked smile, she placed it in front of the weeds.

"What should I write on the card?" Hannah asked.

"Most hazardous."

When watching the three-legged race, she and Martin's mother cheered the loudest as he and Poppy hurtled along the final stretch, leading the field. They would have claimed their elusive victory if they'd remained upright instead of stumbling and falling to the ground in a heap.

"I hope nothing more than their pride got bruised," Isobel said.

"There's always next year," Hannah responded. "That's what Grampa says if the Boston Red Sox have a bad season, or get eliminated from the baseball World Series."

According to Martin, only the Christmas Eve candlelight service and Easter Day mass drew more worshipers than Sunday in Flower Fete weekend. Every pew in St. Anne's Church was occupied. The grand prize winner in the flower arranging competition adorned the altar, and the others were placed in window niches. Some discriminating—or disapproving—person had removed Martin's beer bottles filled with nettles.

After the recessional hymn, he took up a position near the lych-gate, shaded by ancient yew trees, and hawked garden tour maps. He enlisted Hannah as money-taker, and her plastic envelope soon bulged with pound coins and fivers.

"What else will you be doing today?" she asked. "Another stint as target for wet sponges?"

He shook his head. "My duty there is done. Each of our

parish councilors has a turn. And our Member of Parliament. I predict the afternoon takings will far exceed whatever I brought in yesterday. Where are you headed?"

"To watch the Morris dancers. After that, more shopping. Not for myself. I want gifts to take back to my friends." Belatedly, she added, "And family."

At midday, when the church bell rang twelve times, Hannah joined the queue at the Volunteer Fire Brigade tent, intending to purchase a sandwich. She recognized the young man beside her.

"You're Andy," she greeted him. "From The Peacock."

"Hullo," he responded. "You're the movie lady. Jack says if our pub's in your film, it'll bring in more customers. I might get paid a bigger wage."

"If you're interested in part-time work for extra money, plenty of people will be needed for odd jobs. Or as background extras."

"You'll put in a good word for me?"

"I definitely will," she assured him.

By the time cast and crew descended on this corner of Somerset, she'd be thousands of miles away. But that didn't preclude lobbying Liz on Andy's behalf. All that Martin and Poppy had told her about this solemn kid elicited a sense of kinship. When not in school, he labored at the Home Farm or served patrons at The Peacock, activities that prevented him from playing team sports with other boys. Hannah had carried out her daily chores at Bear Knoll, in addition to filling in at the vet practice if Dad needed extra help. Her parents expected her to excel in her studies so she could earn a college degree. Film jobs, volunteer or paid, had thrust her into an adult world at a young age.

Which was one reason she appreciated Martin's sense of playfulness. Remembering the nettles, she wondered what his next trick might be.

Chapter 14

By late afternoon, storm clouds darkened the horizon. Martin presided at the closing ceremonies, inviting winners of the various competitions, if present, to join him on the platform. A man handed up a paper, from which he read the amount the duck race and raffle had earned for the Youth Club. On the board members' behalf he extended thanks for the support. Accompanied by the brass band, the Women's Institute warbled "Jerusalem." After the vicar offered a prayer expressing gratitude to the Almighty for fair weather when it counted, Martin named the dates of the next year's fete and declared this one closed.

Attendees hurried home or rushed to the car park. Artisans and shop staff packed up their wares. Booths were dismantled, and the deflating of the bouncy castle drew a gaggle of spectators. Hannah joined Jan and Gosia and Kateryna in the tea tent. They washed and dried cups and saucers while Ron disassembled the espresso machine.

The festival's aftermath wasn't the anticlimax Hannah expected.

Martin's aunt, Julia Duncanson, arrived from Edinburgh to spend time with her sister. Short and round, she was physically Isobel's opposite, and she led a far more active social life as wife of an army officer. Daughters of a university art history professor and a sculptress, both were artists who spent pleasant afternoons sketching in the gardens.

During breakfast one morning, Isobel announced, "The Royal Academy's Summer Exhibition is open, and there's an interesting lecture listed on the website for the Tate Modern. Don't you agree that we need a day or two in London? It's been years since we took on the city together."

Julia nodded her exquisitely coiffed and expertly colored head. "I'd enjoy that."

Martin looked up from the piece of toast he was buttering. "I've memorized the Newbridge to London train schedule. Let me know what time you want to go, and I'll make the booking. I can also have groceries delivered to the flat in advance of your arrival, if you tell me what you want."

"He turned out rather well, this lad of yours," Julia observed. "We did have doubts."

He frowned. "I don't dare ask who 'we' might be. You're shattering my belief that the Scottish relatives didn't entirely disapprove. Whereas the Latimers regard me as a disaster."

"Darling, that can't be true," Isobel protested. "When Alicia rings me with family gossip, she says you've calmed down and become . . ."

"Respectable?" he supplied. "She certainly isn't. And hasn't even been a Latimer for—how long? Decades."

When the ladies settled on a departure time, Julia went upstairs to get prepared. Martin excused himself so he could arrange their travel before his morning meeting in Newbridge.

Isobel set down her napkin and asked Hannah, "Would you like to go with Julia and me? He can easily add a third ticket to our booking."

"I appreciate the invitation, but I should savor the countryside while I can. I'll be back in the heart of big, busy Boston soon enough."

"You live in the city?"

"In Cambridge. Across the Charles River."

"I traveled to Boston some years ago. But we had no opportunity for sightseeing."

"Martin told me." Hannah toyed with her knife. "You and he have a very close relationship."

"He was so young when we lost his father. And I was too bereft to resist when the Latimers advised me to send him back to Eton, though I hated doing it. We always spent his half-term with my parents, or in Scotland with Julia. Rufus invited us to come here, of course. Without Richard, we both found staying at Stanwell quite hard. During my illness and treatments, Martin was my rock, and afterwards he supported my decision to move to France. We both cherish our privacy and our independence and prefer pursuing our interests without interference. He's stubborn. I have a temper. But we get over our little quarrels fairly quickly."

"I'm an only child, too. But I hardly ever see my parents."

"That's a pity. They must miss you."

"If I'm not off scouting somewhere on my birthday, Mum drives down to Boston and takes me to lunch." She withheld the fact that she usually tried to form advance plans with her circle of friends in order to stave off the visit. Not from pettiness, or vengeance, but as a means of self-preservation. Even her fleeting trips to Bear Knoll dredged up a resentment dating from the day of Chase's arraignment, which had escalated throughout his trial. Because she loved Mum and Dad, despite her tumultuous feelings, she hadn't entirely cut herself off from them. "I try to get home for Christmas. Although when the weather's too snowy or icy, they don't want me on the roads."

"Perfectly understandable."

Hannah stood up. "I suppose I ought to let them know where I am. And when I'll be Stateside again."

In moments of honest reflection, she could acknowledge that her ingrained habit of avoidance was damaging to herself. She'd considered seeking therapy, since her long-standing grievances were unlikely to miraculously vanish, but her travel schedule was an obstacle.

Maybe, she mused, having Chase back in Falmouth will help me find my way home.

He's the one I need to talk to, she realized. More than Mum and Dad.

His voicemail was full, either because he didn't bother to retrieve messages or wasn't rigorous in deleting. She searched online for the Penobscot Nation and found the link to Indian Island's volunteer services.

"You want Chase? I'll check the schedule," said the woman on the opposite shore of the Atlantic. "Okay. I see he's in Community Recreation. Hang on, I'll connect you."

She waited, heart pounding, trying to decide on her opening line.

"This is Chase Ballard."

"That's who I asked for. Although I could've said I wanted to speak with the darts champion of Falmouth, Maine."

"Hannah-Banana?" Astonishment rang clear across several thousand miles. "What's up? Everything okay on Bear Knoll?"

"Far as I know. I'm still in England."

"When'll you be home?"

Where was that, really? Cambridge, or Falmouth? "Less than a week. Before my next gig, I'll have some free time." Plenty of it, since she hadn't a clue where she'd be working—or for whom. "I can drive to Old Town."

"Helluva long way from Cambridge."

"After ten years, totally worth it." The prospect of seeing her hadn't elicited the expected enthusiasm. "I'll give fair warning before I head your way. I'm sure you're busy."

He didn't reply immediately. "I'd figure out how to make time for my favorite niece."

"You haven't got another one."

He cleared his throat. "Coupla weeks ago, Pop came by. Talked about you almost the whole time, Han. 'Cept when he complained about the cost of fuel and the selling price for bugs."

It was good to hear his lobsterman's lingo. Knowing Chase's chronic dislike of interrogation, pre-dating his legal issues, she didn't ask whether he'd return to Falmouth. More than ever she hoped he would, because it could help to ease her emotional separation from her parents and reconnect her to Bear Knoll in a healthy and lasting way.

After a single night and two days in London, Isobel and Julia returned to Stanwell House, laughing over sore feet and inside jokes. Julia gleefully described the distinguished gentleman admirer who approached her sister in Fortnum and Mason's top floor restaurant.

"He must be married," Isobel said dismissively. "And probably has a couple of mistresses. At the minimum."

"You've lived too long across the Channel," Julia accused, "if you assume Englishmen are as duplicitous as Frenchmen."

"Introducing himself with an Irish surname? You think that was genuine?" her sister asked, her tone laden with skepticism.

Within a day of Julia's departure for Edinburgh, Isobel declared her intention of returning to her rental house in La Rochelle. With commissions to fulfill for British ex-pats and holidaymakers, she would spend the summer producing their children's portraits.

Another guest, unrelated to Martin, arrived in a sleek silver Jaguar.

Hannah cast a dubious glance at the solicitor's briefcase, guessing that it contained production contracts and site access agreements.

"Here's Hannah," Martin said by way of introduction. "She did the location scouting for Acorn Films."

"Your colleagues were more demanding in the negotiations than I expected."

Daniel Wheeler might be tall and dark and handsome, with an athletic physique, but she struggled to smile back at him. "And you advised Martin to concede as little as possible."

"That's my job, protecting his interests and shielding him against liability. But it's been an amicable process. No hard feelings on either side."

He exuded confidence and competence, characteristics she missed in herself. "Great."

Poppy told her, "He loves movies, Dan does. I think there's a special word for people like him."

"Cinephile," she supplied.

"That's right," he confirmed. "Classic films, primarily. Black and white era. I don't know much at all about modern film production. Your expertise will be quite useful to our discussions. You know exactly the kind of upheaval that Martin and the other district residents are facing."

First you re-opened my wound, she mourned. Then you rub salt in it.

Martin, apparently aware of her dismay, said quickly, "No need to involve Hannah, she's having a holiday. I've studied advisories and guidelines published by the Historic Properties Association. So has Poppy. And the household staff."

"McLaren, the location manager, sent an email I'll share

with you. He has helpful suggestions about the community forum.”

The threesome headed for the estate office.

Hannah escaped to her bedroom, fully intending to purchase an airplane ticket from Heathrow to Boston Logan.

But for reasons she couldn't identify, she didn't click the link to secure the only remaining seat on her preferred Boston-bound flight. With summer's approach, fares had soared on the airline where she banked her frequent flier miles. After reviewing less costly options, she rejected the Reykjavik layover that would add hours to her journey.

She'd wait to complete the reservation until she found out which day would be most convenient for Martin to give her a lift to the railway station.

The roar of Dan's Jaguar faded after it reached the bottom of the drive and pulled out onto the roadway. Martin shoved his hands in his trouser pockets, well pleased with recent developments.

Flower Fete proceeds had increased over last year. Although he seldom exploited his title and local prominence, he'd had a jolly good time playing marquess. A lucrative film production would be based at Stanwell House and the Milver Vale region, and within the hour Dan would hand deliver those signed contracts to Hartcliffe Studios. After years of collaboration and consensus-building, several land use and property development projects were underway or about to begin.

He did have one lingering frustration. As best he could discern, Hannah didn't like him nearly as much as he liked her. He made every effort to be an exemplary host, a pleasant jogging and riding companion, and an inventive cook. An undemanding guest, she seemed content to fall in with whatever activity was on offer. Or to do her own thing, as happened during his solicitor's brief visit. Aware that Dan outclassed him in looks, Martin had worried he might spark Hannah's elusive interest. Especially when Poppy teasingly suggested that Dan could replace dishy Lucas Daltrey as the male lead in *Forsaken Fortune*.

She emerged from her office, mobile in one hand and car keys in the other. "The Holly Cottage tenant's done a bunk—his neighbor rang me just now." She shook her head, ponytail swinging. "His rent's two months overdue. Payment stopped after his mum moved into the senior community in Sherborne, and I was waiting till after the festival to go storm trooper on him. I'd better find out if he took anything away that he shouldn't have. Too bad our legal eagle left so soon."

"If I'd asked him to stay longer, you could've improved your flirting technique."

She stalked over to him. "I didn't flirt with him."

"You said he should be a movie star. Awfully blatant."

"Not my type," she said emphatically. "You haven't a clue what I . . ." She trailed off and glared at him. "Bugger off, Mart."

"Sure. But first, a request. Dan bringing those documents put Hannah in a low mood. If you could do something to buck her up, I'd appreciate it."

"I'll try." Poppy climbed into her Volvo. She flung one waving hand through the open window before reversing and driving out of the stable yard.

Chapter 15

Hannah, heated from an early evening run, was pressing her damp back against the stony stable wall to cool it when the estate manager's station wagon rolled into its place in front of the estate office. Twirling her headband between her fingers, she watched Poppy raise the rear gate and lean inside to open Millie's crate.

"Don't be shy," she crooned, gently tugging a leash. "Nothing to be afraid of here."

A black and white dog leaped out, its feet crunching the pea gravel. The head turned to Hannah, and the white-tipped tail waved back and forth.

"New companion?"

"Not for me. Millie's been through a lot lately and deserves my undivided attention. This one's yours, if you want her."

"Very funny. I can't begin to guess the hassles involved with transporting a dog from England to the States. I'm a city girl, remember? Whose livelihood depends on constant travel."

"Right." Poppy studied the dog, now sniffing the plants in the stone troughs flanking the office entrance. "The vet checked her out. Weight, eighteen kilos. Health, excellent. As for her breeding, she looks like a mix of collie and black lab. With a powerful jaw. Granny must've been a bull terrier." Glancing at Hannah, she explained, "An unreliable cottage tenant scarpered off and left her tied to the fence. His neighbors think she's called June. Or Jewel."

At the second name, the floppy ears lifted.

Hannah crouched down. "Hello, Jewel."

Brown eyes stared back with recognition so intense that she shrank from it. This animal, suffering a profound personal crisis, sensed that she also was.

Oh, no you don't, she silently protested as the dog licked her chin. I'm unavailable. I live a whole ocean from here.

She stood up and asked Poppy, "Do you have a plan?"

"Begging Mart to foster until I can re-home her. Preferably with him, although Ariel will decide about that." Poppy fumbled in her jeans pocket. "I need a cigarette. *And* a drink. Care to stroll over to The Peacock?"

"Okay."

"We'll take Jewel. She needs a ramble after being confined. Maybe she'll meet her perfect new person."

Hannah succumbed to a childish desire to hold the leash. Jewel marched beside her on white-stocking legs, rear end swinging side to side. Her chest and belly were also white, as were her furry ruff and a patch at the end of her muzzle near her nose. The curving rib bones protruded through her black fur.

They proceeded along the footpath that cut across the lower end of the Home Park. Poppy, reliable as ever, had the key for a padlocked barrier they had to pass through to reach Milverston Magna. Seeing that the pub's outdoor benches and tables were wet from a recent downpour, they went inside.

"My treat," Poppy said on their way to the bar.

"You can't persuade me to take Jewel off your hands by plying me with drink."

"Duly noted."

"Cider, please," she told Jack. "Milverston Gold."

"Vale Ale for you, I reckon," Jack said to Poppy.

"Right. Isn't this usually your day off?"

"It varies," he replied, setting a pair of pint glass on the bar. "Any crisps? Chips? Biccie for the beast?"

"Cheddar and onion crisps for me," Poppy decided. "Nothing for the dog. Hannah?"

"Prawn flavored."

They chose a booth beside a window. As soon as Hannah was settled onto the cushioned banquette, Jewel leaped up beside her.

"Springs in those legs," Poppy observed. "She's a natural for agility. You'll have fun training her."

Hannah covered her ears. "Stop it!" She gave the off command, and the dog obeyed. "Good girl."

Andy Riddell brought their drinks and crisps on a tray. Tucking it under his arm, he said, "That one's from Holly Cottage."

Quickly Hannah said, "She's Poppy's now."

"Untrue." Poppy passed him a twenty-pound note. "Back in a second." She headed in the direction of the lavatory.

Andy laid down two beer mats for the brimming glasses. "Her Millie's healing from the operation?"

"Quite well, according to the vet."

"Shame what happened. She shouldn't of got so close to—she shouldn't go wandering off like that." His face reddened, and he beat a swift retreat.

She recalled seeing Andy on a quad bike, riding at high speed, shortly before she and Martin found the injured Millie. His anxious question about the dog, followed by a hastily corrected comment, made her suspect that he was withholding information about the accident. Or perhaps had caused it.

Feeling Jewel's weight pressing her calf, she placed one hand on the smooth head. "Beware of wheeled vehicles."

Poppy slid into the opposite seat. After a couple of swallows of ale, she ripped open the crisps packet.

They talked at length about dogs and horses before dwelling briefly on parental loopiness. Poppy hadn't fully accepted that her father left Somerset for a foreign country, no matter that it was both sunnier and more economical for a retiree. Hannah confided a few of her lesser issues with Mum and Dad. Coping with their eccentric employers was another common theme of their dialogue.

"Liz Gregorio is incredible. I've known her forever, and we've always been simpatico," Hannah said. "But personally, and professionally, she lives on a higher plane than ordinary mortals. Either she forgets or doesn't realize I have a stress-inducing workload and an unpredictable income. Liz was born with a silver spoon in her mouth, and it's entirely possible that Paul Revere made it. Her mother belongs to one of Boston's oldest families. Her dad descends from Portuguese merchants who arrived shortly after the American Revolution. If New England had aristocrats, she'd be one."

Poppy's head bobbed. "I can relate. Mart is mad as a bag of badgers. To his credit, he doesn't give a toss about the title. Mind you, the shit he deals with on a regular basis would drive me right round the bend. Anyone who's lived here a long time takes him for granted. But upwardly mobile nouveau riche and city transplants try ever so hard to batten on, as if his magical marquess dust will rub off and make them super-special."

Ordering a second round, they compared musical tastes and identified additional areas of compatibility.

Poppy, pressing her empty packet into accordion folds, glanced up at her through half-shuttered eyes. "I've been of two minds about telling you, but what the hell? Mart fancies you rotten."

Taken aback by this forthright pronouncement, Hannah said, "Impossible."

"Don't sell yourself short. If you tell me you don't fancy him back, I'll call you a liar."

"You're a mean drunk, Poppy Deane. Careful, or I'll sic my dog on you." From the floor, the drowsing Jewel heaved a deep sigh. "I'm not trying to steal him from you," she insisted. "Honest."

"You couldn't." The other girl's chuckle became a cackle. "There's nothing between Mart and me. Never was. Or will be. Crikey, I've known him since I was in nappies. I'm interested in somebody else."

"A man?"

"As a matter of fact, yes. My cousin is the only lesbian in our family. That I know of."

"Who is it? You can tell me."

"Keep your voice down, or he'll hear."

She followed the direction of Poppy's gaze. "Andy? Isn't he kind of young?"

Poppy snorted. "Not him."

"Jack?"

"He's years older than me. Not that I care. But he would."

Martin wasn't involved with his estate manager. A potent combination of relief and two pints of Milverston Gold cider was making Hannah giddy.

"This place was my dad's preferred local. In this country, at sixteen you can serve alcohol. Soon as I was old enough, I got a job here. Jack and his wife were already separating when I—when I starting liking him. Their divorce was amicable. She has a job in Bristol, and their daughter attends a school there. He visits Chloe often, and she comes here at half-term and for every other bank holiday weekend."

She remembered something Martin had told her. "Why

do you always go to The Huntsman's Horn instead of coming here?"

"My pash is one-sided. Being around Jack makes me uncomfortable." Peering into her empty glass, Poppy added, "I keep schtum about it, so Mart doesn't know. And if I hadn't been drinking on a very empty stomach, I wouldn't have blabbed to you."

"Let's order food."

"I might not be able to keep it down. One doesn't win a man's heart by retching in his lavatory." Poppy rested her chin on her hand. "As for Mart, he's had no better luck in love. Too bad for the Latimers and their assorted kindred. I reckon they're impatiently waiting for Lord Cary."

"Who's he?"

Poppy's smile was sly. "Ask my boss." She looked down at her phone. "Shit, I'm late feeding Millie. I left her at home, and my car's at the office. Not that I'd risk driving it. The local constabulary is awfully strict."

"I'll walk you to your house," Hannah offered. It would clear her own head.

On their way to the door, she saw Jack raise a hand in farewell and responded in kind. Holding Jewel's leash, she guided her unsteady human companion across the car park.

Abruptly halting, Poppy faced her. "Mart isn't bothered by what they think. The relatives. You needn't worry about that."

"I don't. Because I'm heading back to Boston. Soon."

A car horn made them flinch. Jewel responded with a sharp bark.

"Speak of the devil," Poppy caroled.

Hannah giggled as they staggered towards the Vauxhall.

"Can I give you ladies a lift?" Martin called.

"Come on." Poppy grabbed Hannah's arm. She opened the front passenger door and climbed in. "Home, please."

Jewel, as if aware that the back seat was allotted to

canines, hopped in without hesitation, and Hannah followed her.

"Who's your furry friend?"

"Jewel of Holly Cottage," Poppy told him. "She adopted Hannah. You two are taking her to Stanwell so she can dine on a superior brand of dog food. Take the bends *really* slow," she advised him, sinking lower.

"She's drunk," Hannah contributed.

"Hannah's a bitch."

She let the insult pass without comment.

Like her father before her, the estate manager occupied a Georgian-style dwelling beyond Milver Cross, technically located within the parish of Milver St. Mary. Martin supported her along the front walk and unlocked her door.

Hannah remained in the rear seat, reluctant to remove the dog stretched across her lap. She stroked the velvety fur of one dangling ear.

Shortly before Martin turned off onto Home Farm Lane, she said, "When Poppy sobers up, she'll be asking you to foster Jewel. Until a suitable home can be found."

"I've no objection, though Ariel might—at first. I'm counting on you to help me sneak your friend into the house."

Jewel trotted into the kitchen as though she owned it, and sat politely next to the Aga while Martin prepared her meal.

"No telling when she last had food," Hannah pointed out. "Don't give her much. And limit her water intake. According to your vet, she weighs eighteen kilos. How much is that in pounds?"

"About forty."

"You're quick."

"I occasionally spend time in a cheese shop, as you know. Whenever an American asks the weight of a purchase, I have to convert." He patted the dog's head. "Take her to your room. I'll nick a bed of Ariel's. There's a spare in the library."

Forgetting the cider's effect, Hannah bounded out of her chair.

Poppy's most significant revelation rushed back into her muddled mind, and she felt herself sway towards him. Not trusting her legs to hold her upright, she gripped his shoulders to brace herself. Then she rose on her toes and pressed her mouth on his in an off-center smooch.

"Jack Elliston must be serving half-price pints."

"I'm only a little bit tipsy." She leaned against him in a way that lent no credence to her denial. With her cheek pressed against his chest, she could feel its rise and fall. "I shouldn't have done that," she murmured into his shirt.

"I'm glad you did."

His kiss was an improvement on hers, deep and sensual and thoroughly satisfactory. Strong fingers combed through her hair, making her entire body tingle.

He lifted his head to ask, "Why did you wait so long to make your move?"

"I assumed you were taken."

"By whom?"

"Doesn't matter." She blinked up at him. "You wanted me to kiss you?"

"You'd be shocked to know when I started yearning for a nice, long snog." He draped his arms over her shoulders. "Much to my regret, I've got a Milverston Parish Council meeting tonight, and my participation is necessary. Between half-eight and nine o'clock they're receiving the report from the Flower Fete committee. We'll vote to transfer the monies to the Youth Club."

"Oh." Her sigh was heavy with sorrow.

"Worse, in the morning I'm off to London for the whole damn day. Would you be willing to drive me to Newbridge railway station and meet my return train? There's an Italian restaurant in the High Street with an authentic menu and a fantastic selection of wines. Linen tablecloths. Bespoke fine china. Perfect for a proper date."

"I'd like that." Since her abrupt severance from *Forsaken Fortune,* she'd nearly forgotten what joy felt like. Martin's kisses had revived a sensation that greatly resembled it.

Chapter 16

Without consulting the wine list, Martin decided which prosecco he wanted for the *aperitivo*. Hannah chose an *antipasto* they could share, Parma ham with mixed roast vegetables. He was amused by the frown creasing her brow as she considered the *primo* offerings.

"If you like wonderfully prepared duck, I recommend the Anatra Croccante. The sauce is a combination of peach and ginger." He endorsed their server's suggestion of Brunello di Montalcino as the appropriate vintage to accompany their main dish.

"Did you have a productive day?" Hannah asked.

"At my morning meeting, I learned about changes to guidelines for rural development grants. In the afternoon, I presented survey findings at an entrepreneurship forum. In between I lunched in the Wincott & Sons staff room and stopped at Latimer House to pick up the post."

"You could've brought my party dress. And the shoes."

"Never occurred to me, I'm afraid." Just as well. He was happy to keep them as placeholders, until she was there again. With him.

And then he remembered something else he hadn't brought.

"Will you excuse me? Back in a tick."

Leaving the restaurant, he hurried along the pavement towards the chemist's down the block, relieved that its neon green cross was still illuminated. Just inside the door stood a vat of bouquets in cellophane wrap. He grabbed the least hideous one before looking for condoms. The young woman at the till, luckily, was a stranger to him, and vice versa. He paid for his purchases and hurried out, aware that the same transaction at the Milverston village shop would result in a gossip avalanche.

He removed the condoms from the box, dropping it into the nearest recycling bin, and shoved them into his jacket pocket. After prying the plastic from the flowers, he disposed of it as well.

Presenting the bouquet, he said, "Never tell the famous Wendy Edney that the first flowers I purchased for you were utterly dismal. Those rosebuds are a shade of orange unknown to nature. I think two of them were white before being dyed green. Ghastly."

"Nobody ever interrupted a date to buy me flowers."

When he asked how she'd spent her day, she described the process of introducing Jewel to Ariel and Millie.

"Poppy suggested we take them on a run—with Jewel on her lead—and by the time we returned to the house they'd formed a pack bond. I wasn't worried about leaving Ariel and Jewel alone. Ron's off duty tonight, so Nico is keeping an eye on them." She speared a slice of ham with her fork and reached for her knife. "Who is Lord Cary?"

"Me. I'm also Baron Latimer. Although by law my offspring will be commoners, the eldest son's courtesy title would be Earl Cary. If he takes after me, he'll call himself Rufus Latimer."

She looked up. "I wonder how he'll feel about that for his first name."

"You make a good point. I've always been thankful my parents put Martin before Rufus and Antony when they had me christened."

"Rufus. Antony. You could be a character in a P. G. Wodehouse novel."

He savored a mouthful of wine, relishing its fruitiness. "My relationship with the little lad might start off better if he's Richard. For my father. I could also insert Cadbury, in recognition of our Arthurian connection. Although everyone would assume it was because of the chocolates."

"You're related to King Arthur?"

"Presumably. A cousin, many times removed. If he ever existed, that is. And procreated. According to legend, that red dragon on the Somerset flag belonged to him." He put down his wineglass. "Dragon. Now there's a staggeringly good name for a boy."

She laughed until tears filled her eyes. Drinkers and diners looked over at their table, no doubt wondering what he'd said to amuse his fetching companion.

"This is . . . surreal," she gasped. "I'm on a date with an English lord whose family tree includes King Arthur. Pinch me."

"With pleasure." He grinned. "Soon as I get you home."

She flattened both palms on the table, saying in an altered tone, "I almost booked my Boston flight yesterday."

He seized one of her wrists. "You can't."

"I have to."

"Why?"

She pulled her hand away and waved it aimlessly. "Lots of reasons."

"When we met, you planned to be in England for months and months. Why should that change?"

"Getting fired is bad enough without being deported. My

work visa requires me to be employed. By Hartcliffe Studios. I'm not. Which means I'll soon be in big, big trouble."

"I can get that sorted. Rather, Dan Wheeler will. He handled all the immigration paperwork when Kateryna Bereza came over from Ukraine. As a war refugee, her situation was far more complicated than yours."

"I'm serious, Martin."

"So am I."

Their server presented the main course, slices of roast fowl artistically arranged on plates, exquisitely sauced and garnished. Hannah, doubtless to reinforce her intention of returning to Boston, described its North End, crammed with Italian eateries. He shared tales from his time in the kitchen at the Venice restaurant. They reviewed the dessert menu but didn't order, capping off their meal with liqueurs instead— limoncello for her, grappa for him.

Driving back to Stanwell, he veered off the road into a lay-by.

"I can't wait a moment longer to kiss you again." Their lips met and melded together. "You're lemon-flavored," he murmured.

He ran his hands under her silk shift, acquainting himself with the warm, soft flesh of her inner thighs and the slight swell of her hips. "I've been imagining this," he confessed, "ever since the party in your London hotel suite. You wore this same dress."

"When you lured me to Stanwell House, you said it has twenty bedrooms. Why are we writhing around in your car?"

"Privacy. No staff. No dogs. Just us." He drew back so he could read her face. "You won't mind if I turn up at your bedroom door later?"

"I'm counting on it."

Hannah came awake with a vague sense that it might be morning, although the thick curtains gave no hint of whether the sun had already risen. Her phone could confirm the hour, but it was buried beneath the garments piled on the chintz armchair.

Martin lay stretched out beside her, his right arm curved over his head, his hair sticking out in all directions. The sheet covered the lower portion of the body that had been fused to hers last night, and his bare chest was exposed. On several occasions, his jogging clothes had revealed most of his physique. Last night, she'd become familiar with the rest. His skin felt smooth under her fingers, his arms were firmly muscled, and she now knew the places he most liked to be stroked.

By opening herself to Martin in every possible way, she'd cast aside her protective shield of reserve. After so many weeks as the recipient of his generosity, she was a giver. Because he'd admitted his ulterior motive for twice luring her to Somerset, she felt confident that when he woke, he wouldn't behave as though nothing meaningful had happened. She sank back against her pillow and stared up at the floral fabric canopy overhead, trying not to overthink. But she couldn't suppress the persistent fluttering of delight in the region below her breasts and above her navel.

Martin turned towards her, leaning on one elbow. "What a perfect start to the day." He stroked her shoulder, his hand sliding along her arm. He traced her fingers with his. "Nice to see you again."

"Nice to be seen."

"Let's have breakfast on the terrace. When I was a boy, and meals were served there, the adults permitted me to join them. The dining room was off limits, until I was old enough to not drop my cutlery or make some sort of mess."

"Where did you eat?"

"In the kitchen. Which wasn't nearly as pleasant as it is now."

"Were you aware that the estate would eventually be yours?"

"Not then. Or for years and years. There was the chance—admittedly remote—that Uncle Rufus might marry a title-seeking female willing to accept his sexuality and produce a son. He had his heart set on Dad inheriting. They were devoted to each other, as kids of divorcees can be, despite having so little in common. Our Stanwell weekends were infrequent, so they loom large in my memory."

"I vividly recall visiting my grandparents in Portishead, when I was little. And during the study year I spent in Bristol."

"Imagine if we'd met as teenagers. No chance I could've got you into bed."

"How do you know?"

"I was a prat."

"I was a film nerd."

"My favorite type." His hands were busy—stroking, squeezing. "How old are you?"

"Twenty-seven."

"Born on?"

"December sixth. You?"

"I turned thirty in April, the day you walked into Wincott & Sons. Best birthday present ever."

"That's amazing." She pressed against him, reveling in the contact with his nakedness. Her lips traced the contours of his face—cheekbones, jaw, chin.

His arms encircled her waist, his torso straining against her. In the night hours they had learned much. He was aware of exactly how long to tease, and where a caress would evoke the most intense response. Despite his readiness he held back, waiting for her to sheathe his arousal with the condom and draw him inside. She wouldn't have believed such pleasure existed, if she hadn't already experienced it. Her entire body was overwhelmed, not just by sensation, but also by emotion.

After Martin gathered up his clothes and left the room, she took a speedy shower. She pointed the blow dryer at her hair, fluffing the curls, then applied just enough foundation to cover the faint abrasions his chin stubble had left along her jawline. Buoyed by adrenalin and happiness, she also required a caffeine infusion and sustenance.

She found Martin in the kitchen. He was brewing the coffee and had poured juice and toasted slices of Jan's whole meal bread. Ariel and Jewel were watchful, alert to each item that emerged from refrigerator and cupboard.

"Scavengers," he accused them.

Hannah cut up fresh strawberries and placed them in bowls, adding a generous dollop of *crème fraiche*.

He repeated his question about how they should spend the day. "You haven't seen King Alfred's Tower."

"You're related to him, too?"

"Wouldn't surprise me." He chewed his toast, and after swallowing, explained, "It's a fairly easy climb up to Cadbury Castle. Not a royal residence, but an Iron Age hillfort to which King Arthur's name was later appended without any basis whatsoever. We might take a picnic lunch. Or we could drive over to Montacute House. Same age and period as Stanwell, roughly."

"I'm not a tourist," she protested.

"If I don't keep you occupied and entertained, you'll buy an airplane ticket."

Setting down her spoon with a strawberry still on it, she met his gaze. "Not today, I promise. But I can't exist in limbo indefinitely."

"I'm aware it's a hardship for such a highly organized person."

"I dislike the implication that my life is excessively structured."

"I respect what you Yanks refer to as 'work ethic.' In fact, Ms. Ballard, I've been thinking that my enterprises could benefit from your experience and your credentials."

"In exchange for which I receive room and board. And you enjoy the occasional shag."

"It wouldn't be occasional. Judging from recent experience, the enjoyment will be mutual." His sudden grin was replaced by a sober expression, and a tone to match. "That came out wrong. I'll set aside the personal—for the moment. I'm juggling an overwhelming number of projects. The affordable housing initiative. Promoting local farms and their products. Developing eco-tourism in the district. Creating an environment for small business start-ups. Securing the necessary financing, through banks or government grants, to complete our Rural Heritage Center on schedule. Not to mention the vocational education and apprenticeship programs."

"I lack expertise in all those areas."

"You told me you worked in marketing, when you weren't scouting. And you're a born manager. I'm asking you to remain in Somerset, gainfully employed and amply compensated. Within arms' reach." He returned his attention to his strawberries.

During the past twelve hours, she'd wondered if she was capable of settling for a pleasant holiday fling that was destined to end with goodbyes outside Newbridge railway station. She certainly hadn't expected Martin to pursue what amounted to a major commitment. Unaccustomed to the leisurely life she'd experienced at Stanwell, she was tempted by the challenge of restoring his finances and assisting in the completion of his ambitious and worthwhile plans. But to do that, she'd have to abandon the career for which she'd worked so hard and so long.

Could I?

She shied from the question. Impossible to base a life-altering decision on a dinner date, a bunch of flowers, and a single night sharing a bed.

"No," she said firmly, her reverie interrupted by Jewel, attempting to climb into her lap. She shoved at the solid black and white bulk. "I'm eating. Keep off."

The dog obediently backed away. Sinking on her haunches, she regarded Hannah with solemn brown eyes.

She felt trapped between two individuals determined to hold her here. Hannah's relationship history—with men, not animals—hadn't prepared her for this dilemma.

Chapter 17

After exploring Montacute House and its formal gardens, they proceeded to South Cadbury. The public pathway led them to a broad, flat hill. The ascent to the long-vanished fort wasn't difficult, and the reward was a vista of lush woodlands interspersed with ridges and valleys. Hedgerows crisscrossed the meadows, dividing them into squares and rectangles of green wheat or yellow rapeseed flowers.

"I can see why King Arthur chose this spot for his Camelot," Hannah commented.

"All those centuries ago, the view would've been quite different." Martin turned and pointed. "He's buried over there, in Glastonbury. Not far from the Tor—that mound in the distance, topped with the tower."

On their way back to Stanwell, he remembered that he had an errand in Milverston Magna.

"Poppy asked me to go to Holly Cottage and decide what work needs doing before we publicize its availability. I can drop you at the house. I shouldn't be gone for long."

Jewel greeted Hannah exuberantly, clearly in need of activity as well as companionship, so she clipped a leash to the dog's collar and took her into the garden. Beyond the tennis court, they met Poppy and Millie.

"Martin seemed especially chipper when I popped over from my office this morning. He couldn't stop yawning while he spooned out the coffee grounds, as though he didn't get much sleep. Care to confess?"

"No." Although Hannah wouldn't reveal exactly what had transpired, she said, "If you hadn't swilled so much beer at The Peacock, I'd be packing my bag. Leaving for Boston."

"I'm glad you're not. Mart deserves to be happy."

"So do you. Why not transfer your allegiance from The Huntsman's Horn to The Peacock? Let Jack decide if your age difference matters. Any man would be glad to be fancied by a younger woman who looks like you."

"Thanks." Threading Millie's leash through her fingers, Poppy added, "Caring for Mart as much as I do, I feel a responsibility to enlighten you about his previous relationships. Unless you don't care to hear."

"I'm not sure," Hannah hedged. Poppy's candor, her most consistent feature, could be a blessing or a curse.

"He went through a weird, wild child phase. Dyed his hair purple and wore leather trousers and a bicycle chain round his neck. When he and his mates went clubbing in London, their vibe scared away the society girls. Nobody knew his Uncle Rufus had executed a deed of gift, making him legal owner of this place and the castle up north and the London properties."

"Something to do with avoiding inheritance tax, he said."

"Exactly. After Eton, Mart went to his father's Oxford college. When Isobel got sick he left, wanting to be with her during her treatment. After she recovered and moved to La Rochelle, he took off for Italy and explored a bit of Asia. He came back to England because the marquess was failing. For a while he was enrolled in the agricultural college, taking courses in land management and rural affairs. So did I. But unlike yours truly, he didn't complete a degree. Because of his uncle dying, he didn't finish. About three years ago, at a country wedding somewhere in the Three Counties, he met Jessica."

Jess, who had left a message on Martin's answering machine at the Latimer House flat.

As they proceeded along a wooded footpath that led to the river, Poppy continued, "The jolly hockey-sticks type—very sporty. Not a brain in her head. Teddibly, teddibly tedious. She made the fatal error of introducing him to Natalie." She stopped so Millie could relieve herself. "An effing nightmare. Hatefully gorgeous. Hard eyes."

Hannah ran her hand over the marbled bark of a silver birch. Jess had mentioned Natalie during her telephone call.

"How she got those shiny red claws into him, I'll never understand. They were quite the item. She dragged him to parties and premieres and charity auctions. He put up with it. As daffy as he can often be, at heart he's a traditionalist. I have no doubt whatsoever that he plans to get married. Become a dad. Create the kind of family he didn't have. Natalie was in no way a likely candidate for a Somerset landowner's wife."

"Did his mother get on with her?"

"We never had the chance to find out. Late last year, that pesky virus put Mart out of commission for a fortnight. Natalie refused to give up her holiday on the Alpine slopes. As a souvenir of the trip, she brought back an Italian duke. Whirlwind romance. They married on Valentine's Day."

Her kissable marquess with the impressive bedroom technique wasn't exactly the lady-killer she'd imagined him to be. Poppy had identified only two exes.

"Mart gives the impression of being confident, able to handle anything life pitches at him. God knows, he's had his share of hard blows. Losing his dad so young. Isobel's illness. Natalie's treachery. Don't hurt him, Hannah."

"He asked me to stay," she admitted. "And work for him. Or with him."

"Doing what?"

"I haven't heard the specifics."

"He's an idea-man. Unlike a lot of dreamers, he's got the determination—and the stubbornness—to make a success of whatever he sets out to do. In the process, he drives the rest of us bonkers. But it's worth it. As you'll discover, if you do stick around."

Martin was pleased to find that shortly before closing-up time, the shops of Milverston Magna were filled with people scanning the shelves and queuing at the tills. The elders moved slowly, supported by a cane or Zimmer frame. Children dragged their mothers to the sweets aisle clamoring for a treat. Teens clustered in front of the drinks cabinet.

Entering the pet emporium, he noted the pervasive aroma of bagged kibble and the wood shavings in the rodent cages. He located a right-sized bed for Jewel, a round cushion, amply stuffed, with a tartan outer cover. Among the array of harnesses, he found the type Susan the dog trainer preferred. Unable to decide between a leather or nylon collar, he purchased both, and an identification tag. A machine at the ironmonger's engraved Jewel's name and his mobile number and that of the estate office on the brass disk.

He paused at the edge of the village green to inspect the community notice board. The Milver Beekeepers Society flyer offered an apiary tour in the orchard across from Stanwell's Home Farm. He glanced at the summer schedule for the Pre-School Playgroup, which met in the morning at the cricket pavilion. Below it, surrounded by colorful and informative clutter, he spied a timely notice: Susan's Agility Class, presented by Milverston Clever Dogs Club.

Andy Riddell ambled by, mobile at his ear and vape cigarette in his other hand. Observing Martin's struggle to raise the car boot without dropping his purchases, he offered to help.

"Thanks, mate. On work break?"

"Nah. Jack needs a rubber gasket and plumbing tape. Kitchen sink's leaking."

"What's tonight's special?"

"Fish pie."

"Can I reserve the table by the big mullion window?"

"It's yours. What time?"

"Half seven. Eight. Something like that."

No better place than The Peacock to make public the fact that he and Hannah were a couple. His mother and Poppy had already guessed that he'd found his dream girl, and now he wanted his whole world to know.

Contrary to Hannah's expectations, the interior of *Emotional Rescue* was spacious and comfortable. Martin, just over six feet tall, didn't need to hunch over as he moved about. He was placing loose items in a box while she rinsed their lunch plates in the narrowboat's galley. Green tiles lined the work surface and backsplash. Ash wood cabinetry provided ample storage. A window faced the sun-dappled bank and drooping willow trees.

In a flash of pure blue and bright orange, a kingfisher darted from a ferny clump and dove into the river. It quickly surfaced and skimmed over a reed bed. Perching on a branch, it fluttered its wings to shake off the water.

"You're sure you want to sell this treasure of yours?" she asked Martin, sweeping her cloth over the stainless-steel sink and worktop.

"Positive. *Em* was perfect for me, during the confusing,

carefree time before I hared off from London's Little Venice to the original Venice." His head emerged from the cabinet he was excavating. "Where did you experience your greatest happiness?"

"Lots of places. As a little kid, my first time lobstering with Grampa. In the 4-H show ring with my Sheltie, when we won a blue ribbon. On early summer mornings while milking our goats and the birds started singing. In London, seeing my student film on the big screen at the British Film Institute."

The day she was invited to meet Liz at Acorn Films and learned of her promotion to location manager on *Forsaken Fortune*.

"Stanwell doesn't get a mention?"

"I thought you were referring to the past," she responded. "Not the present."

Martin might be upside down financially, and apparently reluctant to admit it, but he was handsome, funny, serious, sexy as hell—and for the time being, a source of bliss. Hard to put all that into words without sounding soppy.

"When we get back to the house, I'll show you some paperwork I was asked to review. Milverston Village Hall is applying for a rural economy grant available to community buildings, to reduce environmental impact through eco-audits and upgrades. And Milver Vale Dairy is seeking support from a small business booster scheme. They hope to enlarge the display stand they set up at food product trade exhibitions."

"Are supplemental materials permitted?"

"We can check."

"I could put together a short video for each of the sites to submit with the forms. Interviews with dairy workers, and some of their customers. Footage of the village hall, testimonials from members of the groups that use it. A cameo from you."

"You can do all that within a fortnight? Before the dead-line?"

"It would take only a few days. Provided I get access to people and places."

"You're amazing. Come here." He pulled her down to sit beside him on the carpet. "Hark back to your time in advertising and tell me everything you know about tourism development and promotion."

"You know exactly what draws visitors. History. Architecture. Museums. Art galleries. Recreation. Shopping. If you have something unique to offer them, it's a bonus."

"Our area is the primary location for a major motion picture."

"That's not unusual. Or uncommon. The Milver Vale isn't as well known as Lacock and Stamford. Or Bath. Your other challenge," she added, "would be the cost of a campaign."

He ran his hand through his hair. "My advisory board has fifty thousand pounds available for regional promotion."

"Any guidelines for its use?"

"Donated funds. No restrictions. A website is already under construction. I also want an illustrated informational brochure in downloadable format, listing the sights and activities in the vale. A map that includes each village and its attractions. Our artisans' studio and shop in Little Milver. The tithe barn. The river walk. And so on. Would you be willing to take the photographs?"

"Of course. And write the copy, if you like. You could also hire somebody to create a phone app. But even a very simple one requires a bigger budget."

"I'll find more money."

After a thoughtful pause, she said, "You'll want to put the Milver Vale on the itineraries of the tour bus companies that take day-trippers into the countryside from London and

Bristol and Bath. And you can place your brochure in the racks at railway station lounges and hotels and restaurants."

He demonstrated his approval by kissing the tip of her nose. "I've obtained preliminary approval for an electric vehicle charging station in Milverston Magna. The next step is deciding where it ought to go. Someplace close to the shops."

"Next to The Latimer Arms car park," she suggested. "On the short side of the village green. There's probably space for two."

His phone chirped, notifying him of an incoming message. "It's from the film's leading lady." He dipped his head to read.

"Caroline Bryden has your mobile number?"

"When I found out she'd be starring in *Forsaken Fortune*, I got in touch. We're distant cousins, with a common great-great grandfather, a famous and highly revered cabinet minister. He was too sensible to go after the top job."

"Small world."

"Small country. Caroline says she'll be here in about six weeks."

Hannah was painfully aware of the timing. "Do you know her well?"

"Not really. I see her on the telly now and again. It's been years since we were together in person, at a family wedding. She was still in boarding school."

The gorgeous redhead would spend two and half months at Stanwell, portraying a wanton lady of the manor. Hannah, despite her awareness of the storied romances and notorious liaisons between aristocrats and actresses, would not allow her imagination to lead her in an unpleasant direction.

Although Jewel never showed much interest in the horses or

sheep or cattle she observed when walking with Hannah, if she scented field mouse or a hare, she desperately wanted to track it.

"Don't pull. Heel."

No breeze stirred the hot air as they walked from Stanwell House to the pet shop in Milverston Magna. Before departing for a series of meetings, Martin had scribbled a list of required items for agility practice.

"Isn't that the poor creature Poppy found abandoned at Holly Cottage?" asked Lois, the proprietor. "I told Martin he could change that bed he bought if she doesn't like it."

"She does," Hannah assured her. "Very much."

"No need to give me your list, I know what Susan wants you to have." Lois took them to the aisle where she kept the boxed agility kits. "You're with the film company, right?"

Accustomed to this designation, Hannah gave her usual response. "That's what brought me here."

"In yesterday's post I received a letter from Alistair Somebody, asking to use my old ramshackle barn. Doesn't want me to make changes or clear it out. I must say, I'd rather not let anyone in, it's that filthy."

"He won't mind. The production crew will take charge. The set dressers don't just rearrange things, they'll tidy up before they leave."

"That'd be payment enough," said Lois. "Though I won't turn down the fee. Let's see—we've got your flyball and disk and whistle." After placing items on Hannah's list in a carrier bag, she asked, "What to do about this big box with the jump and the hoop and the tunnel?"

"Martin can collect it on his way back from Newbridge. I'll let him know."

A spaniel sat outside the butcher's, patiently waiting for its owner. To prevent a confrontation, she led Jewel in the opposite direction.

Through the bookshop's open door, she saw a water

bowl. Because dogs were obviously welcome, she took hers inside. Moving past a table of current bestsellers, she found a special section with hardcover and paperback editions of *Forsaken Fortune,* obviously created to capitalize on local interest in the film's source material. Stacked between the books was the new issue of *Posh* magazine. A familiar face, stunningly beautiful, beamed up at Hannah from the cover. A banner headline proclaimed "It's Caroline Bryden's Year!"

She picked up the magazine and paged through it—until she came to an article titled "The Maverick Marquess: Debutante's Delight, Countryside's Champion."

Martin.

During Hannah's first visit to Stanwell, a *Posh* reporter telephoned an uncooperative Poppy, inquiring about an interview with Martin. Later, when she stayed in the Latimer House flat in London, his friend Jess left a message about someone seeking photos. He'd shared many aspects of his past with Hannah, and Poppy had provided additional details. Hannah didn't expect to learn anything she didn't already know, but reading other people's accounts of him might be interesting.

She examined a series of captioned photographs. A younger version of Martin with a group of Eton College classmates, wearing black tail coats and striped trousers. On the Milver St. Mary pitch, in his cricket whites. As an attendee at a society wedding, his arm linked with a brunette beauty in a fancy hat, identified as Natalie. Lying beside her on a beach, bare chested and wearing sunglasses.

Hannah closed the magazine and carried it to the till. She preferred to read about him in private, not in view of any villager who wandered in.

"I'm trying to re-order from the supplier," the bookseller told her. "Very popular." He winked.

She'd persuaded Martin to let her make dinner tonight. While Jewel and Ariel engaged in a play-fight, Jan made sure she was aware of recent additions to the kitchen cupboards and the pantry, treasure troves of staples and gourmet ingredients.

Studying the refrigerator meat compartment she decided, "Chicken breasts for a main course with a champagne mushroom sauce."

"He'll like that," Jan said. "Though being so easy to please, you could serve him fish fingers and he wouldn't complain."

She laughed. "I'm tempted to test that theory. But not tonight."

Going to her room, she carried the magazine to the window seat and turned to the section of greatest personal interest.

She studied a full-page collage of candid pictures, apparently shot by paparazzi. A casually dressed Martin strolling in Latimer Row. As a teen, his hair dyed vivid purple, his face colorless in the camera's flash. On the deck of his narrowboat, moored on the London canal. Girlfriends, official and suspected, were listed in a sidebar. Jessica. Natalie. The Honorable This and Lady That. In the aftermath of a romantic disappointment, according to the author, he had withdrawn to his Somerset estate. Adjectives applied to him made Hannah smile: *eligible, elusive, eccentric, erratic.*

Her body tensed when she read the estimate of Martin's net worth. Three hundred million pounds.

A typo, she told herself. Thirty million, possibly, based on the combined value of all his property in Somerset and London, minus mortgages and other debts. Which were probably substantial, because English landowners were reputed to be so hugely leveraged.

But magazines employed fact checkers to prevent reputational harm and ward off legal action. *Posh* wouldn't dare print an erroneous, misleading calculation. It was hard enough, accepting that Martin was a celebrity aristocrat—

something she hadn't realized. Worse, he was unimaginably, outrageously, disturbingly rich.

Her arrival in England had coincided with the onset of the Sterling Scandal, and the feverish coverage from traditional and online media. The fever hadn't broken. Cameramen still camped outside the disgraced politician's London residence and his country house, inconveniencing and annoying his neighbors. They pursued the flashy mistress who swanned about London in designer clothes allegedly purchased with illicit earnings. Her relatives' criminality was as much the focus of attention as her liaison with a prominent Parliamentarian.

Panic surged when Hannah considered the ramifications of Martin's appearance in *Posh*.

What if the scribe who had chronicled his distant and recent past discovered her existence, and their relationship? Martin would be tarnished by his association with an ex-convict's niece. His ambitious plans for promoting the Milver Vale could be adversely affected. Tabloids would feast on the fresh scandal. Curious reporters would have no difficulty uncovering and divulging details of the barroom knifing and the manslaughter trial and Chase's incarceration. Exposure by the unscrupulous British press would inevitably result in similar disclosures in the American media, attention that could block his path back to a normal life—whatever he envisioned the next normal to be.

That prospect made her queasy.

For the past decade, she'd protected her uncle by voluntarily keeping silent. Now she had less incentive to tell Martin about Chase, despite regret over withholding a crucial incident in her past and its everlasting impact.

Her connection to a convicted killer ultimately destroyed her relationship with Joel. Because he was an attorney—though uninvolved in criminal cases—she'd expected him to have sympathy for her uncle's experience in the justice system. But she could tell, without hearing him state it, that the felon in her family was problematic. Because her travel schedule separated them at frequent intervals and for extended periods, she didn't acknowledge the widening rift. Nor had she been sure what to do about it. Until the final hours of last year, during the New Year's Eve party at Joel's law office, in a skyscraper with a fantastic view of the First Night fireworks display over Boston Harbor. Before midnight, he made a derisive and hurtful comment about Chase that she couldn't tolerate and wouldn't excuse and hadn't forgotten.

Martin wouldn't be so crass. Even so, she saw no reason to be forthcoming.

Chapter 18

After squeezing the outfits she'd brought to England and recent clothing purchases into her roller bag, Hannah successfully zipped it closed. This was an experiment, a test of her emotions and fortitude. She hadn't decided whether to take the essential step that would facilitate her departure.

On her way to the kitchen, she hoped meal preparation might alleviate a minuscule portion of her despondency. The two dogs, captivated by the presence of cutting board and knives, took up strategic positions, closely watching her remove items from fridge and cupboards. She no longer fretted about the fortune Jan spent stocking the shelves. The master of the house could afford any and all delicacies, regardless of cost.

She combined tinned chickpeas and artichoke hearts, added lemon juice, oil, and balsamic vinegar, crumbled feta cheese on top. Using the stand mixer, she whipped heavy cream from Milver Vale Dairy into stiff peaks and placed the bowl in the fridge. She dredged each chicken breast in flour and spices and set them aside and began slicing mushrooms. When the knob of butter in the sauté pan melted, she added the meat.

Martin sauntered in and stepped close to the stovetop. "Smells wonderful." His arms enclosed her waist. "What can I do?"

"Open a bottle of champagne, please. Or prosecco."

"Is this a celebration?"

"It's for my sauce. I need less than a cupful."

When she measured out the amount, he divided the remainder between two coupe glasses. "I'll fetch a cloth and cutlery and lay the table on the terrace. It's such a pleasant evening, we should take advantage."

He returned, and she handed him the bowl of salad.

She transferred the cooked chicken pieces to a platter and heated the mushrooms in the pan juices and wine before pouring on just enough cream to thicken the mixture. She ladled it over the meat and garnished the platter with parsley cut from the herb garden.

Martin praised her creation as a triumph.

Verbally impaired by the shock of the magazine article, she asked a single leading question about his afternoon activities. At intervals she looked up from her plate to nod or make a murmur of acknowledgement.

This could have been so romantic, she realized.

Dinner for two. A view of blooming roses and other plants against a background of evergreens. Purple flowers dangled from the thick branches of the enormous wisteria clinging to the wall. A bird, concealed by the foliage, trilled an unfamiliar tune. And with the sun's retreat, the blue sky faded, gradually changing to amber.

They both cleared the table. While Martin packed everything into the dishwasher, Hannah concocted Eton Mess, crushing store-bought meringues, folding them into whipped cream, and swirling in diced strawberries and lemon zest.

"Did they really serve this at your school?" she asked when he had polished off his portion.

"Not often. Always for our annual cricket match with

Harrow. Jewel's agility kit is still in my car. Lois and I studied the instructions printed on the box. We can assemble the pieces before dark."

"All right." Hannah dredged her spoon through the pool of whipped cream at the bottom of her bowl.

Millie trotted onto the terrace. Ariel rose and bounded to meet her.

Poppy marched over to the table, ponytail swinging with each footfall. "You need to see this." She slammed a copy of *Posh* on the tabletop. "It was polluting the bookshop."

Martin peered at the cover. "She isn't the Caroline Bryden I used to know. That one had a mouth full of metal and wore hideous gold-rimmed spectacles." He flipped the pages until he came to the fashion spread. "Quite a transformation."

"Turn back. There's another feature you won't like so much."

Hannah's heartbeat thundered in her chest.

"Damn."

"The writer rang me, weeks ago," Poppy told him. "I didn't tell her a thing. None of those unattributed quotes are mine, Mart. I swear."

"It's true," Hannah contributed. "I was there."

"So this is what Jessica was on about. She kept leaving phone messages that didn't make much sense."

"Do you think Natalie cooperated?"

"Hard to say. During our St. Barth's holiday, her brother was constantly taking pictures, but there were several others in our party. This photo on the beach could've come from anybody."

"Would you like to finish the bit of pudding that's left?" Hannah asked Poppy. "It won't keep."

"I'm due at The Peacock. I was asked to be scorekeeper for tonight's darts tournament. You two should come."

Martin gave a noncommittal response. After Poppy vanished around the corner of the house, he pushed the magazine across the table. "Have a look. Tell me how bad this is."

"I've read it. I bought a copy this afternoon when I was in the village." She stood up and placed their empty bowls on the serving tray. "Can I bring you something else?"

"A bottle of single malt, doesn't matter which. And a glass."

She took her time tidying the kitchen. After she wiped clean all the surfaces and handed each dog a biscuit, she returned to the terrace and sat across from him.

"This is nonsense. Lots of speculation and a certain amount of exaggeration."

Gripping the table edge, she said, "About your net worth, you mean."

"It fluctuates. Her estimate is on the low side."

"Seriously?"

His gray eyes widened. "That can't be a surprise. I'm sure you go on the internet to gather intel about blokes before giving them the time of day. Checking for an arrest record, or the number of ex-wives and children."

"The staff at Wincott & Sons convinced me you were legit, so I didn't have to do much digging. I found a couple of links to an investment firm. You attended the opening of an Indian restaurant in one of the villages. At the time, I wasn't interested in you. I wanted to know about your house." Her hand swept towards the stone façade. "Which, as you said, has almost no visibility on the web. Until a couple of hours ago, I believed you were flat broke. Or very nearly."

"You're having me on."

"According to my liaison at the location agency, no aristocrat would allow access to a film production for weeks on end unless he was practically impoverished or massively in debt. Which sounded all too probable. Even more so after you said you sold your castle to a hotel company."

"I never liked the place."

"Then I saw your car. Not exactly what multi-million-aires drive."

"The countryside is no place for showy vehicles. Although I did follow a branding consultant's directive to purchase a custom-colored fleet of electric vehicles. Vans and pickups, emblazoned with an estate logo." He changed chairs, moving to the one nearest hers. "You're upset. Why?"

"I can't help feeling like a peasant girl who met a prince pretending to be a commoner. So he'll know for sure she isn't shagging him only because he's rich and lives in a castle."

"Maybe America is different, but round here we don't usually introduce ourselves by quoting the sum total of our personal wealth. I didn't know what you didn't know about me."

"I know that now." She produced a semblance of a smile. Her forefinger stabbed the open magazine. "Three hundred million pounds."

"More than that. I think."

"Martin!"

"Hannah."

"I'm wondering how I'll make my next rent payment. On a one-bedroom apartment. According to this writer, you're richer than some members of the royal family."

"She's better informed about them than I am. Here are the facts. When my grandfather died, Uncle Rufus inherited the bulk of the family fortune, in addition to the properties in Somerset and up north and in London. My father received a sizeable trust that was set up to provide him with significant income, not that he needed it. He had this." He pointed to a line of type. "Latimer Global Investments. He founded it."

"You never told me he was businessman."

"Younger sons in our family usually joined the military, but when a congenital heart defect turned out to be disqualifying, he chose to take an economics degree. By the time he married my mother, he was a chartered accountant, based in Reading. Not long after my arrival, he rose to chartered financial analyst. That was his springboard into hedge funds."

"I don't know much about those," she admitted. "Only that they're a popular source of film financing."

"When I was five, we moved to London," he continued. "Every morning Dad walked from our house in Gibson Square to his office in the City, headphones on, listening to a favorite album on his portable compact disc player. I've got his entire collection in my study at Latimer House." He sipped his drink. "In the evening, a taxi brought him back to Islington. We were never sure when he'd arrive, because he was doing business in so many time zones. The firm spread itself around the globe. New York, Toronto, Los Angeles, Sydney, Hong Kong, Singapore, Tokyo."

"Wow."

"And Jersey, in the Channel Islands. We spent every August in our house near St. Helier, where Dad had his other primary office. Mother spent the entire month painting—she'd studied art in Paris. I messed about on the beach with my bucket and spade, constructing sand forts and dreading my return to school. We'd ferry over to France and explore the Normandy coast. Happy memories."

Hannah placed a hand on his.

"Dad wasn't greedy. But he was determined to ensure his financial security, and eventually mine, in ways that could withstand erratic stock markets and the rise and fall of property values. He'd seen how periods of economic uncertainty and recession affected owners of large estates, and he was destined to become one himself. Nobody expected that he would die before his older brother. But his defective heart couldn't hold up to the pressures of the job and the strain of his terrible work hours."

"When you were at Eton."

Martin stretched out his arm and grasped the bottle. Adding whisky to his glass, he said, "Latimer Global is one of the world's most respected fund management companies. I'm heavily invested, of course—a major shareholder. I also have a permanent seat on its board of directors." His attention returned to the open magazine. "My being a millionaire can't possibly be as objectionable to you as these stupid pictures. Especially the purple hair one."

"That wasn't a surprise. You've mentioned it. So did Poppy."

Slowly he turned the pages. "When I was young and rebellious, paparazzi used to trail me in and out of clubs, restaurants, and concerts. They never hacked into my phone or trawled through my bins. But I knew full well that their keen interest could damage people I cared about. Any girl I dated. My uncle, gay and closeted. My mother, after her diagnosis."

Hannah empathized. She had vulnerable loved ones. Her uncle, the former prisoner. Mum, whose television career had stalled in the aftermath of Chase's difficulties. Dad, a hardworking veterinarian. Grampa, struggling against the demise of the lobstering trade.

"You must be the source of the fifty thousand pounds earmarked for the Milver Vale promotional campaign."

"A worthwhile investment."

"And a means of keeping me here?"

"That was an afterthought."

"Here's something I don't understand. If poverty isn't your reason for letting a film company take over your ancestral acres, what is?"

"Publicity about *Forsaken Fortune* and its worldwide release will spotlight this area. I expect the movie to draw tourists and new residents, whose money will boost the profits of our small businesses and agricultural producers. I'm sacrificing privacy to build up our local economy and increase entrepreneurial activity." He flashed a grin. "And I was instantly attracted to the location manager."

By remaining, she would put him and his various business initiatives at risk. One simple, sleazy headline—*The Marquess and the Murderer's Niece*—could imperil all his grandiose plans.

"Why the tears?"

She reached up to brush them away. "It's a lot to absorb. At the worst time of the month." Gazing at the distant woodland, she saw that the sun was about to slip behind the treetops. Mental and emotional agony blunted the discomfort of menstrual cramps. "I should take paracetamol and lie down."

"I'll join you later. Unless you don't want me."

She did. She didn't.

"Jewel—stay." He grasped the dog's collar to prevent her from following. "I'll put together the hurdles and obstacle course before the light goes."

Pausing on the staircase landing she peered through the arched window. Sections of the agility set lay scattered over the lawn—cross-posts, the bar, the hoop. Martin held his phone flashlight against the box so he could read the instructions again.

Industrious and thoroughly absorbed. That's how she would remember him.

In her bedroom, she removed her toiletries kit from the pocket of her packed bag and fished out the bottle of paracetamol. After swallowing two, she switched on her laptop and clicked the bookmark for the airline website.

Confused and angry, Martin was stuck somewhere between the disbelief and denial phases of grief. Heavy rainfall was the least of his concerns as he left the Newbridge roundabout and joined the stream of vehicles zooming along the A303.

"I've known plenty of women attracted to my useless title and my mountain of money. You're the first one to be repelled. If I ever meet that reporter, I'm having her arrested."

"On what grounds?"

"Disturbing the peace. *My* peace. And our happiness." His gaze shifted from the road when he asked gently, "You were happy, weren't you?"

She adjusted her seatbelt, tugging at it as though desperate to free herself from confinement. "I've never had a nicer vacation."

He ground his teeth. "That's all it was for you?"

"I wasn't sure it could ever be anything more."

"Just going through the motions, were you? I've got no complaint about your motions, they're wonderful." Determined to rein in his frustration, he said quietly, "We're sleeping together. We planned an entire promotional campaign. I'm about to ask my solicitor to initiate a work visa sponsored by Milver Vale Properties, Limited." His eyes shifted to the side, and he saw how tightly she gripped her mobile. "You never explained why you broke up with what's-his-name. Your ex. Did he have too much money?"

"He's a corporate lawyer at a major Boston firm."

"How did he handle your desertion?"

"I don't know. I told him to never call me again and left the party."

"Harsh."

"Justified," she insisted. "I'm sure Joel was relieved that I saved him the hassle of breaking up. And I couldn't bear starting out the year with someone who no longer wanted to be with me. The worst part was being stranded downtown and trying to find a cab on New Year's Eve. Impossible. Huge crowds, because of the First Night celebrations. Hordes of people had come to see the ice sculptures and fireworks. It was freezing cold and the streets and sidewalks were covered with slippery patches. Getting a rideshare took forever." Her gaze hadn't wavered from her phone.

"If you want a coffee, we've got enough time to stop at Amesbury services before we join the M3."

"My hotel room will have a kettle. I've just completed remote check-in."

Short of running out of petrol—his tank was half-full—or puncturing a tire, he couldn't delay the parting that she decreed absolutely necessary.

"It just about killed me, seeing you cry when you said goodbye to Jewel."

"She didn't understand what was happening."

"Neither do I."

Hannah turned her head towards him. "Imagine the awkwardness of remaining at Stanwell when my former colleagues arrive. They would assume I was living with, and leeching off of, Britain's millionaire marquess. And they'd be correct."

"You'd be working for him. I mean, with him. With me."

She drew a long, shaky breath. "After so many years as a scout, I wanted to reach the next rung of the ladder. Through no fault of mine, I lost my chance to be location manager. I know Liz has other development deals in the works. She'll do whatever she can to make amends for the way Owen Parry and Alistair McLaren shafted me."

From the earliest days of their acquaintance, her pragmatism and dedication to her odd profession had fascinated him. Now it was the wedge separating them.

Hurtling along the M3 wasn't at all conducive to conversation. Martin switched on the radio and pretended he preferred jangling guitars and husky vocals to a dialogue that increased his wretchedness.

A traffic jam to block the ramps and roundabouts would

be heaven-sent. But the signals were working beautifully. There wasn't a single breakdown in his or any other lane.

Instead of pulling up to the front of the hotel, he drove to the car park.

She dropped her mobile into her handbag and zipped it.

Saying nothing, he stepped out and removed her case from the back seat.

She looked up at him. "Don't come inside, or you'll make this way harder. For both of us."

He couldn't think of anything else to say except, "All right."

"Be careful driving home."

He slid his fingers into the springy dark-brown curls and tipped her face upward. Placing her hands on his shoulders, she rose on her toes to meet his mouth.

Backing away, she said unsteadily, "I'll look for you on the big screen. As the village idiot." Her eyes filled with tears.

"Typecasting."

Her response was a fleeting, off-kilter smile.

Watching her hurry away, head lowered, Martin knew she was weeping. He drew no comfort from proof that this farewell affected her as much as the one involving the dog.

The bellhop glared in his direction, exhibiting no sympathy for a shattered man. After a final, heart-wrenching glance at the tiny figure pulling her wheeled bag through the glass doors, he climbed into the car. He sat motionless, staring at the wet windscreen, wondering what, if anything, he could've said or done to change Hannah's mind.

Part 2

Everything about filmmaking is incredibly weird.

—**Eddie Redmayne**

Chapter 19

Summertime was advancing, but its heat hadn't yet conquered Boston. Young leaves on the willows in the Public Garden fluttered in the breeze, shading the Swan Boats that glided over the water. On Beacon Hill, flowers bloomed in planters and window boxes decorated the brick fronts of the row houses.

Hannah's tentative hold on optimism slipped by the time she reached Charles Street. Before leaving for England, she would enter the Acorn Films office with verve and confidence, buoyed by her promotion to location manager. She had returned as an unemployed scout.

Rounding the corner of Mt. Vernon Street, she heard her cellphone buzz.

"I can see you from my window," said Liz. "Wait there. I'm surrounded by madness and need to get out. No coffee for me—because, breastfeeding. But I'll buy yours."

"Okay."

As usual, Liz looked amazing. Her long, dark tresses were loosely piled atop her patrician head. A gauzy orange tunic flowed past her hips to her thighs, and she wore brown slacks and leather sandals.

"Love the haircut." She hugged Hannah. "Nice sundress, too."

"From the secondhand clothing stall at the Milver Vale Flower Fete. Two pounds."

"Not a fan of the shoes."

Hannah looked down at her sneakers. "I'll probably walk back to Cambridge."

Physically, Liz seemed unchanged, her step as energetic as always, her chin thrust forward as she proceeded to the French café she often used for a satellite office. She marched to the counter to order Hannah's coffee and a fruit smoothie for herself, and two of their favorite apricot danish.

"Let's go over to Acorn Street so you can meet your goddaughter. I need to top her up before my ten o'clock." She'd named her film company after the historic cobblestone where she lived with her scholar husband and their infant. "Online meeting with a distributor in L.A. No airplane trips for me till I head overseas." Liz heaved a sigh. "I hate that you aren't going with me."

Hannah looked down and broke off a piece of pastry. Any reference to the film, direct or implied, was a bitter reminder of what she'd lost—Martin, and the movie.

"I've recommended you to an independent producer based in New York," Liz continued. "The script was adapted from her late sister's novella. She's very committed. You'd be scouting in Nova Scotia, territory you already know."

"Sounds interesting."

"I recently had an alert about a network television series pilot that shoots next winter, literally on your parents' doorstep. An hour-long dramedy based in coastal Maine. On an island, I think. Quirky Down East characters, boats and lobsters and clams—all that shit. If that team doesn't hire you as location manager, they don't deserve a network pick-up. I'll be your reference. Your pimp. Whatever you need."

"How's the Texas project?"

"I expect to see the rough cut any day. The final will be shown at the Toronto Film Festival. If you aren't otherwise occupied, you should join our Acorn contingent. I'll be stuck in Somerset."

She felt it again, that nasty double stab of envy and regret. "When do you leave?"

"We haven't decided. Tom survived the tsunami of childbirth, exam week, and commencement. He's on sabbatical now and envisions many happy hours deciphering obscure Reformation manuscripts in the British Library and the Bodleian and God knows where else. We're taking Telma, to look after Lexi. And us. So perhaps I can maintain a modicum of sanity while overseeing a film with baby brain and bouts of postpartum depression. My mother will join us so Telma can have two weeks of vacation with her family in Portugal."

"The executive producer doesn't have to be on set every moment. Most never appear at all. They let their director and department heads handle everything."

"You know that's never been my style." Liz tucked a drooping strand of hair behind her ear. "Tell me about Hartcliffe Studios. Give me a preview of any problems I might confront there."

"For me, Alistair McLaren."

Liz responded with a low growl. "I've made my displeasure very clear to Owen and Nigel."

"Don't let what they did to me affect your relationship with them."

"It hasn't. It won't."

"Hartcliffe is a state-of-the-art facility. As good as any production studio in Los Angeles or Atlanta or North Carolina. Advantageously located within an hour of Stanwell House and the Milver villages."

"A camera unit is setting up soon to capture seasonal footage. Landscapes and exteriors, establishing shots.

They're going to fly a camera drone along the river, low and slow over the water. Bird's eye view, to go under opening credits."

After leaving the café, they covered the short distance to Liz's historic brick townhouse on Acorn Street. She scrounged deep in her soft leather satchel for her key, but before she found it, Dr. Thomas Picton opened the front door.

"Hi, Hannah. It's been a while."

Liz tilted her head. "I don't hear Lexi's starvation wail."

Following her up the staircase, Hannah turned back to ask, "Enjoying your sabbatical?"

"Sleepless nights don't matter as much, now that I'm not commuting to Cambridge for classes and student appointments and departmental meetings."

A mural of cotton-puff clouds and soaring doves decorated the pale blue walls of the upstairs nursery. Liz gently lifted her daughter from the crib and carried her to a platform rocker by the window.

"She's beautiful," Hannah said. "So tiny. What color are her eyes?"

"We call it mud season brown." Liz kissed the dark down atop the baby's head before unbuttoning the orange tunic.

Hannah had previously witnessed the mechanics of nursing—several of her college classmates had become mothers. To her surprise, she was profoundly moved. "You look like a post-modern Madonna." She sank onto a loveseat upholstered with Winnie-the-Pooh toile.

"Nobody ever speculates on whether the Blessed Virgin suffered postpartum blues."

"You look plenty content to me."

"When focused on her, I'm okay. There's no lack of maternal attachment—all the instinctive stuff is going on. But everything else in my life feels out of whack. I don't get enough rest. At night, between feedings, I toss and turn. I wonder whether it's right to expose my newborn to unfamiliar places and foreign germs. Not that I have a choice. But when we're in Somerset we won't be in a hotel. Tom's been looking online for a rental house and found a couple of good ones."

"Where?"

"Newbridge." She glanced down, then nudged the baby's mouth back onto her nipple. "I worry that *Forsaken Fortune* won't live up to my lofty expectations—or those of the industry. And our investors. It might be a high-profile and outrageously expensive disaster."

"That's nuts. If you need a reminder of what you're capable of, and your accomplishments, I'll run to the office and bring back an armful of those awards in the display case."

"I'm not so nuts that I don't realize my greatest achievement is right here in my arms."

Lexi finished, and Liz let Hannah carry her to the changing table.

"Better not stick around for what comes next. Go downstairs and ask my husband to show you the rental house webpages. I'd like your opinion."

Descending the stairs, Hannah paused at intervals to examine the framed engravings. The one at the bottom bore Albrecht Dürer's initials and appeared to be genuine.

Tom called from his study, "Everything all right up there?"

Joining him, she said, "Far as I could tell. Lexi is exquisite."

"You enjoyed your trip to England? Except for—" He broke off.

"Except for that, yes. I spent time with my grandmother in Wales, and saw other relatives. The natives are friendly. You and Liz will like the people at Stanwell."

She had a vision of Martin and the Gregorio-Pictons seated at the long mahogany dining table. She mentally filled more chairs with Poppy and Owen Parry and Nigel Rossiter. And Caroline Bryden, the host's beautiful cousin. Not Alistair, though—he wasn't important enough to receive an invitation to the imaginary dinner party, and didn't deserve one. The double chandeliers glowed and the Latimer silver service gleamed. Laughter and erudite conversation filled the room.

And she would be scouting in rugged Nova Scotia, driving a rental car across windswept terrain. She'd stay at a cheap motel. Or, if lucky, a bed and breakfast with a resident dog.

Liz came into the study, holding up her phone. "I've just sent you the contact info for an ad agency downtown. They're looking for a producer, if you wanted to give up freelancing for a permanent position. They have huge accounts all over New England."

"You're an excellent pimp. Thank you."

She didn't take the Red Line back to Cambridge but stuck to her original plan of returning on foot. She appreciated the spirit-lifting sight of the Charles River and the view of the city from the Longfellow Bridge. On the other side, she followed a favorite jogging route on the MIT campus perimeter. Spotting an unoccupied bench, she sat down to answer a group text from her college friends, seeking a mutually convenient date for a get-together.

Instead, she pulled up the *Milver Vale Messenger* website. She scrolled through community news bulletins, looking for Martin's name. It didn't appear in any of them.

Returning to the rambling stucco residence where she lived, Hannah found her landlady watering the flower containers on the porch.

"Hey, Hannah. I finally got ahold of an electrician who can check out the wiring in the basement apartment. He said he'd come sometime this week, and that he might need to switch off fuses elsewhere. I'm not sure if the upstairs rooms will be affected."

"Thanks for the warning. Let me know if you need someone to weed your vegetable garden. I'm available."

"So am I, for a change. Now that the semester is behind me."

Erica, a widowed priest, taught theology in Harvard's religion department. Her son from a prior marriage was a legislative aide.

"How's Elliot?"

"Busy as ever. He'll be house-sitting for me later this summer when I lead a clergy retreat to Scotland. We'll be staying on Iona."

Before becoming involved with Martin Latimer, she would have relished the prospect of having the very attractive and unattached Elliot in residence. "That's great."

"My first trip without Helen. I'm ready. I think."

"A Scottish island will be better than Boston when the summer heatwave comes."

"How right you are."

At every Palindrome Posse gathering, alcoholic beverages were consumed, sometimes to excess. Hannah made the prudent choice of taking the train to Newton and a rideshare car delivered her to her college roommate's condo.

"C'mon in. Mim just got here," Eve said. "I've never seen your hair that short."

"Souvenir from a very fancy London salon. Sort of. My hairdresser did her best to copy the cut, from a photo on my phone." One Poppy had taken, of Hannah and Martin standing in the stable doorway. "But she chopped off way too much."

"It'll grow."

Eve's jeans were cropped just enough to expose the discoloration on her dark brown legs. On a fateful April afternoon, she and a multitude of spectators had stood in viewing distance of the Boston Marathon finish line. She'd been waiting for her brother to complete his run when the bombs exploded. Surgery to remove the metal projectiles embedded in Eve's flesh left permanent scars.

Hannah followed her into the kitchen, where the lethal drinks were being concocted.

"Here's to us." Mim lifted her martini glass. "Together again! Let the commiserations begin."

"Why? What happened?

"My ex-husband moved in with his former girlfriend," Eve announced. "Last week, I got dumped by the guy I've been dating on the rebound."

"Your personal life is a mess," Mim drawled. "Big deal. I've had a professional setback."

"I read about it in the *Globe*," Eve told her. "The judge on your case declared a mistrial."

"I was fired from my dream job on a major motion picture," Hannah contributed.

"You'll have to do better than that," Mim said.

"I could have been arrested on a visa violation. I had a torrid affair with a multi-millionaire aristocrat who begged me to stay with him. Which was impossible, for lots of reasons. My heart is broken. And unlike you two, I don't have a job."

"Here's to Hannah, champion of the misery stakes." Eve raised her martini glass.

Hannah said reflectively, "Sometimes I wonder if attending a women's college messed up our ability to develop uncomplicated relationships with men. Do you think that's possible?"

"No," Mim answered.

"Yes," Eve contradicted.

"Seems like girls from coed schools manage their dating lives better than I ever have. And enjoy plenty of great sex without commitments and drama."

"Is that what you want?" Mim asked her. "A fuck buddy? No strings?"

She shook her head. "Definitely not. Though I feel like I should want to want it." Uncomfortable with her reply, she clarified, "I'm not the type."

"Neither are we," Mim affirmed.

"The topic of men is off-limits," Eve declared, pounding the chair arm for emphasis. "What are you doing about a job?"

"I'm waiting to hear if I landed a scouting assignment in Nova Scotia. The person who makes the final decision is out of the office for Canada Day. There's also a location manager gig in Maine, for a television pilot. Or I can return to the advertising biz, producing promos for web and broadcast."

"You don't sound thrilled about any of your options," Mim observed.

"If we're going to drink, we'd better eat something. There's a box of Chinese dumplings in the freezer, and I have a jar of spicy Asian peanut sauce. And ingredients for salad."

During their improvised meal, the catching up continued. Eve, temporarily liberated from the myriad challenges of teaching elementary school, spent more time at her gym. Mim expressed the hope that the mistrial might enable a plea bargain favorable to her client or dismissal of charges by the prosecution.

"What will you do for the Fourth of July?" Hannah asked, carrying plates to the kitchen.

"Sleep in," Mim replied. "My neighbors invited me to the Pops concert on the Esplanade, and the fireworks. The weather's supposed to be good. Want to join us?"

"Maybe."

Eve said, "I'll keep my noise-canceling headphones on and listen to an audiobook and podcasts. I can't bear to hear the pop-pop, bang-bang." This was a rare reference to her post-traumatic issues. "What the hell?" she cried, as Big Ben's deep boom rose from the depths of Hannah's purse.

"Sorry about that." With multiple professional balls suspended in the air, she wasn't leaving any call unanswered. "Hannah Ballard speaking."

Her friends smirked at her businesslike greeting.

"Hannah, dear, it's Isobel. Latimer."

"Hello." She glanced at the illuminated digits of Eve's microwave. "I guess I should say good evening."

"I'm not in France. I'm at a hotel near Copley Square."

Chapter 20

"You're in town? For how long?"

"I'm not certain," Isobel said. "I arrived two days ago. It occurred to me that you could provide some much-needed travel information. And useful advice."

"Sure. Happy to help."

Eve and Mim erupted in laughter.

"I've caught you at a bad moment. Shall I get in touch tomorrow?"

"No, no, it's okay. I'm hanging out with my girlfriends." She held her finger to her lips before moving away from the kitchen island.

"I've got appointments in the morning for a series of medical tests. The holiday will delay lab processing. Instead of staying in Boston, which I'm informed will become very crowded, I'd like to go elsewhere. I know there are mountains and lakes and the seaside not far from here, and I haven't any preference. I wondered whether you could perhaps recommend a pleasant inn or a bed-and-breakfast."

"Easy enough," she said brightly. "For a location scout."

"Wonderful. I'll give you my mobile number. Better wait till the afternoon to get in touch."

"Is there anything else I can do?"

"Good wishes would be appreciated. Prayers, too, if you're so inclined."

"You've got them. I hope all goes well in the morning."

"I appreciate that, Hannah. And I look forward to hearing from you."

"You definitely will," she said. She returned her phone to her purse and resumed her clean-up tasks.

"Didn't sound like a job offer," Eve commented.

"A woman who's visiting from France, asking if I know of a traditional New Englandy inn or B&B." She wouldn't get tangled up in explanations of how she became acquainted with Isobel Latimer or identify her as the parent of the wealthy aristocrat she'd referenced.

Odd, thought Hannah, for Isobel to travel alone to the States for medical purposes. If Martin had accompanied her, wouldn't she have said so? Perhaps her sister Julia was with her, and planned to stay in the city over the holiday. That was possible.

"Does she have a car?" Mim asked.

"Didn't ask."

"If she drives in France, she won't have any trouble here."

"Our traffic is worse," Eve pointed out. "Especially before and during and after the Fourth."

Hannah was troubled by the prospect of Isobel attempting to maneuver through Boston's clogged and confusing one-way streets or busy highways where motorists would be speeding towards the beach or the mountains. Or just as bad, relying on the scheduled tour buses. An obvious solution presented itself, one that depended on her ability to handle the awkwardness of looking after the mother of the man she'd loved and left. It also forced her to make a journey that she'd postponed since returning from England.

"Back in a minute." She retrieved her cellphone and opened the sliding door to the wooden deck.

Don't overthink, she told herself. Just do it.

She pressed the number at the top of her list of contacts.

"Ballard residence."

"Hi, Mum. Do you and Dad have any special plans for the Fourth?"

"He's got the day off. I'll be in the garden and the kitchen. Are you able to come home? We'd love to see you, sweetie."

"Is it all right if I bring someone?"

"I didn't realize you and Joel were back together."

Perish the thought. "It's Isobel Latimer. Her son owns Stanwell House in Somerset, where Liz is filming *Forsaken Fortune.*" She relayed Isobel's requirements, adding, "Bear Knoll matches her request perfectly. It's quiet and secluded, and near the coast. It's a chance to repay the hospitality I received from the Latimers."

"Of course. We've got loads of room, and it gives us a reason to be festive. Your grandfather can supply us with lobsters. We'll recreate the American Revolution, just for fun. She and I can sit together on the British side of the table. The Yanks—your dad and granddad—will go on the other. You'll be the piggy in the middle. When do you plan to join us?"

"Day after tomorrow, most likely. I doubt she'll want to travel immediately after her procedure. I'll let you know. Thanks, Mum."

Two days later, Hannah's Subaru station wagon joined the mass migration from Cambridge to Boston. She threaded her way to Back Bay and Copley Place, and eased the car into an open space close to the front entrance of one of the city's most historic and luxurious hotels. She hopped out to tell the doorman which guest she was meeting, and he signaled to a uniformed porter in the lobby.

Watching the wheeled cart roll along the red carpet, she saw a single hard-sided suitcase and three pieces of soft luggage.

A lot for just one person, Hannah realized, with a frisson of alarm.

"The lady and gentleman are on their way," the porter informed her.

Gentleman . . .

Isobel exited first, her pace slow and deliberate. Martin followed.

Hannah dropped her keys and leaned down to pick them up.

"You changed your hair," Isobel said. "It's very becoming."

"Shorter for summer," Hannah responded. "And job interviews," she added, glancing at Martin.

"He won't be coming with me," his mother said.

"I most certainly am," he stated.

"Darling, we agreed—"

"There was no agreement. You're not haring off to the wilds of Maine by yourself after the ordeal you've just been through."

"I'll be with Hannah. And her parents."

"And I'll stay at a hotel."

"No, you won't," Hannah heard herself say. "Our house has only four bedrooms, not twenty like Stanwell does, but that's exactly enough. I'll phone Mum now so she can prepare one for you. She'll be delighted."

While he helped his mother into the front seat, she stepped into the shade of the awning to make her call. What a strange homecoming it would be. Having Isobel for a houseguest could've helped her cope better with the usual stressful situation. Martin's presence imposed a completely different kind of stress.

Waiting at an intersection for a red light to change, she asked her silent passengers, "Did everything turn out all right yesterday?"

"We won't know," Martin said, "until the doctor reviews the lab reports."

"Is there a reason the tests weren't done in London?"

Isobel replied, "My specialist there advised me to consult the hematologist in charge of my prior treatment. Has Martin told you about my disorder?"

"I did not."

Hannah's gaze wavered from the stoplight to her rear-view mirror. He'd put on a pair of sunglasses and faced the window. She saw only a portion of his brown head.

"I had a blood cancer with a silly name: hairy cell leukemia. It was in remission for many years, but HCL has a high rate of recurrence. When the blood draw ordered by my La Rochelle physician indicated a spike in my white cell count, he sent me to my London doctor. She got an identical result and submitted her report to the Boston specialist who treated me a decade ago. Back then I was prescribed a course of chemotherapy. I'll either have another, or doses of interferon. Or a bone marrow transplant."

"I'm really sorry you're going through this again."

"Since my initial diagnosis, I've led quite a productive life. With advancements in treatment, I expect to continue it."

Hannah waited until after merging onto the interstate highway to ask Martin whether Poppy had found a home for Jewel.

"Detaching her from Stanwell was impossible. Popster is taking her to agility class while I'm away."

"She's a lovely dog. I'm glad you kept her."

"I'll let her know."

Martin's headache, the product of jet lag and dread, accompanied him from Massachusetts to New Hampshire, and he doubted it would subside before he entered Hannah's native state.

She broke her silence to ask his mother about her current commissions.

"Before I left La Rochelle, identical twin boys sat for a double portrait. So wriggly, like puppies. I finished that one but had to cancel the August sittings. If parents don't mind my working from photographs, I hope to take on a few projects to complete by Christmas. Is that the ocean underneath this bridge?"

"The Piscataqua River. It separates New Hampshire from Maine. If you'd like to stop for lunch, I know a place on an inlet near Kittery. Part of the outdoor deck is covered. It's shady, and there's usually a breeze. They serve fried clams, lobster rolls, crabmeat salad, and lots more."

"That sounds perfect. Doesn't it, darling?"

"Quite." He'd never been less interested in food.

Picnic tables painted in rainbow colors covered the waterside restaurant's large outdoor deck. After placing their orders, Isobel inspected the Lobster Pound, where water-filled bays teemed with crawling crustaceans, claws bound by rubber bands.

Martin followed Hannah, who had wandered across the dining area to watch a man tie a motor launch to the dock. Resting his elbows on the wooden rail, he said, "This excursion is what she needs right now. I hope we won't inconvenience your parents."

"I doubt they know the meaning of the word." She put a hand to her hair, tossed by the strong breeze, and faced him. "My small way of reciprocating. You provided me with refuge in Somerset."

Unable to hold back, he blurted, "God, I've missed you." He wanted to run his fingers through those flyaway curls and kiss her pink mouth and press his palms to her round bottom. "I've never felt this way about anyone else."

"I haven't either. But there are . . . obstacles."

"What, specifically? I know you're not working."

"Not yet. I have prospects, thanks to Liz." Her attention veered to the opposite shore. "Look over there," she said, pointing at towering evergreens. "Do you see the bald eagle?"

"No. Where?"

"At the top of that giant pine, perched on the snag—the bare branch—near the top. I'll get my binoculars."

Off she went, racing up the steep ramp and climbing a set of wooden stairs to the roadway.

"Abandoning us so soon?" his mother called, coming towards him. "What did you say?"

"She went for her binoculars, to get a closer look at an eagle. I didn't know she was a twitcher." He scanned the treetops, silently cursing the invisible bird for interrupting a crucial conversational moment. "I don't see it."

"On a branch, quite high. Oh—there it goes."

He watched the enormous dark shape glide above the woodland and out of view. Clutching the wooden rail, he confided, "I'm in love with that woman."

"Yes, darling."

"And I'm worried about you."

"That's pointless, when we don't know whether there's any reason to be."

When Hannah returned and learned her quarry had vanished, she promised future opportunities to observe America's national bird.

"I'll take you to a place where they forage for fish to feed their young at this time of year. Ospreys, too."

Tucking in to thickly battered onion rings, Martin held out hope for a private bird-watching expedition. He was pleased to see his mother polishing off her crab salad.

Amply fed, they climbed back into the Subaru. Beyond Portland, Hannah left the turnpike to follow a winding roadway bordered by dense forest. Most of the dwellings were constructed from wood, painted white or gray or pale blue, with a neatly cut lawn, colorful flowerbeds, and productive vegetable plots. Farmhouses and their outbuildings were large. Fields of maize stretched to the horizon. Holstein cattle grazed the meadows. He identified equestrian properties by their outsized stables, extensive paddocks, and indoor riding facilities.

"Plenty of money around here," Hannah said. "New residential developments are springing up all over, for commuters to Portland who want to live near the country club and the golf courses." She turned at a four-way intersection and accelerated up an incline. "This is Bear Knoll."

At the summit stood a handsome multi-story house of faded red brick, appealingly antique. The Subaru stopped near the enormous red-painted wooden barn and a series of sheds, where the packed dirt drive ended.

A pair of yapping Shetland sheepdogs trotted round the corner of the house. A tri-color border collie raced ahead of them and added ear-piercing barks.

The woman who stepped out of the barn was small-boned like her daughter and graying brown hair framed a similarly shaped face. "That's enough, dogs! Away!" The collie retreated but the Shelties tensely stood their ground.

"Mum, this is Isobel Latimer."

"So very pleased to meet you. I'm Gwen. Neil's sorry he's not here to welcome you, but he'll be back for an early supper. Once a week he has evening work hours—he's a veterinarian—and tonight's the night."

"This is Martin," Hannah said.

"The first nobleman to visit Bear Knoll." Gwen slipped an arm around Hannah's waist—they were exactly the same height. "We've missed you so much, sweetie. Come out of the sun, Isobel. I'll have the tea ready in no time."

Martin and Hannah carried the luggage from the car to the house. She led him up the narrow stairs. At one end of the long corridor were two spare rooms with a bathroom between. He chose the smaller one and placed his mother's suitcase and carry-on in the other. When they returned to the ground floor, Hannah showed him a parlor furnished with Victorian-era chairs and marble-topped tables. The adjacent dining room had a coffered ceiling and a large wooden table with eight chairs.

"Do you want tea?" she asked.

"Something cold, if it's available."

She led him to the attractively and incongruously modern kitchen and opened the refrigerator. "I could've told you without looking. Goat milk. Apple juice. Lemonade. Chardonnay."

"Lemonade, please."

They took their drinks to the screened porch overlooking an expanse of gardens. The two women were seated at a painted table, conversing as easily as though they'd been acquainted for years. Although Gwen retained her English accent, it wavered.

"Are there really bears here?" he asked when he could get a word in.

"Too many," she replied. "And very active at this season. They seldom roam onto our property during daytime, mostly they come after dark. Before nightfall I take my bird feeders into the garden shed and lock the door. Although bears are a nuisance, they're actually rather shy. And harmless, as long as you don't get between a sow and her cubs."

"Too bad we can't arrange an on-demand sighting," Hannah said. "Unless I take them to the transfer station at dusk. Otherwise known as the town dump. Near Scittery-gusset Creek."

"What a curious name," Isobel marveled.

Neil Ballard arrived in a truck labeled with his vet practice logo on its doors. He was exceedingly tall—Martin had to look up to see his face—with a solid handshake and hazel eyes like Hannah's. Whenever he looked at his daughter, his expression indicated that she was his pride and joy, and something of a mystery. Martin could relate.

The evening meal was served in the dining room. It consisted of salad made from home-grown lettuce and herbs, roast chicken, and freshly picked peas. The windows were kept open to catch the breeze flowing through mesh screens that kept out mosquitos and flies.

"Is this your family home?" Isobel asked their host.

"My folks were salt-breathers, living in Falmouth Foreside, next to the ocean," Neil told her. "After Gwennie and I married, we found this place and put all the money we had into it. Lots of work had to wait till her American television series got popular. I doubt we could've made it livable if she hadn't been so famous."

"It's charming."

"I got grief from the family for moving inland from Ballard's Landing, even though we're barely two miles from the coast." Nodding at his daughter, Neil added, "Punkin, your Grampa wants you to drop by."

"I'll go tomorrow."

"Here's the Hannah-Banana pudding!" Gwen carried in a crystal bowl topped with whipped cream. "That's what my brother-in-law always calls it. Her favorite."

"And his," Hannah said in a strange voice.

"I'll have mine later," Neil said, and excused himself from the table. "Sorry to leave, folks, but my patients can't wait."

The trio of dogs trailed him to the kitchen as though expecting a handout.

Gwen cleared the table, with Hannah's help, and they stowed the plates in the dishwasher. Isobel asked to see the renowned gardener's gardens. They sprayed on insect repellent and went outside.

Martin hung back on the porch with Hannah. As soon as the two women rounded the clump of trees, he drew her into his arms for a deep and needy kiss.

"I've wanted to do that all damn day. Don't fly away from me, like your eagle."

"We're *not* having sex in my parents' house. With your mother here."

He pulled her closer, bringing her pelvis in contact with his. "Where? When?"

Her eyes were half-closed, her mouth parted. "I'll think of something. Soon."

For now, he had to be content with a brief session of what she called "necking" before their mothers returned.

His temporary bed was comfortable, but as he lay beneath a quilted cover—reportedly cut and sewn by a Ballard ancestress—he had difficulty falling asleep. Hannah's proximity should have soothed him, but it had a contrary effect. And from the woodland at the edge of the property, an owl hooted repeatedly and mournfully.

Chapter 21

Waking early, Martin blamed his inability to adjust to the time zone difference on a lack of exercise since leaving Stanwell. He dug into one of his bags for his running clothes and trainers. As quietly as possible he made his way down the staircase and went to the kitchen for a glass of water.

Hannah, in shorts and an oversized t-shirt, sat on the granite worktop drinking orange juice.

"I'm in the mood for a run. Care to join me?"

"If you don't mind waiting." She pointed to the white enamel pail on the worktop. "I've milked the goats, but I'd better release the hens from their coop and put Rascal in the paddock. There are plenty of ripe strawberries to pick for breakfast, too. Have your coffee. Dad made a pot before he left." She poured it into a mug and handed it to him, and removed a cream jug from the refrigerator. Picking up a ceramic bowl, she said, "I won't be long."

He stepped onto the porch and saw her unhook a mesh gate. A flock of chickens darted out, scrambling over the dewy grass in search of insects. She led the gelding out of the barn into a white-railed enclosure. Kneeling between parallel rows of low, green-leaved plants, she plucked red berries and dropped them into her bowl, occasionally popping one into her mouth.

Overnight, a Maine farmgirl who hadn't completely uprooted herself from her hillside home had replaced the well-traveled, assertive film professional. Martin marveled at the transformation, amazed by how completely she'd eased back into this place so familiar to her, and utterly alien to him.

He could hear her mother and his chatting.

"After the late service at church, we could drive to Portland," Gwen was saying as they came into the kitchen. "The art museum has a fine collection. Good morning, Martin."

"Good morning."

"And the Old Port is worth a visit. Lovely shops and interesting galleries."

"Your roses are wonderfully inspiring," Isobel said. "If there's an art supplier in the city, I could pick up paper and pencils. Perhaps a watercolor set."

"Along the coast there's rugged and dramatic scenery. Rocks and beaches and lighthouses."

The porch door banged, heralding Hannah's return.

"We're going for a run," she said, depositing the bowl of strawberries in the sink. "If I don't keep an eye on Martin, he'll get lost. Or end up as a bear's breakfast."

"Ready when you are."

While they stretched, he described her mother's itinerary. "What's your preference?"

"Church. Mum's in charge of the Flower Guild, she likes to see how the altar arrangements turned out. After lunch, I'm taking you to meet my grandfather. Then we'll find a place to—to be together. I had a plan, but I'm changing it."

"Oh? Why?"

"It involved checking into the fanciest hotel in Portland. For the afternoon."

"I like the way you think."

"But I'd rather go where our mothers won't be. So it's Freeport instead. You can't come to Maine without seeing L.L. Bean."

"If you say so." Surveying the terrain in all directions, he asked, "Do we head uphill, while we're fresh, or downhill, and leave the worst for the end?"

"Up."

They encountered no bears and few passing vehicles as they loped past farms and timber lands, and houses Hannah identified as Cape Cod style, Federal, or McMansion.

"I needed this," he huffed. "Too much sitting. On the plane. In a hospital waiting room trying to read the *Financial Times* and the *Wall Street Journal* on my mobile while Mother had her blood and bone marrow extracted."

She stopped to retie a shoelace. "If she's nervous, she doesn't let on."

"I'm scared enough for us both."

Back at the house they showered and changed. After breakfast, Neil Ballard remained on the porch with the dogs and his copy of *The Portland Herald* and waved to the others as they left for church in Hannah's Subaru.

The service was similar to the one at St. Anne's, Milverston, but the pews contained more worshipers and the priest's sermon was considerably shorter. Sunday lunch at Bear Knoll was a casual combination of sandwiches and salads.

"When you see your grandfather today," Gwen said to Hannah, "ask what time he'll be bringing the lobsters on the Fourth. I'll make your Granny Jane's yeast rolls. And bake some sort of fruit pie. What should we have for dessert tonight?"

"Your daughter's Eton mess," Martin suggested.

"We've no shortage of eggs," Hannah said. "I'll whip the meringues." She smiled at him. "You might be tired of strawberries by then."

"No danger of that," he assured her.

"Dad will be home for supper tonight. When you're shopping, get something for him to grill."

"Oh, he *would* enjoy that," Gwen replied. "He hasn't done kebabs for ages. I'll buy lamb and mushrooms and potatoes."

Martin followed Hannah to her car, veering from getting in on the wrong side at the last minute.

"A genius move on my part, bringing you and Isobel here," she muttered before starting the engine. "She's in her element planning meals and talking about her gardens and going to Portland art galleries."

"She's awesome." He removed her hand from the steering wheel and kissed it. "So is her daughter."

"A lord, is he?" Arthur Ballard was a stocky senior citizen whose face and arms appeared to be permanently tanned. "We had one in our family."

"We did?" Hannah stared at her grandfather.

"On my ma's side, long time ago. He's written down in the old Desmond Bible. Far as I can tell, it's the woman who brings the good blood into a family. Lord Desmond, he was."

"An Irish title," Martin guessed.

"Could be. Ma came from Ireland. After the war, when times were hard, her family sent her over here."

"Grammy Jane came down from Quebec for the same reason."

"Ayuh. She and her sisters. To work in the shoe factory in Brewer. Penobscot County."

"What county is this?" Martin wondered.

"Cumberland," they answered together.

Hannah wanted her grandfather to take their photo in front his stacked lobster traps, and patiently showed him how to press the camera button on her phone. When he realized Martin was about to send it to Poppy in England, he shook his silvery head in amazement.

"You young folk and them gadgets. Neil set me up with a computer and the email. It's all but useless, 'cept for gettin' long range weather forecasts and the tide chart. C'mon down to the wharf. If I know this one, she wants a swim."

Hannah lifted her shirt to reveal a peacock blue swimming costume. "You're right. I'm going in. His lordship wouldn't survive the water temperature."

She skinned off her shirt and shorts and slipped off her sandals. Without another word, she headed for the edge of the dock and dove into the water. She bobbed to the surface, shrieking. "Fuck, it's cold!"

"Watch your language," her grandfather chided. "Your grammy's up in heaven, listening to every word."

"Back atcha," she shouted, and dipped below the water's surface. Bobbing up, she added, "I learned that word from you."

"Chase says it more'n me. She's gonna need a towel. Knowin' her, there's one in the car. Thinks of everything."

"I'll get it."

Martin met her at the top of the metal ladder. Her fair skin dripped and was pimpled with goosebumps.

"Did I say it was cold? Jeezum crow!"

Her grandfather sat on a bench, smoking a cigarette and listening to his radio. He and Hannah discussed the number of lobsters required for tomorrow's feast.

"How 'bout fireworks?" he asked. "They're legal now, I don't have to go to New Hampshire no more to get 'em."

"Definitely. Not the ones that make really loud booms—they terrify the dogs. Just things that light up and whirl and sizzle. Lots of the Chinese chickens with the sparks that fly out of their butts."

"All righty. Are you takin' him out on the boat? Her engine's overhauled, runs real sweet."

"Maybe tomorrow. We're going to Freeport today."

When Martin and Hannah resumed their journey, he asked whether her grandfather made a living from harvesting lobsters.

"Not like he used to. The industry has been sinking for years. Catch limits, low prices, bad economy. Sometimes the fishery is totally shut down for whale conservation. He has a charter boat license, so he earns money taking sportsmen way out to sea to catch stripers and trophy fish. And summer tourists hire him for eagle-spotting trips on the river. Off season, he ferries supplies to the islands in Casco Bay."

"His granddaughter inherited his work ethic."

"His *unemployed* granddaughter."

He leaned against the car seat, stifling his urge to point out a job tailored to her skills and interests waited for her at Stanwell House.

"What happened to your parents' Morris Minor? I haven't seen it."

"Dad sold it about ten years ago, when Chase needed help paying his—" She began again. "My uncle was in debt. And I started college sooner than the family expected and too late to apply for financial aid. But I got it for my sophomore year. A scholarship from the Film Education Institute covered my year at Bristol University."

Each disclosure about the Ballards' finances helped him better comprehend her reaction when she discovered his net worth exceeded the hundreds of million pounds reported by *Posh* magazine.

She made a detour to a strip of land accurately named Sandy Point. Hannah removed her sandals, obviously intending to walk along the strand.

"Brave enough to wade into this part of the Atlantic Ocean?" she asked.

"If that's a challenge, I accept." He took off his shoes and socks and rolled up his trouser legs.

Hand in hand, they approached the waves. How bad could it be?

Worse than bad, he discovered as soon as he stood ankle-deep in the water. His feet and toes tingled, then lost all sensation. "Crikey!"

Hannah splashed ahead of him, stopping when the hem of her shorts got wet. "So refreshing."

"It's torture!" He inched forward. Gazing towards a group of young swimmers, he said, "Their parents should be charged with child endangerment."

She held up a hand to shield her eyes from the sun. "Harsh winters make thick blood."

Having proved his mettle, he retraced his steps back to the damp, firm sand. Hannah marched across the beach, picking up items the most recent high tide had deposited. She carried her gleanings to the car and dropped them into an empty paper cup marked with a fast-food logo.

"You saw all those the jars lined up on the wooden ledge on our porch? Mum collects beach glass. I gather shells."

During their journey he noticed a semi-circle of identical pastel-colored huts built close together, set back from the roadway.

"Do people live in houses that small?" he asked.

"They're old-fashioned rental cottages, for tourists. I always wanted to stay in one." She shifted her gaze from the road. "This could be my lucky day. I was thinking we'd go to a motel in Freeport, but a Kozee Kabin might be better."

"Jesus crow."

Laughing, she corrected, "Jeezum, not Jesus. We don't have to go to L.L. Bean. But we need to get home in time for supper."

"Let's stop at the store, just long enough to purchase

something. A carrier bag is proof that we stuck to our stated plan."

Martin had never seen car parks as vast and full as the ones in a town famous for its outlets and souvenir shops. Hannah, familiar with the layout of the sporting emporium, steered him to the display of canine accessories. He chose two toys, for Ariel and Jewel, then stood in a long queue to buy them. Hannah insisted on taking his picture beside wild creatures preserved by taxidermy—a moose, a black bear, a beaver—and forwarded all of them to Popster.

She drove back to the Kozee Kabins and parked in front of the small office building.

"Tell me what to do."

"Rent a unit for the night." She reached into the center console for a pad and pen and wrote down a combination of letters and numbers. Tearing off the page, she handed it to him. "They'll want this. Tell them it's a Massachusetts license plate."

When prompted by the woman at the desk, he provided the required information and presented his bank card. In return, he received the key to Unit Ten, two bottles of water, and a bucket of ice. He walked to the designated cottage while Hannah followed in the car.

"Seafoam green," she said, stepping onto the shallow porch. It barely had enough space for the two white plastic chairs and a small stack of cordwood. "I love it."

Inside they found a compact stone fireplace, a queen-sized bed, a small wooden table with four chairs, and basic kitchen appliances.

"Knotty pine paneling, chenille bedspread, hooked rug!"

A basin, a toilet, and a fiberglass shower stall had been crammed into the tiny bathroom.

"This is almost like being on the narrowboat," Martin observed.

She lowered all the window shades and closed the curtains. "Do you have any—necessities?"

"When you stopped for petrol yesterday, I bought one. There was a metal box in the men's lavatory. I used all my coins to get this." He placed the condom on the nightstand.

"Presumptuous."

"Optimistic. Shall we resume where we left off last night?"

Gradually he unbuttoned her floral cotton blouse, pausing for kisses. She carried his hand to the zipper of her khaki shorts, and he slowly lowered it. Confronted with the skin-tight swimsuit, slightly damp, he pulled the straps down, uncovering the round breasts, and eased it down her torso. He knelt on the rug to tug off the rest of the suit. When she stepped out of it, he pressed his cheek against the curve of her bared hip. He felt her fingers in his hair as he stroked the dark, feathery tuft between her legs. Her gasp of pleasure faded into a hum of delight.

After shedding his clothes, he had just enough presence of mind to tear the condom wrapper.

They moved to the bed and continued reacquainting themselves with each other's bodies, searching for all the most sensitive and responsive places. Desperate anticipation built up until he could bear it no longer. He clenched his jaw, determined to prolong their pleasure. They moved together, slowly at first, luxuriating in the contact, until their need for fulfillment speeded them along. She came in a rush, palms tapping against his back in that excited way of hers, and that brought him to a glorious, shuddering release.

"That was worth the wait," he whispered in her ear. He rolled onto his back and took her by the hand, placing it on his chest.

"Your phone is buzzing," Hannah murmured.

"I don't care." It was in his trouser pocket, somewhere on the floor.

"What if the doctor's trying to reach you? He might have gotten lab results before the holiday."

That was incentive to check the source of the missed call. "Popster. Probably ringing me to bitch about the cool pics we've sent her and to moan because she's missing out on the fun. She didn't leave a voicemail." He studied the figure in the bed—dark curly head, naked shoulders and breasts above the sheet—and raised his mobile.

"Don't you dare!" She pulled up the cover.

"No? I could make a packet by selling your photo to *Posh*."

"That's not even remotely funny."

Before returning to the bed, he took the water bottles out of the mini fridge. "You wouldn't believe the fallout from that asinine article. Ex-girlfriends were outraged, thinking I'd passed on their names. Milver Vale old-timers weren't fussed about it. New people, enlightened about my purple-haired past, give me strange looks." He swallowed some water. "During all the furor, Mother told me about her dodgy blood test. I promptly forgot about *Posh* and almost everything else. Except you." His fingers roamed across her collarbone.

She shimmied beneath the sheet. "And the wicked awesome sex?"

Their hope of showering together was thwarted by their inability to fit themselves into the shower stall. Martin let Hannah go first. When it was his turn, she laughed to see him crouching under a shower head several inches too low. He stepped out and pulled her close. Slipping his hand under her knickers, he tickled her bum until she shrieked.

She unwrapped the towel from her hair and combed out the tangles. Reapplying sunscreen, she told him to hurry up and dress. "Take the key back to the office. Say we've been invited to have dinner with some people in Falmouth, and we're spending the night at their house. And that's absolutely, indisputably the truth."

Chapter 22

Their return to Bear Knoll was delayed by heavy holiday traffic on Route 1. Dinner preparations were underway by the time they arrived. While Hannah sliced strawberries and whipped the cream, she recalled doing the same in the Stanwell House kitchen after discovering so many troubling facts about Martin in the *Posh* article. The pint of fresh blueberries on the counter inspired her to create a variation of Eton Mess to satisfy the British and the Americans—both nations had a red, white, and blue flag.

Because they would eat on the porch, she covered its table with a red-checked cloth and laid out plates and cutlery and arranged an assortment of chairs. The shish kebabs and couscous were a big hit with the Latimers. She crushed the perfect meringues Mum had baked and added them to her Eton Mess variation, which received enthusiastic accolades.

When they moved to the living room, Martin sat down to read a local author's book about a shipwreck recovery. Isobel sketched. Mum and Dad discussed the weather outlook and plans for a Fourth of July boat excursion.

"Rain coming," he said, his fingers scratching behind Bess the border collie's upright ears.

"Late in the day. Not that English people mind getting wet," her mother insisted.

Martin laughed. "We whinge about it all the time."

Hannah, seated on the rug with Sasha and Sadie, the Shelties, was relieved that Martin had asked her about the missing Morris Minor instead of her parents. She'd very nearly slipped up and given the reason Mum and Dad sold their beloved British motorcar. Chase's sentence included a fine of several thousand dollars, far beyond his ability to pay.

Although his name had surfaced several times, none of her relatives had mentioned his prison years. She hoped they wouldn't. Despite her curiosity about his plans, she couldn't ask questions when the Latimers were present. She'd have to join Dad in the goat barn during milking. Or offer to help him shuck corn on the porch steps, when no one else was around to overhear. Looking up, she caught Isobel staring at her with those gray eyes so similar to her son's.

She's drawing *me*, Hannah realized. Curiosity was stronger than self-consciousness, and she wondered how she was being depicted. "May I see?"

Isobel handed down the sketchpad.

Even in its unfinished state, the portrait was eerily precise. Her curly head filled the entire page. Her expression was thoughtful, perhaps even wistful, and graceful lines indicated her neck and the curve of her shoulders.

"It's a start," Isobel said, reaching for the pad. "Even before Martin asked me to sketch you, I was thinking you'd be a lovely subject. I hope you don't mind."

"I'm flattered." By Martin's request even more than his mother's complimentary version of her.

Clouds marred the morning sky, but no rain was falling when Martin and three Ballards—Hannah, her father, and her grandfather—boarded *Jenny's Dream*. Arthur Ballard guided his vessel into Casco Bay, as far as the shore of Chebeague Island. Hannah stood beside Martin and pointed out the shiny rounded heads of the harbor seals, and cormorants standing on jagged rocks. The water surrounding the vessel seemed to intensify the sun's glare, and the breeze whipped his hair into a quiff.

On their way back to Ballard's Landing, Arthur pulled up next to each of his bobbing white-and-green buoys, and the flock of rapacious gulls swooped low, clamoring for morsels of fish. He and Neil, both wearing orange waterproof overalls, winched up the traps. They used a gauge to measure each greenish-brown creature, and tossed most of them back to the sea.

"The breeders have to be v-notched before being discarded," Hannah shouted over the roar of the diesel engine. Rubber gloves protected her hands and she used special pliers to band the claws of the legal-sized lobsters before flinging them into the keeper tank. Holding up one whose pincers were safely bound, she explained to Martin how she determined its sex.

He was reunited with several of the same lobsters later that day, when Arthur Ballard delivered a portion of their morning harvest to Bear Knoll.

"Wow, that's a lot," Hannah commented.

"Steam 'em all. You'll have plenty of meat to chill or freeze for lobster rolls or salad." Grinning at Martin, he added, "Girl eats up them bugs like she was a seal."

Martin and Neil lugged the cooler into the kitchen. Before they were out of earshot, Martin overheard her grandfather tell Hannah, "I like your Limey fella. But if he don't treat you good, I'll start a whole 'nother revolution."

He was setting the bowl of coleslaw on the table when a red pickup pulled into the area between the house and barn.

Hannah arrived with a basket of nutcrackers, picks, and miniature forks—necessary utensils for a lobster dinner.

"Oh, my God." She froze, watching the dark-haired man who was greeting the trio of barking dogs.

He came up the porch steps and let himself in.

"Happy Fourth of July, Hannah-Banana. Long time no see."

She ran to hug him. He wrapped his arms around her and lifted her off the floor. "I can't believe it," she told him. "Did everyone else know you were coming?"

"Pop did. We wanted it to be a surprise."

"Best ever, swear to God." She faced Martin. "This is my Uncle Chase. Dad's brother."

"Hey, man. You're the English dude. She sent me your picture."

"Right," he said.

Chase Ballard had the same hazel eyes as Hannah and her father. His bushy hair curled almost as riotously as hers, and was a shade closer to black.

She seized his hand and dragged him into the kitchen. "Mum, Dad, look who's here."

Gwen shrieked. Neil, laughing, pounded his brother's back.

Perplexed by the exuberant welcome being extended to a family member, Martin went in search of his mother. He found her in the rose garden, refining the portrait he'd commissioned.

"Hannah's uncle just turned up," he announced. "And the lobsters are about to meet their fate."

In the kitchen, they found the five Ballards in a scrum, their excited voices rising to be heard over each other.

"Grampa *knew.*" Hannah held a tissue against her face to soak up her tears. "That's why he brought so many bugs."

"Gwennie, you're looking fine as ever."

"You drove from Old Town today?" Neil asked.

"Sure did. Through wicked bad traffic." Chase was short, like his father, but was lean and wiry instead of stocky and broad-chested.

"When did you get that truck?" his brother wondered.

"Not long after I was sprung. Bought it used, and cheap, with some of that money you sent. No bells or whistles, but it gets me where I need to go."

Hannah leaned against him. "Why didn't you come back sooner?"

"Too busy at the canoe factory. And they keep giving me more assignments at Indian Island." He scanned the ring of faces. "I couldn't show up till I felt ready. Ya know?" He bobbed his head at the Latimers. "I s'pose you've told your friends where I've been. And why."

Hannah turned towards Martin. In a tone he'd never heard before, she said, "I haven't seen Chase in over a decade. I wasn't allowed to."

Her simple statement changed the celebratory atmosphere. Her relatives' facial expressions shifted from joy to something else. She went to the oven and took out the yeast rolls.

"They're done." She slammed the metal tray on the worktop and rushed off. Her feet pounded each step on her way up the staircase.

Shattering the silence, Chase asked, "What's the matter with her?"

"You gave her a shock," his father said.

"I wouldn't have minded advance notice," said Gwen quietly. "Martin and Isobel must be wondering what's come over us all."

"I'm the Ballard black sheep." The younger man's dark head jerked backward, and he shoved his hands into his pockets. "Served near ten years in the state prison. I got paroled for good behavior and completed my sentence on work release. I've just graduated to unsupervised probation. No liquor allowed. No firearms, neither."

"Not even during deer season?" Arthur asked. "Can't we go on a turkey shoot next spring?"

"Never again, Pop."

Isobel intervened, saying calmly, "I hope it's not too uncomfortable for a Yankee to mix with English people on Independence Day."

Chase flashed a grin, baring bright teeth. "Doesn't bother me one bit, ma'am." The scratch of claws drew him to the sink. "Jeezum crow, that's a lotta bugs."

When Hannah came downstairs to resume her kitchen tasks, Martin took note of her freshly scrubbed face and suspiciously red eyes. She placed the yeast rolls on a wicker tray lined with a tea towel.

"We need another place setting." She yanked open a drawer.

"Feeling better?"

She shook her head. Her ragged breathing told him she was about to break down again.

"I've had an idea," he said, in an effort to distract her. "I'd like to create a meal for your family. When I was in Italy, a cook from Chioggia taught me to make *bigoli in cassopipa,* a traditional pasta dish of the Veneto. All the seafood ingredients can be sourced easily round here—clams and mussels and squid. I sauté them in olive oil with garlic and leeks and carrots and celery. Add some herbs and spices. Then they simmer in a bath of white wine and tomatoes."

"Ambitious."

"I wouldn't expect to find *bigoli* pasta round here. But I could substitute with *parpadelle* or *tagliatelle.* I'll need you to be my sous-chef."

"All right." She removed pieces of cutlery from the drawer.

Using tongs, Chase pulled each red and steaming crustacean from the enormous pot and set them on a plate to be taken to the table. Each member of the party tied on a plastic bib and embarked upon the messy business of cracking claws and tails, extracting the meat and dipping it in lemony melted butter or aioli. As dusk fell, Neil lit the candles in lanterns hanging from the porch rafters. Gwen presented a blueberry pie decorated with a hissing sparkler. When the thunder of fireworks echoed from neighboring properties, the two shelties cowered under the table, and the border collie fled to a secluded region of the house.

Martin and his mother made themselves useful by carrying dishes and serving bowls to the kitchen. Hannah, her father, and her uncle inspected the ordnance that Arthur brought. They produced a brief pyrotechnic display on the strip of lawn between the flower beds.

"Say, Hannah-Banana, how about a game of checkers?" Chase asked.

"You're on."

Everyone gathered in the den, facing the television to watch or listen to the Boston Pops orchestra perform patriotic music. Neil and his father played cribbage. Gwen handed Isobel a book of paintings by members of the Wyeth family, Maine artists associated with the coast. Martin intended to read the shipwreck book but was attentive to the battle being waged over the checkerboard.

Arthur and Chase departed after the Boston Pops concert ended, the red truck following the white one down the sloping drive. Soon the others scattered to their separate rooms for the night.

In the morning, Martin, already showered and dressed, answered a soft rap on his bedroom door.

"The doctor rang," his mother announced, an anxious quiver in her voice. "He scheduled an appointment for early tomorrow."

"You let Gwen know. I'll tell Hannah."

"I feel bad about dragging you away. From here. From her."

Positive news would probably have been communicated with a telephone call. As he knew from prior experience, bad results were given in person.

Hannah was meandering through the rose beds, choosing which blooms to cut for an arrangement in her mother's favorite vase.

"I'll drive you back to Copley Place," she offered. "I need to head back to Boston anyway."

"You can't. Your uncle just came home. I'll hire a car." His forefinger traced her cheek. "I'm staying long enough for you to explain why you were upset last night. Was it because of Chase?"

"Seeing him again stirs up all the awfulness of ten years ago. I wanted desperately to be a character witness at his trial, to make sure that jury knew he's one of the kindest people in the whole world. But Mum and Dad wouldn't let me. Or take me to visit him after he went to prison. I was heartbroken—and furious. That's the reason I started college a year before I was meant to. As soon as I got away from Bear Knoll, I contacted Chase and said I wanted to see him. He said no, without explanation. I guess because he knew my parents didn't want me there. Then I did my study abroad in Bristol. After graduation, I chose a profession that keeps me moving all around the country."

"I wish you'd told me."

"I almost did. Before I left Stanwell. Only I . . . I just . . . couldn't. It was important to me, protecting Chase. And you."

He frowned. "That makes no sense."

"When I saw that gossipy *Posh* article about you, and all your former girlfriends, I was afraid our relationship would become public. The Sterling Scandal was inescapable, a prime example of how your country's press targets the privileged.

You want positive publicity for the Milver Vale. I'm related to a convicted felon. Just imagine the consequences for you if the tabloids found out. And revealed to the entire world that my uncle stabbed his ex-girlfriend's abusive husband in a bar fight. It would destroy Chase's ability to rebuild his life."

She hadn't fled Stanwell because of his financial status. Or to find her next job. Her deeper, unacknowledged reason for abandoning him couldn't be discounted, or easily resolved.

"Instead of trusting me with the truth, you ran away. You gave up on me. On us."

Hannah winced. "Let's not part in anger the way we did at Heathrow. That was a horrible way to say goodbye."

"Quite right. I can think of a better one." He infused his kiss with passion and promise. "This is definitely not goodbye."

Hannah and her mother were browsing in the bookshop when her cell display flashed Martin's number.

"Hannah, it's Isobel."

"Yes." She held her breath.

"My tests confirm that I've come out of remission."

"I'm so sorry. What happens next?"

"Martin booked our seats on a London flight for the day after tomorrow. From Heathrow we'll transfer to Stansted and fly to La Rochelle. He'll help me pack up my things for removal to Somerset. My treatments will take place in London, so I'll stay at the Latimer House flat for the duration. Please tell Gwen and Neil we enjoyed our time at Bear Knoll. Very much, indeed."

"They were happy to have you there. So was I."

"I'm putting Martin on."

She leaned against a bookcase, weak with sorrow.

"Hannah?" His voice was as vibrant as ever, filling her ear.

"Will she be all right?"

"The doctor says so. I'd hoped we might still be in the city when you return, but it isn't possible. I've been thinking of everything you said yesterday. And all that I wanted to and didn't. We'll be all right, too. You and me." In a hushed tone he added, "Promise you won't visit the Kozee Kabins with anybody else. Ever."

"You don't have to worry about that," she assured him.

Chapter 23

Hannah handed Chase a cedar shake from the stack and held up the can of nails. He'd spent the morning re-shingling the windward side of the weather-beaten fish house at Ballard's Landing and had recruited her as his helper.

When he pulled off his baseball cap to fan his face, she said, "You should take a break. It's lunchtime. I'll get the cooler."

They sat down at the edge of the dock with their egg salad sandwiches.

Picking up a discarded cigarette butt, Chase shredded the filter. "I wish Pop would stop smoking."

"I was afraid you might start up again when you were— during your time in Warren. Or Machiasport."

"And get lung cancer for a souvenir? No thanks."

"Was prison as awful as it looks in the movies?"

"Nah. A thousand time more boring. Most of the guys were doing time for stupid juvenile shit, drugs and burglary and check-kiting. Soon as they get out, they'll keep screwing up. I buddied up with the Passamaquoddy and Penobscot inmates. Like me, they kept their heads down and followed the rules. That's how I knew I could do work release at Indian Island Reservation. They said I'd fit right in with this dark skin and hair."

"The tribe could've adopted you. Like Natty in *The Deerslayer*. And *The Last of the Mohicans*."

"That don't happen in real life, Han. But my experiences in their community made me think I could mentor other parolees. 'Specially the ones who aren't lucky enough to have family support, like I do."

"Can you do it in Falmouth? Mum and Dad are hoping you'll stay. Grampa, too."

"That's the plan. Pop's worked a helluva long time without reliable help. I put in my application to the Department of Marine Resources to get my license for lobstering and crabbing. A lot's changed in the trade—it's not the same as it used to be—and won't get any better. I'll need another paying job."

"Doing what?" Hannah rubbed at a mosquito bite acquired when taking the dogs outside before bedtime.

"Anything I can on the water. I talked to a guy in Falmouth Foreside who's starting up whale watching tours and needs a pilot. He took me out on his catamaran—sweet and smooth, easier handling than *Jenny's Dream,* or any other fishing boat. And I already interviewed to be a janitor at Discount Depot. The manager knows me from high school, we played football together. He still calls me Shrimpy. I was littler than the rest, but couldn't nobody catch me. Didn't want to get near me, either. They said I smelled of fish."

"Bet they did, too. Or something worse. Cow manure stinks way more than lobsters and crabs."

"He said Buck had it coming. That pissed me off. What I did wasn't deliberate. I don't want no praise for it."

Her gaze darted to his hands. He favored the left one, which must have delivered the fatal stab.

"Nobody ever talked to me about what happened at the Anchor Bar. I read the part of the trial testimony that was printed in *The Portland Herald* and heard news radio reports. I bet a lot was left out. Can we talk about it?"

"I s'pose., if you really want to know everything. After all this time."

She nodded. "I need to."

"Okay." After a moment, he said, "The trouble started when Buck was yelling at his wife, calling her a dirty whore, and I told him to shut up. He pulled her out of her chair and dragged her over the bar. Asked if his kid was mine. She was close enough I could see a bruise on her cheek. All us guys knew he knocked her around, we'd heard him talking about it. Almost bragging." Chase's breath came in short bursts.

"Is that when you hit him with your beer mug?"

"I never did that. I poured beer on his head. I was half-drunk and wicked mad. He let go of Shannon and reached for my throat. I moved my hand along the bar, to grab a pitcher or something hard enough to knock some sense into him. Out the corner of my eye, I saw the knife by the lemons and limes. I figured waving it at Buck would make him back off. Instead, he lunged at me. That's how he got cut. Pierced artery."

"I guess if the ambulance had reached him sooner, he'd still be alive."

"You know what our crappy roads are like in winter. Potholes. Snowplows in the way." Chase tossed a scrap of bread to the seagull floating nearby. "According to the prosecution's medical expert, the paramedics couldn't have saved him."

When he stared down at the water beneath their dangling legs, Hannah saw several gray hairs mixed in with his dark curls. "Shannon should've gotten a restraining order."

"Things have been tough for her and her boy. My probation officer told me I could contact her, after he checked that she'd be okay about it. I can help out, after I start earning some dough."

"Do you still care about her?"

"Not like when we were young, before she started going with Buck. If she'd left that jerk when he started beating her up, gotten a divorce, who knows what might've happened?" His head shifted towards her. "I'm wondering what's going on between you and your duke of earl."

"He's a marquess. To describe our situation as complicated would be a massive understatement."

"I saw how he looked at you. And you at him. That don't seem complicated."

"Until you arrived at Bear Knoll on the Fourth, he didn't know anything about you. Or where you've been. I never told him. I was so afraid the press would find out and hassle him. And you, which would mess up your future. When he asked me to stay in England, I decided I'd better come back to Boston."

His eyes bored into her. "Did Martin and his mom leave all of sudden like that because of me?"

"No! Isobel had an appointment with her Boston doctor."

Chase climbed to his feet. "I don't see a problem."

"You can bet there will be a big one if tabloid newspapers and gossip websites and scandal-obsessed television programs find out about Lord Milverston being involved with an ex-con's niece. I won't let that happen."

"Sounds kinda self-serving. Like maybe you just don't want to be embarrassed about my going berserk in the Anchor Bar."

Affronted by the accusation, she shoved his shoulder. "Wrong."

"Who cares what a bunch of stuffy Brits think?"

"I do. Martin's working hard to increase tourism in his part of Somerset, and I want him to succeed. If a sensationalized version of your story got traction here in the States, it would be hard on Dad and Grampa. Mum's career nose-dived after you—" She couldn't say it.

"You gotta stop treating me like I'm your own personal Boo Radley."

"What do you mean?"

"I don't need you protecting me. I've had counseling—the psychology kind and the employment kind. My head's on straight. Straighter than it used to be. I'm tough, I'll deal with whatever comes my way. And I know damn well you can, too. So what if you're related to an ex-con? Why would anybody judge you or your mom and dad for a felony I committed? Stop being a weenie, worrying that stupid media fuckers might say or write bad stuff about us."

"Don't call me a weenie—Shrimpy! I'll do whatever I think is best for everyone. Including Martin."

"Okay. Just remember, you can't blame me for wrecking your love life. Or causing the weird vibe I get whenever you're with your parents. Yeah, I've noticed. What's that all about?"

"A longstanding grievance."

"Well, that sure clears it up. C'mon, tell me. Maybe I can help."

"It's more than ten years too late for that."

"Oh, yeah? I spilled my guts. Your turn."

"They didn't let me testify in front of the jury. Or before the judge handed down your sentence. I wanted to be a character witness."

His eyes narrowed. "Not them. I'm the one who didn't want you in court. No way was I involving you in that trial. My lawyer—the public defender—wanted you on the stand. But without my okay, it wasn't going to happen. You were a teenager. And you couldn't have said anything that would've done me a damn bit of good."

His admission, a convincing contradiction of her assumptions, stunned her into silence. She couldn't shift all her pent-up resentment from her parents to Chase. Her determination to spare him from public exposure and media intrusion had been so strong that she'd turned away from the man she loved. Battling her shock, confusion, hurt, remorse, and regret, she realized she couldn't justifiably criticize her uncle's effort to protect her. Not when she'd done the very same thing on his behalf.

"I can't understand why Mum and Dad didn't tell me it was your decision. They should have."

"Don't be mad about that, either. Water under the bridge, Han. Get back to work. Break's over."

With that, he disposed of an entire decade of hardship and turmoil and misunderstanding as easily as he discarded cracked and broken shingles.

"It's Grampa's night at the Legion Hall, hanging out with his buddies," she told him when they stopped work for the day. "Come to our house for supper. Shepherd's pie."

"Can't say no to that. See you later, Hannah-Banana."

Dad stood at the stove, browning minced lamb, and Mum used her mixer to whip the potatoes. On the counter stood a bottle of champagne, beaded with water drops, and three crystal flutes.

"We waited to start the celebration," her mother said, "until you got back."

She dropped her bag onto an antique thumb-back chair. "This isn't an anniversary or a birthday. What are you celebrating?"

"Good news. The best we've had in ages."

Not a drop of bubbly had been consumed, yet her parents were giddy.

Dad pulled the cork and poured sparkling, foaming liquid into each glass. "To Wendy Edney!"

"To Mum!"

"To me! To the multi-book contract! To my television series!"

"Wait, back up. You're going on television again?"

"*Wendy Edney's Great British Gardens*. A US-UK production by Acorn Films, for streaming on ServeFlix. Six one-hour segments, two or three gardens per hour. Not a travelogue," Mum said excitedly. "Each episode will include the history and development and contents and maintenance of each garden. I'll interview the designers and groundskeepers as well as property owners. Shooting starts in spring and summer. The scripts will be used to create the tie-in book, which will be illustrated with photographs."

"That's fantastic."

"*Wendy Edney's Great Irish Gardens* will follow, and its book. If all goes well, there's a chance of doing a European series. After that, the Caribbean."

"Jeezum crow! Say, Dad," she said, looking up at him, "you'll be spending a lot of time all alone."

"I'll survive. Just like I did all the other times."

Mum looked up at him. "I'm counting on you to take that long overdue vacation. When I'm not filming, we'll visit my mother and George and Barbara in Wales. And it's been yonks since we've spent time with my brother James, and Lisa. Their Will was a schoolboy when I last saw him."

"I'm trying to bring another vet into the practice. Plenty of time to get it done before I have to make travel plans. Did you invite Chase for supper, Punkin?"

"He said he's coming."

"Better polish off the bubbly before he gets here. His probation officer advised him not to drink any alcohol."

Dad's lamb went into the pie crock with steamed carrots and mushrooms. Mum piled the mashed potatoes on top and made artistic swirls with her spatula.

They used up the champagne in additional toasts—

to Liz, and the literary agent, the television networks, the streaming service.

Hannah had enough religious faith to believe that God had pressed a celestial re-set button. Mum was ecstatic about her high-profile television series and book deal. Chase was helping Grampa and was evidently about to become gainfully employed. Dad planned to expand his veterinary practice. She was settled in at Bear Knoll, temporarily but no longer uncomfortably in the aftermath of her uncle's revelations.

The night brought a shift in the weather, the start of a protracted heatwave predicted by the forecasters. A few minutes in the blazing afternoon sun prompted Hannah to bathe the dogs and cool them down. Her first victim was the reluctant Sadie, and nervous Sasha was the second one to endure a soaking. While the two Shelties raced around the yard, shaking off the excess water, Hannah whistled for the water-loving border collie. Bess trotted over and leaped into the galvanized metal tub.

"Such a *good* girl," Hannah said, reaching for the dog shampoo.

Her mother, who was holed up in the den with the window air conditioner going full blast, came outside.

Reaching for the hose, Hannah said, "I should've started by brushing the girls. They're shedding fur like crazy."

Mum sat down on the picnic table bench. "For a long time, your father and I have been worried about you, sweetie. We try not to pry into your personal life. But we've wondered what happened to you and Joel, and if work stress and all the travel might be responsible."

"Partly." Mostly it had been Joel's attitude towards Chase that caused the rift. But her habit of withholding information about her relationships kept her from saying anything more.

"Well, I hope you won't let your career affect whatever

the situation is with you and Martin. We like him very much indeed. It was hard, but I refrained from asking Isobel questions that I daresay she could've answered. How the two of you met. Whether you both are as serious about each other as it seemed when he was here."

Soaping the collie's fur, Hannah laughed. "This is your way of not prying?"

"It's my way of saying I'm glad if you're happier. Whatever the reason."

"My romantic life is too complex for unadulterated joy," she admitted. "But now Martin knows where I come from. He doesn't mind about my uncle doing time for manslaughter. And I'm really glad Chase is home. I've been able to talk things out with him. That helped. A lot."

"Last night, you told us you'll soon be returning to Cambridge. Before you go, I need to share an idea of mine. I haven't mentioned it to anyone else yet."

"I'm all ears." She wiped her wet hands on her shorts.

Mum's tone was reflective when she said, "You might not know, but my happiest time, professionally, was making that initial program for public television—my American debut. You and I drove all around New England with Liz and her crew. Remember?"

"Sure. It was fun for me, too."

"I was so proud of my teenager—mature, creative, responsible. At twenty-seven, you have production credits somebody twice your age would envy. It might not be fair to tell you this, but I'll regret it if I don't. I want us to work together again. On my series."

Hannah's sponge fell into the tub. "In England?"

"Ireland, too. And Europe, if it's renewed. There's no other person as familiar with my style of presenting or more capable of finding the right locations and taking care of logistics. I could also use your help writing scripts for the segments."

Thinking hard, Hannah pointed the hose at Bess and rinsed off the last suds.

"If you're interested, my agent can negotiate the details with Liz and her people. She'll have to decide whether to add you to the Acorn Films payroll, or arrange to put you under contract with the British production studio."

"I'm definitely interested." She would seize any opportunity that placed her in England.

"I'm so glad. And I'm not pressing you to decide about this next bit. But if you moved back here, we could start planning the first series."

Reaching for the towel, she contemplated the invitation. Before yesterday's conversation with Chase, accepting it would have been impossible, unthinkable. But now that she was aware of having misjudged her parents, she wanted to seal the cracks in her relationship with them.

Liz would soon jet over to England. Eve and Mim were about to take their summer vacations. Without work, and no friends to hang with, Hannah saw no reason to keep her Cambridge apartment, letting monthly rent eat up what was left of her savings. Transporting her small collection of belongings to Bear Knoll could be accomplished with two trips in the Subaru. Erica would have no difficulty finding another tenant. In a matter of weeks, students would descend on Harvard and MIT, seeking accommodations.

She shoved her hair out of her face. "Will you let me have a pony?"

"The usual rules still apply. You can keep any animal you like, so long as you take care of it yourself."

"Mum, I was kidding! I can ride Rascal."

"Anytime you want. Except today. It's far too hot for him."

"And the rest of us." She adjusted the nozzle of the hose, changing the stream of water to a spray and playfully turned it towards her parent.

By suppertime, Hannah's move to Maine had morphed from intriguing possibility to firm decision.

Late that night, after drawing up a detailed to-do list, she composed a lengthy explanatory email for Martin. She inquired about Isobel. She asked whether Poppy still favored The Huntsman's Horn over The Peacock, but without referencing Jack Elliston. She hoped Jewel was excelling in agility and that Ariel hadn't done anything lately to annoy Andy Riddell's lurcher-loathing dad. She didn't mention *Forsaken Fortune*. Not because her exclusion from the production was a source of pain, but because it no longer mattered.

Hannah scheduled a farewell get-together with the Palindrome Posse at her favorite North End Italian restaurant. They started with a pitcher of chianti, indulged in dishes of handmade pasta, and after demolishing their servings of tiramisu they finished with amaretto. Throughout the meal they flirted shamelessly with the waiters.

The next morning Hannah woke feeling sluggish and headachy. She was debating with herself about whether a run would have a beneficial or detrimental effect when Liz called.

"Can you come to the office? Right now?"

"I guess." She wouldn't mind postponing the rest of her packing. And the only other item on her schedule was scrubbing the bathroom fixtures into a shining state that would delight the apartment's next occupant, who had already put down a security deposit.

The Red Line train carried her over the Longfellow Bridge to the stop at Charles Street. The air was thick and muggy, and low-hanging clouds hinted at thunderstorms to come late in the day. Thankful for the climate-control system in the building that housed Acorn Films, she climbed the glass-walled stairs to the executive suite.

"Hi, Pam," she greeted the receptionist. "Liz is expecting me."

"I'll tell her you're here. Can I get you something to drink?"

"Just water, thanks."

Pam left her post.

A Fed-Ex package sat on the desk, awaiting pick-up. It was addressed to Alistair McLaren, Hartcliffe Film Studios, Bristol. Hannah leaned down and stuck out her tongue. Then she wandered to the case where awards were displayed. Framed certificates were arranged along the walls, papered with grass-cloth.

Pam returned with a full glass. "She says you can go in."

Liz stood in the doorway of her inner sanctum.

"How was your Vineyard holiday?" Hannah asked.

"The weather couldn't have been better."

"Ditto for Maine. We had company. Lord Milverston and his mother."

Liz's mouth curled in a smirk. "Poppy Deane told me. She assumed I knew all about it. I gather your secret romance with his lordship started while you were staying at Stanwell House. I'm crushed that you never said anything about it to me."

"When I came back from England, Martin and I were on hiatus." She crossed over to the plush sofa and sat down. "Honestly, Liz, what happened between us had nothing to do with Mr. Darcy and Pemberley fantasies. I thought I was getting involved with a charming guy who has a title and an enormous country house. But he's also one of the richest men in the realm."

"As problems go, that's not a bad one."

"For me, it is. He's too high-profile for a privacy nut. The internet is a petri dish of gossip. The tabloids are rapacious. Reputations are destroyed in a split second, regardless of facts or truth. I was concerned about Chase being victimized by the media. With Mum doing more television, it could definitely happen."

"I can name any number of celebrities with a felon in the family. Not a few have their own criminal background." Liz shoved an envelope across her desktop. "Open it."

Hannah extracted a document printed with her name and an airline code and a departure date. It was an itinerary for travel to Heathrow Airport. One way. "What have you done?"

"I can't spend months in England without an assistant. You're it."

"From location manager to PA? Major demotion."

"The perks are considerably better, I promise. A healthy compensation package. Medical insurance. Expense account. A car. Staying at the manor house hotel instead of slumming it with the crew. You'll be my plus-one for all the fancy parties Tom won't give a shit about."

"Will I have to babysit?"

"Smart ass, you know we're taking the nanny." Liz's beautiful, fine-boned face conveyed dismay. "I thought you'd jump at the offer."

"It's tempting." Then, remembering why she'd spent the first part of the day boxing up her belongings, she said, "But I already promised Mum I'd work with her on *Wendy Edney's Great British Gardens.*"

"That's my production. There's no conflict. You'll be in exactly the right place to begin preliminary groundwork and research. Let's brainstorm about a more impressive title than PA. I want your name in the closing credits."

"Deal. Where do I sign?"

Liz extended her arm. "Handshake will do for now. Gentlewoman's agreement till I have a chance to work things out with the Contracts Department. My travel maven will email the link for your e-ticket. You're on the flight with Tom and Lexi and me. And Telma."

Hannah glanced again at the date on her itinerary. "Better start moving my stuff to Falmouth. Today."

She'd departed Bear Knoll as a creative partner on Wendy Edney's next television series. Now she was an Academy-award winning producer's new employee. Fingering the envelope Liz had given her, she told herself that it wasn't an instant cure for unresolved conflict and potential controversy. But she wouldn't let that consideration impair her present state of euphoria.

Chapter 24

A Mercedes-Benz stretch limousine delivered the Gregorio-Picton-Ballard party to the Ritz Hotel's entrance. The doorman ushered the passengers from the dark street to the lobby, where bellhops took charge of the hard-sided suitcases and Liz's array of Louis Vuitton luggage—carry-all, garment bag, and toiletry case.

Tom set Lexi's car seat on the grandiose carpet and unfastened the straps so he could pick her up. Hannah claimed her new wheeled case, larger than the one that had accompanied her on her trip in the spring.

"Tomorrow," Liz said, "I'm buying an English pram. So Lexi can travel to the park in style."

The infant, cradled in Telma's arms, let out a wail. The Portuguese woman crooned soothingly and shielded the sensitive eyes from the brightness and glitter of the chandelier.

"I'll take her." Liz said exchanging her designer handbag for her daughter. "Hannah, go ahead and check in. Sleep as late as you want, and enjoy your free morning."

She stepped aside to make way for a group of men and women in formal dress and was reminded of the springtime night when she and Martin had attended a dinner in these same opulent surroundings. She concluded that a similar event was taking place this evening.

Her room was located on the hotel's Arlington Street side. Pulling aside the pale blue curtain, she looked over the rooftops and wondered which belonged to Latimer House. If Martin was there, only a few blocks of Mayfair separated them.

She relied on ibuprofen and a hot shower to combat the headache brought on by her day-long transatlantic flight. If she could fall asleep right away, she could more easily re-set her body clock to British time. But her restless brain refused to cooperate. She checked her phone again and found a message from Liz, enthusing about her deluxe suite's lavishness and reminding her of their scheduled conclave tomorrow with the director and associate producer. Reaching for the television remote, Hannah searched for a program dull enough to lull her into unconsciousness. A foreign language channel did the trick.

At an advanced hour of the morning, Hannah left the hotel and was swept up in the steady stream of foot traffic in Piccadilly. Mayfair teemed with summer tourists and traffic, and the noise and fumes from the cars, cabs, and buses assaulted her senses. She turned the corner of St. James's Street, seeking a quieter, less crowded route to Latimer Row.

Pausing at the curved window of Wincott & Sons, she admired the display of cheeses. Staff members were waiting on customers, but she didn't spot Martin. Moving on to the florist's shop, she purchased a bouquet of pale roses and green berries bound with strands of ivy, then made her way to Latimer House.

The porter—she struggled to recall his name, something Irish—buzzed her into the lobby.

"Nice to see you again," he said.

Lorcan. That was it. "Didn't you used to be on the evening shift?"

"My fiancée pressed me to take on daytime hours, when the last chap retired. Says it'll keep me out of the betting shop. And with my nights free, I can take her out more often."

"These are for Lady Richard Latimer. Can you make sure they're delivered?"

"She might be home to visitors. I can ring the penthouse and find out."

After a brief hesitation, Hannah agreed.

During the call, he nodded at her, and when he put down his phone he said, "Fourth floor. Lift's round the corner."

She remembered.

"Welcome back," Isobel greeted her. "Oh, how lovely."

"Coals to Newcastle," she murmured. The round table in the foyer was covered with arrangements.

"Yours are by far the nicest. Excuse me a moment, and I'll put them in a vase. Would you care for tea, some biscuits?"

"Thanks, but I had a late breakfast."

"An ample one, I should think, at the Ritz."

"Liz Gregorio travels in style. So does her entourage. Mum insists that we have afternoon tea in the Palm Court, and she's sure to ask if we did. Won't you join us?"

"I wish I might, but I don't go anywhere except to medical appointments. My treatments were delayed until we were certain I hadn't caught anything flying back from Boston or La Rochelle. I go into hospital day after tomorrow for my initial infusion of cladribine. The rest will be done right here, by a nurse."

"Martin says it's the same chemotherapy drug you had before."

"Most fortunately, I tolerated it without any terribly troublesome side effects. I'll be immune-suppressed afterwards. I'm hopeful I'll soon have sufficient energy to move to Somerset. I won't be at the big house, because of all the filming activity, and people in and out. Martin's letting me have a vacant house in Milverston Magna. A bungalow, really. No stairs."

"Holly Cottage?"

"That's the one. Freshly painted, with fitted carpet installed in the three bedrooms. Martin ordered a new cooker for the kitchen and is replacing the white goods in the utility room. There's a patch of front garden and a larger one behind. Kateryna Bereza might live there with me, although her host family is quite fond of her. Come and see the picture I'm determined to finish before going into hospital."

Isobel had set up her easel in her son's south-facing, sunlit sitting room. Her current watercolor depicted a colorful garden of pink roses and mixed perennials—magenta cranesbill, purple irises, deep blue delphiniums, and green-leafed hosta plants.

"That's the long border at Bear Knoll."

"A gift for your parents."

"They'll be thrilled. I'm thrilled for them."

"Gwen sent a lovely, long email, full of news about her upcoming projects. She mentioned coming over later this year, for a recce."

"She's eager to see the Stanwell House gardens."

"I expect Martin will try and persuade her to include them in her television series."

Hannah laughed. "He'll probably succeed."

"I've just remembered something. I'll be right back." She returned with a shoe box and a dress encased in protective dry cleaner's plastic. "I imagine you'll be needing these."

"Did Martin explain why they're here?"

"Yes. And I told him that the day after the countryside association annual dinner, Alicia rang me to inquire about a little American my son was squiring around town."

"It wasn't a date," Hannah said.

"You're aware, I'm sure, that my son is a very transparent individual. There's never any mystery about what he may be thinking or feeling. At Stanwell I saw quite clearly that his interest in you wasn't merely casual. During our time at Bear Knoll, the situation became considerably clearer."

After carrying her belongings to the hotel, she went shopping in the arcades and fashionable boutiques, looking but not buying until flagging energy sent her back to her room for a cup of tea. Examining the items hanging in her closet, she selected a plum-colored trouser suit.

"You look fab," Liz said when they met down in the lobby. Her hair was arranged in an upswept hairstyle that accentuated her thoroughly classical profile. The woman who determined which movie stars would appear in her films could easily pass for one herself.

"So do you."

Throughout their taxi journey to the Savoy, Hannah experienced a strong sense of déjà vu. Immediately after her cheese shop meeting with the man she didn't know was a marquess, she'd followed this same route to the Savoy Hotel. Since then, she'd fallen in love, reunited with Chase, and reconciled with her parents. Her smart leather satchel, a gift from Liz, contained items connected to her new responsibilities: a state-of-the art electronic notepad loaded with documents and schedules and checklists and personnel contact details.

"It doesn't seem right," she commented, "going to the place where Owen prefers to hold court. He and Nigel should've met us at the Ritz."

"Not show-biz enough, I guess."

"Are they aware they're about to see me again?"

"Of course. You're executive assistant to the executive producer."

"A title not officially sanctioned by the Producers' Guild."

"Doesn't matter," Liz stated emphatically.

"A film set is a hierarchy. People want to know who fits where. Who do you suck up to? Who do you treat like shit?"

"Nobody's treating my executive assistant like shit. That's for shit sure."

They passed through the hotel portals and entered the American Bar. The gentlemen wore the requisite jackets and ties.

Sir Owen kissed Liz on both cheeks. "Hannah Ballard. Such a pleasure."

Was it really? Not if he also recalled that strained meeting at Hartcliffe Studios, when he told her she'd been replaced by Alistair McLaren. She took vengeful delight in the knowledge that her successor wasn't important enough to be included in this high-level meeting. While she hob-nobbed with a knight of the realm, that creep was stuck at Hartcliffe, figuring out which sites were suitable for setting up craft services and the honeywagons.

When everyone was seated, the director told Liz, "We look forward to meeting Tom."

"You soon will. Tonight he's spending quality time with his daughter. Meaning she sleeps while he devours one of the scholarly history books he picked up at Hatchards. We'll arrange for social time when we're in Somerset." Looking at Nigel, she added, "I haven't seen your husband since Cannes. When was that—two festivals ago?"

Her co-producer nodded. "Remind me, Hannah, are you married?'

Avoiding Liz's close-mouthed smirk, she replied that she was not.

"She does have a significant other, an Englishman who swept her off her feet when she was over here scouting. I'm lucky she was still available to work with me on this shoot. And as showrunner for Wendy Edney's next garden-ing program."

"Isn't she your mother?" Nigel asked.

"Yes," Hannah said. "She and Liz gave me my start in show business."

"Acorn is producing her new series for ServeFlix," Liz continued. "Six episodes will film in Britain, six more in Ireland. After that—the world!"

When Liz alluded to Martin, Hannah had been tempted to kick her under the table. Now she wanted to give her a hug for championing her in the presence of people who had discounted her expertise.

Liz asked about the progress of rehearsals and sought assurances that casting of minor roles was completed. From there, the discussion turned to the shooting script, and other critical matters. Hannah typed brief notes and reminders into her tablet and occasionally posed a clarifying question. The director ordered a second round of drinks. Her energy ebbed from the combination of sparkling wine and jetlag. The nursing mother, who limited herself to still water, must be thinking it was nearly time for Lexi's next feeding.

Sir Owen downed the last of his gin and tonic. "Apologies for dashing off," he said. "I'm dining at the Garrick Club with friends. My PA will ring Hannah to schedule a meeting at my Soho office so both of you can meet our department heads. Some are in town. The rest will participate remotely from Hartcliffe or their home offices."

The Ritz doorman welcomed them with a smile, a bow, and a cheery greeting. They responded in kind.

Before speeding to the lift, Liz said, "Let's do the afternoon tea tomorrow. Can you arrange it with the concierge?"

When he asked the number in their party, Hannah discovered her sense of recall was significantly impaired by a recent transatlantic flight and multiple glasses of wine. "Two. I think." She doubted Tom Picton would join them, but to be on the safe side, she added, "Perhaps one more. For the three-thirty seating."

"Very good. Lord Milverston asked us to convey a message. He wishes you to know he's in the Rivoli Bar."

Martin, uncharacteristically dressed in coat and tie, sat beneath a shiny bas-relief panel of Leda and the Swan.

"This is an ambush," she said. "Why didn't you text and let me know you'd be here?"

"I wanted it to be a surprise. Gosh, you look smashing. Nothing at all like the damp person I watched banding lobster claws on the deck of *Jenny's Dream.*"

That made her smile. "We lead double lives. In your spare time, you work in a cheese shop."

"Not today. Back to back to back meetings. Mother was delighted by your visit, and the flowers. She sent me over to offer myself as her substitute for the Palm Court tearoom."

"Three-thirty tomorrow. Liz will be thrilled. Champagne cocktail, please," she told the white-coated waiter who had glided to their table.

Frowning into his whisky glass, Martin said, "I know I ought to be grateful to her for making you her executive assistant, and bringing you back to me. And I am. But I hoped to present you with an alternative."

"You already did. Tourism promotions manager."

"That was before I decided on something better. I wanted to hire you as my personal location manager. Monitoring all that goes on during the filming. Serving my interests as property owner and landlord. You've already built relationships with the crew. And you know the territory. My territory."

She looked towards the bar, watching the wizard mixologist create her drink. In no time it arrived in a tall glass with a curlicue of orange peel trailing down the side. Fidgeting with the scalloped edge of the gold-embossed cocktail mat, she said, "Every conversation brings me another job offer. From Mum. Then Liz. Now you."

"Would you have accepted, if I'd got mine in first?"

"No."

"Why not?"

"The usual reasons. Uncle Chase. Keeping my name out of the press. Unwillingness to essentially become a kept woman." To prevent him from pursuing the subject, she asked, "How's Poppy?"

"Busy as ever. Soon to be even busier. Jack Elliston asked her to give his daughter Chloe riding lessons during the half of August holidays that she spends with him."

Hannah wondered if he knew of Poppy's interest in The Peacock's owner. "I'm sure she agreed."

In a determined tone, he said, "I ambushed you, as you put it, so we could continue the conversation that began as I was leaving Bear Knoll. Now that I'm fully aware of all your concerns, I understand them. To an extent, I share them. I'd prefer to maintain a low profile while at the same time turning the spotlight on Stanwell House and the villages. I believed the press no longer regarded me as an object of interest. Unfortunately, that magazine article proved I was mistaken. But there's a simple way to ensure that nobody will find out that we're a couple. I've got a cunning plan."

"What is it?"

"A cover up."

"Way too late for that. Half the population of Milver Vale saw us together. Villagers. Your household staff."

"They won't, not any longer."

"Various media outlets will arrange access to our cast members, for interviews. Reporters and photographers will sometimes be on the set."

"We can be careful. The filming lasts only a couple of months, right? Where will you be staying?"

"Newbridge. The country manor hotel. Where you can't visit me. Or stay overnight."

"Afraid the boss will find out?"

"She and Tom have a rental house. Anyway, she knows about us. Too much," Hannah acknowledged.

"Tomorrow, at tea, we're telling her that you won't be available except during working hours. When not on the job, you'll be with me. We can search for the nearest equivalent of your Kozee Kabins."

"On location, free time is practically nonexistent," she countered. "Liz brought her husband and her baby. She'll be pulled in more directions than on any other production. Her executive assistant gets pulled with her."

He gestured to the waiter, indicating his desire for the bill. "I've already got Poppy onside. I'm sure Mother will support the conspiracy."

"She says you've done up Holly Cottage."

"It's similar in size to her La Rochelle house, and the furniture and other things we brought over from there are already in place. She can draw and paint in the front room, which has an enormous south-facing window. I must say, it's a most convenient place for an assignation."

"Did you pick up that word from *Forsaken Fortune?*"

"My vocabulary isn't as limited as you think. Not that I've ever used the term in conversation."

Hannah reached for the leather wallet containing the bar tab. "Till now, I never had a chance to treat a zillionaire." She scribbled her room number on the check and signed her name.

"And I've never spent a night at the Ritz."

"It won't be this one." Her mouth and jaw stretched as she struggled to hold back a yawn.

"You're knackered, I know. What if I just tuck you into bed and leave you there? To dream of future assignations."

"I'm too tired to argue."

They left the Art Deco bar for the rose and cream splendor of the Long Gallery. In her near stupor, she couldn't locate the guest lift. Realizing they were approaching the restaurant, she paused to get her bearings. Martin's hand closed on hers.

He drew her behind a pedestal topped by a giant floral arrangement and pulled her into an embrace. The whisky-flavored mouth teased and tasted hers, and she melded her body to his.

"Martin?"

Two young women on their way from the dining room had stopped nearby. Hannah recognized Martin's dark-haired former girlfriend from the magazine article. The same issue contained a multi-page photo feature on her lavish wedding to an Italian duke. On that occasion, she'd worn a Venetian lace gown and a pearl coronet. Tonight her dress was red, short, and tight, and all of her jewelry was gold—necklace, earrings, and cuff bracelets.

"Hello, Natalie."

"You didn't used to bring dates to the Ritz. For me, it was either a naff club or your silly old boat." She gestured to her blonde companion. "Adriana, my sister-in-law."

"We've met. At your wedding," he said pointedly.

This is bizarre, Hannah thought. She's had more of his kisses than I have.

Natalie's eyes fell on Hannah. "Hang on to him as long as you can. He's got a habit of violating his exes' privacy."

"I had nothing to do with that magazine piece, Nat," he responded. "Ask your brother how *Posh* got the picture of us on St. Barth's."

Hannah wondered whether this bickering was habitual.

Natalie patted Martin's cheek. "Good to know you've come out of hiding. I miss seeing you. *Ciao*." She hooked her arm through Adriana's, chattering to her in Italian as they continued along the gallery.

"That was fun," Hannah commented.

"Wasn't it? Quite the charmer, Natalie."

"Poppy called her a nightmare."

"I'm not disputing the description. Fortunately, I woke up several months before meeting my dream girl."

"I can't say I'm impressed by your method of keeping a low profile."

His arms fell to his sides. "It was a kiss, Hannah."

"In a public place."

Turning a corner, she wandered aimlessly, her confusion mounting. Opening a glossy wooden door, she found herself surrounded by the porphyry columns of a staircase hall. She'd been here before, months ago. With Martin.

He wasn't here now.

The eighteenth-century courtiers depicted in the colorful mural decorating the wall and upper landing could have stepped from the pages of *Forsaken Fortune*. The fashionable ladies in lace and flounces leaned over the painted balustrade and seemed to regard her critically—disdainfully. No doubt about it, any one of them would have invited a handsome and wealthy marquess to her bedchamber.

/ Chapter 25

Not since childhood had Martin experienced the ritualistic and impeccably served afternoon tea at the Ritz. Alicia, determined to do her grandmotherly duty, had introduced him at an early age to the grandeur and gentility of the Palm Court.

"Mother bribed me into submission by promising a visit to Hamleys toy shop. Greedy as I was for all this," he said, gesturing to the three-tiered serving piece filled with petite cakes, macarons, scones, and crustless sandwiches, "I was desperate to escape."

"And now?" Liz Gregorio asked.

"There's no place I'd rather be. Unless my grandmother should appear. She's no less intimidating now than during my childhood."

"I had a granny like that," said Liz. "Crucifixes and pictures of the Pope and the Blessed Virgin Mary all over her house. She scared me to death when I was little. When I was older, I could tell that deep down, she was a softie."

"If Alicia has a soft spot, I've yet to detect it."

Hannah sat across from him, her pretty face tense. Was she constrained by the presence of her boss or cold-shouldering him because he'd gone off in a huff last night? He'd meant no harm by sneaking a kiss. To Hannah, it was proof that he was a careless and overly demonstrative lunatic. And Natalie's unwelcome and inconvenient presence had made the situation worse.

"How was your production meeting?" He directed his question at Hannah.

Liz answered him. "Longer than it needed to be. We were with the director and co-producer and staff at an office in Soho. Most of the department heads joined in from Hartcliffe Studios. Hannah was reunited—virtually—with Alistair McLaren, her favorite Scotsman. He blew her a kiss and called her a bonny lass."

She nodded. "You'd have thought I was his long-lost—something."

"It was sexist," Liz said.

"Embarrassing. And demeaning."

Liz went on, "Then Hannah and I had a session with a group of finance people. I came back here to feed the baby and discovered Tom and Telma were packing up for the move to Somerset."

"Where in Newbridge is your rental house?"

"Carleton Close. Contemporary, five bedrooms, fully furnished, with an enclosed garden. And a granny flat for the nanny."

"After you're settled, I'll have you over to Stanwell for drinks and dinner."

"Martin's buttering you up," Hannah interjected. "It's his ambition to be cast as a village idiot."

Liz's black eyebrows slanted downward as she studied him. "Really?"

"Not seriously. I've been teasing Hannah about it ever since I've known her. You've already got one member of my family in your epic."

"Oh, right—Caroline Bryden. How exactly are you related to her?"

"We share a set of great-great grandparents," he clarified. "I believe that makes us third cousins."

He was impressed by the Oscar-winning producer. He thought her extremely brave, embarking on motherhood while burdened with ultimate responsibility for the major motion picture version of an adored bestselling novel. During his long separation from Hannah, he had viewed all the available Acorn Films television programs and movies. Judging by what he'd seen, *Forsaken Fortune* was certain to succeed.

He prided himself on his impeccable behavior at the tea table. Even Alicia, insistent on proper etiquette, would be pleased. He hoped Hannah noticed—and approved. Nobody in the Palm Court could possibly guess that they had ever shared a bed.

Hannah guided the hire car through the roundabout until she came to the road connecting Newbridge to Milverston Magna. The wipers whipped back and forth, clearing cascading raindrops from the windshield. Liz, seated on her left, paged through a binder of multi-colored papers.

"I can't find today's scene. Where's the revision?"

"Pink pages. 28A. Interior. Harvest supper."

"Got it! And the call sheet."

After they passed through Milver Cross, traffic thinned. The vivid yellow rapeseed flowers that brightened the fields in May and June had vanished. The sides and tops of the hedges had recently been shaved. Hannah missed the bright white clouds of hawthorn blossom and nodding daisies that had rendered this drive so magical earlier in the year.

Beyond the crossroads, signs warned that entry was

restricted to Hartcliffe Studios personnel. Liz presented their photo identity badges to the security officer—everyone, even the executive producer, had to follow the stringent security protocol.

Driving on, Hannah entered the familiar universe-within-a-universe, where creativity, artistry, and heavy equipment collided. People in wet weather gear tramped about—cable pullers, set dressers, gaffers. Rows of vans and trucks covered the sodden ground. She spotted the larger trailers of the leading performers and the smaller one where medical staff administered Covid rapid tests and distributed face masks to those who wanted them.

"A ten-hour day," Liz commented as Hannah searched for a parking spot. "I'm good for about half that. How about you?"

Hannah stifled a yawn. "Whatever you say."

"Here's your other boyfriend. Holding what looks like the world's biggest umbrella."

For the past two weeks, Alistair McLaren had brought her cups of coffee, engaged her in conversation, and shared the on-set gossip and jokes. His attentiveness provoked no end of commentary from Liz.

"Does his lordship know our location manager has a crush on you? Not that he has any cause for concern. Your room at the Ritz should've been designated the Honeymoon Suite. Every time I passed by, the fancy Do Not Disturb was hanging on your doorknob."

Hannah didn't respond.

"Martin must wish you were staying at Stanwell House."

He definitely did. "I've told him that's impossible. And unprofessional."

"How's his mother?" Liz asked, as the rain pounded the car roof.

"I haven't seen her yet, but we've spoken on the phone.

She's not quite strong enough to resume painting sessions or gardening. I'll visit her sometime this week."

Alistair opened Liz's door. "Loove-ly weather we're having today, ladies. What's your pleasure? Craft service breakfast, or shall I escort you to the set?"

"We've eaten. Coming, Hannah?"

"Step under the brolly," he said. "Plenty of room."

"My raincoat has a hood. I'll follow in a minute."

Hannah checked messages. Nothing from Martin.

The scene being filmed inside the tithe barn was the most complex to date. Participants included many members of the cast, multiple musicians, and dozens of extras who would be dining and dancing. The cavernous space contained mismatched trestle tables. Set decorators arranged pitchers and tankards and pewter dishes. A food historian was inspecting items on the serving platters for accuracy. Electrical technicians—the sparks—positioned the light stands.

Sir Owen Parry conferred with the director of photography, waving like an orchestra conductor to illustrate a point. Production assistants chattered into their headset mics.

Caroline Bryden looked remarkably alert and cheerful, despite her early morning call for corseting, dressing, and make up. She wore a brown wig, and a hairdresser was using a pick to arrange curling tendrils over her temples and forehead.

Lucas Daltrey, her handsome co-star, didn't need a hairpiece. He'd grown out his dark hair, now tied behind his head by a black silk ribbon. In frock coat, vest, and breeches, he resembled the quintessential Georgian gentleman as he posed for the still photographer. One of those images, Hannah suspected, was destined for the cover of the tie-in edition of *Forsaken Fortune,* to please all those female women readers who had sent the novel soaring up the bestseller lists.

Nigel Rossiter beckoned Liz to her canvas chair. Her full name was stitched on the front and back panel.

Alistair came over to Hannah and said, "If we wrap on time, we'll have a proper night off. Meet at the pub later?"

Her evenings had been exceptionally quiet—and dull. This week Tom Picton was in London, accessing archival materials. Either she invited Liz to her hotel restaurant for dinner, or they worked their way through the limited number of Newbridge restaurants. At night she landed in her bed, exhausted.

In addition to the variable demands of her working day, she did her best to boost Liz's spirits. Although the postpartum depression had subsided, stress affected her moods.

Hannah would have preferred to spend her free night with Poppy Deane, catching up. But she was determined to maintain a positive working relationship with Alistair. "Can we go to The Huntsman's Horn?" she asked him, knowing the likelihood of finding the estate manager there.

"Suits me."

The process of blocking the harvest supper took up most of the morning. The number of participants and the lively action required careful direction and a lot of coordination before everyone was clear on what to do when. And where. After the lunch break, Liz told Hannah she was leaving.

"Tom caught an earlier train than he thought he would. If I take the car, can you get a lift to the hotel?"

"Easily."

"What's tomorrow's schedule?"

"Owen and the first unit will be at Stanwell House for a Granville and Rosalind scene, pages seventy-three through seventy-nine. No script changes—that I know of. The assistant director and the second unit and the extras will come back here for pick-up shots."

"I might play hooky. You can too, if you want. Have fun tonight. But not too much. I'm on Team Martin."

Hannah laughed. "So am I."

She rode to Milverston in a minibus with the members of

the supporting cast lodging at the Latimer Arms. The Huntsman's Horn, derided by Martin as too tarted up for his taste, was popular with the film crew and packed with locals. Disappointed by Poppy's absence, Hannah went to the only vacant booth. She placed her rain-drenched coat on the protruding hook attached to the bench seat. Seeing Alistair, she waved him over.

"At last, I get you all to myself," he said. Surveying the room, he added, "Sort of. What'll you have?"

"A pint of Milverston Gold." Martin would've known.

He placed their order at the bar and returned with a foam-topped glass of lager and her cider.

"I've been reet fashed about our executive producer leaving the set early. Was she not pleased?"

Hannah had no intention of sharing Liz's impressions of the shoot, or her opinion of dailies. "If she were here, she'd tell you it's Owen's opinion that matters most."

"A fortnight in, we're on shed-yule. You'll be glad to get back to that big house tomorrow. I well remember how chuffed you were after your recce."

"It meets our specs. Practically all of them, which is rare."

"Aye. I remember going there the first time, and how pleased we all were with the place. And with you for discovering it."

"That's why I was so surprised," she said, "when Owen fired me. To make you location manager."

"I did feel bad about that."

"You might have told me so. You had my phone number."

"I didn't think you'd answer if I rang you."

A woodcut of a hunting horn was imprinted on the small square of a beer mat. Covering it with her glass, she suggested that they order their food. They both selected fried haddock, served with mushy peas and a mound of chips fresh from the deep fryer and glistening with oil.

Hannah, mellowed by the meal and the cider, countered her companion's tales of demanding shoots and on-set disasters with her own.

"I always dreamed of working with Owen," she confided.

"And so you are."

"Not exactly." A vinegar-soaked chip limply dangled from her fingers.

"Even though you don't report to him, we're colleagues. And I hope we will be for a long time yet."

Her eyes narrowed. "It's an eight-week location shoot. With six remaining."

"After we wrap *Forsaken Fortune*, I'll start my own agency. Should be up and running by year's end. I'd love to get you on board as my chief location finder."

The irony of it drew a laugh from Hannah.

"I'm dead serious."

"I can't go anywhere without getting a job offer," she said shakily.

"That wasn't one. Not yet. But I could use your help developing my business plan."

"Sorry, I'm already booked. Double booked, in fact." Glancing at her phone display, she was startled by the hour. "I'd better call for a car."

"I'm bound for Newbridge myself. I'll take you."

She collected her belongings and scooted across the bench. He placed a hand on her back as they proceeded towards the door. From her break up with Joel until now, Martin was the only non-relative male to touch her, and the unwelcome contact made her increase her pace. Poppy sat at the bar, where other drinkers formed an impenetrable barrier. She smiled and wagged her fingers before exiting the pub.

Alistair drove a Mini, a vintage specimen, not a newer model. He admitted it wasn't the most practical of vehicles for location work. "But in a car park, she fits into even the smallest space," he allowed.

When she got out, in front of the manor house hotel, she didn't tell him that she wasn't going to Stanwell tomorrow.

Chapter 26

After ascertaining that Isobel Latimer was feeling well enough to receive her, Hannah drove from Newbridge to the cul-de-sac where Holly Cottage was located. During her initial stay in Milver Vale she'd driven around it unintentionally, the result of a wrong turn off the Milverston road. She found a single-story house matching Isobel's description and parked in front of the detached one-car garage.

Kateryna Bereva, the young Ukrainian, answered the bell. "Hi, Hennah. Nice seeing you."

She presented the box of pastel macarons that had magically appeared in her hotel room. "For Isobel."

"She has surprise, too, is so heppy to show you."

A front hall connected to a spacious sitting room. A set of glass doors at the far end of the kitchen opened onto a paved patio.

Isobel was seated in a lounger. The small lump of fur in her lap stirred and raised its head, revealing round brown eyes.

"A puppy!"

"From Martin, for my birthday. Ernie is a cavalier spaniel, not quite two months old. They're both training with Susan. Macarons—my favorite!"

The little dog hopped down and shook his long, fluffy ears. As he sniffed Hannah's shoes, she placed the confectionary box on the table. "How are you feeling?"

"Each day there's noticeable improvement." At the sound of vehicle doors shutting, Isobel said, "That will be the gardeners Martin sent from Stanwell to plant my rose bushes."

The gate opened to reveal a man wearing work clothes and wellies. He pushed in a wheelbarrow overflowing with shrubs, and his co-worker followed with a bag of compost.

"You gentlemen certainly don't require supervision, so we'll leave you to get on with your task. Step inside, Hannah. I'll put the kettle on, and we can sample those sweets."

While waiting for the water to boil, she gave Hannah a tour of the cottage. Ernie padded after them on miniature feet, his tail constantly wagging.

"I know better than to offer you the spare bedroom," Isobel said. "Martin says you turned down his invitation."

"I've got to stay within shouting distance of Liz. Although she's making an effort to follow her husband's advice to avoid stress. Tom is constantly telling her to pace herself."

"I can't imagine how she produces a major movie and meets the needs of a husband and an infant. I borrowed my son's copy of *Forsaken Fortune*. A cracking good tale, as he says. Even if you weren't making the film here, I'd be eager to see it."

"We hope the rest of the world feels that way."

After their tea-drinking session, Hannah promised to return soon.

Seeing her to the front door, Isobel said, "If you happen to be available when it's time, come back to help me put my tulip and hyacinth bulbs in the ground. I'd love to boast that Wendy Edney's daughter planted some of them. And do, please, give Gwen and Neil my best. Your uncle as well.

Those days in Maine are a happy memory for me. And Martin."

Hannah studied the sage-colored minivan parked near her hire car. A new logo was printed on its door beneath the full name Milverston Estate in classic lettering. Martin had taken possession of his fleet of electric vehicles.

Her introduction to the spaniel pup led to an impromptu visit to Stanwell. Not in connection with her job, but because she wanted to see Jewel.

She found both dogs in the kitchen, watching Jan whisk egg whites in a copper bowl.

"Hello, girls. Behaving yourselves?"

"You should know better than to ask," said the cook, returning to her task.

As Hannah knelt on the stone floor, Jewel lunged forward, almost knocking her back. She ran a hand along a glossy black shoulder. When she hooked her arm around the lurcher's neck, the other dog responded with a jealous snarl. "Mind your manners," she chided.

"They're jumpy today, like they can sense Martin's due back from the city." After this remark came a disparaging sniff. "All these years I believed my mortal trial was dealing with his antics. Now there's caravans everywhere, engines running constantly, electric wires all round. Ron and Nico and the security men had to tuck away all the valuables. Gosia frets because she can't clean the rooms as thoroughly as she wants to. At day's end, we almost have to tie Freya down to stop her putting furniture back where it belongs. And our Poppy goes about looking like a thundercloud."

"A temporary disruption," Hannah reassured her. "If you have specific concerns, let me know, I'll pass them on to the location manager."

"To be honest, I expected worse. Though I did grumble t'other day when I got to Milver Cross and found the cars stopped and hardly any pedestrians allowed through. Now the paved walk at St. Anne's church is covered over with dirt, all the way to the lych-gate. When it rains, what a mess that'll be!"

No part of this commentary was unfamiliar to Hannah.

"And," Jan went on, "when Martin's away, those poor beasts are shut in here, or put into Ron's quarters. Can't have them knocking over any of that expensive equipment blocking the passages."

Hannah, dividing her attention between the two dogs, said, "Martin wanted this house to become a film set."

"If he didn't hare off to Newbridge or London so often, he mightn't be so keen."

"Every night this week I've seen them at The Huntsman's Horn," Poppy informed Martin when he was guiding Jewel through the agility course. "After filming—they sometimes carry on till evening—the crew and some of the cast head for the pub. Not the stars."

"Clever girl!" When the dog dashed out of the nylon tunnel, Martin handed her a treat.

"Did you hear what I said about Hannah and the Scotsman? They always leave together. He drives her back to the hotel in Newbridge."

"And they say chivalry is dead."

"Aren't you concerned?" She glared at him, chin lowered and hands on hips.

"That bloke stole her job, Popster."

"He isn't stealing anything nowadays. Looks like he's getting what he wants."

"That's slanderous."

"Not if it's true," she shot back.

Martin kept his eyes on Jewel, seated at his feet and waiting for the next hand signal.

"You went to Maine. You met her parents. I suspect Isobel's already deciding what to wear to the engagement party and the wedding. Take my advice. Pop into Huntsman's tonight and see for yourself what's going on."

"I'll meet you there. What time?"

Her head swung back and forth. "I'm wanted at The Peacock. Andy needs backup while Jack's in Weston-Super-Mare with Chloe. They go every September, before term starts. He asked me to help keeping things running smoothly at the pub. If the kitchen gets busy, I'll have to do the odd fry-up."

"There's a reason to keep clear of the place."

She retaliated by lobbing a ball at him. It landed on the grass. Jewel promptly retrieved and returned it.

"What's today's location, do you know?" he asked.

"The river, on the Milver St. Mary side. First thing this morning, they closed the bridge. I've taken lots of calls from aggrieved villagers." Poppy watched him work the dog, and after Jewel completed another series of jumps, she asked, "Have you auditioned for the role of village idiot?"

"I've grown camera-shy in my dotage."

"Here's more movie gossip. Étoile and Meg might end up on the silver screen instead of you. The horse master—mistress—asked Shona if she knew of an attractive animal capable of carrying a lady on sidesaddle. For some reason the gelding for Caroline Bryden was withdrawn. Meg's owner is a member of the Sidesaddle Association and competed in their annual show, and uses her for teaching. I let her be checked for health and temperament, and she passed with flying colors."

"Do we have the owner's permission?"

Poppy affirmed it. "I've already forwarded paperwork to sign and return. Your cousin has started sidesaddle practice. Because Étoile is comfortable with Meg, Lucas Daltrey might ride her. Lucky girl."

"Presumably we receive a fee."

"Of course. The firm that hired out the carriage horses and the shires gave me an estimate of what we should charge. We can set Meg's payment against her boarding expenses, and whatever Étoile brings in goes towards oats and hay. Dr. Allason's assistant is the on-set vet, and having the time of his life. I must say, despite the hardships this production brings, it does wonders for our local economy. As you'll discover tonight at The Huntsman's Horn."

After Jewel's training session, he changed into running gear and hung the lanyard with his identification badge around his neck. He trotted across the Home Farm acres towards Milver St. Mary. The air was heavy and humid, no clouds shaded the sun. His t-shirt and the laminated card he'd tucked inside were sticking to his chest. Beyond the cordon erected around the film set, crew members gathered at long tables. He had no trouble finding the person he'd come to see—the only one in costume, she was surrounded by hangers-on.

"Martin!" Handing her plate to an assistant, Caroline Bryden hurried to meet him as hastily as her long, full skirts allowed.

He held up his hands to ward off an embrace. "Don't touch. I'm damp."

"Me, too. Impossible to keep dry inside this tent I'm wearing. I'm surprised you recognized me in this misery of a wig. How long has it been?"

"Years. But I've seen you more recently, on the cover of *Posh*."

"And I saw that article about you. I'm too weighed down with fabric to walk to my caravan and felt too famished to wait for a cart to take me there. Why don't you get some food from craft services and join me? I'm at the table under the trees. They said I'd feel cooler in the shade. They were wrong."

The shortest queue was for people seeking vegan, vegetarian, or gluten-free fare. He received a serving of orzo salad and joined his cousin. A wardrobe woman was winding a sheet around her to protect the costume.

"Just what I needed—another layer." Caroline plunged a straw into a water bottle and held it to her rouged lips. "Whose idea was it to film a period piece in the hottest summer month?"

"Liz Gregorio's I should think. Or Sir Owen's."

"How's your mother? I heard from mine that she's dealing with another bout of cancer."

"She's doing famously. Lives near here and would enjoy seeing you. What time do they set you free?"

"According to my call sheet, six o'clock. Shooting finishes before then, but Lucas and I have a blocking session. With our intimacy coordinator."

"Fancy a pub dinner? Based on my reading of *Forsaken Fortune,* your character wouldn't refuse an invitation from a titled gentleman."

"Definitely not. As my horse-mad grandfather would say, Rosalind is mare-ish. I haven't had a night out since coming to Somerset," she admitted. Daintily she touched a paper napkin to the corner of her mouth. "Usually at day's end I'm so tired I can't think of anything but a hot bath and room service. Vegetarian options on the country house hotel menu are limited. And monotonous."

After polishing off his final forkful of salad, he said, "Message me after your rehearsal, and I'll collect you. Where will you be?"

"The big barn. Hayloft scene."

He hadn't forgotten the eroticism of that episode. "All in a day's work, right?"

He added his empty plate to the recycling bin. Scanning the crowd, he saw Hannah pacing the riverbank, phone clamped to her ear, tablet in the crook of her arm. She couldn't wave back, but she acknowledged him with a nod and a smile that made his heart race more than his run had done. The giant Scot loomed beside her.

The sun sat low in the sky when he drove to the parking area beside the tithe barn. Set carpenters had constructed an accurate facsimile of a hayloft from weathered wooden joists and beams. The director stood at the base of a stepladder, and a woman perched on the top rung addressed the couple on the pile of straw. Lucas Daltrey sprawled across Caroline, and her legs were splayed.

Peeping over her co-star's shoulder, she asked, "Is this what you want me to do?"

"Move your head a bit to the right," Sir Owen told her, "so the camera can frame your face. That's better."

The actor let out an explosive sneeze. Everyone laughed.

"Allergic to hay?" the intimacy coordinator asked.

"I didn't think so."

"That's all for now. Lucas, go to the medic first thing tomorrow morning for antihistamine tablets. We'll have another quick run through in costume, with lighting and mics, sound and camera."

Caroline descended the ladder and brushed away the hay from her top and leggings. Her flaming hair was shorter than it had been when posing for the *Posh* feature, to accommodate the period wig. After her assistant handed over her backpack, she asked Martin where he was taking her.

"The Huntsman's Horn in Milverston Magna. Five minutes from here."

During the short drive to the village, he repeatedly pulled into the lay-bys to avoid film company lorries transporting equipment.

"Are you satisfied with progress?" he asked Caroline. "And the performances?"

"I try not to analyze. Owen is the most demanding director I've ever had. The notes he gives makes me wonder if I should abandon acting for another job."

"Like what?"

"No idea. Reckon I'm stuck with this crazy profession."

"Don't be offended, but it's hard to connect the movie star with a girl who had shiny railway tracks on her teeth and wore her hair in two bunches."

"And I remember when your hair was purple and you wore black eyeliner. My grandparents predicted you'd be remanded into custody on drugs charges. Or worse."

"I've always been notable for my sobriety. How are they?"

"Living in pampered isolation in a luxury care home near Salisbury. An enormous country place like Stanwell, converted into residential suites."

"When you see them, let them know their fears about my future were unfounded."

The pub's car park was full. All the outdoor tables were occupied, and they heard the din before they stepped inside.

"Popular spot," Caroline commented.

"Not with me. I'm rarely here." If The Peacock was this busy, Poppy and Andy and the kitchen staff must be run off their feet.

Glancing around the room, he spotted Hannah and the Scotsman in a booth. They sat with a group of people, chatting and laughing over drinks and food.

To Caroline he said, "We'll have to wait for a table."

"This suits me." She hopped onto a stool and beamed at the barman. "A glass of house white, please."

Martin eyed the taps. "Milver Vale Bitter. And the menu." He positioned himself so he could observe Hannah and her companions. Three chaps and the woman got up to go, leaving her with the location manager.

He couldn't tell if she'd noticed him yet, she appeared to be completely focused on McLaren. Watching her, he recalled an article in a woman's magazine he'd read when he and his mother had traveled by train from London to Newbridge. It was titled "What Signals Are You Sending Him?" and provided a guide to decoding female body language. Hannah exhibited a disheartening number of the items on the list. Toying with her hair. Angling her head sideways. Maintaining eye contact. Was she actually giggling? He suddenly understood all too well what people meant by the phrase *too much information.*

Chapter 27

After a protracted and frustrating day on the set, Hannah drove Liz to her Carleton Close house. They found Telma pacing the back garden, soothing a fractious Lexi. After the weary mother changed into an un-Liz-like combination of pajama top over faded maternity jeans, she joined Hannah in the sitting room.

Lowering the lights, she bared her breast for the feeding process. "The most effective form of therapy I know. When she was a newborn, and my emotions threw me into a tailspin and my hormones kicked up, I doubted I'd ever get this motherhood thing right. Living up to my own expectations seemed like an impossibility."

"Now you're a pro." Hannah sat cross-legged on the plush area rug.

"I feel guilty that I didn't love her enough at the beginning. This sounds bizarre, but traveling halfway across the world to supervise my most demanding project, proves what's truly meaningful. Somehow, surrounded by all the madness and mayhem, Tom and I have developed an intense parental bond with this tiny person. And we feel even closer to each other because of her."

"That's lovely."

She was happy for Liz, but her observations yesterday by the river and last night in The Huntsman's Horn heightened her loneliness and sense of disconnection. Martin's on-set lunch with the beautiful and vivacious leading actress, immediately followed by their dinner date, loomed large in her thoughts.

Caroline is his cousin, she reminded herself for the hundredth time. *After years of not seeing each other, they want to catch up.*

"There's wine in the fridge—for Tom. Help yourself."

"No thanks."

"I suppose you're going to that pub later. Who else do you see there?"

"On an average night, most departments are represented. Script supervisor, continuity, assistant camera, sparks, grips, gaffers, wardrobe."

"Anybody from the cast?"

"Supporting players. Last night, Caroline. With Martin."

"Today they had lunch together on the terrace at Stanwell. He'd better not take her out tonight. She should stay in her hotel room and prepare for tomorrow's seduction scene."

"Not with Martin's help, I hope." Hannah's comment didn't come out as jokey as she intended.

Dropping her voice to a murmur, Liz said, "Looks to me like he's following the plan, keeping your relationship under wraps."

"That did occur to me," she acknowledged. No one in cast or crew had any idea they were casually—or intimately—acquainted.

Liz tweaked the blanket and peeked at her sleeping daughter's face. "He'll get in touch soon."

Hannah felt in her pocket for her phone and pulled it out to check that it was charged and powered on.

"The weather's been perfect for shooting outdoors.

Which means by Friday evening we'll be close to seventy-two hours of work this week. Carrying on past that would violate union regulations. Owen and Nigel and I plan to shut down for the entire bank holiday weekend. Cast and crew will have time off to spend with their families. You and Martin can hook up, with none the wiser."

Rising later than usual, Hannah put on her running garb and left the hotel, relishing this rare opportunity for exercise. She followed the busy road that eventually passed through Newbridge town center. She stopped at the bus shelter to adjust her bra strap and study the notice board. An eye-catching pink flyer invited her to *Join the Pub Dashers on their Bank Holiday pub-to-pub. 5 p.m. Four mile run across level ground. Mixed running ability. Members £8 entry, non-members £10, proceeds designated for Milver Vale Youth Club. Start and Finish @ The Peacock car park, Milverston Green.* That eight-pound fee was a brilliant money-making strategy. Most members probably handed over a tenner and let the nonprofit keep the change.

She held her phone to the poster and took a picture to send Martin. It was an activity they could share without inciting the type of rumors they hoped to suppress by keeping their distance from each other. On she jogged, until her pedometer informed her that she'd completed two miles. Turning around, she headed back to the hotel. Four miles in an hour was far from her best time, but at least she was covering the same distance as Monday's run.

Her cool-down began at the hotel entrance sign. She left the drive and walked beneath the tall evergreens, refreshed by the shade underneath the thick branches. When she arrived at the front lawn, she saw Martin's Vauxhall parked near the door. He must have found out she'd be free all weekend.

Whipping off her headband, she used it to blot the sweat from her temples and neck, and hastily finger-combed her curls.

When he exited the hotel, she was startled to see him in a suit with a paisley tie dangling down the front of his crisp white shirt. A Vuitton keep-all was slung over one shoulder, and he carried a matching dress bag. He opened the boot and placed both items inside.

Caroline Bryden, holding her phone, joined him. "Does everything fit?" she asked.

"Looks like it."

Hannah's footsteps on the gravel drew their attention.

"Good morning, Hannah," Caroline said brightly. "We're off to a wedding. A friend is getting married in Salisbury Cathedral. Thanks to union rules, I can attend all the events and stay at the hotel with other guests. Three whole days away from the set—isn't it wonderful?"

"Very."

"I'm hoping Alicia won't be there," Martin said. "The bride is her goddaughter."

"Are you invited?" Hannah couldn't help asking.

"He's my plus-one," his cousin explained. "And my chauffeur."

"Have a nice time," she told them, trying to sound like she meant it.

Fantasies of a long weekend with Martin, in and out of bed, were well and truly dashed. Going up the stairs, she wondered if he would also remain in Salisbury overnight. It couldn't be more than an hour away.

Fresh lilies scented her bedroom. She'd have plenty of time to enjoy them, with nothing to do and nowhere to go. Liz and Tom had departed for Bath earlier, in their rental Range Rover, taking Lexi and her fancy English pram.

She removed her sweat-damp clothes and turned on the faucets in the glass-encased shower.

I've got a car, she reminded herself, as hot water streamed onto her head.

She could embark on a scouting mission for Mum's television series, and visit some of the famous gardens in the vicinity.

By Sunday afternoon, she'd toured multiple properties in Somerset and Dorset and had shot hundreds of photographs. She hadn't been able to consult with anyone about obtaining access for filming purposes, or gather names of individuals for her mother to interview. But she'd collected a stack of brochures, with links for websites that would provide contact information.

Having performed her daughterly and her professional duty, she stopped in Sherborne. Retail therapy, in the form of spiffy running togs, failed to vanquish speculation about Martin. And Caroline. At a wedding.

Considering worst-case scenarios was a feature of her job. Toiling in the film industry demanded that she prepare herself for any—and all—contingencies. In Maine, and more recently in London, Martin had expressed and demonstrated his feelings, quite convincingly. He wasn't the fickle type, or the careless playboy she'd mistakenly assumed him to be early in their acquaintance. For a man of thirty, attractive and titled, he'd had remarkably few serious relationships. He wasn't a closet chauvinist. He liked women. He relied on them for advice and support and companionship. Especially strong-minded, stubborn, and opinionated ones—Isobel, Poppy, Jan.

And me.

Still, he should have let her know he would be going away for the weekend. With Caroline.

Many weeks ago, Poppy told her that Martin deserved happiness. Hannah recalled specific times when she'd made him extremely happy. The first time she kissed him. During their dinner date at the Italian restaurant in Newbridge.

While brainstorming the Milver Vale tourism campaign. When exploring each other's bodies—in a fourposter bed or a rented Kozee Kabin or her stately room at the Ritz.

Why did it have to be so hard—seemingly impossible—to integrate a rewarding work life and a satisfactory love life?

The question forced an examination of her own responsibility for her present woes. Hard-wired to expect disaster, major or minor, she'd voluntarily imposed distance between herself and the man she loved. Avoiding publicity was only possible in the short term. In trying to protect others from harm, she was harming herself. In retrospect, she saw that Martin and Chase had both correctly accused her of over-reacting to the media's mania for gossip and scandal. Her present and future contentment depended on remedying that mistake.

Chapter 28

On Monday she woke to a gray, misty morning better suited to reading than running. By early afternoon, the sun had pushed through the clouds. Joining the Pub Dashers had been more appealing two days ago than it was an hour before the meet-up. But after consuming gooseberry yogurt, her current addiction, and drinking a cup of coffee, she felt ready to face the lanes and paths of the Milver Vale. She covered her sports bra with the new pale blue midriff-baring tank top and put on the navy cropped leggings. She wanded mascara onto her lashes and added a dash of lip crayon, then pulled back her hair with a stretchy headband.

Martin was with the other runners in the pub car park. Three other men and two women of diverse ages and physiques bent from the waist and the knees, stretching their limbs.

"A newcomer," a woman commented. She appeared to be in her forties. "Welcome."

"This is Hannah Ballard," Martin informed the group. "She's with Acorn Films. Hannah, here's Joyce. And Eileen." Pointing at each of the men in turn, he added, "Bob and Rory and Thomas."

"Glad you joined us," Rory said. "We wondered if any Hollywooders might turn up."

"I don't actually live in Hollywood. And I'm a very casual runner."

"Us, too," Joyce responded. "We're not competitive, either. If there's a ridge loop, plumpies like me and some of our sixties take the low road."

"Which is to say," Bob added, "we don't all finish at the same time. We used to make the first person who reached the pub buy our first round, but we discarded that rule. Otherwise, Rory would've had to re-mortgage his house to keep the tortoises in drink."

Martin chimed in, asking, "Ready for the off? Doesn't look like anyone else is coming."

They set out as a pack but as Joyce said, there was no effort to keep together. Rory shot ahead after the first mile, cheered on by his friends—except for Thomas, who shook his fist in mock-fury.

"This is half our usual number," Eileen huffed as she came up beside Hannah. "One member has back strain, and Gareth is nursing a bad knee. Plus it's a holiday. Some regulars are relaxing at home, or on family outings."

"I work at the bank in Newbridge," Joyce said. "There'll soon be filming in the town, I hear."

"I hope it won't be disruptive," Hannah said. "Part of the street outside the Guildhall will be covered with dirt and the curbs concealed for exterior and establishing shots. We're using the interior for courtroom scenes."

"Sounds exciting," said Eileen. "When term begins, my students would enjoy watching, if that's allowed. I teach at Milver Vale Comprehensive."

"Members of the public can observe, from a distance. And they have to keep quiet. I can ask the location manager to place your class close to the action."

"That would be grand. I'll give you my contact info."

Martin suddenly speeded up, moving well ahead of the ladies as though intent on catching up with Thomas and overtaking Bob.

Bob dropped back, wailing, "Sod it—forgot my phone! I'm supposed to take pictures for the website blog."

"Never mind," Eileen said, as though consoling a pupil. "I brought mine. And I'll get a group photo at the pub. But this time I won't do the write-up for you."

Farther on they found Martin seated on a wooden bench, studying the verdant landscape and wooded hillside beyond.

"Gosh," said Joyce, "you never wait for us to catch up. Leg cramp?"

"Admiring the view."

"Hannah, sit beside him." Eileen had whipped out her phone.

Her eyes met Martin's. He shifted to make room, and she sank onto the bench. Her fingers curled on the edge, gripping it tightly.

"Give me happy expressions. Our blog visitors need to know what a splendid time you're having!"

She responded with her picture-posing smile.

"Perfect!"

The two women jogged on.

Martin's hand moved to Hannah's thigh. "I'm surprised you came."

They were alone and unobserved—except by the sheep over the hedge—in a beautiful setting on a gorgeous evening. The pasture, lit by the sun's lingering rays, belonged to him. So did the oak tree behind them. And the grass under their feet. Months ago, when he drove her to the hotel at Heathrow, she hadn't imagined running with him again. Or loving him. Or yearning for a durable connection to his home and these villages and acres and the interesting people who inhabited them.

Their shared silence stretched beyond a minute but felt longer.

"If you don't want our picture posted on the blog," he said, "I'll intervene."

"It's all right. Really."

"You're sure?"

She nodded.

He stood. "Shall we carry on?"

She'd had another type of carrying on in mind, and disappointment flowed from the perspiring crown of her head to the toes of her running shoes. A sheep bleated, a mournful noise that accurately expressed her feelings.

The track led them away from agricultural land to a paved roadway bordering the grassy park in Milver Cross. Instead of overtaking Joyce and Eileen, Martin suggested they all head straight for The Peacock.

"If Rory took the long way," Joyce commented, "we'll beat him to the bar."

He hadn't, and they didn't.

Hannah waited her turn for the ladies' loo. She rinsed her flush face at the sink, careful not to streak her mascara or smudge her rosy lips.

She found the runners on the terrace behind the pub, seated at a round table. Martin had already ordered her cider. Jack Elliston brought out three servings of chips, fresh from the fryer basket and so hot they couldn't be touched. Eileen handed him her phone and everyone squeezed close together, holding up their glasses.

After comparing their completed run to prior outings, the Dashers talked of summer holidays, work activities, family matters. Bob managed Milver Vale Dairy. Rory, an estate agent, had two properties under offer, subject to conditions. Thomas, a motor sports enthusiast, worked as a mechanic and attended rallies in his spare time. Hannah listened passively, entertained by teasing remarks addressed to Martin, who clearly relished them. He possessed a noble title and doubtless held the deeds to their homes and business sites, but she could tell how much he valued this camaraderie.

After Joyce—the first defector—departed, there was a mass exodus.

Martin accompanied Hannah to her car. "Caroline said you'll be at the flour mill tomorrow."

"For a scene that was delayed until the set carpenters could construct a fruit press. Miraculously, the props people sourced a working reproduction at a museum down in Dorset, which is being delivered and set up today. Owen wants to finish filming by the riverside before Sir Francis Cooke arrives. He plays Rosalind's father. After that, we'll be back at Stanwell."

"And our horses will go before the cameras. Then it's on to Newbridge, right? Before finishing up at Hartwell Studios."

He must have learned these details from his cousin. She'd probably already invited him to the wrap party.

"Counting the days till we leave you in peace?"

"It hasn't been bad. Even Popster admits it. She might actually miss all the activity."

Martin waved to tenants and acquaintances who had gathered near the mill to observe the proceedings. Liz and Hannah stood on the spectators' side of the cordon, with an agitated man who flailed his hands. He stalked off before Martin reached them.

"Is that fellow causing trouble?"

Hannah turned to him. "It's Simon, our historical advisor. We actually pay him to complain that we have the wrong type of apples."

Liz added, "According to him, the ones Props brought

in by the bushel are a modern variety, most likely imported from France. I couldn't tell which of those facts is most offensive to him."

"You need heritage apples."

"Apparently."

"I can solve your problem. Shouldn't take long."

"Define not long," Liz replied.

After considering, he told her, "Within the hour. I could use a couple of helpers."

"You can have Hannah." Liz was clearly too flummoxed to realize how Martin would interpret her words. "And Logan, Alistair's intern."

"The orchard where you filmed the other day grows old-fashioned fruit, and there's plenty of it at the cider factory. I'll exchange your apples for theirs. I can transport them in the van we keep in reserve at Stanwell. For emergencies."

"Which Simon insists this is," Liz said.

"The factory will expect me to return their lot, of course. Hannah drinks so much Milverston Gold, they need every apple in the Vale." Turning to her, he said, "Let me have the key to your car. I walked here, and it's plain that speed is essential."

She dug around in her satchel for the fob and handed it to him. "Not too much speed."

When he returned, she was waiting at the security gate with a young man and two bushel baskets.

"This is all?"

"Yes," Hannah answered. "I came up with a work-around. We aren't replacing all the bad apples. We need just enough to cover the ones Simon dislikes, and some to scatter on the ground. Logan's going with you. He'll text photos to Simon for approval."

Logan pulled a bright red apple from his anorak. "At

least I won't miss my brekkie." After taking a big, noisy bite, he laughed.

Hannah glared at him, not amused.

Martin's mother was burying tulip bulbs at the base of the yew hedge when he brought her tiny spaniel back to Holly Cottage. The instant he unsnapped the lead from the collar, the pup raced to greet her.

"How did he perform?" she asked.

"He was attentive and responsive. I haven't yet convinced him that nibbling the legs of his larger classmates is counterproductive to forming friendships. We're registered for the next course. Susan offered to schedule a private session before it begins. She'd like to see you working him. Can I help with your digging?"

"And deprive me of this pleasure? No, thank you. Come, sit."

"Not if you speak to me like I'm Ernie."

She smiled. "Be a good boy, and I'll give you a biscuit."

"I'd rather have some of your motherly wisdom and advice," he told her. "I'm in such a muddle." Running his fingers through his hair, he added, "Actually, it's far worse than that."

"Romantic troubles?"

"Heaps of them."

She reached out to grasp his arm. "Stop. You're giving yourself hedgehog head. A sure sign something's gone very wrong."

"Many things. And I can't think how to resolve them. I've got to leave Stanwell straightaway." His hand raked his scalp more forcefully than before. "London. Latimer Global board meeting. The timing couldn't be worse."

"Stay."

"You're doing it again."

"You'll always be my pup—the most precious one. Darling, don't let that company damage you the same way it did your father."

"I haven't. I won't." He stretched out his legs. "That's not the only reason I'm going. The other is considerably more important. And urgent. If I explain, you can't say a word about it. To anyone."

"Very well."

He breathed deeply, exhaled slowly, and plunged into his confession.

Chapter 29

After a fortnight of sidesaddle practice, Caroline Bryden and Meg the Welsh cob were about to have their joint performance captured for posterity. Lucas Daltrey, mounted on Martin's Étoile, looked outrageously dashing in eighteenth-century riding attire.

As the couple guided the animals around the Home Park to relax them, Poppy turned to Hannah. "Isn't she gorgeous?"

"Caroline? Always."

"I was referring to Meg. Shona and I gave both horses a wash yesterday and kept them blanketed when we stabled them. I curried Meg's mane and rubbed baby powder on her socks to whiten them, like I was preparing her for the show ring."

"When her owner leaves boarding school, she'll be more interested in boys than ponies. Why don't you offer to buy Meg?"

"I've considered it. She's a dream to ride. And perfect for Chloe's lessons."

"Did the Ellistons enjoy their seaside holiday?"

"I should say so. Jack's been in quite a cheery mood since he came back. I reckon he's relieved Andy Riddell and

I managed not to burn down The Peacock. And the takings were good."

"Any developments to report?"

"With Jack?" Poppy shrugged. "Nothing's changed. For the better part of a week, I proved myself a trustworthy and reliable temporary pub manager. He's still older than me, without a clue how I feel."

"This isn't the eighteenth century," Hannah replied. "Be proactive. Tell him."

"And risk rejection? I think not." Poppy went quiet, but not for long. "When we were working together, Andy was really, really weird. More dejected than usual. One night, after dropping a pint glass, he was practically in tears. While we cleaned up the mess, he admitted he was responsible for Millie's injury."

"I'm glad he told you. How did it happen?"

"He'd taken out his dad's quad bike, without permission. Millie was in the field and he called her over to race him. When he was doing a wheelie, the daft kid, the tire struck her leg hard and she went down. He was so scared he'd be found out that he took the bike to the shed first. By the time he went back to check on Millie, you and Mart had taken her to the vet."

"You must know why he kept quiet so long. He thought you'd be furious."

"What would be the point? I reminded him that if he'd fallen off, he could've been very badly hurt as well. He's been saving up his wages to reimburse me for Millie's operation, but I can't take his money. Instead, he's going to walk Millie after school, before he has to be at the pub."

"Community service," Hannah said approvingly. Chase's post-prison experience was evidence of its many benefits.

"And he'll come to the estate office at weekends to study. He needs to get good marks his GCSEs. Especially now that he's thinking he wants to be a vet. I had to answer a lot of questions about Millie's surgery." Poppy peered past the assembled spectators. "Isobel's here. Looking quite hearty, too. Let's say hello."

The older woman greeted them warmly.

"Does Martin know you're breaking quarantine?" Hannah asked.

"I promised to remain outdoors and keep my distance. He brought Caroline to Holly Cottage last week and prepared dinner for us. She told us about learning how to ride on the sidesaddle, and invited me to watch the filming. Ron drove me over and will take me home when I'm ready."

Hannah's smile wavered. Martin and the leading lady had eaten meals together on set and at the pub and on the terrace here at Stanwell. She'd taken him to a wedding. They visited his mother at Holly Cottage. He'd cooked for her.

"In that riding habit," Isobel said, "she looks like she stepped out of a painting, doesn't she?"

"Always," Hannah acknowledged. Determined to say something nice, she added, "Her performance will force film critics to invent new forms of praise."

If only Caroline was a bitch, she silently fumed, and an ego-maniacal diva. Then I could detest her as well as envying her for spending all her precious free time with Martin.

The leading actress was a firm favorite with everybody involved in the production. She'd made friends with some of the lowliest crew members, preferring their company to that of her co-star and their castmates. Instead of bemoaning protracted set-ups, she waited patiently under her caravan's awning, studying her lines or knitting or playing solitaire on her phone. And chatting with anyone who passed by. Gorgeous, gregarious, gifted . . . no wonder Martin enjoyed her company.

"She had to overcome a significant amount of parental objection to her acting career," Isobel said. "The Brydens were appalled when she left university for RADA."

Fascinated by the complex mechanics of an action scene, Isobel remained until midday.

Caroline ruefully announced that if they kept her on Meg's back any longer, she wouldn't be capable of walking to her trailer to eat her lunch. Owen Parry pulled Lucas aside to give performance notes. For the duration of the one-sided conversation, the actor wore a sullen expression and tapped his riding crop against the top of one boot.

"I detect friction between the director and the leading man," Hannah commented to Liz when their paths crossed.

"Owen wants to draw maximum passion and desperation from his performers. By speaking to Lucas and Caroline separately, he forces real-time reactions, unrehearsed."

"Divide and conquer."

"You've seen the dailies. Spine-tingling scenes, with depth and beauty. And that's without editing. Or a musical score."

"I wonder what the novel's author will think when she gets here."

"Frankly, I wish she'd stick to her keyboard and finish the sequel to *Forsaken Fortune*. But it's important to keep her happy. She hasn't fussed about the slight adjustments. In fact, she phoned me to say what a good job the scriptwriters did. Not the usual eat-shit-and-die-for-fucking-up-my-masterpiece tirade I often get."

Hannah and Liz returned to Stanwell House the following day. Two indoor scenes were on the morning schedule, and Liz wanted to run interference in case her director's dictatorial methods annoyed Sir Francis Cooke.

"And if somebody, anybody forgets to call him 'Sir Francis,' trouble will ensue. He's easily offended."

"Fun times ahead," Hannah muttered.

During the first set-up, she and Alistair debated which of two bedchambers would be better for a deathbed scene.

"All along, I intended for them to shoot in that very large

one called The King's Room, which has the most sumptuous furniture and fittings. I couldn't get permission."

"Why not?"

"No reason given. I'm not fussed about the number or position of the windows," Alistair continued. "We can use a light balloon. Let's measure each of the available spaces to make sure the actors can move about after the equipment goes in."

She had no decision-making authority on locations—he'd taken it from her, months ago. Nevertheless, she went with him, stepping around the boom arm of a microphone stand blocking the entrance hall. She almost collided with the helium canister that would be used to fill the floating light balloon. When a sound tech buttonholed Alistair, she waited by a window and watched Martin in motion on the tennis court, driving the ball across the net to Ron. Nobody had told her he'd returned from London.

Conscious of Alistair's looming presence, she turned.

"How about dinner tonight? Latimer Arms."

"Liz wants me to review the video press kit footage. The file came today."

"That takes twenty minutes, at most. I'll book a table for seven o'clock and pick you up at your hotel."

"I'll meet you there," she said, to underscore that this was not a date.

Sometime after Hannah's April stay at the Latimer Arms, its dining room had been refurbished. Striped wallpaper replaced the busy floral she remembered, and the chairs were covered with pale brocade. The influx of movie money, or the expectation of it, must have inspired the updated décor.

"Miss Ballard," the hostess greeted her. "Good to see you again. It's been quite the adventure, having your movie people here. T'other day my son and his mates got paid to be in a crowd scene. He skived off from class to do it, but I didn't mind. Does 'im good to start earning his own dosh, 'stead of asking me for it all the time." She handed over the evening menu.

Without looking, Alistair asked, "Any specials?"

"Baked halibut. What'll it be for drinks?"

"A glass of Sancerre," Hannah replied.

"I'm drouthy. Bring me a pint of Milverston Bitter."

"Righty-oh." The woman lit the candle in the center of the table and departed.

"What does drouthy mean?" Hannah asked.

"Dry. Thirsty for drink."

"Are you bilingual?"

"Not me. Though I've got family who enjoy speaking Gaelic. To confuse the tourists looking for Nessie in the loch."

A young server delivered their beverages and asked if they were ready to order.

"I'll start with a house salad," Hannah told her. "Mushroom tortellini for my main."

"Leek and potato soup. Somerset Pork Chop. Might as well do the locavore thing, right?" Peering closely at Hannah, he asked, "Does meat eating bother you? Are you vegetarian?"

"No. And no." She sampled her wine.

The girl arrived with her salad and his soup. "It's hot," she warned Alistair. "Have a care."

He left his spoon on the table and fumbled in his jacket pocket. "I had an ulterior motive when I invited you to dinner. I hope you don't mind."

"Tell me what it is, and we'll find out."

He placed an object in front of her. "Two days ago, this was taken from Stanwell House."

Hannah stared at a portrait miniature approximately

the size of her palm, of a lady in Georgian dress. The red gems surrounding its gold frame glistened in the candlelight. "Taken," she repeated. "You mean stolen."

"Tragically, yes. Found on a crew member. During a pat down."

"Logan. Your intern."

"Ex-intern. How'd you guess?"

"He shamelessly pilfered a prop apple and ate it. Right in front of me. He didn't ask permission." She pierced an arugula leaf with her fork. "Was he vetted? Did he receive a recommendation from his university film program?"

"My assistant made the referral. Logan told her he'd completed a video production course at Bridgewater." He placed his finger over the elegant lady's painted face. "You'd best soon return it to your friend Latimer, or Milverston, or whatever he calls himself. Discreetly. Apologize. Assure him our unit manager and I will beef up security. Tell him nothing like this will ever happen again. We need him to keep quiet about it. Can't have any adverse publicity."

He'd pushed her out of her dream job. Now was asking her to tidy up a mess that he should've prevented.

And she would—she had to. Not only out of loyalty to Liz, or to preserve the good reputation of Acorn Films. But because she was the one person on the production familiar with the way Martin received really bad news. Not that she'd be capable of soothing his outrage when he learned a family treasure had been purloined.

Gingerly she picked it up and thrust it into her bag. "Conceal this travesty from Owen and Nigel, if you feel you must. But I'm telling Liz."

Mrs. Gregorio had recently arrived from Boston to look after her granddaughter during Telma's visit to family in Lisbon. Liz had often been absent from the set lately, temporarily giving domestic matters priority over professional ones.

Hannah abandoned her feeble effort to eat her salad, rendered tasteless by dismay. Pulling her napkin out of her lap, she dropped it on the tablecloth. "I've lost my appetite. I'm going to Stanwell."

Striding through the car park, she decided Poppy's house would be her first stop. The estate manager had years of experience dealing with Martin and his responses to disappointments—or disasters. She would be a supportive, objective presence.

But as she drove by The Peacock, she noticed the Volvo parked in front. Making a sharp turn, she circled the village green and rolled up to the pub's door.

As usual, the place was buzzing. Andy Riddell, behind the bar, was manning the taps.

"What'll it be?" he asked.

"I'm looking for Poppy."

"She went outside. Reckon she wanted to sneak a smoke."

Hannah barged between the tables, barely acknowledging members of the film crew on her way to the terrace. The floodlight wasn't turned on and the tables were empty, their umbrellas tightly closed. She heard soft voices over by the stand of trees. When her eyes adjusted to the darkness, she made out two figures.

A brown head with dangling ponytail was fused to another head. Two bodies, entwined. Two people, kissing. Poppy and Jack.

Rejoicing at evidence that her friend's crush on the pub's proprietor was reciprocated, she hurried inside. Passing through the room as quickly as before, she returned to her car.

At the crossroads, she swerved onto Home Farm Lane. Halfway to her destination, she noticed flashing blue lights in her rearview mirror.

Chapter 30

Hannah eased into a lay-by. She told herself to stay calm, as if that were possible while a policeman approached her car.

He tapped the window.

Her hand jerked towards the control panel. She lowered the glass. "Hello."

"You were traveling at a dangerous speed."

"Sorry. I'm in a hurry. I guess that's no excuse," she added.

"Have you consumed any alcoholic drinks this evening, miss?"

"Half a glass of wine."

"*Half* a glass." His tone and the raised eyebrows communicated disbelief.

"Maybe less. I left the restaurant during the salad course. I was at the Latimer Arms."

"How long since you were drinking?"

She tried to calculate the time. "Ten minutes. Fifteen. I'm not sure."

"Please switch off the engine. I need to see your driving permit."

As she reached inside her purse for her wallet, her trembling fingers brushed the framed miniature. Getting pulled over on a traffic violation was bad enough. If he searched for drugs and found a stolen antique, she was doomed.

The policeman pointed his torch at the Massachusetts driver's license. She watched him study the information printed on both sides, hoping her organ donor status would count in her favor.

"Miss Ballard, I'm going to administer a breath analysis test to check for alcohol impairment. Refusal is grounds for arrest."

"Okay. That is . . . I mean . . . I don't refuse."

He pulled a bright yellow device from a pocket in his hi-vis jacket. Before presenting it to her, he inserted a white plastic tube into a hole at the top. She listened carefully to his instructions, inhaling deeply before she blew into the mouthpiece. She waited, pulses pounding, while he studied the readout.

"Pass. Looks like you were being truthful about the wine," he acknowledged. "Where are you headed in such a rush?"

"Stanwell House. I work for the executive producer. I've got a Hartcliffe Studios-Acorn Films identification badge, if you want to see it."

"That won't be necessary. You must be aware that security guards are posted around the property at all hours."

"I'm familiar with their duty rota." She'd helped create it.

He handed back her license. "Take it slow, Miss Ballard. This isn't an American speedway."

"I'll be extremely careful, I promise. Thank you."

She swallowed to soothe her throat, parched from panic.

Because the lane was too narrow for the officer to reverse his vehicle, he followed her all the way to Stanwell's private entrance. Checking her mirror, she saw him turn into the drive, back out, and drive towards Milverston. The mercifully brief ordeal had shredded her nerves, already shattered by Alistair's revelation. And she hadn't even begun her mission.

When she reached the stable yard, her car set off the security light motion sensors. The sudden illumination drew Martin to the kitchen window. He opened the door before she reached it.

His shirt was untucked and he had a dishcloth draped over one arm. "This is a surprise. Do come in."

She crossed the threshold. Ariel and Jewel trotted over, clamoring for attention. Placing her handbag on the trestle table, she stroked Jewel's smooth black head and Ariel's shaggy brownish one.

"Care for a drink?"

"No thanks. I'm driving." She wouldn't admit that her extreme caution resulted from being pulled over by a cop. "I won't stay long." She removed the miniature from her bag and held it up. "Logan stole this. The intern who went with you to the cider factory with the apples. He's been sacked. We're not pressing charges. I realize I'm asking a lot, but I hope you won't either."

"No reason." He plucked the portrait from her unsteady hand. "She's not mine."

"You're sure?"

"Positive. A late Victorian copy of a Georgian piece. The frame is silver gilt, not gold. The image is painted on enamel instead of ivory. These aren't rubies, they're paste." He tossed it in the air and caught it. "See how light it is? You'll come across plenty of similar items at any car boot sale. That's probably where your props master found it. Tell him—"

"Her."

"Tell her if she prefers a genuine eighteenth-century miniature, I can provide one. A Marchioness of Milverston."

"You'd do that?"

"Her ladyship will be well protected. Ron and Nico and a member of the security team can stand guard. Ariel, too."

Hannah's heart and lungs were resuming normal function when she noticed the empty wine glass and a half-full whisky tumbler on the marble worktop. Wedged between them was a small brown leather object, scallop-shaped. A ring box.

A flash of color drew her attention to the hallway. Caroline Bryden, wearing a short silk kimono, paused at the open door. Her legs and feet were bare.

She twirled her sash. "My patience wears thin, Martin." Glancing at Hannah, she added, "Oh. I didn't know you were here."

"I'm going," she said, blindly reaching for her purse. "See you later."

A stolen prop. A brush with the law. Finding another woman, half-dressed, with the man I love.

Worst night of my life.

As soon as she stepped outside, she heard a motorcycle's roar. So did the horses in the stable. They responded with a chorus of startled whinnies.

The machine sputtered along the drive and pulled in next to Martin's car. The rider turned off the engine and dismounted. Removing his helmet, he placed it on a handlebar.

Lucas Daltrey looked across at her. "You didn't see me on this thing. If you blab to Liz, she and her production insurers will have my balls."

"Your secret's safe with me."

"Is Caroline here?"

"Inside. I believe she's about to . . . be busy."

"Got it in one. Truer words were never uttered."

Perplexed by his grin, she said lamely, "You seem to know more than I do."

"Explanations would take too long. I'm late enough as it is."

"You made it." Martin paced through the darkness, his shoes crunching against gravel.

"Barely." Lucas gestured at the motorcycle. "Borrowing a set of wheels took longer than expected. An audio technician came to my rescue."

"Brave man, venturing out on that old scooter at night. Step inside, make yourself at home."

The actor clapped Martin's shoulder. "Thanks again, mate."

Watching him enter the kitchen, Hannah said, "I'm quite certain their intimacy coordinator is unaware that they use your house for a rehearsal studio."

"They're here because they need a bedroom. And privacy. They're married. To each other."

This was one of the better shocking revelations of the night. She ranked it just below seeing Poppy and Jack kissing behind the pub. "Since when?"

"Early June. I begged Caroline to let me tell you. Pestered her while driving to Salisbury. And the whole time we were there. All the way back. When I finally got her to agree, it was conditional. They needed a place where they could spend the night together without anybody finding out."

"Unbelievable. Those two are even better actors off camera. I never guessed they liked each other all that much."

"They went for coffee after their first audition together, and things moved along rapidly. Before they were cast as Rosalind and Granville, they were seeing each other in secret. Not long after the announcement that they'd be co-stars, they eloped. They told their parents first. Then their agents, who prefer that they time the announcement for the Cannes Film Festival."

"That's the middle of May. Practically their first anniversary."

"They won't wait that long for the big reveal. The subterfuge is too stressful. I empathize."

"Does your mother know?"

He shook his head. "Caroline thought it safer not to tell anyone else. I hope you don't mind that I confided in her about us. After she heard the full saga, she suggested that my being seen with her would prevent people from finding out about you and me. I didn't think you'd be bothered. Any more than I was every time I saw you with that infernal Scotsman."

"I've been way more bothered by hiding our relationship," she confessed. "Chase told me to stop worrying about the media. I should've listened to him. After thinking about it a lot, I realized that even if you and I do eventually end up in a gossip column, the attention won't be lasting. I've missed you more here in Somerset than I did when there was an ocean between us."

He spread his arms outward, an invitation that she happily accepted. He slid his hands along her waist, settling on her hips, and pulled her closer.

Their mouths met in a long, satisfying kiss.

From the depths of her skirt pocket, her cell phone clanged. "Sorry," she said. Glancing at the screen, she found Liz's image. "I'd better answer." She swiped to take the call.

"Where the hell are you?"

"Stanwell House."

"I'm sitting in the hotel lobby, waiting for you. We need to talk."

"Right now?"

"Yes. No questions. Get your skinny ass over here."

Martin's hand had shifted to that part of her anatomy. "Okay. Bye." After a quick kiss, she said apologetically, "She wouldn't bother me so late if it wasn't really important. Or a crisis. Maybe she heard about what Logan did."

"Go." Before she could open the door to her car, she heard him call her name. When she turned around, he said,

"I was so relieved by what you said that I forgot to say how much I love you."

"Good. Because I love you, too. And guess what?"

"What?"

"I don't care who knows it."

Chapter 31

She found Liz waiting for her on an overstuffed sofa, clutching a large manilla envelope.

"My mother offered to babysit Lexi so Tom and I could have a romantic dinner at the restaurant."

Hannah looked around. "Where is he?"

"At our house, checking that Mom is coping with the grandbaby, and vice versa. He'll be back to pick me up. Soon." She held out the envelope. "This is for you."

"Thanks. I think. What's inside?"

"Your enrollment application for the British Film Producers Association. I filled out the form, but it needs your signature. And your Acorn Films credit card number for the annual dues payment."

Hannah opened the flap and pulled out the papers. Staring at the BPA letterhead and logo, she said, "I've had a crazy evening like you wouldn't believe. When you explain why you did this, please go very slowly and speak very, very clearly."

"Mom's visit isn't the only reason you haven't seen much of me this week. I've been wrapping up negotiations on a major development deal. A union of Acorn Films and Serve-

Flix, the largest streaming service in the known universe. Our offices and legal departments have approved the press release. It's going out—actually, I don't know. Tomorrow, I think. We provide them with an infinite amount of content—feature films, series, documentaries. I'll be staffing up on both sides of the Atlantic. I want you to set up my outpost over here. You won't be managing it, though. Because you'll be my producing partner. For everything. Not just *Wendy Edney's Great English Gardens*. Is that clear enough?"

"Perfectly." Hannah sank against the sofa. "Liz, are you sure?"

"You've got vision. You're creative. And organized. You keep your wits about you when under the most intense kind of pressure." A manicured forefinger tapped the envelope. "I put Hartcliffe Studios as a placeholder address. Before submitting the paperwork, you can change that. If you need to. I have a hunch you will. I see headlights—that'll be Tom." She stood. "Shit!"

"What's wrong?"

"I look like hell." Liz stared at the ornate mirror on the opposite wall. "I'm surprised I didn't put him off his dinner."

"Oh, stop."

"I've been living on New York time for days. Lexi doesn't need to wake me up for her middle of the night feed. I'm expecting another call, extremely important. Can't talk about it yet. As soon as the file comes, I'll send it over. A very special surprise." Bending down, she pressed a quick kiss on Hannah's cheek. "See you soon, partner."

Hannah remained in place, numbed by contrasting and rapidly shifting emotions. True to form, Liz was playing fairy godmother, turning this bizarre night into the nicest.

When she got up, she felt lightheaded. Not in reaction to a series of shocks, but from gnawing, aching hunger. If she didn't eat something, and soon, she was going to pass out.

She wandered into the restaurant. No host on duty, and

the tablecloths had been removed. In the kitchen two young men in aprons loaded plates into an industrial sized dishwasher.

"Sorry to bother you," she told them, "but I missed dinner. Can I please have some kind of food to take to my room? Anything will do."

"There's a leftover pear crumble in the fridge," said one. "It'll be cold, though."

"Doesn't matter."

He located the oval dish and peeled away the clingfilm. "Some custard in the jug. Shall I pour it on?"

"Yes, please."

In addition to the crumble, he supplied her with cutlery wrapped in a napkin.

"Enjoy," he said.

"Thanks, I will."

Making her way up the staircase to her floor, she wondered whether Alistair had eaten her tortellini as well as his pork chop.

Whoever performed turndown service had already visited. The floral chintz counterpane was neatly folded back and its pillows were plumped and stacked, and the curtains were drawn. Such a pleasant change, this country house hotel—classic décor, unobtrusive yet accommodating staff. The big chains tried too hard. During her scouting years, she returned to her room each night to find a bath towel contorted into an animal figure—elephant, swan, monkey, or frog. She'd always taken a photo and sent it to Chase for his amusement.

Light glowed from the gooseneck lamp on the antique corner desk. She walked straight to it and sat down to eat her crumble. The topping wasn't crispy like Mum's, but the fruity pudding underneath it was ever so slightly warm.

After changing into her silk camisole and sleep shorts,

she remembered to plug her phone's charging cord into the bedside outlet. The telephone on the nightstand rang.

"Good evening, Ms. Ballard. There's a person here at the front desk with a delivery for you. Shall I send him up?"

He must be bringing that file Liz mentioned, she thought fleetingly. Maybe more paperwork I'm supposed to sign.

Unwilling to get dressed for a trip downstairs, she gave permission. She covered herself with the complimentary terrycloth bathrobe, several sizes too large. Hearing the soft rap of knuckles on wood, she opened the door.

Martin stood in the hall. He held a bottle of champagne in one hand and a bouquet of velvety red roses in the other.

Stepping aside, she said, "I've stayed in dozens of hotels. Maybe a hundred. I never had finer room service than this."

"Our earlier parting was unsatisfactory." After kissing her, he placed his offerings on the sofa table and pulled a champagne coupe glass out of each jacket pocket.

"You think of everything," she said appreciatively.

"Your planning expertise is contagious." Gradually he eased the cork from the bottle. He poured the pale golden liquid into each glass. Handing her one, he touched it with his. "To us. To our future. To being together."

She sipped the bubbly.

"Your turn," he prompted.

"To new beginnings," she said. "And next adventures." She recounted her brief conversation with Liz. "I'm not sure how I survived six months of job title changes and shifting responsibilities. Location scout to location manager to executive assistant to the executive producer."

"Now you're a producer yourself."

"And starting up the UK division of Acorn Films. Which probably requires some other type of visa."

"I'm about to resolve that issue." He placed his glass on the table before kneeling on the carpet. "Don't laugh."

"I won't." She didn't have enough breath for it.

"Will you marry me? Please."

She joined him on the floor. "Absolutely. Yes. Definitely."

"No need to think it over?"

She shook her head. "For an ultra-modern marquess, this is a surprisingly old-fashioned proposal."

"I'm predictably unpredictable. You should know that by now." From his inside pocket he removed the brown leather ring box and raised the lid.

She'd never seen, or imagined, a diamond so large. When he put it on her finger, she felt the weight of it. "It's real, isn't it?"

"Of course. Just before you arrived at the house, I was showing it to Caroline. Our great-great grandfather purchased it in Paris. He wanted a stone that would impress a Belgian princess. The Prince of Wales attended their wedding, representing his mother Queen Victoria, in 1898. That date is engraved on the inside of the band."

"Stop right there. You never told me you're related to Continental royalty."

"They barely acknowledge the connection. Anyway, this treasure of mine was sitting in a London bank vault. Waiting for you." He started untying the robe's thick sash. "Although that ring seals our engagement, I came here with another ritual in mind." He pushed away the voluminous terrycloth covering, revealing her scanty attire.

She pulled off his jacket and unbuttoned his shirt. "I didn't think this evening could get better," she murmured. "How wrong I was."

They finished undressing and moved to the bed. Their foreplay didn't last long, their mutual need was too intense.

Hannah, shaken to her soul and thoroughly sated, lay comfortably within the curve of his body, conscious of the simultaneous rise and fall of their bare chests.

"What do you think about a December wedding? On your birthday. Can you wait till then?"

"If you can," she said drowsily.

"A small and private ceremony at St. Anne's in Milverston Magna. We can fly your parents over. We'll include your Gran and your aunt and uncle in Wales, and the ones near Wimbledon. Perhaps your violinist cousin and some of his orchestra mates will provide the music. Afterwards, an intimate family dinner party at Stanwell."

"What about Alicia?"

He scrunched up his face.

"She's your grandmother, Martin."

"I suppose we ought to invite her. She'll come."

"Grampa and Chase can't. They don't have passports."

"We'll spend Christmas and New Year's in Maine and arrange a blessing ceremony in your parish church. Your grandfather and your uncle will be there. Plus anyone and everyone you and your parents want to include. And Liz and Tom. All your Boston friends. Followed by a huge reception."

Hannah released a long sigh. "I could get used to this."

"What do you mean?"

"Being presented with a very detailed plan that covers every contingency and all the logistics. And I didn't have to develop it."

"Mother helped me," he admitted. "She suggested a candlelight wedding, because by December it gets dark at such an early hour. She's impatient to discuss church flowers with your mother. And she planned a dinner menu. But none of it happens unless you approve."

"When did you two start conspiring?"

"Before I left for London."

Big Ben clanged. She reached across Martin to pick up her phone from the bedside table. "Liz—again."

"Go ahead. Tell her your news."

Hannah swiped and said, "Your timing is terrible."

"Just a quick heads-up. I'm about to email the file. It's

a book manuscript. *Tender Treasure,* the sequel to *Forsaken Fortune.* I just got off the phone with the author's literary agent. Acorn Films has the option. I'll adapt it as a television series for ServeFlix instead of a film for cinema release. Production will be based at Hartcliffe. I want to lock Stanwell and the surrounding villages for the location. Find out if Martin is okay with that."

Hannah glanced at him. He nodded. "It's a yes."

"He's there?"

"Mmm hmm."

"Nigel won't be co-producing," Liz stated. "I want you."

"I'll have to discuss it with my fiancé."

"Wait, what? You two are getting married?"

"In about three months."

"Did he give you a ring?"

"It's the only thing I'm wearing."

"Too much information! A diamond?"

"Yes."

"How big?"

Hannah held up her left hand. "Way bigger than yours. Wait till you see. It's an antique. A Latimer family heirloom."

There was a pause, then a gasp. "Oh, my God. You'll be the Marchioness of Milverston."

Martin murmured, "She's right."

"I've got to go. He wants to rehearse what he'll say when he phones Dad and Mum."

"Oh, my God," Liz repeated. "Am I the first person to find out about this?"

"Almost. As you should be. You're responsible for bringing us together."

"Damn right I am! When I hang up, I'm calling the front desk and telling them to send up a bottle of champagne."

"No need, Martin took care of that. Listen, Liz. I'm not ditching you, I promise. But tomorrow I'll be checking out of this hotel."

"Sure, whatever."

"Time for a change of location. I belong at Stanwell."

The mattress beneath shook. Martin had raised his arms to pound the air with his fists in a silent show of victory.

When she ended the call, she snuggled against him and asked, "Which of your twenty bedrooms will be ours?"

"Only nineteen left, because I gave one to Caroline and Lucas. I've been thinking we ought to have the King's Room. Too big for one person. Just right for two. And a pair of mongrel dogs." He reached for her phone. When she didn't surrender it, he said, "I'm ready to ring Bear Knoll."

"Dad's at work. Mum's either riding Rascal or in the garden. We'll tell them first thing tomorrow." She took his hand in hers. "After you take me home."

Epilogue

Screen Monitor Daily, May

From Cannes. Festival favorite *Forsaken Fortune* was awarded the *Palme d'Or* and other prizes as follows: *Prix de la mise en scene*—Sir Owen Parry, *Prix d'interprétation masculine*—Lucas Daltrey, *Prix d'interprétation feminine*—Caroline Bryden, *Prix du scenario*—Louisa Jensen and Frank Walters.

Milver Vale Messenger, June

Martin Latimer and Hannah Ballard of Stanwell House enjoyed a brief holiday in the South of France following last month's Cannes Film Festival, where locally produced *Forsaken Fortune* received numerous prizes. The film's world premiere will take place in September at the cinema in Leicester Square, London, with members of the royal family in attendance. Later that month, during autumn Harvest Week, the prince will perform the ribbon-cutting at the Rural Heritage Center, Little Milver.

Isobel Latimer of Holly Cottage and her cavalier spaniel Ernie took the blue rosette for his breed class at the Somerset Hills Dog Show. Isobel invites Vale residents to an exhibition of her paintings and portraits on the second May Bank Holiday Weekend, in the Little Milver Art Gallery.

Newlyweds Poppy Deane and Jack Elliston, married a fortnight past at St. Anne's, Milverston Magna, are grateful to all who celebrated with them at The Peacock. Their honeymoon is postponed to a later date, as Poppy and her Welsh cob Meg are competing in the Main Ring at the Royal Somerset County Show. Daughter Chloe Elliston, a budding equestrienne, will also ride. Best of luck to both ladies, and their horse!

In three weeks, renowned garden expert Wendy Edney will present a workshop titled "Raising Roses the Right Way" at the Tithe Barn. Contact the Milverston Estate Office for details and bookings.

Advertisement in Academy Announcements, December

For Your Consideration
Forsaken Fortune, Acorn Films

British Film Bulletin, February

BAFTA Film Awards. Building on its resounding success at Cannes and in Toronto, and recipient of too many critic awards to list, *Forsaken Fortune* received the lion's share of awards at the ceremony hosted in London by the British Academy of Film and Television Arts. During the star-studded after-party, director Sir Owen Parry said he wasn't offended by certain off-color jokes the emcee and certain presenters made when referencing the film's romantic scenes. Of all the honors the period drama received, he is most pleased by its win for Outstanding British Film.

Posh Online, March

Red Carpet Report. Married co-stars Lucas Daltrey and Caroline Bryden were a popular target of camera lenses when making their entrance at the Academy Awards post-ceremony gala. In addition to receiving matching gold statuettes for their performances in *Forsaken Fortune,* the glamorous twosome were prominently featured on every Best Dressed list. Their film swept up awards in the majority of its nominated categories, and the producers, cast members, and production team celebrated through the night and into the wee hours of the morning. Executive Producer Elizabeth Gregorio was a standout in sweeping red satin and rubies. Producing partner Hannah Ballard, escorted by the Marquess of Milverston—her husband—was a petite vision in tea-length emerald velvet and designer diamonds valued at £12 million. The collet necklace and drop earrings, loaned by a Rodeo Drive jeweler, were chosen to complement the heirloom eight carat diamond ring her ladyship received last year on her engagement.

In the Pipeline, May

Tender Treasure (sequel to *Forsaken Fortune)*, multipart series for streaming service ServeFlix. Elizabeth Gregorio, executive producer. Hannah Ballard, co-producer. Acorn Films UK/Hartcliffe Studios.

Location Log, June

Currently in Production. Acorn Films UK/Serve-Flix. *Tender Treasure,* starring Caroline Bryden and Lucas Daltrey. Hartcliffe Studios. Locations: Milver Vale, Somerset; Stanwell House, Milverston Magna, ancestral home of the Marquess of Milverston. The marchioness, known professionally as Hannah Ballard, co-produces.

Production Completed. Acorn Films US-UK/ServeFlix: *Wendy Edney's Great British Gardens,* six-part series. Hannah Ballard, producer.

Advertisement in Television Talk, May

For Your Consideration
Tender Treasure, Acorn Films US-UK/ServeFlix

Location Log, June

Currently in Production. Acorn Films US-UK/ServeFlix. *Wendy Edney's Great Irish Gardens,* six-part series. Hannah Ballard, producer.

Milver Vale Messenger, October

Jewel, the mixed breed dog belonging to Hannah Ballard and Martin Latimer, qualified for the All-Shire Agility Trials. Are she and her Stanwell House companion, Ariel the lurcher, aware that their owners expect a new arrival—not a canine—next year?

Milver Vale Messenger, March

Congratulations to Martin Latimer and Hannah Ballard, the Marquess and Marchioness of Milverston, on the arrival of their firstborn, Richard Dragon Rufus Latimer, whose courtesy title is Earl Cary. After the Easter Sunday christening at St. Anne's, Milverston Magna, the couple will host a celebration on the village green. Catering by The Peacock. All are welcome.

Author's Note

Although *A Change of Location* is not autobiographical, Hannah Ballard and I do share certain interests and pursuits and professional experiences.

In the region where I spent my formative years, filming for cinema release or television broadcast was a common occurrence. As a very young actress performing in local and regional theatre, I was accustomed to drop-ins by producers and directors and casting agents working in the area. I observed or participated in major motion pictures filming on my college campus. During my graduate studies in Radio-TV-Film, a television series filmed in and around the university, providing additional opportunities for extra work. Making the transition from performance to production, I worked on informational and educational documentaries.

In addition, this novel's English settings are extremely familiar. My connection to South Somerset, a specific location I've fictionalized, goes back generations. I've explored ancestral villages and churches containing effigies and other memorials to my ancestors. Since my teenage years, I've been hanging out in London's Mayfair and St. James's neighborhoods. I know exactly where Latimer Row would be, if it existed outside of my imagination. Only a short walk from the nearby Ritz Hotel.

Coastal Maine, the story's other setting, is within driving distance of my home. Many years ago, on the outskirts of Falmouth, I discovered the model for Bear Hill farm.

Animals I know, have known and loved, frequently appear in my books. This one features Jewel, my dearly departed and intensely devoted border collie-black Labrador, who was blessed with a long and happy life and is much missed. Several of my canines have possessed what I would describe as lurcher habits, although I've never shared my home with a genuine one like Martin's Ariel. However, Ernie the Cavalier spaniel, companion of dear friends and neighbors, lives within walking distance. Thank you, Kate and Michael, for letting me borrow him!

As ever, I extend deep gratitude to the Gallica Press crew. Other valued members of my production team include Kristine Braley of Finalize Editorial, for her stellar work on the pre-production manuscript. Deborah Bradseth always creates the ideal cover design. Michelle Argyle at Melissa Williams Design once again proved her brilliant formatting skills. And the amazing Jon Abbiss miraculously transformed my very rough sketch of the story setting into a detailed map of the imaginary Milver Vale.

Throughout my career I've relied on a vast community of writers—local, national, and international—for comradeship, support, amusement, and inspiration. Too many to name, but each one is uniquely cherished. I hope my cohort of historical novelists will excuse this detour into contemporary fiction!

The greatest contributor of all is my husband, whose presence and patience are a precious gift. His ability to chauffeur me along the narrowest of Somerset lanes is unsurpassed. And I'm endlessly appreciative of his willingness to take on dog care and household responsibilities when I'm deeply embedded in the universe of my work-in-progress. There were no clauses in our marriage vows about being an author's spouse, and I don't dare ask which part of "for better or for worse" covers that. But I am so grateful to you for living into this adventure. You are the essential part of it.

About the Author

Margaret Porter is the award-winning and best-selling author of sixteen novels in multiple genres. A former stage actress, she also worked profession-ally in film, television, and radio. Additional writing credits include nonfiction, newspaper and magazine articles, and poetry. She  and her husband live in New England. Information about her books and aspects of her life and career can be found at www.margaretporter.com.

www.ingramcontent.com/pod-product-compliance
Lightning Source LLC
Chambersburg PA
CBHW021217310726
48971CB00006B/1599